I0630648

ABOUT THE EDITORS

LIZ GRZYB was born in the middle of a thunderstorm in Perth, Western Australia. She is the editor of acclaimed paranormal romance anthologies *Scary Kisses* and *More Scary Kisses*, the Orientalist pantomime *Dreaming of Djinn*, the website Ticon4.com, co-editor of paranormal noir anthology *Damnation and Dames* and *The Year's Best Australian Fantasy and Horror 2010* and *2011*.

TALIE HELENE is a musician and writer, from Melbourne, Australia. She has poetry published in journals including *Voiceworks*, *Avant*, and *Inkshed*, and Mary Manning's *About Poetry* (Oxford University Press), and a co-authored short story (with Martin Livings) "The Last Gig of Jimmy Rucker" in *More Scary Kisses* (edited by Liz Grzyb), winner of a Tin Duck Award, and nominated for Best Short Story in the 2011 Ditmar Awards. Talie was News Editor for the Australian Horror Writers' Association for four years; she is serving on the Short Fiction Jury for the 2012 Bram Stoker Awards. With a background in music journalism—especially extreme genres—Talie has performed with many artists including The Tenth Stage, Wendy Rule, Sean Bowley, Saba Persian Orchestra, Maroondah Symphony, and Eden. A member of the SuperNova writers' group, she is currently developing a new audio arts anthology titled *The Unquiet Grave*. You can find out more at taliehelene.com

Also edited by LIZ GRZYB

Scary Kisses
More Scary Kisses
*The Year's Best Australian Fantasy & Horror 2010 (with
    Talie Helene)*
*The Year's Best Australian Fantasy & Horror 2011 (with
    Talie Helene)*
Damnation and Dames (with Amanda Pillar)
Dreaming of Djinn

Also edited by TALIE HELENE

*The Year's Best Australian Fantasy & Horror 2010 (with
    Liz Grzyb)*
*The Year's Best Australian Fantasy & Horror 2011 (with
    Liz Grzyb)*

THE YEAR'S BEST AUSTRALIAN FANTASY & HORROR

~ 2012 ~

EDITED BY

LIZ GRZYB & TALIE HELENE

THE THIRD ANNUAL COLLECTION

THE YEAR'S BEST AUSTRALIAN FANTASY & HORROR

~ 2012 ~

EDITED BY

LIZ GRZYB & TALIE HELENE

Tᴍ
pᴍ
Ticonderoga
publications

for

Russell
(L.G.)

Betty McInerney
(T.H.)

The Year's Best Australian Fantasy & Horror 2012
edited by Liz Grzyb & Talie Helene

Published by Ticonderoga Publications

Copyright © 2013 Liz Grzyb & Talie Helene

All rights reserved. Without limiting the rights under copyright reserved above, no part of this publication may be reproduced, stored in or introduced into a retrieval system, or transmitted in any form or by any means (electronic, mechanical, recording or otherwise) without the express prior written permission of the copyright holder concerned. Pages 487–8 constitute an extension of this copyright page.

Introduction copyright © 2013 Liz Grzyb & Talie Helene
"The Year in Fantasy" copyright © 2013 Liz Grzyb
"The Year in Horror" copyright © 2013 Talie Helene
"The Year in the Industry" copyright © 2013 Liz Grzyb & Talie Helene

Designed by Russell B. Farr
Typeset in Sabon and Poor Richard

A Cataloging-in-Publications entry for this title is available from The National Library of Australia.

ISBN   978-1-921857-48-5 (hardcover)
       978-1-921857-49-2 (trade paperback)
       978-1-921857-50-8 (ebook)

Ticonderoga Publications
PO Box 29 Greenwood
Western Australia 6924

www.ticonderogapublications.com

10 9 8 7 6 5 4 3 2 1

The editors would like to thank Joanne Anderton, R.J. Astruc, Lee Battersby, Alan Baxter, Jenny Blackford, Eddy Burger, Isobelle Carmody, Jay Caselberg, Stephen Dedman, Felicity Dowker, Terry Dowling, Tom Dullemond, Thoraiya Dyer, Will Elliot, Jason Fischer, Dirk Flinthart, Lisa L. Hannett, Narrelle M. Harris, Kathleen Jennings, Gary Kemble, Margo Lanagan, Martin Livings, Penelope Love, Andrew J. McKiernan, Karen Maric, Faith Mudge, Nicole Murphy, Jason Nahrung, Tansy Rayner Roberts, Angela Slatter, Anna Tambour, Kyla Ward, Kaaron Warren.

Liz would like to thank Talie Helene, Helen Grzyb, Angela Challis, Shane Cummings, Amanda Pillar, Tom Bicknell, Kate Dunbar-Smith, Kate Williams, Andrew Williams, Debbie Wilson, Jacinta Rosielle, Ambre Hillier, Michael Hillier, Tasmar Dixon, Kylie Dainton, Mel Barbarat, Mel Donald, Phil Ward, Angela Rega, Annie Backshall, Ruza Foster, Lina Piscitelli, Nikki Irwin, Andrea Orlowsky, Anna Frankie Bertolini, Hilary Donraadt, Angie Irwin, Jane Hebiton, and of course the Department of Fabulous.

Talie would like to thank Liz Grzyb and Russell B. Farr, Kirstyn McDermott, Jason Nahrung, Rocky Wood, Ellen Gregory, Sarah Endacott, Claire McKenna, Gillian Pollock, Sharyn Liley, Kaaron Warren, Michelle Goldsmith, Martin Livings, Stephen Gleeson, Peter Hickman, Catriona Sparks, Robert Hood, Jason Franks, Chuck McKenzie, Trudi Canavan, Lucy Sussex, Julian Warner, Kyla Ward, Brendan Duffy, Terry Dowling, Mariangelina Maccarone, Alisa Krasnostein, Janeen Webb, Jack Dann, Anna Tambour, Sonia Tamarri, Tessa Kum, Jason Fischer, Felicity Dowker, Juvairia Khalid, Bill Bamford, Samantha Escarbe, Shelley Slater, Joanna Giradon, and Josephine Wilson.

CONTENTS

THE YEAR IN REVIEW 13
   LIZ GRZYB & TALIE HELENE

PAUL HAINES 41
   CAT SPARKS

BELLA BEAUFORT GOES TO WAR.. 45
   LISA L. HANNETT & ANGELA SLATTER

RIVER OF MEMORY 61
   KAARON WARREN

A MOVEABLE FEAST.. 81
   JENNY BLACKFORD

CROW AND CAPER, CAPER AND CROW 93
   MARGO LANAGAN

THE BLACK STAR KILLER 105
   NICOLE MURPHY

THE LAST BOAT TO EDEN... 119
   JASON NAHRUNG

KINDLING 137
   KATHLEEN JENNINGS

TIED TO THE WASTE 149
   JOANNE ANDERTON

THE DOG WHO WISHED HE'D NEVER HEARD OF LOVECRAFT 161
   ANNA TAMBOUR

TINY LIVES 177
   ALAN BAXTER

ANVIL OF THE SUN... 183
   KAREN MARIC

TORCH SONG.. 199
   ANDREW J. MCKIERNAN

JIMMY DEAN, JIMMY DEAN 205
   ANGELA SLATTER

A SMALL BAD THING 209
   PENELOPE LOVE

TO WISH ON A CLOCKWORK HEART 223
   FELICITY DOWKER

THE STONE WITCH.. 239
   ISOBELLE CARMODY

SLEEPING BEAUTY 265
    THORAIYA DYER
PIGROOT FLAT 275
    JASON FISCHER
THE FALL 289
    STEPHEN DEDMAN
YOU AIN'T HEARD NOTHIN' YET! 305
    MARTIN LIVINGS
BEAUTIFUL 313
    JAY CASELBERG
STALEMATE 321
    NARRELLE M. HARRIS
POPULATION MANAGEMENT 335
    TOM DULLEMOND
SWEET SUBTLETIES 349
    LISA L. HANNETT
THE BULL IN WINTER 359
    DIRK FLINTHART
SATURDAY NIGHT AT THE MILK BAR 375
    GARY KEMBLE
THE WITCH'S WARDROBE 387
    EDDY BURGER
COMFORT GHOST 399
    LEE BATTERSBY
HUNGRY MAN 407
    WILL ELLIOTT
THE COOK OF PEARL HOUSE, A MALAY SAILOR BY THE
NAME OF MAURICE 417
    R.J. ASTRUC
THE LOQUACIOUS CADAVER 419
    KYLA WARD
WHAT BOOKS SURVIVE 425
    TANSY RAYNER ROBERTS
ORACLE'S TOWER 441
    FAITH MUDGE
NIGHTSIDE EYE 451
    TERRY DOWLING

ABOUT THE CONTRIBUTORS 469
RECOMMENDED READING LIST 475
AUSTRALIAN & NEW ZEALAND FANTASY & HORROR AWARDS 479
ACKNOWLEDGEMENTS 487

THE YEAR IN REVIEW

LIZ GRZYB & TALIE HELENE

THE YEAR IN FANTASY

Fantasy in Australia in 2012 seemed to start moving away from the dark vampire fantasies that have been prevalent for a while, and into the realms of fresh new paranormal creatures, revisited fairy tales and more epic adventure stories.

2012 was the year of Margo Lanagan! As well as releasing her novel *Sea Hearts* through Allen & Unwin and her boutique collection *Cracklescape* with Twelfth Planet Press, Lanagan's work was short listed for and won many, many awards, both in Australia and internationally. *Sea Hearts*, a reworked and extended take on her 2009 novella of the same name, won Aurealis awards in both the Fantasy and Young Adult Novel categories, the Ditmar for Best Novel, the Australian Independent Bookseller Awards for Children's works, the Norma K. Hemming Award, and was short listed for the British Fantasy Award Best Novel (as *The Brides of Rollrock Island*) the Stella, the NSW, WA and Qld Premiers' literary awards, as well as the Children's Book Council Book of the Year Award! Two stories from *Cracklescape*, "Bajazzle" and "Significant Dust" were awarded the Fantasy and Science Fiction Short Story awards in the Aurealis Awards, respectively.

Tansy Rayner Roberts also had a very busy year, releasing the third in her *Creature Court* series, *Reign of Beasts*, and producing various non-fiction work which has won and been nominated for many awards. She has been nominated for a Hugo Award for Best Fan Writer, as well as another nomination along with Alisa Krasnostein, Alexandra Pierce and Andrew Finch for their Galactic Suburbia Podcast in Best Fancast category. Roberts' critical writing in 2012 has also won her two Ditmars (William Atheling Jr. Award for Criticism or Review for "Historically Authentic Sexism in Fantasy. Let's Unpack That." (Tor.com) and Best Fan Writer). The Chronos Awards, although awarding Victorian residents, recognised two of Roberts' projects in the shortlist—Snapshot 2012 for Best Achievement with Alisa Krasnostein, Kathryn Linge, David McDonald, Helen Merrick, Ian Mond, Jason Nahrung, Alexandra Pierce, Tehani Wessely and Sean Wright, and winning Best Fan Written Work for "Reviewing New Who series", with David McDonald and Tehani Wessely.

Jonathan Strahan has continued to be recognised worldwide for his editing: he was nominated for a Hugo Award for both Best Editor, Short Form, and Best Fancast for *The Coode Street Podcast* which he co-presents with Gary K. Wolfe. Strahan also won an Aurealis Award, and his anthology *Under My Hat* was nominated for a World Fantasy Award.

RECOMMENDED NOVELS

Juliet Marillier released the first installment in her *Shadowfell* series through Pan Macmillan with the eponymous novel. This is a wonderful young-adult adventure which won the Tin Duck Award for Best Novel, the YALSA Best Book for Young Adults, and was short listed for the Sir Julius Vogel Award in New Zealand.

Margo Lanagan's *Sea Hearts* is a must-read. This Selkie story is captivating and powerful, and will mesmerise both fans and new readers of Lanagan's work.

Rapunzel retellings seem to be the order of the year, with James Bradley releasing a novelette *Beauty's Sister* through Penguin, and Kate Forsyth giving us Aurealis and Ditmar award-nominated *Bitter Greens* through Random House, in addition to Faith Mudge's Ditmar-nominated short story *Oracle's Tower* from *To Spin A Darker Stair* which is reprinted in this volume. *Bitter Greens* is another for the must-read list for fantasy lovers this year, especially those who enjoy fairy tale retellings. While it certainly captures the "fairy tale" spirit, it is also a well-researched historical novel and will please readers of this genre as well.

Harper Collins released two novels in the continuation of Rhonda Roberts' Timestalker series in 2012. *Gladiatrix* (2009), the first in the series is a very entertaining novel, and both *Hoodwink*, set in Hollywood in the 1930s, and *Coyote*, in the Wild West, are just as intriguing and lead the reader on two very different episodes in Kannon Dupree's career. *Hoodwink* has deservedly been long-listed for the Davitt Award for Australian women's crime fiction.

Angry Robot is going from strength to strength at the moment, especially with Australian authors. Jo Anderton's sequel to *Debris*, the Ditmar and Aurealis-nominated *Suited*, is a highly recommended read from Angry Robot this year, as is Trent Jamieson's followup to *Roil*, *Night's Engines*.

OTHER NOTABLE NOVELS

Random House was a great supporter of Australian fantasy this year, publishing many series in the world of children's and young adult fantasy. Deborah Abela began a new children's series Ghost Club with *The New Kid* and *The Haunted School*. Karen Brooks rounded out her excellent Curse of the Bond Riders series with *Illumination*. Martin Chatterton also started a new humorous fantasy series for children following Mort, a 10,000 year old boy, with *Mort* and *Mortal Combat*. Stuart Daly continued his young adult Witch Hunter Chronicles with *The Devil's Fire*. Marianne de Pierres concluded her young adult Night Creatures trilogy with the fantastic *Shine Light*. John Flanagan continued his New York Times Bestselling List series Brotherband with the second and third installments, *The Invaders* and *The Hunters*. In *Vulpi*, Kate Gordon continued the tale of shapeshifters she began in *Thyla* last year. H.J. Harper started a new adventure series for children with *Bureau of Mysteries*. Rhiannon Hart continued her vampiric princess Lharmell series with *Blood Storm*. Sophie Masson released two titles in 2012, her Bollywood ghost story *The Maharajah's Ghost* and Cinderella retelling *Moonlight and Ashes*. Colin Thompson continued his How to Live Forever series with *The Second Forever*.

Harper Collins Books published many Australian fantasy novels this year, both as standalone novels and in series, such as A.A. Bell's next Mira Chambers story *Leopard Dreaming*. Kylie Chan released *Small Shen*, a novel interspersed with manga, illustrated by Queenie Chan. Gary Crew's newest novel, *The Architecture of Song* was released, as was Rosie Dub's *Flight*. Jennifer Fallon's *Dark Divide*, the second installment of her Rift Runners series, has been included on the long-list for the David Gemmell Legend Award. Traci Harding continued her Triad of Being series with *The Light Field*. Duncan Lay began a new epic fantasy series, Empire of Bones with *Bridge of Swords*. Fiona McIntosh's standalone novel *The Scrivener's Tale*, and Jo Spurrier's first novel in her new trilogy, *Winter Be My Shield*, were both also long-listed for the David Gemmell Legend Award. *Winter Be My Shield* was also short listed for an Aurealis Award for Best Fantasy Novel. Tracey O'Hara continued her Dark Brethren series with *Sin's Dark Caress*, which was nominated for the Australian Romance Readers Awards for Favourite Sci Fi, Fantasy or Futuristic Romance. As previously mentioned, Tansy Rayner Roberts concluded her wonderful Creature Court trilogy with *Reign of Beasts*. K.J. Taylor also began a new series, *The Risen Sun*, with *Shadow's Heir* this year.

Hachette Australia continued their pattern for the past few years, focusing mainly on continuing series. Sam Bowring released his *Strange Threads* duology this year, with *The Legacy of Lord Regret* and *The Lord of Lies*. Trudi Canavan completed her Traitor Spy trilogy with *Traitor Queen*, which made the long list for the David Gemmell Legend Award. Ian Irvine and M.K. Hume continued their trilogies this year with Book 2 for each: Irvine's The Tainted Realm trilogy with *Rebellion*, and Hume's Prophecy trilogy with *Death of an Empire*. Helen Lowe resumed her Wall of Night series with *The Gathering of the Lost*, which also made it onto the Legend Awards shortlist. K.E. Mills released a fourth installment of her Rogue Agent series with *Wizard Undercover*. Nalini Singh's 2012 releases, continuations of her Guild Hunter and Psy-Changeling series respectively, were *Archangel's Storm* and *Tangle of Need*. Both were short listed for Australian Romance Readers Association Awards.

Allen & Unwin published many Australian fantasy novels this year, and similar to Random House, focused mainly in the young adult and children's markets. Asphyxia released three Grimstones books: *Hatched*, *Mortimer Revealed* and *Whirlwind*, children's "gothic fairytales" which have been nominated for APA Book Design awards amongst others. Marianne Delacourt's *Stage Fright*, the third crime-with-a-hint-of-paranormal Tara Sharp novel was deservedly long-listed for the Davitt Award for Best Australian Women's Crime Novels. Kaz Delaney's paranormal novel *Dead, Actually* won joint Aurealis Best Young Adult Novel and Favourite Paranormal Romance in the Australian Romance Readers Association Awards, as well as being long-listed for the Davitt Awards. Andrew McGahan's second novel of his epic Ship Kings series, *The Voyage of the Unquiet Ice* was listed as Highly Commended at the Fellowship of Australian Writers National Literary Awards and Notable in the CBCA Book of the Year Awards. Garth Nix had two novels published this year: the science fiction/fantasy novel *A Confusion of Princes* which was nominated for an Aurealis Award and an Inky, and the continuation of his collaborative Troubletwisters series with Sean Williams, *Monster*. Louis Nowra released *Into That Forest*, which was nominated for the Ethel Turner Prize (Young People's Literature) at the NSW Premier's Literary Awards and Best Young Adult Novel in the Aurealis Awards. Gregory Rogers and Frances Watts began a new children's series, Sword Girl, and released four titles this year: *Secret of the Swords, Poison Plot, Tournament Trouble* and *Siege Scare*. Lian Tanner concluded her Keepers series with *Path of Beasts*.

Penguin Australia published a growing number of Australian fantasy authors this year. Allan Baillie released his science fiction fantasy thriller *Outpost*, and Gary Crew and Ross Watkins produced the environmental fable picture book *The Boy Who Grew Into A Tree*. Kirsty Eagar brought out her gothic *Night Beach*, which was nominated for an Inky. Leah Giarratano began a new young adult paranormal series, *Disharmony*, with *The Telling*. Kylie Griffin released two novels in her new paranormal *Light Blade* series, *Vengeance Born* and *Alliance Forged*, with Penguin Putnam. *Alliance Forged* was the winner of the Australian Romance Readers Association Favourite Sci Fi, Fantasy or Futuristic Romance. Sonya Hartnett's new novel, *Children of the King*, was also released this year, which was awarded CBC Notable Book for Young Readers, short listed for the Melbourne Prize for Literature for Best Writing and the Prime Minister's Literary Award. It was also a winner in the APA Book Design Awards. Erica Hayes began her erotic urban fantasy series *Seven Signs* with *Revelation* at Berkley Sensation, which was a finalist in the Australian Romance Readers Association Awards. Steve Lochran began a new children's superhero series *Vanguard Prime* with *Goldrush*. Doug MacLeod released a creepy young adult fantasy novel, *The Shiny Guys*, and Fiona McIntosh released a sequel to her children's novel *The Whisperer* with *The Rumpelgeist*. Melina Marchetta concluded her young adult *Lumatere Chronicles* with *Quintana of Charyn*. Bernadette Rowley also released her fantasy romance *Princess Avenger* as an ebook with the Penguin Australia imprint Destiny.

Pan Macmillan has continued supporting fantasy fiction this year, although only a few of their authors are Australasian in this genre. Juliet Marillier released two novels with Pan Macmillan this year, the entrancing *Shadowfell*, which was mentioned previously, and the sixth installment of her Sevenwaters series, *Flame of Sevenwaters*. This novel was a finalist in the Aurealis Awards as well as the Tin Ducks. Jaclyn Moriarty released the first in her new Colours of Madeleine series about the cracks between worlds, with *A Corner of White*. This novel won the Ethel Turner prize for young people's literature at the NSW Premier's Literary Awards. Tara Moss released the third in her young adult fashion/paranormal Pandora English series, *The Skeleton Key*. Pan Macmillan's digital publishing arm, Momentum Books, also published many Australian authors. Greig Beck began a new young adult series Valkeryn Chronicles with *Return of the Ancients*. Nina D'Aleo released the science fiction/fantasy/crime *The Last City* and Josephine Pennicott released her *Circle of Nine* trilogy. Louise Cusack released her Shadow Through Time series, and Gillian Polack published her horror/fantasy tale *Ms Cellophane*. *The Final Wish* from Tracey O'Hara was an erotic paranormal fantasy novel this year, which was nominated this year for the ARRA award for Favourite Paranormal. Simon Brown's epic Chronicles of Kydan trilogy was also re-released through Momentum.

Solaris continued their relationship with Rowena Cory Daniells this year, releasing three new novels in her *Outcast* series: *Besieged*, *Exile* and *Sanctuary*, which all made it onto the David Gemmell Legend Awards long list. They also published a novella which is part of Daniells' King Rolen's Kin series, *The King's Man*.

Winterbourne Press added three titles to their catalogue this year, Kate Smith's *What Night Hides*, Shaune Lafferty Webb's *Balanced in an Angel's Eye*, and Anneque Malchien's *Ain't No Rest for the Wicked*.

Clan Destine Press has begun reissuing Kerry Greenwood's Delphic Women trilogy: *Medea*, *Cassandra*, and *Electra*. They also released R.C. Daniells' *The Price of Fame*, and Narrelle M. Harris' very entertaining *Walking Shadows*, sequel to her refreshing vampire story *The Opposite of Life*.

Dragonfall Press, another boutique Perth publishing house, released a number of Australian horror/fantasy titles this year. A.L. Brooks introduced his Mortifera series with *Strangeworld*, and D.J. Daniels released *What the Dead Said*. R.J. Ashby began a science fiction/fantasy series The Airmen with *The Pirates of Aireon*.

Walker Books released a couple of fantasy titles, with Carole Wilkinson continuing her children's Dragonkeeper series with *Blood Brothers* through Walker imprint Black Dog Books. Alison Croggon also released a young adult novel, *Black Spring*.

Angry Robot Books published a number of notable Australasian fantasy titles this year. Jo Anderton's science fiction/fantasy *Suited* has been mentioned previously, as has Trent Jamieson's *Night's Engines*. Lee Battersby's comic fantasy/horror *The Corpse-Rat King* is an enjoyable read which was nominated for a Ditmar for Best Novel. New Zealand author Adam Christopher released two novels with Angry Robot, *Empire State* and *Seven Wonders*. *Empire State* was nominated for a Sir Julius Vogel Award for Best Novel, and Adam Christopher was also nominated for the Best New Talent award.

Text Publishing brought out Leanne Hall's *Queen of the Night*, her Inky Award-short listed sequel to *This is Shyness*. Myke Bartlett's *Fire in the Sea*, a young adult thriller, was also long-listed for an Inky Award. *Shadows* is Paula Weston's first novel in her new paranormal *Rephaim* series.

University of Queensland Press dipped their toes in the fantasy waters by releasing *Word Hunters: The Curious Dictionary* by Nick Earls and Terry Whidborne, and Rosanne Hawke's *The Messenger Bird*.

Anna Tambour had her World Fantasy Award-nominated novel *Crandolin* published with Chômu Press. Kirstyn McDermott brought out her second horror/fantasy novel *Perfections* through Xoum Books, which won an Aurealis Award and Australian Shadows Award for Best Horror Novel. Jay Kristoff released his novel *Stormdancer* with Tor, which was a finalist for Best Fantasy Novel in the Aurealis Awards and was short listed for the David Gemmell Legend Award. Craig Cormick released the young adult science fiction/fantasy novel *Time Vandals* with Scholastic. Rebekah Turner released *Chaos Born* through Escape, an imprint of Harlequin, which was short listed for the Australian Romance Readers Awards Favourite Fantasy/SF/Futuristic Romance.

Dane Richter released the first in his epic fantasy *Eldon Archives* series *Hunt for the Star* through Acashic Books. Demelza Carlton released her paranormal siren story *Ocean's Gift* through Lost Plot Press. Joanna Fay began her new *Siaris* series with *Daughter of Hope* with Musa Publishing, and Tobias Troy released his magical realism novel *Subterfuge in Heart* through Xlibris.

Simon Haynes continued his humorous science fiction/fantasy series *Hal Junior* with *The Missing Case* and *The Gyris Mission* from Bowman Press. Stephen Measday continued his young adult time travel series *Send Simon Savage* series at Hardie Grant Egmont with *Return of the Black Death*. Shona Husk continued her *Goblin King* series with *Kiss of the Goblin King* through Sourcebooks, which was a finalist for the Australian Romance Readers Awards in the Paranormal section.

Sharon Ann Rowland released three titles in her *Crystal Channelers* series with *The Last Reincarnation*, *The Sohtym Stone Trials*, The *Revenge of the Kolob* and Tor Roxburgh released *The Light Heart of Stone* through Curious Crow Books. Bruce Gregor Hodge released the first two books of his *Scarpthorne* series: *The Return of Merling* and *The Wrath of Absynth*.

ANTHOLOGIES

As usual in Australia, most of the genre anthologies released this year were from independent publishers. The exceptions to this rule were *Corrupted Classics* from Harper Collins, and Jonathan Strahan's young adult fantasy anthology *Under My Hat* through Random House, which was nominated for a World Fantasy Award and an Aurealis Award. Strahan's other two anthologies this year, the Aurealis Award-winning *The Best Science Fiction and Fantasy of the Year Volume Six* and his science fiction anthology *Edge of Infinity* were published by Night Shade Books and Solaris Books respectively.

Ticonderoga Publications released three anthologies this year. *The Year's Best Australian Fantasy and Horror 2011* was nominated for an Aurealis Award, Ditmar, Australian Shadows and a Chronos Award, and won a Tin Duck Award. Amanda Pillar's fantastic new look at urban fantasy and paranormal, *Bloodstones*, was nominated for an Aurealis Award and Liz Grzyb and Amanda Pillar's paranormal noir anthology *Damnation & Dames* was nominated for a Tin Duck Award.

Fablecroft Publishing released two anthologies this year, both edited by Tehani Wessely. *To Spin a Darker Stair* is an exquisite chapbook including two fairytale-inspired stories. *Epilogue* was a longer anthology exploring a hopeful view of the future, which was nominated for a Ditmar.

Permuted Press released David Conyers' *Cthulu Unbound 3*. Edwina Harvey released the Sir Julius Vogel Award-winning *Light Touch Paper, Stand Clear* with Peggy Bright Books, also nominated for a Ditmar. Black House Comics released *Terra*, edited by Jason Franks. Jodi Cleghorn released *From Stage Door Shadows* with Emergent Publishing. Paul Collins released his second young adult *Trust Me* anthology, *Trust Me Too* with Ford Street. Stephen Thompson's *Mythic Resonance* anthology was published by Specusphere.

COLLECTIONS

As with the anthologies released this year, the single author collections remained the domain of the independent presses with a couple of exceptions. Allen & Unwin released Isobelle Carmody's new Aurealis-nominated collection *Metro Winds*, and Michael Pryor's futuristic collection *10 Futures* by Random House.

Ticonderoga Publications released three fantasy collections: Felicity Dowker's chilling fantasy/horror *Bread and Circuses* which was nominated for an Australian Shadows and a Chronos Award; Greg Mellor's science fiction/fantasy *Wild Chrome*; and Lisa Hannett and Angela Slatter's collaborative collection *Midnight & Moonshine* which was nominated for an Aurealis Award and a Ditmar.

Twelfth Planet Press also released three boutique collections this year. Kaaron Warren's amazing *Through Splintered Walls* which won an Australian Shadows and Ditmar Award. It included the critically acclaimed novella "Sky", which also won Warren many short fiction awards across the country and a Shirley Jackson Award, and is also up for a World Fantasy Award. As previously mentioned, Margo Lanagan's diverse and intriguing *Cracklescape* was also nominated for many awards this year. Narrelle M. Harris's collection with Twelfth Planet, *Showtime*, showcases Harris' vivacious and engaging writing style.

Dark Prints Press published two horror collections with fantasy elements this year: Craig Bezant's collection *Surviving the End* which won an Australian Shadows Award and Martin Livings' *Living with the Dead* which was also nominated for an Australian Shadows and an Aurealis Award.

IFWG Publishing released Michael Fletcher's *Kings of Under-Castle*. Fresh New Zealand publishers Steam Press released the Sir Julius Vogel Award-winning *Mansfield with Monsters*.

K.J. Bishop and Kate Krake both self-published their collections: *That Book Your Mad Ancestor Wrote*, which won an Aurealis Award, and *Revealing Curiosities* respectively.

MAGAZINES/E-ZINES

Aurealis Magazine is available electronically through iTunes and occasionally Kindle, and other formats through Smashwords. *Aurealis* released ten issues in 2012, combining fiction with opinion pieces.

Andromeda Spaceways Inflight Magazine released four issues this year, from #53–56. ASIM is available both electronically and in print through their website.

Cosmos Magazine regularly publishes speculative fiction edited by Cat Sparks, both in the print magazine (now available as an iPad app) and on the website. While these are primarily science fiction, some stories have fantasy elements.

Antipodean SF has continued to prolifically publish speculative fiction online, releasing monthly issues. *Ticon4.com* publishes fiction irregularly throughout the year.

PODCASTS

Kirstyn McDermott and Ian Mond's *The Writer and the Critic* won the Ditmar this year for Best Fan Production, reflecting its ever-growing popularity. Gary K. Wolfe and Jonathan Strahan's *Coode Street* Podcast and *Galactic Suburbia* have been short listed for the Hugo Award for Best Fancast. Other podcasts which discuss Australian fantasy include: Ion Newcombe's *Antipodean SF Radio Show* and *The Bad Film Diaries Podcast* from Grant Watson and Sonia Marcon.

OTHER MEDIA

Kathleen Jennings has gone from strength to strength in her artistic endeavours this year, being awarded the Ditmars for both Best Artwork and Best Fan Art, and being nominated for a World Fantasy Award.

Peter Jackson's *The Hobbit* is the biggest thing in fantasy movies from Australasia this year. It was short listed for a Hugo for Best Dramatic Presentation, Long Form, a Saturn Award, a Sir Julius Vogel Award and a British Fantasy Award among others.

THE YEAR IN HORROR

ANTHOLOGIES

Avatars of Wizardry (P'rea Press), edited by Charles Lovecraft, offers poetry inspired by George Sterling's *A Wine Of Wizardry* and Clark Ashton Smith's *The Hashish-Eater*, with a foreword by noted anthologist and scholar S. T. Joshi; featured fantastical poets include Australians Leigh Blackmore, Earl Livings, and Kyla Lee Ward.

Bloodstones (Ticonderoga Publications), edited by Amanda Pillar, collects seventeen dark urban fantasy stories concerning esoteric creatures of myth. Featured Antipodean authors include Joanne Anderton, Alan Baxter, Jenny Blackford, Dirk Flinthart, Stephanie Gunn, Richard Harland, Pete Kempshall, Karen Maric, Nicole Murphy, and Dan Rabarts; standout darker tales are "A Small Bad Thing" by Penelope Love (about the Malaysian Toyol),

Thoraiya Dyer's delicate study of impending mortality "Surviving Film".

Damnation and Dames (Ticonderoga Publications) edited by Liz Grzyb and Amanda Pillar, offers sixteen stories of speculative noir. Antipodean authors featured include Jay Caselberg, Dirk Flinthart, Donna Maree Hanson, Chris Large, Penelope Love, Nicole Murphy and Brian G. Ross; both the co-authored stories— Alan Baxter & Felicity Dowker's "Burning, Always Burning", and Lisa L. Hannett & Angela Slatter's "Prohibition Blues"—are highly engaging; Pete Kempshall's "Sound and Fury" and Rob Hood's "Walking the Dead Beat" are also stand out tales.

Cthulhu Unbound 3 (Permuted Press), edited by Brian M. Sammons and David Conyers, offers three long Lovecraftian mythos stories including a co-authored tale by the editors, "The R'Lyeh Singularity", that featured a recurring character, Harrison Peel, from Conyers' *The Spiraling Worm* collection.

Corrupted Classics (HarperCollins Australia), authored by the un-credited "Corrupted Classics Team" is a HarperCollins in-house "project runway" style concept anthology featuring six zombie-themed re-workings of classics. Stories were individually authored as follows—"Alice in Zombieland: A Mad Z Party", "Capulet's Garden of Horror", "Hood and his Undead Men: Eating the Rich and the Poor", "Swiss Family Robinson: A Tale of Zombie Survival" by Tim Miller; "Hector The Undead Prince of Troy" by Melanie Saward.

eMergent Publishing brought out two anthologies in 2012. *Deck the Halls: festive tales of fear and cheer*, edited by Jodi Cleghorn and with art by Andrew McKiernan, is a huge book of traditional Christmas horror tales, and includes Australian writers Benjamin Solah, Rebecca Dobbie, Rebecca Emin, Graham Storrs, Nicole R Murphy, Jo Hart, Jonathan Crossfield, Lily Mulholland, Janette Dalgliesh, Laura Meyer, Stacey Larner, Jodi Cleghorn, Steve Cameron and David McDonald. eMergent also published *From Stage Door Shadows*, sporting a lovely cover by Blake Byrnes; the anthology collects twenty-six stories about the spooky space of theatre in its many guises, with Antipodean authors Graham Storrs, Andrew J. McKiernan, Alan Baxter, Joanne Anderton, Jennifer Muirhead, S.G. Larner, Melanie Saward, Laura Meyer, Jodi Cleghorn, Rebecca L. Dobbie, Janette Dalgliesh, and Tom Dullemond.

FableCroft Publishing produced the wonderful *Epilogue* anthology, edited by Tehani Wessely; twelve tales exploring ideas of post-apocalyptic society, with notable darker tales being "The Mornington Ride" by Jason Nahrung, "Ghosts" by Stephanie Gunn, and "Cold Comfort" by David McDonald.

Dark Prints Press also published a post-apocalyptic collection, *Surviving the End* (edited by Craig Bezant); nine horrific stories linked together with framing narrative by the editor. Antipodean authors in the mix include Amanda J Spedding, Ashlee Scheuerman, Martin Livings and Kathryn Hore. Stand-out story is Jason Nahrung's relentlessly bleak "The Last Boat to Eden", arguably the finest horror story from 2012.

The Specusphere (in cooperation with Esstee Media) forayed into publishing with *Mythic Resonance* (edited by Stephen Thompson), a mythology themed anthology. Notable darker tales are "The Everywhere and The Always" from Alan Baxter, and "Wetlands" by Jen White. Steve Rossiter edited *Possessing Freedom* (The Australian Literature Review); twelve stories from four writers, Beau Hillier, Belinda Dorio, Rhiannon Hart, and the editor. Karen Henderson edited the *Night Terrors Anthology* (Kayelle Press), collecting supernatural horror and published as an ebook; includes a story by Andrew J. McKiernan.

Kaaron Warren placed "Blame the Neighbours" with *Slices of Flesh* (Dark Moon Books). "The River of Memory" by Kaaron Warren was published in *Zombies vs. Robots: The River of Memory* (IDW Publishing). Kaaron Warren's "The Pickwick Syndrome" appeared alongside her AHWA protégé Michelle Goldsmith's "The Hound of Henry Hortinger" in *Pandemonium: Stories of the Smoke* (Jurassic London).

"King Wolf" by Anna Tambour appeared in *A Season in Carcosa* edited by Joe Pulver (Miskatonic River Press). Christopher Sequiera had two short stories, "The Scion of Fear" and "The Adventure of the Lost Specialist" included in *Sherlock Holmes: The Crossovers Casebook* (Moonstone Publishing). "Sayuri's Revenge" by Helen Stubbs and "The Kiss" by Jason Nahrung appeared in *Tales From the Bell Club* (Knightwatch Press). "The Loquacious Cadaver" by Kyla Ward was published in *The Lion and The Aardvark: Aesop's Modern Fables* (Pelgrane Press).

Pete Kempshall had "Closure" and Dave Hoskins had "Collisions" in *World's Collider: A Shared World Anthology* (Nightscape Press). Kempshall placed "Dry Run" in *Beast Within 3: Oceans Unleashed* (Graveside Tales). Eugene Gramelis published "2109" and "The Milepost Motel" in *Night Gypsy: Journey Into Darkness* (Indie Gypsy). Marty Young had "A Monstrous Touch" in *Dangers Untold* (Alliteration Ink), and "Addiction" in *Tales From The Mist* (Anessa Books). Steven Gepp saw publication of "A Visit From Zombie Nicholas" and "Another Endless Night" in *The Undead That Saved Christmas 3: Monster Bash* (Rainstorm Press), and "Second Chance" in *Tales Of Terror And Mayhem From Deep Within The Box* (Evil Jester Press). "Dark Spaces" by Suzanne J. Willis appeared in *A Rustle of Dark Leaves: Tales from the Shadows of the Forest* (Misanthrope Press). "Life in Miniature" by Tracie McBride appeared in *Scared: Ten Tales of Horror* (Scimitar Press).

Charles Lovecraft saw publication of "Apocalyptic Vision: The End II" in *Buzzkill: Apocalypse* (NightBallet Press). Jay Caselberg had "Beautiful" in *The Washington Pastime*. Talitha Kalago published "Blood For Bone" in *Demon Lovers: Succubi* (Storybones Publishing). "Duck Creek Road" by S. G. Larner appeared in *Bloody Parchment: Hidden Things, Lost Things and other stories* (Random House). Gerry Huntman published "Creation's Flaw" in *Penny Dread Tales, Volume Two: A Phantasmagorical Calliope of Clockwork and Steam* (RuneWright), and "Raindrops In His Eyes", and "They Can Never Find Out" in *Dark Dispatches* (Static Movement), and "Whatever Happens Happens" in *Tales Of Terror And Mayhem From Deep Within The Box* (Evil Jester Press).

"Hungry Man" by Will Elliott appeared in *The Apex Book of World SF 2* (Apex Publications). "Old Mabel's Stray Cat" by Cameron Trost appeared in *Fear: A Modern Anthology of Horror and Terror 1* (Crooked Cat Publishing). Tom Dullemond had "Population Management" in *Danse Macabre: Close Encounters with the Reaper* (EDGE Publishing). "The Girl from Odessa" by David McDonald appeared in *Night of the Nyctalope* (Black Coat Press). Gitte Christensen's "The Snowy River Feral" was in *Return of the Dead Men (and Women) Walking* (Bards and Sages Publishing). Steven Gepp published "The Seeker and the Dark

One" in *Tough As Nails* (NorGus Press) and *"Wrestling Gators"* in *Lucha Gore: Scares from the Squared Circle* (Cruentus Libri Press). "Thumping" by Rachel Towns appeared in *Unnatural Tales of the Jackalope* (Western Legends Press).

MAGAZINES

Andromeda Spaceways Inflight Magazine (Andromeda Spaceways Publishing Co-op) published three issues in 2012, although it was a light year for dark stories from ASIM. The issues notable for dark content is Issue 55 (edited by Jacob Edwards) which came out in December and featured the claustrophobic social horror story *"First They Came"* by Deborah Kalin.

Aurealis magazine went forward as an emagazine in 2012, charging for issues through Smashwords. The magazine published an impressive ten issues, with two short stories per issue, ranging across the speculative genres. Issues notable for horror content are Issue 47 (February, edited by Dirk Strasser) featuring Jason Nahrung's rural vampire story "Breaking The Wire"; Issue 49 (April, edited by Michael Pryor and Dirk Strasser) featuring Jason Fischer's "Rolling For Fetch"; *Aurealis* 52 (July, edited by Scott Vandervalk and Stephen Higgins) featuring Robert N. Stephenson's demon hunting thriller "Do You Want To Live Forever?"; Issue 53 (August, edited by Stephen Higgins) featuring the creepy teddy tale "The Karma Tree" by Benjamin Allmon; Issue 55 (October, edited by Dirk Strasser) features a reprint of Lisa L. Hannett's Aurealis Award winning story "The Short Go: a Future in Eight Seconds"; Issue 56 (edited by Dirk Strasser) featured reprints of Thoraiya Dyer's Aurealis Award-winning "Fruit of the Pipal Tree", and the Aurealis Award-winning "The Past Is A Bridge Best Left Burnt" by Paul Haines.

Dark Edifice proved an interesting new literary speculative magazine, publishing two editions as PDF in 2012, including writers active in academic circles rather than mainstay Australian speculative practitioners; featured writers included Eddy Burger, J. Michael Melican, Shannon Bell, Candace Petrik, Jo Clay, Sam Sperling, Helen Haloulos, Guy Salvidge, Nicholas Ordinans, Travis McKenzie, and Katya Becerra.

Exotic Gothic 4—Postscripts 28/29 (PS Publishing) featured a number of wonderful Australian writers. "Escena de un Asesinato" by Robert Hood was one the stand-out stories of the year, blending haunted images with creepy fetishism; other offerings included "Blooding the Bride" by Margo Lanagan, "The Fall" by Stephen Dedman, and "The Lighthouse Keepers' Club" by Kaaron Warren.

The Australian Horror Writers Association published two issues of *Midnight Echo*. Issue 8 published in November (edited by Amanda J. Spedding, Mark Farrugia, and Marty Young) featured "The Girl from the Borderlands" by Felicity Dowker, "Hello Kitty" by Jason Nahrung, "They Don't Know That We Know What They Know" by Andrew J. McKiernan, "Tooth" by Kathryn Hore, "Jar Baby" by Michelle Jager, "The Boy With the Hole in his Heart" by Caysey Sloan, and "Pigroot Flat" by Jason Fischer. The winners of the AHWA Story competition were also published in this issue—"Always A Price" by Joanne Anderton (AHWA Short Story winner), and "Blood Lillies" by Shauna O'Meara (AHWA Flash Fiction winner). Issue 7—The Taboo Issue came out in May (edited by Daniel I. Russell), and included "Saturday Night at the Milk Bar" by Gary Kemble, "Brand New Day" by G. N. Braun, "The Final Degustation of Doctor Ernest Blenheim" by Andrew J. McKiernan, and "Ghosts of You" by Lee Battersby.

Margo Lanagan published "Mouth to Mouth" in *The Big Issue*, 28 August–10 September, 2012, and "Titty Anne and the Very, Very Hairy Man" in *Meanjin, Volume 71, Number 4*. Terry Dowling's "Nightside Eye" appeared in *Cemetery Dance 66*, and "The Way the Red Clown Hunts You" appeared in *Subterranean*, Winter 2012. Jenny Blackford published "Their Cold Eyes Pierced My Skin" in *The Pedestal Magazine 70*. Gerry Huntman published "The Weight of Sin" in *Blood Moon Rising 49*. Barry Rosenberg published "Arachnid-Man" in *Penumbra eMag, Volume II Issue 2*, and "Two Minus One Makes Three" in *SNM Horror Magazine* (April/May 2012). Charles Lovecraft had "Choir (of the Damned)" and "The Rhymeless Sonnet of Fear" in *The Weird Fiction Review 3* (Oct 2012), and "Temple of Nyarlathotep" in *Eye to the Telescope 6*. Leigh Blackmore's "The Last Dream (for Ambrose Bierce)" appeared in *The Weird Fiction Review 3* (Oct 2012).

"Creeper" by Daniel I. Russell appeared in *SQ Mag 2*. "Crossroads and Carousels" by Alan Baxter appeared in *The Red Penny Papers*, Fall 2012. "Dawn's First Kiss" by David Kernot and "If You Give This Girl a Ride" by Steve Cameron appeared in

Cover of Darkness 11. "Dead on the Doorstep" by Peter Cooper appeared in *Kaleidotrope, Spring 2012.* Tracie McBride's "Drive, She Said" was published in *Lovecraft eZine 14*; Anna Tambour's "The Dog Who Wished He'd Never Heard of Lovecraft" appeared in *Lovecraft eZine 13.* "Hours on the Voodoo Clock" by Kelly Matsuura appeared in *Free Flash Fiction.* "In the Dark" by Ian Nichols was featured in *Apex Magazine 37.* Eugene Gramelis published "Live Girls" in *Night to Dawn 21.* "The Haunting" by Jay Caselberg was published in *ChiZine.* "Night Music" by Pete Aldin appeared in *Niteblade 19.* Jacinta Butterworth's "Zombies" saw publication in *Wet Ink 27.*

COLLECTIONS

Living with the Dead (Dark Prints Press), the debut collection by Martin Livings, is simply the strongest single-author horror collection of the year. Collecting the best twenty-three stories from twenty years of publishing, including three stories original to the collection ("Birthday Suit", "You Ain't Heard Nothing Yet", and "The Ar-Dub"), and an introduction from Kaaron Warren—drawing on two decades of work really shows in quality, the breadth of work on offer here is quite outstanding.

Bread and Circuses is the debut collection by Felicity Dowker, edited by Russell B. Farr (Ticonderoga Publications); showcasing fifteen stories and boasting an introduction by Trent Jamieson. Of special note are Dowker's fabulously original feminist zombie story for which the anthology is named.

Midnight and Moonshine (Ticonderoga Publications) co-authored by the inseparable 'Brains' Lisa L. Hannett and Angela Slatter, and edited by Russell B. Farr, and with an introduction by Kim Wilkins and an exquisite cover by Kathleen Jennings; this collection of thirteen stories explores territory of myth and folklore as interconnected tales, described as a "mosaic novel". A beautiful collection showcasing the elegant craft of these wonderful collaborators.

James Doig edited two fascinating historical collections for Ash Tree Press. *The Devil of the Marsh and Other Stories*, published as a limited edition of 500, collects fifteen stories by the Australian-born H.B. Marriott Watson (1863–1921), a prolific Gothic writer, and a contemporary of Thomas Hardy, Henry James, and H.G. Wells in London literary society. The book is also available as a Kindle edition, and includes the vampire classic "The Stone Chamber". *A Natural Body and a Spiritual Body: Some Worcestershire Encounters with the Supernatural* by J.S. Leatherbarrow (1908–1989) unearths rare works from an Australian writer active in the 1930s, creating his own ghost stories in homage to M.R. James.

Twelfth Planet Press released a number of single author collections from women as part of The Twelve Planets series edited by Alisa Krasnostein; *Cracklescape* by Margo Lanagan collects four stories, most notable among them "Bejazzle" and "Significant Dust"; *Showtime* by Narrelle M. Harris contrasts the serious dysfunction of "Stalemate" with comedic contemporary vampire and zombie tales, including the title story featuring the recurring characters Lissa and Gary (the world's most inept vampire); *Through Splintered Walls* by Kaaron Warren features four literary horror stories, the stand-out being the luminous story "Sky".

Sophie Masson's *The Great Deep and Other Tales of the Uncanny* (Sixteen Press), while not horror, traverses dark folkloric territory in a poised literary style and truly earns the title "uncanny". Dark Continents Publishing published the co-authored *April Fool and other antipodean horror stories* by New Zealand born authors John Irvine and Tracie McBride; the collection offers three stories from Irvine, and two from McBride.

Self-published collections for the year include—*Revealing Curiosities: Collected Tales both Peculiar and Grim* by Kate Krake; *Hoffman's Creeper and other disturbing tales*, the debut collection by Cameron Trost, a robust volume of twenty-three tales; *The Flesh Trade and other nineteen drabbles* by Marcelo Rinesi, twenty flash stories shorter than one hundred words, mostly literary SF, with some mortality concerned stories evoking a horror atmosphere. David R. Grigg published two collections through Rightword Enterprises—*At the Dark Lighthouse and other tales*, an ebook collected seventeen short stories ranging from horror to fantasy, and a science fiction anthology.

Books for children that touched on horror themes included *Monstrum House* by Z. Fraillon (Hardie Grant Egmont) collects four short stories of YA monster hunting, all set in the same unusual boarding school; *Not Bog Standard and Other Peculiar Stories* (Scholastic Australia) is the debut collection of humorous, fantastical, very Australian stories for children, by Perth-based writer Mark Pardoe; *Witches' Britches, Itches & Twitches!* a book of jokes and puzzles by Mark Carthew (Interactive Publications).

NOVELLAS

In 2012 stand-alone eNovellas became a major area of output, both for small press and especially for self-publishing authors. Dark Prints Press launched their eNovella series with *Rope* by Martin Livings, an oppressive portrait of a hangman at Freemantle Prison; Greg Chapman's *Vaudeville* was the carnivalesque follow up.

Dark Continents published Daniel I. Russell's *Critique* about a nasty food critic who gets his just deserts, and Matthew Tait's *Slander Hall* which explores the ghostly aftermath of a cult suicide in an affluent gated community in the US. Tait's other novella of 2012, *The Grief School* (Dark Meridian) concerns a grieving gambler, and Daniel I. Russell self-published the novella *Penanggalan! An Aussie Vampire Tale.*

Dark Water by Mike Pieloor is a self-published ebook novelette about a prescient child. Erica Hayes published a stand-alone Kindle edition novella *Hunter's Blood*; a demon huntress and vampire slayer team up against soul-munching demons. *It Hides In Darkness* is a Southern Gothic eNovella by Canberra Science Fiction Guild member Ross C. Hamilton.

Zombies continue to be popular. *Dawn of the Zombie Knights* (JoJo Publishing) by Adam Wallace is a comedy zombie romp in the Pete McGee series, and John e Normal's zomedy *Land Down Undead: The Backpacker's Guide* is a self-published post-apocalyptic travel guide. Patty Jansen's *Looking for Daddy* is a self-published stand-alone Kindle edition about a child's quest in zombie plagued world.

Anomaly, co-authored by Jason Fischer and British fantasist Steven Saville and Jason Fischer, is a stand-alone thriller in the Viral Novellas ebook series from Swedish publisher Foxrain. *Beauty's Sister* by James Bradley, is a dark re-imagining of the Rapunzel myth published under the Penguin Shorts imprint. Alan Baxter's *The Darkest Shade of Grey* (The Red Penny Papers) is novella-length supernatural noir. Eleni Konstantine's *Gateway to Hell* (Musa Publishing) is a paranormal romance novella, first in the series of Warder Tales. Shona Husk's *Brightwater Blood*

(Samhain Publishing) is a rather dark paranormal romance stand-alone ebook novella concerning shamanism and shape shifters, and witchcraft and blood magic.

YA and children's novella length works were also notable. Deborah Abela's *Ghost Club 1: The New Kid and Ghost Club 2: The Haunted School* (Random House Australia) are kids adventure novellas. K.C. Webb's *Soul Trader: A Johnny Marsh Adventure* is the second in the dark YA series published by Dark Wind Books, and illustrated by A.R. Puttee. Libby Gleeson's *Red* (Allen & Unwin) is a YA crime-thriller with an amnesia-stricken protagonist, set in Sydney after a cyclone. *The Grimstones 1: Hatched, The Grimstones 2: Mortimer Revealed* and *The Grimstones 3: Whirlwind* (Allen & Unwin) by an author/illustrator publishing as Asphyxia, are novella-length illustrated books for children based on a stage production with Gothic puppets.

Novella length works also appeared in many anthologies. Sylvia Kelso's "Sister Anne" is a retelling of the Bluebeard story in *Beyond Grimm* (Book View Café). Kaaron Warren's novella "The History Thief" in *Visions Fading Fast* (Pendragon Press) is a whimsical, Gaimanesque ghost story. "Elyora" by Jodi Cleghorn, a supernatural horror novella published in the *Review of Australian Fiction, Special 'Down The Rabbit Hole' Issue 2012*.

NOVELS

Lee Battersby saw publication of *The Corpse-Rat King* (Angry Robot), a unique take on the quest to the underworld motif. Will Elliott's *Nightfall* (HarperCollins) is another darkly fantastic adventure in the underworld. Kirstyn McDermott's *Perfections* (Xoum) is an urbane gothic story concerning the interwoven lives of two sisters and a doppelganger. Jason Nahrung's *Blood and Dust* (Xoum) wryly and engagingly details the exploits of a monaro-driving vampire named Kevin, caught in a vampire biker war in North Queensland. *Salvage* (Twelfth Planet Press) by Jason Nahrung, a short novel, an Australian Gothic using the vampire archetype with subtlety. Jason Fischer's *Quiver* (Black House Comics) is a zombie novel, the first of *The Tamsyn Webb Chronicles* following a young archer protagonist, originated in the *After The World* magazine.

Margo Lanagan's *Sea Hearts* (Allen & Unwin) a complex selkie myth novel about doomed love. *Beneath A Rising Moon* (Dell) by Keri Arthur is the third installment in the *Ripple Creek Werewolf Series*; Arthur also saw release of *Darkness Devours* and *Darkness Hunts* (Penguin), part of the *Dark Angels* paranormal series. *Black Mountain* (Pan Macmillan) by Greig Beck is a supernatural thriller exploring the Yeti myth. Alison Croggon's *Black Spring* (Walker Books) is a dark fantasy inspired by Emily Brontë's *Wuthering Heights*. *Bloody Waters* (Possible Press) by Jason Franks is a Faustian rock'n'roll adventure mixing up witches and succubus and crime. Trent Jamieson's *Night's Engines* (Angry Robot) concludes *The Nightbound Land* duology.

Adrian Scott's *A Vampire's Tale* is the first novella in a sixteen-part series titled *Society of Vampires* (Rebecca J. Vickery Publications); *Gateway to Hell* is a cursed mansion stand-alone novel from the same author. Cin Eric's *Baker Street Inquisitor* (MuseItUp Publishing) is the second in a supernatural noir crime series. *Beneath A Cold Moon* (Equilibrium Books) by Keith Williams is a crime thriller set in Glasgow, Scotland and Geelong, Australia. Ex-pat Western Australian Tracy Cooper-Posey's *Blood Stone* and *Byzantine Heartbreak* (Stories Rule) are part of a vampire paranormal romance series. Eleanor Coombe's self-published novel *Burying Ground Point* is a ghost story on the Tasmanian coast. *Chaos Born* (Escape Publishing) by Rebekah Turner is dark steampunk crime.

Kaz Delaney's *Dead, Actually* (Allen & Unwin) is a YA paranormal adventure. Jack Heath's *Dead Man Running* was released exclusively as an ebook by Pan Macmillan Australia. *Death By Beauty* (Hachette Australia) is installment #5 in the *Gemma Lincoln PI* series by Gabrielle Lord; this time Lincoln is on the case of a vampire attacking beautiful women. Jessica Shirvington's *Endless* (Hachette Australia) is part four in the *Violet Eden Chronicles* of angel paranormal romance. Myke Bartlett's *Fire in the Sea* (Text Publishing) concerns ancient mythical creatures battling through Perth, and won the Text Prize for YA and Children's Writing in 2011. *Flesh* (Momentum) by Kylie Scott is the first in a zombie apocalypse series, with a romantic ménage à trois twist. Aaron Dries published two novels through Samhain Publishing; *House of Sighs*, a thriller about a bus driver kidnapping her passengers, and *The Fallen Boys*, a splatter-punk abduction novel.

How to Disappear Completely is a surreal novel from Annika Howells, self-published to Kindle. *Love notes from Vinegar House* (Black Dog Books) is a YA Gothic flirtation with the haunted house archetype from Karen Tayleur. *Night Beach* (Penguin Books Australia) by Kirsty Eagar is a YA Gothic romance, and garnered a nomination for The Gold Inky Award. Andrez Bergen's *One Hundred Years of Vicissitude* (Perfect Edge Books) is the follow up to *Tobacco Stained Mountain Goat* with the continuing protagonist Wolram E. Deaps—new weird with horror overtones, this novel follows a now dead Deaps as he travels through the memories of a twentieth century geisha ghost named Kohana.

Erica Hayes *Revelation* (Berkley) is a paranormal romance featuring fallen angels, demon princesses, in a zombie plague. Paula Weston's *Shadows* (Text Publishing) is part one in *The Rephaim*, a gritty YA paranormal series about angels. *Shine Light* (Random House Australia) is the third installment in the *Night Creatures* YA series by Marianne de Pierres. Tracey O'Hara's *Sin's Dark Caress* (HarperCollins) is book three in the Dark Brethren series, concerning a "forensic witch". *Team Human* (Allen & Unwin) by Justine Larbalestier and Sarah Rees Brennan is a YA parody paranormal romance. Brett McBean's *The Awakening* (Tasmaniac Publications) explores the traditional Haitian zombie trope.

Daniel I. Russell's *The Collector—Book One: Mana Leak* (Dark Continents Publishing) is a small town horror melodrama about dysfunctional people confronted by death embodied. *The End Of Ever* is a post-apocalyptic horror novel self-published by Troy Barnes. *The Flats* by Craig Bezant is Dark Prints Press foray into kids fiction with the Darklings imprint. *The Skeleton Key* (Pan Macmillan Australia) from Tara Moss is the third *Pandora English novel*, with continued romantic intrigue and an unlocking of secrets in the protagonist's haunted mansion. *Disharmony* (Penguin Australia) by Leah Giarratano is the first in YA paranormal *The Telling* series concerning supernaturally gifted twins. *Walking Shadows* (Clan Destine Press) by Narrelle M. Harris is the sequel to *The Opposite Of Life*; geek-girl Lissa and her best mate Gary (the world's most inept vampire) take on killer vampires in a comedic romp around Melbourne's very exclusive Western Suburbs Goth club scene. Sometime rock chick and celebrity Wiccan Fiona Horne has forayed into YA paranormal with *Witch: A Summerland Mystery* (Allen & Unwin) where an Australian teen witch turns California girl.

GRAPHIC NOVELS, COMICS & ILLUSTRATED WORKS

Black House Comics had a prolific year publishing Australian horror; comic book *The Dark Detective: Sherlock Holmes Vol 7*, written by Christopher Sequiera, with cover art by Dave Elsey and interior illustrations by Phil Cornell; retro-horror anthology *Eeek!* written and illustrated by Jason Paulos; Jason Franks "gonzo-SF-noir adventures of Whiteface McBlack" saw publication through the Black Glass Press imprint as *McBlack*. *Terra Magazine* edited by Jason Franks launched—a triannual comics magazine with newsstand distribution. Talent on show includes Tom Bonin, Ben Michael Byrne, Michal Dutkiewicz, Jason Franks, Jason Fischer, Greg Gates, Nicholas Hunter, Leigh Kuilboer, Bruce Mutard, Luke Pickett, Jason Paulos, Harry Purnell, Jan Scherpenhuizen, Christopher Sequeira and Yuriko Sekine.

Hayden Fryer wrote and illustrated the *Darkest Night: Acts 1 and 2* graphic novel series (Siberian Productions). John Stewart wrote and illustrated the first in a five part comic series titled *Giants*. Jason Paulos had three horror comic designs commissioned to adorn wine bottles through The Creative Method. *Ghost Doll and Jasper* by Fiona McDonald is blurbed as "an Edward Gorey-esque graphic novel for kids" from Sky Pony Press.

Darren Koziol published three issues of *Decay* horror comic magazine in 2012, which included work by numerous Australian creators. *Decay Issue 14* (December 2012), the 'End of the World' themed issue, featured work from Koziol, Lachlan Creagh, Dave Heinrich, John Fitch, Alister Lockhart, Kurt Stone, Jan Scherpenhuizen, Charith Wijewardane, Paul Briske, and Jason Paulos. *Decay Issue 13* (August 2012) includes work from Australian creators Frantz Kantor, Lee Smith, Hayden Fryer, Jason Paulos, Erin McGregor, Melissa Waterman, and Nahum Ziersch. *Decay Issue 12* (April 2012) was the Cthulhu Special edition with twenty pages of colour, and contained offerings from Lee Smith, John Stewart, Darren Koziol, and Glenn Lumsden; the issue featured Cthulhu pin-up pages from Jason Paulos, Ryan Wilton,

SCAR (Steve Carter & Antoinette Rydyr), Danikah Harrison, Nahum Ziersch, Tanya and Owen Nicholls, Colin Wells, Emerson Ward, Jan Scherpenhuizen, Dénes Nagy, David Williams, and Dave Heinrich.

FILM

Crawlspace (dir. Justin Dix), a sci-fi horror set at Pine Gap, premiered at Cannes. Isolate (dir. Martyn Park) premiered at the 2012 Los Angeles Fear and Fantasy Film Festival; Jacinta John took out the Best Actress award at the LA Festival, and also Best Actress at the Indie Gems Film Festival in Paramatta, New South Wales. *Bait 3D* (dir. Kimble Rendall), a joint Australian/ Singaporean schlock giant shark feature, premiered at the Venice Film Festival in September 2012. *100 Bloody Acres* (dir. Colin and Cameron Cairnes), a comedy horror feature set around a blood and bone fertilizer factory, premiered at the Melbourne International Film Festival in August 2012. *6 Plots* (dir. Leigh Sheehan) filmed in Williamstown in Victoria, was released to DVD in Japan and had a TV premiere in Sweden as *Six Graves. As Wonderland Goes By* (dir. Marc Windham) an Australian/Bulgarian production filmed on location in Bulgaria, Hungary and Austria; this parody thriller has notable technical production, filmed to 65mm film using a Panavision Super 70 lense, and stars adult film star Kayden Kross. *Nowhere Else* (dir. Danial Donai) premiered at the Goldcoast Film Festival; the feature follows a documentary crew who stumble upon a Olitiau, a gigantic mythological bat. *Inhuman Resources* (dir. Nicholas Hope) received a DVD release in Japan on the Fangoria Presents label; the film details the bloody exploits of a psychopath office manager.

A Night of Horror Film Festival's Australian Horror Gala featured a range of Australia horror shorts—*Defrayment* (dir. Christos Katsaros), *A Dream* (dir. Laurence Rosier Staines), *School For Zombies* (dir. Daniel James Millar), The *Truth* (dir. Martin O'Donoghue), and the music video for Thy Art Is Murder's *Reign In Darkness* (dir. Chris Elder) all premiered at A Night of Horror. A Night of Horror hosted an Exclusive "Online Only" Shorts Program that included the Australian films *Tyson's September Playlist* (dir. Siobhan Mulready) and *Too Late* (dir. Mike Gibson).

The Occupants (dir. Alex Chapman and James Lane) was a semi-finalist in the Action/Cut Short Film Competition. *She's Having A Baby!* (dir. Robert and Chris Smellin) premiered at the Nevermore Film Festival (USA), and received an honourable mention at the Fright Night Film Festival (USA). *Friend Request* (dir. Danny McShane) premiered at the Tribal Theatre in Brisbane, and was an official selection for La Indie Film Festival (USA), received an Award of Merit in the international Indie Fest awards, and won Best Horror Film at the Intendance Film Festival (USA). *Elizabeth* (dir. Adam Johnsson) won the awards for Best Directing in Drama and Most Provocative Film at the 16th Sydney Film School Festival 2012. Animated horror film *Butterflies* (dir. Isabel Peppard) won the Best Animation Award at The Sydney Film Festival, which qualified the film for Oscar nomination.

THE YEAR IN THE INDUSTRY

Many Australian speculative fiction authors attended and/or presented panels at literary festivals across the country, such as Peter Ball, Deborah Biancotti, John Birmingham, Alison Croggon, Brian Falkner, John Flanagan, Jackie French, Narrelle M. Harris, Melina Marchetta, Jason Nahrung, Michael Pryor, Emily Rodda, Lucy Sussex and Kaaron Warren.

Many of the large publishers have been getting on the bandwagon of releasing ebooks only, and having a digital publishing arm to their companies. Pan Macmillan opened their much-discussed Momentum digital publishing arm this year, with a plethora of new and re-released ebooks and print-on-demand titles. Penguin Australia branched out with Destiny, their digital romance imprint, and Harper Collins launched Harper Teen Impulse, dedicated to young adult short fiction. Random House was one of the first, opening Hydra, with controversial terms for authors.

Angry Robot was inundated with submissions for their Open Door submissions period in April this year, receiving hundreds of Fantasy submissions.

Steam Press, a recently opened New Zealand publisher, is off to a great start, releasing a collection and two science fiction novels in their first year of operation, and also winning a Sir Julius Vogel Award.

············

REMEMBERED

Paul Haines, 41, multiple award-winning Australian dark fantasy writer. **Alice Shirley Brine**, grandmother of Ticonderoga Publications editor Liz Grzyb. **Maddy Grzyb-Farr**, 11, beloved Ticonderoga pooch. **Michael O'Brien**, 42, Perth fan and compleat gentleman. **Boris Strugatsky**, 70, Russian science fiction writer. **Margaret Mahy**, 76, New Zealand young adult writer, recipient of the Hans Christian Andersen Award. **Ray Bradbury**, 91, legend. **Maurice Sendak**, 83, U.S. Writer and illustrator of *Where The Wild Things Are*. **Harry Harrison**, 87, SFWA Grand Master. **Gerry Anderson**, 83, co-creator of *The Thunderbirds*. **Jean Giraud**, 73, 'Moebius', artist. **Ralph McQuarrie**, 82, science fiction artist, *Star Wars* developer. **Janet Berliner**, 73, Bram Stoker Award winner. **Leo Dillon**, 79, SF artist. **Kathy Diane Wentworth**, 61, Writers of the Future winner. **John Christopher**, 89, real name Sam Youd, writer of *The Death of Grass* and The Tripods trilogy. **Ardath Mayhar**, 81, SFWA Author Emeritus. **Bryce Courtenay**, 79, Australian best-selling writer.

PAUL HAINES

CAT SPARKS

8 JUNE 1970 — 5 MARCH 2012

A year and a half has passed since Paul Richard Haines, a much loved, admired and missed member of the Australian speculative fiction community, lost his five-year battle with cancer.

Born and raised in Auckland, New Zealand, Haines moved to Australia in the 1990s after completing a university degree in Otago. He attended the inaugural Clarion South writers' workshop in 2004 and was a member of Melbourne's SuperNOVA writers group. Haines had more than thirty short stories published in Australia, North America, and Greece.

Haines won Australia's Ditmar Award three times (Best New Talent in 2005; Best novella/novelette for "The Last Days of Kali Yuga" (2005) and "The Devil in Mr Pussy (Or How I Found God Inside My Wife)" (2007)); and the 2004 horror short story Aurealis Award for "The Last Days of Kali Yuga". His fiction regularly received Honourable Mentions in the annual Year's Best Fantasy and Horror anthologies, edited by Ellen Datlow, Gavin Grant, and Kelly Link (St. Martins). In 2009 his novella "Wives" made the James Tiptree Jr Honours list.

Haines' first short story collection *Doorways For The Dispossessed* (Prime Books, 2006) won New Zealand's 2008 Sir Julius Vogel Award for Best Collection. Two subsequent collections followed: *Slice of Life* (The Mayne Press, 2009) and *The Last Days of Kali Yuga* (Brimstone Press, 2011).

Haines left us with a significant body of potent, thematic storytelling. His prose encompassed a blend of horror, humour and his own unique sensibility, often delving below the skin to itch in uncomfortable places.

Long evenings lingering in convention bars are not the same without him. Nor are anthologies—there's a story missing. A gap that continues to haunt our community as it matures and evolves.

Paul Haines is survived by his wife Julie and daughter Isla.

•••••••••••

THE YEAR'S BEST AUSTRALIAN FANTASY & HORROR

~ 2012 ~

THE THIRD ANNUAL COLLECTION

BELLA BEAUFORT GOES TO WAR

LISA L. HANNETT & ANGELA SLATTER

Volume Twelfth, 2nd Series, No. 312. July 19, 1873

QUERIES, cont'd:——

MAKING FATE & THE INFLUENCE OF NORNS IN THE NEW WORLD

In pursing research for my book, IN THE FASHION OF WOLVES, *I come, time and again, to the same pressing questions: Does the Norns' power stop when* certitude *does? When the idea that they decree* FATE *and tend to* YGGDRASIL *weakens, can such myths continue to exist? When faith in them ceases, to what thread might they cling? Without the lifeline of credulity are these* things *no more than the smoke of memory dispersed on the wind? Or are they weaving still, out of sight and mind, but not out of the world? Opinions and responses are most heartily desired.*

Valdís Brynjólfsdóttir
South Carolina, United States of America

"What do you see?"

Black things flap and snap on the wire fence running around the vacant land adjacent to the Laveau place. The sun is harsh, reflecting on the hard-packed dirt street, glaring off the two-storey house's peeling white paint; yet the old woman insists upon sitting out on the verandah with the heat and light bouncing up at her, hitting the great diamond hanging like a monocle on a silver chain around her neck.

Sweat creeps down Bella's skin, soaking the armpits and back of her green gingham work dress, trickling from her temples, making her scalp itch worse than the lice she'd been afflicted with last summer. What she wouldn't give to scratch like a dog right about now, or to lift the thick russet hair off her crown like an unwanted hat. But she ignores the urge and concentrates on the widow's question. She squints, stares across overgrown cotton fields, and focuses on the shreds of—*what?*—writhing in the distance. While she gathers her thoughts, Eugenia, as usual, leaps in.

"Dead birds. Ravens. Big ones." This last was added in an uncertain tone, as though she realises she's wrong once again. The old lady's lip curls—she doesn't even bother to conceal it from her great-granddaughter nowadays—and then slides her eyes to Bella, who senses the expectation in that look, just as keenly as she feels Eugenia's resentment seething off her. Within the first few days of their apprenticeship, she'd overheard the other girl moaning to her *mémé*, saying it wasn't right, her teaching the two of them together. Her own rightful heir and Bella No-Blood. Bella Know-it-all. Bella Who-wasn't-even-family.

Such a waste of effort, staring so hard at someone else's flaws, the Widow Paris had said. *Take a close look at yourself, Eugenia Laveau, and tell me—what do you see?*

"It's skins," says Bella, who wasn't even family, as she smooths the white pin-tucks of her apron. "Skins taken so they can't fly anymore."

"They?" Eugenia sneers, white-blonde hair a striking contrast against her bronze skin. She props her elbows on the porch railing next to Bella, leans down to take another look from that vantage. Her sharp nose crinkling like there's a bad smell.

"They. Witches. Witches with their wings clipped, with their soul suits taken."

As if in answer, the feathered things wave in agreement, agitating like house-rugs left out for beating clean. The old woman nods brusquely, the closest she ever gets to showing approval. But Bella knows her mentor is pleased, though she covers a smile with her fan, a handsome thing of lace and mahogany. A gift, perhaps, from a grateful follower. The woman's fluttering hands are smooth, ageless. Unlike her face which, in recent months, has sagged dramatically, its rich brown becoming greyish. Against doctor's orders, the widow won't slow down. Knocking on eighty, and still she insists on sitting out in the heat, teaching them, trying to make sure they're receptacles of the knowledge only she can pass on. *Truth be told*, Bella thinks, *Miz Marie feels her time running away.*

"There you have it, child," the old woman says, peering over accordion folds at Eugenia, barely keeping the disappointment from her tone. "Focus. Pay attention. This isn't hairdressing school, no matter what folks been told. Make a mistake with *this* craft and you'll suffer much worse than burnt curls. You need to concentrate: be *certain* before you speak. Words are weapons, girl—you can't just fling them around, willy-nilly. Wield them carefully, accurately, else you'll unleash a world of hurt—on others, sure enough, but first and foremost, on yourself. Stop and *think*."

Eugenia's mouth tightens like she's fit to spit nails. A few seconds pass as she wrangles her temper. Splotches crawl up her neck, blooms of anger and shame. She straightens, pushes away from the bannister, away from Bella, and turns to stand with hands folded, white-knuckled, before the Widow Paris.

"Yes'm," she says through gritted teeth. "I'll bear that in mind."

"You do that. For now, go on in. Tidy up the brushes and arrange the curling rods by size—largest to smallest, handles out, on a tray near the fire—then scrub the combs and scissors. Miss What's-her-name from Olafsson House is coming 'round in an hour, and I haven't yet sussed if her appointment is for plaits or potions."

Eugenia, thus dismissed, bobs a curtsey, and flounces inside. Soon they hear utensils rattling into jars, iron tools clattering against tin, water splashing, the occasional grumble and mutter. When the screen door finally swings shut on its slow hinges, Bella looks over at the widow, whose rheumy brown eyes are fixed on her. Reduced to slits. Assessing.

She freezes like a hare, resists the desire to gulp. *Be* certain *before you speak* . . . The Widow Paris had been chastising Eugie, but Bella has a feeling the old herbwoman was talking double. Directing the dressing-down at her great-grandchild, but expecting them both to listen. Telling Bella that she's onto her. That she more than suspects, she *knows*.

That even though Bella's answer was right, it was obvious, to the widow at least, she had *guessed*.

She did it a lot, actually. Guessing. It wasn't laziness, not really. It's just, she can pick ideas out of the air. Sometimes. Most of the time. Very broad hints. And more often than not, they are precisely right. They are enough. Enough to ensure her instinct wins out over Eugenia's increasingly desperate shots in the dark.

Bella tries to distract the Widow Paris with a smile. It withers on her cheeks half-formed.

What if Eugenia finds out, that Bella guesses? Oh, rage, rage, such a rage. And lightning, no doubt. Whirlwinds. Hail. What Eugenia lacks in reading vibrations, ripples in water, tremors in the earth, the story of human expression, she more than makes up for with dark-limned magic. Spells of destruction, thunderous conjuration, explosions of fire and lava. These were her forté. *These* came to her easy as living.

Eugie would make a powerful ally, if she wasn't such a pain in the backside.

"Lemonade?" Bella asks, getting up from the white wicker chair. The old lady holds her gaze another instant, then shakes her head.

"That's enough for today. Better get home, young Isabella, before your uncle starts a-wondering what can possibly be taking so long."

As Bella collects her satchel and packs away the book in which she writes recipes, for hair tonics and potions alike, two men stroll down St Ann Street. Both pretend they don't know they're being watched, but they stand a little straighter, puff their chests a bit as they walk. One's a local parish boy, spends Sundays ushering people into church. The other's a regular jack-of-all trades—does everything from working the cotton gin to digging graves. The sight of him sets Bella's heart to pounding, as it no doubt does to most girls in town. Tall with blue eyes and bone china skin, a spill of Black Irish hair and a smile that makes the day brighter. Bella averts her eyes, but not soon enough.

"Careful, girl," says the old widow. "The worst thing in the world is getting what we desire. Help me inside before you go."

As she bends close to assist her teacher, their faces almost touching, Bella can smell the decay on the woman's sigh, the gust of death soughing up from inside. She squeezes the old lady's hand.

• • •

The trellis on the exterior wall is rickety, so Bella chooses the oak tree instead. Its branches are strong and thick and spread *everywhere*; one in convenient reach of her bedroom window, another trailing like a truncated staircase, with just a foot-long drop to the ground at the end. She's standing on the sill, ready to make the leap, when a single loud knock shudders the door behind her. Arms windmilling, she manages to hop back down and carefully arrange her face, a mix of umbrage and respect, before the knob slams into the wall. Only one person barges into her *chambre* so abruptly, trying to catch her out.

"Uncle Augustin."

"Evening, Bella. Have I disturbed you?" Her uncle's expression is hopeful, slightly lecherous. A distant cousin of her father's— not a *true* uncle, *not* a Beaufort—Augustin Fabron was willing to adopt poor, orphaned little Bella, after the accident. To take her in, not as a full family member, of course, but as a high level domestic in his plantation house. Daughter and servant and something else altogether. Something in between, not quite pure, existing in the social limbo dictated by her colouring. Hair red and irises green enough to say 'white', but skin a shade too dark, features a tad too Creole, to let her pass without question. Without the protection of papers and a wealthy not-uncle to vouch for her. To provide a room of her own. A safe enough space for now. She's got house duties and other . . . duties . . . Augustin hasn't commanded her to perform. At least, not yet. Not with Aunt Claudette around, and Uncle Augustin's tenure as lord of the manor secure only so long as she is—the property deeds being written in *her* name, after all, not his.

He blinks with eyes like a winter sky, close-set in a long cadaverous face framed with lank hair that greases down to his collar. They are of a height; Bella statuesque, Augustin spindly. It's been a few years since he's been able to look down at her, so he tilts his head slightly back whenever he speaks. Lines her up in his sight, and *peers*.

"Did you do your chores today?"

"Yes, Uncle," Bella says, hoping she remembered them all.

"Only, your Aunt said Evangeline couldn't find you when she wanted her hair done before dinner," he says smoothly. Bella doubts that Claudette's maid reported anything of the sort. "It's not that we mind you learning a trade—indeed we think it a sensible idea. After all, we won't be around to support you forever. But we are, however, here now. You must not forget your first duty."

"How could I," she says, thinking, *with you constantly reminding me*, "when you and Aunt Claudette have been so . . . kind."

"We wouldn't want to have to discontinue your apprenticeship, dear niece." Augustin's reply sounds as empty to Bella as hers must have to him. They both know he won't follow through. Claudette has been *delicate* as long as Bella has known her—as long, she suspects, as the woman has been wed. And Augustin is more than aware of what his ward has been learning at the Widow Paris's knee. He relies too heavily on the witch's remedies to keep his wife in reasonable health; when the old lady passes, he'll need Bella to continue administering Claudette's *treatments*.

To keep her sedate, she thinks. *Sedated.*

"No, Uncle. We wouldn't want that," she says, lowering her chin, feigning humility though it makes her pride squirm.

Mollified, Augustin gives unnecessary orders for the morning—her routine hasn't changed in seven years—and takes his leave. The door clicks shut behind him. She listens, for a minute, then two, waiting for him to move off the landing. The floorboards creak; he is still on the other side, listening for her too. She sits on her bed, wincing as the springs squeak loudly. Another moment passes and she blows out the lamp on her bedside table, knowing he has watched for the snuffing of the line of light under the door. At last, footsteps. Self-congratulatory and solid along the hallway. He thinks his point is made, that Bella remains under the thumb.

She doesn't move, even after she hears his tread on the stairs, wending their way down to the sitting room, where he will smoke cigars, drink whiskey and read those books he imports from France, the ones with the dirty pictures he thinks his wife knows nothing about. He'll be there for hours and now his *job* is done, Uncle Augustin will not stir. To be safe, Bella waits an extra five minutes before setting off. More than enough time to do a cats-eye spell, to help her find her way under the slivered new moon.

The leap from sill to tree branch feels further, more exciting, more liberating than it actually is—a delusion she's happy to enjoy. Half a mile to the Widow Paris's, which Bella covers so quickly and quietly she seems to fly the distance. All the lights in the place are extinguished. A candle flickers to life, briefly, in the round porthole staring out from an attic gable. *Eugie's room.* It winks in and out of sight two or three times before being extinguished. *The fool never can settle, can she? Fidgeting even when she's alone.* Bella grabs a handful of wild sage from the roadside, some flax and a few black-eyed-susans and crushes them between her palms, scattering the bruised leaves and seeds on her toes, whispering ancient words to make her footfalls petal-soft.

The path between the house and the fairy hill beyond the wire fence is overrun with weeds and old cotton. Few dare tread across the Widow Paris's land in broad daylight, much less after dark, but Bella has no such fears. If pressed, she can identify the marks of everyone who's passed this way. The widow's stunted shuffle hasn't flattened the dirt here for years; but a set of Eugenia's prints, small and wide-spread and deep as a running deer's, head off to the bushes on her right. Wild blackberries grow there by the bucket-load, Bella remembers, and thinks she might follow the other girl's path next time. On her left, another series of tracks. Narrow and heavy-heeled, blurred with urgency. With excitement.

These Bella pursues.

Her boots make a *shhhhhhing* sound as she crosses to the field, barely raising a puff of dust. Mist winds through the shrubs, coalescing into sinuous smoke-women that slip around pecan trees along the field's borders. It seems they smile at her as she hurries to the fence and ducks under, careful not to catch her skirts. The witch-skins applaud her arrival. They shoo her toward the man leaning comfortably against the gentle slope of the fairy hill, as if he belongs there.

Tancred Carew sits with his long legs outstretched, crossed casually at the ankle. The hessian sack he always carries, with a flute he made and god-knows what else, is propped like a pillow behind his broad back. With her cats-eyes, Bella can see him perfectly—a bewitching sight that enthralls her. Cotton boles glowing white, little stars of the earth, surrounding his rumpled brown curls. Glints of moonlight winking in his blue eyes, glancing off his teeth as he chews his nails, beaming off them as he smiles.

"Evening, Miz Beaufort," he says, then wastes no more time talking. When they come up for air, Bella's lips are tingling. She bites them, savouring, and inhales the salty scent of Tancred's skin, sweaty underneath his open-collared shirt. He rests his chin on Bella's head and she can feel his Adam's apple bob against her temple as he talks.

"We should bury them," he says, gesturing at the black scraps caught on the fence. For a second, Bella hears a rustle of wings, loud as a dozen ravens taking flight at once. "It's not right, having them exposed like that."

Bella cranes her neck to look up at him. "We haven't any shovels."

"We've got hands, haven't we?"

She smirks. "Why, Mr Carew. I can't possibly go fossicking in the earth wearing this, my Sunday best." She pulls away to give him a better view of her faded, ill-fitting gingham. "If I didn't know better, I'd say you had a mind to see me *digging* out of my petticoat."

"Wouldn't be the first time," Tancred grins.

Bella plays coy only so long, and no longer. Soon her dress, apron, smock and bloomers are tossed like offerings to the fairies. Tancred's buttons seem to melt beneath her fingers; the drawstring on his pants loosens of its own accord. Together they work up a sweat and when they're done, they lie on Bella's clothes like they're the finest bed in New Orleans. She traces patterns into his chest hair with her nails, resting her cheek on his lean bicep, and watches him soften. When he's recovered, Tancred looks down the slope to the rusty fence running along its base.

"We really should give them whatever peace the earth can offer."

"All right," says Bella, loving him for his passion, determination, caring. For keeping a noble thought in his head both before *and after* he's spent. Wearing nothing but their unders, they hoist the ragged skins off the wires. Two of them, a leathery jumble of feather and beaks, strands of long hair, boneless faces, and places that shouldn't have bones. Bella's stomach clenches—not with sick, with certainty. Her guess, as usual, had been right.

Witch-skins.

Collapsed, they are incredibly compact; the pair of them could easily fit inside Tancred's bag. Instead, he folds them in on themselves, ties each bundle off with its own hair, then passes it to Bella while he gets started on the digging. She stands there a moment, just watching. Admiring the way his muscles strain, the way dirt sticks to his chest, his ribs, his thighs. Almost unconsciously, she plucks at the witch-feathers, tearing at the desiccated flesh, at the matted tresses . . . And as she strikes cartilage, she feels a warmth in her belly, a heat of *knowing*. Ingredients potent as these can't go to waste.

Before she hands Tancred the neatly-tied parcels, she tucks a chunk of salvaged flesh up under her arm, unsure why she takes it, but determined to smuggle it home in the pocket of her apron.

• • •

A lamp, turned low, is burning in her room when Bella returns, stepping lightly over the sill. She doesn't really pay attention, happy as she is, reeking of Tancred's sweat, with tender parts tingling as if a charge has been sent through them. She puts her hands to the strings of her apron, the buttons at the back of her dress, doesn't notice the movement in the shadows, her cats-eye spell now thoroughly worn off. It's not until a bony hand closes around the hair at the nape of her neck, fingers gouging into the thick locks, that the magic of the night shatters and she realises she's not alone.

"Insolent little whore!" Spittle froths from Uncle Augustin's mouth, spatters her ear. Waves of malt fumes roll off him as he yells. He shakes her, bolstered by a rage that's simmered since she was a child; unheeded or outright defied by servants who check his orders with a mistress too frail to fulfil her marital duties, maids who lock their doors at night. Augustin fumbles with his trousers, trying to get them undone while keeping a grip on her. "I won't be ignored!"

He hooks a foot around her ankles, jerks hard. There's a jolt, hair ripping, as she tumbles free of his grasp—just for a second. Her head hits the floor. The blow is cushioned by the thick rug, but it's hard enough to make stars and suns pinwheel across her vision. Stunned, she scrambles for purchase, goes nowhere. It gives Augustin time to drop down beside her, shrug out of his suspenders.

With one hand, he urgently shoves his pants down, while the other is busy loosening his narrow neck-tie, looping the noose over her head—as if he cannot decide which punishment will come first.

Bella tries to claw forward, but Augustin tightens the garrotte, pins her petticoat with his knees. Fabric tears. He yanks the ribbon tie, tighter, tighter. Bella tries to get words out, but the only sound she can produce is an animal whimper. Augustin's breath, hot, rank, slides across her cheek. Gagging, she tries to scream, tries to cry. And she flails, she flails, but his fingers jab, her skirts are lifted—

Her not-uncle, her un-uncle, grunts, then his grip relaxes enough to let her draw in great gusts of air. His hipbones dig into her rear, his ribs slam into her spine before he pushes himself upright again. Bella takes advantage, tries to shove him off, but he holds on. She realises there's been another noise, a new sound, unexpected. It's followed by a second, a loud, solid *thud*. Augustin slumps heavily onto her back; he tilts to the right, and drops, his arm draped across her calves. Bella kicks him aside, shimmies into a crouch. She blinks and blinks and finally looks up. Focuses on the shape looming over the fallen man.

Aunt Claudette, with shadows and lamplight dancing across her white nightgown, which is now spotted with a spray of wet red blossoms. In her shaking hand, a poker from the fireplace dangles between slackened fingers. The women stare at each without a word. Eventually, Bella heaves herself forward and checks for the pulse in Augustin's throat. It is slow, sluggish. She knows it won't be long before it stops, unless something is done.

She snatches her hand back, wipes it and wipes it on her torn skirt, turns to her Aunt for a cue.

Claudette is not as tall as Bella, nor as fit. She is *thin*, a bed-bound woman coddled to within an inch of her life. She stands there, swaying a little, her expression flicking between fear, hope, disbelief. Her glazed eyes meet Bella's and again her fingers tighten. She hefts the poker—as Bella gathers her wits and leaps up. She is at the casement in a few steps, out it in one bound and scampering down the tree like a squirrel.

As she hares into the woods, she can hear her name being called. In a small part of her mind—the same part that tells her a fluttering rag is a witch-skin, that interprets voices on the air—she *knows* it's not a cry of panic or condemnation; there is no tone of threat or accusation. In that same small part of her mind, she knows she should go back and help her not-aunt. *What if he wakes? She'll be alone . . .* But Bella is running, feet barely touching the ground. Running away from Augustin, from danger. Running to Tancred and safety. Without magic, her stride goes *thud, thud, thud* in time with her beating heart, and soon she is almost at the fairy hill—*he must still be there*—soon almost in Tancred's arms. On the path, she slows, tries to control her panting, the shaking and shuddering her body is committing without her say-so. Bella walks now, quickly, quietly and as she rounds the stand of trees that hid them both not even an hour ago, she sees Tancred's arms are otherwise engaged.

"Thanks for clearing those nasty old bird-skins."

"Couldn't have my best lady suffering the creeps, now could I?"

"I *am* your best, aren't I?

Naked and gleaming, a girl with white, white hair and smooth bronze skin laughs, riding Bella's lover as if he's a steed, bouncing and writhing much as Bella was not so long—now, forever—ago.

• • •

The Widow Paris's front door is never locked—only the sorriest fool would enter there without permission—and Bella knows where all the fixings are, the ones she requires. In her pocket the pilfered piece of witch-skin weighs heavy; she pulls it out, lays it on the countertop.

She places the basalt mortar and pestle beside it, then begins. Collecting and adding ingredients, grinding and stirring them as she goes, making sure the mix is properly combined. There are scarlet rose petals, hyacinth oil, powdered mint leaves and rosemary, dried lavender, a tiny dash of the gold dust the Widow Paris is always so miserly with, a crush of indigo, a smear of marigold, two pansy petals and then half a spoon of the imported honey. She spits into the mess and whisks it about, hard and fast, then takes a knife, a small thing, fit for peeling fruit, and pulls it across her right palm. From the shallow cut drips fat jewels of blood to seal the deal—for all dark magic, all curses, all dreadful things dearly wished for, cost something personal. Bella needs no recipe for this potion; *this* alchemy comes from the deepest knowledge of heart and hurt.

Soon the paste is thick and dark and red, with a sheen that only hatred can give. So, they want each other, Tancred and Eugenia?

They want to be together? Bella will give them what they want. She pours in a flacon of rainwater, takes the shreds of witch-skin and adds them to the admixture, bubbling of its own accord. The thin membranes float into the pestle and disintegrate as soon as they hit the liquid. Without hesitation, Bella whispers over it, feeling heat rise off the surface. "Here's my wish for you both: to love an ideal of each other without reason, to see an eidolon never a soul. Let your wings be clipped, let your love be a cage, let it trap you both forever." She murmurs their names across the brew so the spell will *know* them, so there can be no mistake, no misdirections. So the enchantment will hook its claws into the fabric of their lives and never let them go. *Happily ever after.*

When the spell leaves her Bella feels exhilarated and empty, as if a part of her soul has darkened in payment for this wicked wish, for this vengeance. The air seems thick and time still—until the front door creaks and Eugie's entrance echoes along the corridor. Hastily, Bella decants the potion into a small vial, stoppers it and slips it into her apron pocket. She runs a hand through her hair and waits to hear Eugie pass by the workroom. *So, what? I'm to sneak out?* Bella snorts. *Why should I creep around?* She opens the door and steps out into the hallway.

Halfway up the stairs, Eugenia spins around. "What are you doing here?"

But before Bella can answer, there is a crash and a thump upstairs, coming from the direction of the widow's room. Both girls race towards the sound.

• • •

"*Mémé!*" Eugenia's cry is heart-wrenching, or would be if Bella hadn't seen what she'd seen earlier. If her heart hadn't hardened.

The Widow Paris is half-on, half-off the bed, the linens caught up around her waist and legs, a knitted shawl 'round her shoulders despite the heat. While they watch, she slides fully to the floor with a thud. Her nightdress is open at the collar, the thin cotton clinging. Curls frizz out of her sleeping-bonnet, sticking to her ashen face, some tipped with droplets of cold sweat. High arched eyebrows, not much more than a few wisps on a shrivelled brow, frame lashless lids, closed on sunken eyes. Until she moans, Bella thinks she's already dead.

Death rattles the old woman's lungs as she blinks awake, her gaze unfocused, searching. "Mémé," Eugie wails, rushing to her great-grandmother's side, hugging her close.

"Get away, child. You're smothering me."

"But we've got to get you on up into bed—"

The Widow Paris waves the girl quiet. "Let me be. We all start low, Eugenia. Ashes to ashes, dust to dust, dirt to dirt—no matter what heights you reach in life, in the end it's all the same. Back to beginnings. I'm just saving y'all the trouble of hauling my old shell down off the bed. *No*, I said." Eugenia's tugging her by the armpits, forcing her upright. She gets the woman into a seated position, then kneels, clings to her hand. The lady extricates her fingers, pushes the girl further away.

"Just let me be. Save your fussing for after I'm gone; I've no use for it." She coughs, long and sloppy, and Bella thinks, this time, the tide of her life must surely have ebbed for good.

"You in pain, Miz M?" she asks, mouse-quiet, coming close enough, but no closer.

"I'd expect more from you, Isabella Beaufort," the widow replies. "Sure you can *guess* what state I'm in." The widow blinks, and this time her eyes stay shut.

Her lips go slack and a puff of rancid meat air escapes them. Bella finds herself crouched beside Eugie, inhaling that stale gust. Finds her head resting on the old woman's scarecrow shoulder, ear pressed to her chest. Finds herself counting the seconds between heartbeats, tracing symbols across the desiccated breast, grasping at words, at spells to keep the faltering thing ticking.

"Take care of this house, Eugenia," the Widow Paris mumbles at last, eyes searching, unfixed. "I may crumble, but there's sure as Hell no reason it has to follow me into the earth."

"Don't say that, *mémé*. We'll get Doc Coffey down here, you'll be just fine, we'll—"

"Hush, now. Mind my house, child, that's all I ask. You do that for me?"

Eugie whimpers, tears coursing down her round cheeks, and nods.

"Good girl," the widow says, before turning to Bella. "Now, you." Marie folds her fingers around Bella's palm. She feels sharp angles, a cold glassy surface, a rough sphere with many facets.

"You," says the old woman, "*you* mind my business. You keep it going, my girl. You keep it going."

Bella opens her hand—there is the stone, the single biggest she will ever see. A white diamond the size of a child's heart.

"I will," Bella promises. "I am."

• • •

There is no moment of silence to honour the dead.

"She gave it to you! You! You're nobody! You're nothing. You're not even family." Eugenia's face boils crimson, and she's making a sound like a kettle left on the heat too long.

"Yet here we are, Eugie. Together with the one person who loved us both," says Bella smoothly. "Close as family."

Eugie weeps until she hiccups, hiccups until Bella thinks the girl might be sick in her own lap. She pours a glass of water from the bedside table and tips one, two, three drops from the vial into it— Eugie is too distracted to notice. The red liquid quickly disperses, tinting the clear fluid with only the slightest shade of pink. She hands it to Eugenia, who takes it without thanks, and gulps it down, down. All of it.

Bella smiles.

It will take. Oh, yes. It will sit inside her, stirring, gestating, ready to come to life the moment she sees Tancred. And when she does, the spell will uncurl, rise up and take hold. She'll be ruined in soulless love—there'll be nothing but obsession. The only tremors Eugenia will feel, the only excitement, the only fireworks, are the ones she casts with magic. It will be like eating, but never feeling full. She'll get nothing from Tancred, empty paragon of lies. And Tancred? Greedy, beautiful Tancred will take anything from Bella's hand, anything at all. He need only take this last thing. And he will.

While Eugenia sobs on the floor, Bella crosses to the window and looks out between the sheers. In the street below is the lady's maid Evangeline, gazing up at the house. Bella raises her hand, guessing, *knowing* she is safe. Aunt Claudette would not have sent Evangeline to *arrest* her; if that were the case, there would be constables roaming about by now. But there is nothing unusual on the road, in the fields. No-one but the servant.

Bella lets the curtains fall shut. Closing her eyes, she turns and perches on the sill. Runs her palms across her tattered apron, her twisted, torn skirt. *Eugie never even commented on it*, she muses, then blocks out all thoughts of the girl, all thoughts but the ones thrilling through the air. Quiet, she listens. Listens to the present, feels the truth of it in her belly. Her aunt's voice, not so feeble as it once was, explaining to Doc Coffey how Augustin has had a terrible accident, how he has fallen down the stairs. Listens to the doctor, who never liked the man, declare it's an open-and-shut case, no need to examine the wounds on his head. Listens to the night, replayed in her mind, and knows she will go back to that uncle-less house. She will tend to Claudette, who may not need her as much, in that uncle-less house, but Bella knows she'll want her there anyway. To keep an eye on her. To ensure her silence.

As she exhales, Bella senses the future, hears it through the other girl's wailing, hears the beat of what's to come, the pulse. Knowing Eugenia will ache for Tancred though he is hers, and Tancred will yearn for Eugenia, both fighting for more, neither getting enough, everyone getting what they deserve. And she, Bella Beaufort, will be there to see it all. To watch how the battle unfolds.

• • • • • • • • • • • •

RIVER OF MEMORY

KAARON WARREN

It took nine days to fall from Earth to Tartarus and all the while, zombies could smell meat not far away, big meat brains close by. They fell in a clump, all tangled together, rolled around, and they gnawed at each other, cracking bone, splitting teeth, until they landed.

Mnemosyne saw all. Understood all. She was ancient and wise and so lonely some days she wanted to die. Punished by the gods to live out eternity in Tartarus, she missed her daughters and thought of Zeus on lonely nights. Her space was filled with mirrors which kept away the tortured souls, the punished sinners, reflecting back their anguish.

She smelled the zombies coming down; she knew the smell of decay.

Zombie stop falling. Zombie watch meat fall. /Zombie eat. /Zombie eat./ zombie stop/zombie smell old meat old meat brains dried/zombie smell fresh meat zombie eat/meat wet/ zombie . . . zombie stop/zombie . . .

They landed. At the bottom of the zombie pile there was some spillage. Some splatter. Those on top were cushioned and they crawled over, down, sniffing for meat because it was close, it was near, and it landed. Four girls *plop plop plop plop*, some zombie skulls cracked but not enough to save those kids. The little one, Pip, queen for nine days, died on the way down. Too young to last for so long without water.

Her face was all pink skull, her eyes dry and wide, her arms and legs stiff, out like stars, because that was the way she fell. Zombies had tried to take random bites on the way down but she was always out of reach; now, they dug their teeth in and tore her to pieces, a zombie at all the pressure points and two at her toes. There was no warm brain left to her but they tore her apart anyway.

Dhysa, with her gold band made by the gods, fought the zombies off for a while but there were too many and she couldn't find purchase, her feet sinking into soft zombie flesh. She sliced her way, rolling, cutting, delirious from lack of water but still that instinct to survive, to save herself. She rolled off the pile, leaving them distracted by the others. Her friends. But the dead pulled her back by the ankles, sucked her into the stinking, writhing mass. She clawed her way toward Pip, but Pip was already gone. She'd been dead when they got to her and Dhysa thought, *at least that.* At least she was spared the desecration of becoming like them.

The zombies, starved and thoughtless, tore at each other to get at Dhysa's brain. She fought and struggled but there were too many, too many. She roared, a deep, primal scream she'd heard when women gave birth, but this was the opposite; this was death.

It was only moments before she rose to join the mass, the pulsing, dragging mass of the dead. No longer named; zombie.

• • •

Mnemosyne had seen a lot in her long, long life, but it was nasty watching them tear into the two young Amazons. These girls could have been her daughters, if she'd moved fast enough. At least she could try to save the other two.

The zombie heap of stink-flesh and black tooth began to move toward the massive cavern entrance. Zombies stumbled in search of brains, clumped like dog shit and sticks. Dhysa with them, lost, absorbed.

Mnemosyne heard them moaning *meat, meat* and she clucked her tongue.

She hated any creature who couldn't speak properly.

• • •

The twins had landed at the edges of the pile. Beka rolled off and ran, blinded by thirst and terror, until she felt water at her feet. The ground dropped away and she found herself flailing, drowning, sucking in the air of this place, this Tartarus, feeling it in her lungs like poison and she sucked air and water until they came for her, zombies braving the water in their hunger. She could recognize some of them. There was Androdameia, and there Clete. There was an older woman; a mother, Beka thought, a few years older and she'd been a mother before she was a zombie. "Help me, Mummy," she called, but she knew her own mother was long dead and far from this place.

She swam from them as best she could but the three persisted, joined now by a tall, broad zombie, a man. He wore a cop's uniform with the shirt unbuttoned to the waist. "Help, police," she called. She took a deep drink of the river, her throat sore and dry. "Help, police." Thinking she'd hit a chord and he'd remember who he'd been, leave her alone. He continued toward her, wading solidly through the water, his teeth bared, the gums pulled back and grey.

"Clete," Beka called out. "Help me, Clete, you remember me, don't you? It's Beka. Remember? We found that little kitty together one day?" But Clete sniffed, smelled brains and kept coming. Androdameia, who had been mean as a girl, a bully, could never be appealed to.

Beka was still firm-bodied, although she has some bites out of her. These had closed over as if cauterized. Body still rotting slowing and smelly as all get out.

Beka ran further upriver, but the bed was soft and silty and she sank to her ankles. They sank too but there were more of them, with inhumanly long reach. The man got her first and dragged her backward and under with his soft, strong hands, pulled her to his chest and sank his teeth into her skull.

The other zombies roiled in the water, sniffing the brains. Clete, Androdameia, and the mother all reaching in for some.

The man had been tall, but disintegration had shortened him. His ears were torn; earrings long since tugged out, dogs and hungry zombies gnawing on the rest.

The mother had been wealthy; she was still covered with her jewels. Glitter of no value to the hungry.

Clete and Androdameia had been too young to be much of anything at all; they had seen very little of life.

They crouched in the river, focused only on their hunger and the good, fresh brains to sate it.

Then Beka rose. *Where?*

• • •

The man felt suddenly, desperately thirsty. Remembered thirst. His name was Steve. He remembered that. The brained girl—he knew those words—had lost her scalp. Her hair floated on the river like a bright red sprawl of seaweed. Not a fish.

I caught fish. I remember the tug of the line between my fingers. I remember the smell of their guts and that makes me hungry again. The slice of the knife.

Eating brains makes me thirsty.

• • •

Isa had rolled off the pile and run in the opposite direction to Beka, because that was where she landed. Running? She could barely move. Luckily the zombies were slower. She felt as if her body had melted, or merged, as if there was no distinction between bone and muscle. She had long ago accepted that thirst was the only thing left to her.

They followed her, the stink of them pushing her forward, their shuffling feet together sounding like a great rolling ball.

Mnemosyne saw all. She watched the girl staggering toward her mirrored room and she saw that this girl was not dead, not yet. But close. Behind her, the massed group, seeking her.

"Come on," she said, appearing before Isa. "In here, you'll be safe in here."

Isa allowed herself to be tugged and dragged into the mirror-filled room. Seeing herself made her scream; she thought she saw a ghost, a monster, she could not imagine this haggard, grey creature was her. She was gaunt, her hair sticking out like straw, her lips swollen, peeling, her tongue protruding. She cried, but the tears were dry, like salt pouring straight out of her eyes, and it hurt.

The room was a dead end. "We have to get out of here. They'll trap us. They'll turn us into them. Living dead."

Mnemosyne smiled. "I'm already immortal. Already in hell. It can't get any worse."

Isa backed away from her, horrified. "Never get yourself into a dead end, idiot. Always have a place to run to. We have to keep moving. They're slow, but they don't give up."

"It's okay, girl. I'll look after you. Your life is still important; I can see that."

She dragged Isa behind the largest mirror and settled her there. "Sit down, rest."

She looked into her small mirror, watching the zombies. They shuffled past, no longer able to smell the brains, or sense them. "I haven't seen these things before. These incarnations."

Isa's tongue rolled out; it was swollen, white and furry.

"You need water," Mnemosyne said. "Not the water from my river, though." She fetched a cup and held it against the wall; water poured down in a smooth, crystal sheet. Isa took the cup greedily, almost dreamily. She'd fantasized this moment many times and she hoped this was reality. The water was metallic but more delicious than anything she'd tasted in her life.

"Sip slowly."

But she gulped, and was almost sick, then she sipped.

"There's a river down here?" She'd been so desperate to get away she'd taken nothing in.

"My river of remembrance. You're too young to be burdened with memories of your past life. I won't allow children to take refreshment there."

"We should keep running," whispered Isa. She wasn't even sure if any noise was coming out, but at least she had water. "We should find Beka and Dhysa." She knew that Pip was dead; had watched, as they fell, the life fall out of her.

Isa heard the sounds of ghosts, chains, groaning. Sounds of lashes.

It was misty behind the mirror. She felt exhausted, but she was also curious. She wanted to explore this place, find out more about it and figure out how to escape it. She thought, *Where's that darn robot? He's supposed to be my protector. Why didn't he jump in straight after us and blow the crap out of these zombies?*

"What about the other girls? Beka. Dhysa," she asked.

Mnemosyne shook her head. "I don't think things have changed so much with you mortals that you can survive without a brain." She saw all but she didn't understand these creatures. "Yet they are walking."

"They'll be coming for me, then. That's what they do." Mnemosyne turned a small mirror toward them and showed Isa the zombie pile, dispersing. She showed her Dhysa becoming part of the mass, stumbling away. She showed her Beka and her new companions, making their way slowly through the spaces of Tartarus.

Isa sipped water to stop herself throwing her guts up.

Mnemosyne looked at her with great affection. A warm, living girl, a needy one. She wanted to smother her with love, take her in, keep her forever.

"We should keep running. They won't stop till they have me, and you. You know what zombies are like."

Mnemosyne shook her head. "These are the first I've seen. Seriously. I've seen all manner of dead people here, and you are not the first real bodies to land. You I can tell are human; but they?"

"Zombies. Living dead. Whatever. They're arseholes, every last one of them, no matter who they were as humans. They want to eat your brains. Even Beka."

"Not my brains, surely. And Beka? Why is Beka special?"

"She's . . . she was my sister. They can sniff us out. We should keep running."

"We'll be safe behind this mirror. It's like another realm in this space. It's a one-way mirror; we can see them, they can't see us. They are close, though, very close. Be quiet." The thought of her sister made Isa cry, dry, dry tears.

"Crying girl. It's a crying girl. That means sad."

"Stay here," Mnemosyne said. "Quiet." She was someone's daughter, this young thing. Mnemosyne had nine once, nine lovely daughters lost to her now.

The zombies hadn't sniffed her out; godflesh wasn't on their radar. It was the girl they were after. They'd been drawn by the sound of her voice, or by the memory of her. Mnemosyne understood they had been changed by her river but she didn't understand how.

The mirrors confused the zombies. *Who, who?* They came forward, saw themselves. *No meat no meat* and Steve hammered in fury. *Zombie ugly. Zombie ugly.* A zombie can get very hungry on a nine-day fall. Mnemosyne and Zeus had spent nine solid days together, and he dined her like a god should. Anything they wanted to drink was there for the drinking. She was exhausted at the end of it but neither thirsty nor hungry. During her nine days of labor, all she did was drink. She felt like a sponge. Afterward, her hunger was so ravenous, she ate half a suckling pig while the babies took turns to feed from her.

So she understood how these zombies must feel. The hunger.

Isa started to pant. She'd recognized Beka amongst the five monsters and this freaked her out. She knew Clete and Androdameia too.

"It's Beka."

Mnemosyne said, "Hush, hush, they can't smell me, and if you stay behind the mirror, quiet, they won't find you."

Isa couldn't bear the thought of her sister, her friends, mindless. She'd seen too many transformed; people she loved, or cared about, turned into mindless, stumbling bone yards full of teeth and hunger.

At the sound of her name, Beka roared on the other side of the mirror. *Beka! Beka! Beka!* She had not had time to regret but still the sound of her own name was painful.

"Do you remember?" Mnemosyne called in a sweet, watery voice. "Do you remember your lives?"

All five stood still, straight. The grey-fleshed woman, her gums tightening her mouth into a grimace, let her tongue roll out of her mouth. The man clawed at his face. Clete and Androdameia leaning together as if glued. And Beka, the young Amazon, the sister, not yet dead long enough to rot.

"You've swallowed water from my river," Mnemosyne said. "My river is the spring of memory. Those who choose to drink go to the Elysian fields. Those who choose Lethe, choose to forget, are reborn."

She gave them the gift of authoritative speech because she was lonely and wanted companions.

Where . . . are . . . we?

"Where . . . are . . . we?" Beka said.

"This Tartarus is vast. Crowded full of those the gods dislike, so many rooms. A dank, gloomy pit. The walls of bronze in some places, of rotting wood in others. Walls of dirt, walls of gold, walls of stone and marble. Dark, always dark, with the minor glow coming from the walls, a humming, as if from the ghosts who are there eternally."

Mnemosyne saw all. The zombies looked at one another, confused. There was instinct to follow, to join the others, but there was also memory.

She stepped out from behind the mirror, curious now they had the power of speech.

• • •

Awareness comes slow when you've been brain dead for six months. Steven blinked, unable to guess where he was, because it wasn't where he was, before.

Around him, the other zombies blinked as well. Steven's mouth was full of the taste of blood and it made him feel hungry again, although by the look of his distended stomach, he really couldn't eat any more.

"Is it coming back to you?" he heard. It was a woman's voice. It could be his mother, if he hadn't eaten her brain himself. He remembered that; there she sat, waiting to visit. All the wives and mothers, waiting to do their duty and visit their men.

The speaker was young but her eyes were old. Her hair was in a bun. Her dress was off the shoulders, flowing. Her shoulders were glowingly white. Very soft around the edges, her hair was a rich red auburn red but streaked with grey. She was strong. Broad shouldered.

She smiled at him.

She was the one who smelled of old meat. Ancient. Not like food at all.

She touched his shoulder and his tongue wriggled.

"You should be able to talk now," she said.

Steven tried to speak but his tongue was thick with rot.

• • •

The other two were now physically merged, as if their flesh was soft and sticky.

"Is it coming back to you?" Mnemosyne asked. She turned to Steve. "You remind me of my brother." The thought of Chronos made her angry; he had been freed and sent to rule the Elysian Islands, yet she was left to suffer for them all. "Why him? Why me, left here lonely? Is it jealousy? When we were children he was the one who threw stones. He was the one always late, and the one dirty. I was the one who shuffled everybody in to place, I was the one who made sure all were happy." She knew she was talking too much. She was desperate for company. It seemed like centuries since she'd had someone to talk to.

Brother? Steve thought hard.

"And you remind me of my daughter, Talia," she told Beka, the dead Amazon twin. "And you . . . you are like my mother," she said to the zombie woman, but she was lying about that. The woman seemed empty. "You . . . ." The two girls, their grins fixed, spun around together.

Food. We know there's food.

Isa still cowered behind the mirror. Lying flat, barely able to lift her head, she absorbed the smells and the sounds. They hadn't found her yet; was the magic so strong here? And what would they do when they did? Beka . . . surely Beka would protect her? Beka was so strong. After all they'd been through, there she stood, brain crazy?

"We are hungry. We are thirsty," the mother zombie said.

She began to spin in circles as her memory returned; she had eaten her own babies. She had eaten them, torn them limb from limb, eaten their brains. Her face changed, if a face half-off can change, becoming monstrous with her terrible guilt. She touched her head, the tender place where some of her skull was missing, and she ran at the brass-plated wall again, again and again, until her skull was shattered and what was left of her dripped down into a dark brown puddle. Her casing slumped and her guilt was gone. In spirit form she would choose to drink from the river Lethe, to forget, to begin another life in complete ignorance of her past. This was the gift; this was her sentence.

"Tired tired when did we sleep when can we sleep?" Steve was not affected by the death of the mother. He didn't know the mother; had never known her. He was tired but he wasn't hungry; he remembered eating.

He saw the woman there and her blood was thick and old and dusty. He had no desire for her. The Amazon at his side, the young woman whose brain he had eaten only minutes ago, sniffed the air.

"My sister," she said, "my twin, my sister, my girl."

The other two, the Siamese twins, sniffed as well.

"I have three daughters now," Mnemosyne said. "One, two, three. No more." She glanced at Isa behind the mirror, knowing she was safe there, protected by the reflection. She was so lonely without her girls and without a man. It was so long ago, so long, that Zeus took her to him nine nights, nine times.

Steve pressed his fingers into the mirror, tilting it. The others joined; pushed against the mirror even as Mnemosyne tried to stand between them.

"My sister, my twin."

"Our sister, our twin."

Isa, so tired, thirsty, hungry, began to cry. Cough and cry, trying to smother it in her hands.

Her sister Beka slumped, exhausted, and spoke her name, but with her tongue half bitten out it sounded like a complaint. She remembered falling, falling, she remembered great thirst, and water, and she remembered being bitten.

"You remember?" Mnemosyne said. We can bring your sister out if you remember she is your sister. If you remember she is a young girl."

"We are hungry," Steve said.

"Go eat *her*," Mnemosyne said, pointing at the mother zombie.

"No, too old. Too old."

"Meat is up above," Isa whispered. "That's where they need to look," knowing full well there were no humans left on the island. That she would have to find a way off the island, find her warbot and make him take her somewhere there were people to meet. Futures to be had.

She cried; called for warbot.

Beka said, "Isa."

Isa stepped out. She screamed; Beka's head was covered with blood, her hair torn off. She hadn't seen that in the small mirror's reflection.

The fused zombies moaned and reached for her but Beka held them back. "No brains. Not here."

"Where are we?" Clete said. Her voice was ragged, wet. "Why are we here?"

"Warbot dropped you in," Isa said. "You stupid zombies. He dropped you in here to get rid of you."

Steve made a noise; perhaps laughter. "And you, too."

"This is Tartarus," Mnemosyne said. "This is a . . . good place. A place of rest. And remembrance."

"It's a place of punishment," Isa said. "I shouldn't be here."

"We shouldn't be here," Steve said. "We have done nothing wrong but be destroyed."

"It is not so bad here," Mnemosyne said. "There is water to drink and you can live with me as my daughters and my brother. We can explore the world down here. You can talk to people. We can laugh at Tantalus."

She led them to a hole in one wall. Isa followed cautiously. Through it, they saw a naked man, standing up to his knees in water. When he stooped to drink, the water vanished. Food was likewise out of reach for him. He starved and thirsted eternally.

"He was a really nasty man. Stole nectar and ambrosia from the gods, then fed his own son to them to test them. Imagine. Eating your own son." She thought that if the mother zombie hadn't killed herself already, she would have at those words. She said, "The punishment he is suffering. He feels no guilt, though, whereas she, that mother, she would rather die than feel it. And we will see if she comes to me, and see what water she drinks from. I can give you anything you want," Mnemosyne said, though in truth all she could give was memory.

Steve and Beka circled the room. They felt a draw to follow the other zombies; the group mind telling them come, come. But they remembered; they were different. And there was group enough; if they could turn Isa, they would be group enough.

"There are plenty of rats down here," Mnemosyne said. "Not sure what they did to deserve it, but they seem happy enough. You are not the first physical bodies to visit Tartarus; they made happy meals of the others, though."

Clete and Androdameia lurched toward Isa. They could not eat rats.

"You are the first living bodies," Mnemosyne told Isa. Isa was sleepy; no longer thirsty or hungry, but desperately, painfully tired. "You'd be surprised at the body disposal methods people use."

"They throw bodies down?"

"They do."

"Where?" Isa said. Thinking, if bodies can come down, bodies can go up. She'd looked on the fall down and seen no place for purchase; perhaps elsewhere there was a rock wall to climb.

"Murder victims, I suppose," Mnemosyne said. "If those other zombies haven't discovered them, we can go and have a look."

Isa's stomach growled. She wasn't hungry enough to consider eating the dead, and the smell of the zombies made her feel like starving forever. Still, her stomach growled. Mnemosyne gave her some thin, salty wafers. These were perfect. Isa could feel them expanding in her stomach but she didn't feel stomach pains from eating.

· · ·

It took them three days to reach the place where bodies were disposed of. The noise made Isa feel ill; the wailing of lost souls, the torture of their torment. Everywhere, spirits reached out for them, as if they could be saved. Steve snarled at these souls and each recoiled as if they had met the devil.

Mnemosyne carried a large supply of the healthful wafers, and Beka and Steve did their best to lower the rat population. It didn't stave off the hunger at all but it gave the impression that it did. Like air-sucking horses, their stomachs felt full although they had no nutrition and the desire, the desperate need for brains was unabated.

Clete and Androdameia refused even the rats and their steps became slower as they fused closer and closer together. They seemed to be almost one, so soft you couldn't touch them without your finger sinking in. They were too weak now to attack Isa, the only food in all of Tartarus. They tried; regardless of their human memory they tried. Androdameia had never cared for others and she didn't care who lived and died now so long as she was fed. Clete was weak and had always been weak; a pack-follower.

They talked along the way, as well as Steve and Beka could with their bitten and swollen tongues. About life above and how warm it was. Mnemosyne told them about the life she'd lived; Beka and Isa exchanged glances, as they always did. Conspiratorial glances meaning, "Bullshit."

"Here," Mnemosyne said. Finally they arrived.

The first body they saw rested in a clump; there was no blood around it. No splat. Steve shambled closer to it, reached out his clumsy fingers.

"Looks like a gun shot wound to the head. Dead on impact. I'd say close to two weeks, but I don't know the environment down here well." This said slowly, torturously.

"What sort of cop where you?" Isa said.

He shrugged. Touched his uniform. "I'm not sure." He sniffed at the corpse. Looked at Beka. "Too old?"

She shook her head; tiny bits of flesh flew off. "Don't look, Isa." And the two zombies ate. They tossed small pieces to the others girls who sucked them up and spat them out. "There's where the brains are," they said, one arm lifted to Isa. "She's who we should be eating. Not this dead stuff."

• • •

Nine days up, nine days fall away, the warbot sat in his shelter, waiting. He would wait ten years or twenty until the robot parts arrived, if that's what it took.

He had dispensed his responsibilities. There was no doubt that as a warbot he had failed; this was clear. He had failed to save the last of the Amazons and instead had dispensed them into the afterworld with the zombies. The warbot kept record of the time and it was 246 hours after he failed that he got the signal; children alive. Deep in his programming; children alive, save those children.

He made the analysis without help from the mainframe. The mainframe had not been of use in some time.

He assessed that the signal came from below. He also assessed that there was no one alive in the labyrinths. He had made an exhaustive search for survivors and had dispatched the female minotaur with a shot to the head himself.

While it made some logical sense to remain above and wait for the robot parts in order to facilitate their offloading, it was imperative he listen to his basic programming.

• • •

It was easy opening the doors to Tartarus last time, with the pressure of the bodies on the flap door. This time, he rigged up a dozen or so dead zombies, then pulled the switch. There was an amount of self-preservation in the design, with the knowledge that his landing would be softer on top of the zombies.

He had made an error of judgment and now was required to repair the damage of the action.

Tartarus was a place of punishment. The humans did not require punishment. The humans were still alive. Therefore the humans needed to be retrieved.

The understanding that at least one of the Amazons had survived made his circuits hum. New information, new planning, slightly adapted programming.

They were calling him.

He leaped into the hole.

Nine days later, he landed. The zombies were as soft as he had envisaged and he squelched right through them. Fortunately he was made him out of shock-absorbent metal; he bounced. He landed in the shallows of a river and righted himself. Water would dry quickly if it was on the surface; any further into his equipment and a technician would be required.

Technician. The word gave him pause. It gave him an image, a mirror image, and it gave him a small short circuit in the shoulder region.

It took him another three days to find the source of the distress call.

Isa. Alive.

Isa saw the warbot and she ran to put her arms around him. "You've come to save me. You're my hero."

The warbot wished he cared. He felt that. He understood it. He also understood that this was abnormal.

Beka. Not alive. But remembering, approaching him with open arms. She seemed unaware of her color, grey rot, and her smell. Unaware that her teeth were loose in their sockets and that there was nothing he could do to save her.

He lifted his weapon up to kill Beka and the decrepit zombie staggering beside her; Isa said, "No, it's okay. They remember; they won't eat me. They remember their past lives and all they want to do is survive. They don't want to eat my brain any more."

How the hell? the warbot thought, and then, *What?* His other shoulder felt stiff and he thought, *Too many hours over the desk.* Though he had never been at a desk.

"Is this it?" he said. "Anyone else I need to deal with?"

"This is it. There were two more but they wanted to eat my brains so Steve killed them. He was a cop."

"Was he just? Hero type, then?" the warbot said, some weird unfamiliar resentment in his circuits.

• • •

Mnemosyne introduced herself. She didn't like the warbot already; she knew he was there to take her girls.

He said, "What's happened down here?"

"They remember. What makes them human is their memory, their past knowledge, and that has been returned to them. It's what lifts us above the other animals. Lets us solve problems, negotiate, survive."

"Kinda cruel, in a place like this. Don'cha think?" This was the warbot stirring up trouble. It was clear to him now; the river of memory had brought back to him his technician. The man who'd put him together, who'd sweated his palms into the circuits, who'd muttered and complained about the world and his part in it.

Mnemosyne nodded.

"I'm gonna take the girls up and outta here. They don't belong, correct? They have done nothing wrong."

She nodded again, but he could see the telltale readying, the *fuck you robot I'll kick your head in* readying he knew very well.

"I think that you should take them away from here. They don't belong here. Take your two girls." She said this with her fingers twitching. Planning.

"You'll need me," Steve said. "No way you can climb out of here without me."

With half a tongue it was hard to understand him. Steve was thinking of the time he'd been a whole man and could beat off wolverines, insane humans, and zombies.

Mnemosyne looked at him. She knew more than he remembered; or he remembered and he was not letting on. She said, "Not you. You stay here with me, keep me company."

"I'm not staying."

"Actually, you're all staying," she said, and she cooooed, a loud and creepy calling sound. Kampe entered, fast as lightning, furious, resentfully. Body of a woman, tail of a scorpion, she spat in fury. "She's the children's guard, you know. She has a way with them. Keeps the children from causing trouble. 'Cos only the naughty children come here. Lots of naughty zombies now."

Kampe grabbed Isa by the hair and lifted her. Beka tried to stop her but her left heel came up and smashed Beka's jaw. The warbot rolled up, guns out, and shot Kampe through the forehead. How long it would last he didn't know; they'd have to move fast.

Steve leaped for Mnemosyne, took her down, tried to tear at her throat.

"I'm immortal, you idiot. Immortal!"

"Leave her, Steve. She can't stop us," Isa said. She didn't want to touch him, so Beka grabbed his shoulder.

"Come on. This old bat is better off dead."

"Come with us," Isa said, filled with pity. "Come up."

"I can't," Mnemosyne said, and she lifted her arm; what had been invisible before was now clear. A long, sharp chain attached to her wrist. "I'm a titan. Not a bat. I am one of the first race," Mnemosyne said, cowering. Words not matching her actions. She pointed at Steve. "You watch him. He's a killer."

Isa shook her head. They were all killers, every last creepy zombie walking dead one of them. She gave Mnemosyne a hug. "I wish you could come with us. I feel bad leaving you behind."

Mnemosyne cried, tears of memory pouring down her chins. "You're a good daughter, a good dear daughter. At least I have your voice to remember. And the way your hair swings. I can remember that."

Warbot said, "We need to go. Now. If we take the water, we can convert all the zombies we meet. If titans were the first race, maybe converted zombies are the last. Maybe we can humanize zombies, make them remember who they were."

"You can't take the water. This is where it belongs," Mnemosyne said. "This is my power, my control. If you take it . . . " Here she paused. She lifted her arm, clanked her chains. "If you take it above ground it becomes ordinary water. No," she shook her head. "No, it will take all memory. It will blur the minds and no one will remember everything. You will cause chaos." The warbot rolled in a circle; he thought, *I remember laughing. I remember this.*

"Not so," he said. "Where can we find the river?"

Isa pointed. "The river runs through here as well. The river runs everywhere."

They tried to scry the water to read the future as they filled bottles and containers, enough to save the world. "I'm no good at this," Isa said. "I'm too self-centered. All I see is me."

"Maybe all there is is you."

"We can always come back for more," Steve said, impatient. He laughed, a fruity, juicy laugh all phlegm and loose bits. The warbot thought, *Tartarus is similar to undercity in that underground. The elite chosen to save the human race. Here are more humans underground, like moles. Except, again, they mostly don't survive.*

• • •

They searched for the tunnel, the escape valve. There's always a way out. Steve and Beka sniffed hard, as if this could lead them up, as if there were people, someone up there ready to be eaten. They were slowing, their skin softening, and it was hard for them to walk on their spongey feet.

There was too much old meat in Tartarus. It smelled bad; almost tempting, almost food, but it made them feel wet on the inside when they ate it.

Then up, up, up, up. The zombies were okay, although the warbot made sure to keep between them and Isa. Isa had to lick the walls, she had to eat rats, she was not happy.

"You gotta survive, girl. You're it. We gotta find you a mate and then off you go again," the warbot said. Isa shuddered at the thought.

"I'm the last person left alive. I'm never gonna fall in love. Never gonna have some guy all over me." She started to cry. She annoyed the others with her noise.

It was slow. To the warbot, it was excruciatingly slow. He kept trying to leave Steve behind, carry the girls and move fast, but he followed. He always caught them up when Isa had to piss, or eat, or drink. He carried her while she slept but she fidgeted and complained so much he wanted to drag her by her feet. This annoyance; it was an interruption. His technician had been a weak man, clearly, and the warbot hated feeling that sense of weakness.

Nine days, ten, they climbed up. Twelve days, fourteen, then the air started to clear and the light began to seep in.

They reached the top.

Isa sucked in the air; none of the others cared. She cried, threw herself about. Beka and Steve staggered out. They were both so green the light reflected off them like it did off the glorious ocean. The warbot stashed the bottles of water in a safe place. Isa looked longingly.

"Not you. Not yet. You don't want to confuse yourself. Live this life alone." He rolled away, seeking food for her.

Steve stumbled over to a pile of corpses, kicking them over with what remained of his toes. He bent down to push some hair aside and inspected the head.

"Too old," he said.

Isa stood close to him, closer than she'd been. Outside she felt safer. "Trying to figure out how they died? I can tell you; they got eaten. Once a cop always a cop," Isa said.

He shook his head; tiny bits of flesh flew off.

"I was the opposite. I know, now. I was a killer. I broke out of jail, in there for killing a dozen or more women. Don't you remember me? I was all over the news."

Isa put her hands on her hips. "That's disgusting."

Steve laughed at her. "What, more disgusting than eating brains?"

"At least as a zombie you're acting on instinct to survive. As a human, you were acting on sick desire."

"Who are you to say murder isn't instinctive?"

"I got an instinct. I got a big one."

And she went for him right there. Even a zombie can look surprised.

But it didn't take long to turn it around. She was weakened from her nine days without water, her limbs like jelly, her muscles like custard. Steve slurred, "Being a live person doesn't make you good. The blood flowing doesn't make you moral."

He held her over his knee, stomach facing up. His hands resting one hard on her forehead, one on her belly. He traced a line.

"They called me the Eviscerator," he said, and with one sharp movement he opened her guts. He and Beka fell to their knees and within seconds had her skull open and her brains out. Grunting, snorting, they ate. Beka's shoulders heaved with disgust but she couldn't help herself.

She lifted her head. Around her mouth, grey matter. Her skin slightly less green and perhaps firmer. But she moaned, clawed at her lips, at her stomach.

Steve stood, his legs apart, his fingers clawed. He remembered other meals, cooked meat, soft vegetables, sweet white bread slathered with butter. Gravy. He remembered eating real food but this was still good.

He wanted more.

Beka staggered to the warbot. "Kill me. Kill me now. I don't want this," and there was enough human in her for the plea to take hold.

"I protect humans. I don't kill them," warbot said.

"Then you failed," Steve said. "You should work for me now. Find me brains. Find me more food. Find me more little girls to tear open, find me women, find me men. Find me a foul old man with brains so fat it'll keep me for days."

"You failed," Beka said. "You let her die. You let him kill her. That's not what you're meant to do."

"I did fail," the warbot said. "I can't read minds. How was I supposed to know he'd turn? I told you I wanted to leave him behind." The warbot killed Steve with a simple shot to the head, and for good measure he killed Beka as well.

He had his stockpile of water. He waited for the robot parts and made his plans, but he wondered, *Is it worth it? What the fuck am I doing here?* And he wished he could sink in the sea then sit and let himself rust.

• • • • • • • • • • •

A MOVEABLE FEAST

JENNY BLACKFORD

"Benji isn't really a baby, you know, Aunty Jessie," Angela said. Fluoro-bright ice cream was smeared orange and green around her wide mouth; more dripped from her fingers onto the floor. "He's a durga-monster."

Jessica nodded, and looked back at the notebook's screen. Angela's world was full of monsters that no one else knew about: moon-leopards hunted through her nights, and stranger things stalked her by day.

Jessica kept staring at the screen, but she could still feel Angela looking at her with those huge brown eyes—as if she didn't have enough problems already. On cue, the idiot, incessant voice inside her head said, *He doesn't love me anymore. I wish I was dead.*

She gritted her teeth and copied some financial data from the company's website into her report, trying not to hear the drip drip drip of melted ice cream puddling on her sister Sophie's floor. She would mop it up off the slate later; poor Sophie had enough to worry about—but Eric needed this report fast, and she was determined to finish it.

Jessica managed to grind out one more painful paragraph, her eyes stinging with suppressed tears, then she saved and closed the file. Eric had torn her heart into small bloody pieces and stamped on them, but that wasn't Angela's fault.

She smiled as convincingly as she could manage, and said, "Okay, chicken, what's a durga-monster?"

Angela beamed a fluoro-bright smile. "A durga-monster looks like a baby most of the time. It's *very* cute. It makes people love it and cuddle it, but it turns into something else when no one's watching."

That sounded nasty; silly, but nasty. The figments of Angela's imagination were seldom cute, or even comfortable. "Oh. Is that why you were screaming last night, possum? Because Benji turned into something?" Jessica still remembered night after night of her own evil dreams, when she was Angie's age.

Angela shook her head so violently that Jessica could almost hear her brains rattle. "No, silly. Benji was in Mummy's bed all last night. He can't turn into something else when he's in bed with Mummy."

"What made you scream last night, then?"

Angela stuck her ice cream-dripping fingers in her mouth and mumbled something incomprehensible.

Jessica said, "Take your fingers out of your mouth, Angel, and tell me what happened in the dream."

Angela looked furtively around the family room. "Don't want to."

Jessica frowned, remembering that feeling. The poor kid was still terrified. "If you don't want to tell me about it, that's okay. Just put the ice cream stick in the kitchen tidy and wash your hands. I've got to finish this report for my boss." (*Even though he doesn't love me anymore.*)

The girl turned her head away and mumbled again.

"Angela," Jessica said, warningly. She remembered her mother saying "Jessica" in just the same tone, each syllable perfectly distinct, and winced. It was strange how all the tiny, niggling pains could still hurt, even when one's whole being was flooded with misery.

Angela stared at her feet. "The lady from the stars was looking at me." Her voice was soft and fast.

"What lady from the stars? An alien? An astronaut?"

Sophie boasted about her daughter's imagination—unlike their mother, who'd labelled Jessica *over-imaginative* as if it were a notifiable disease, and forced her to study accounting instead of Medieval English and the Norse poets.

Angela stamped her foot. "Not from the *stars*, from the *stairs*! Don't you know anything? The lady from the stairs! The scary lady!"

"What scary lady? And what do you mean, she was looking at you?"

Angela almost shouted, "The lady wants me to go to the party!"

"What party?" But by the time the words were out of Jessica's mouth, Angela was gone, stomping down the long corridor towards the front of the terrace house, then up the stairs to the bedroom where Sophie was trying to get Benji to sleep. Jessica put her head in her hands. Another failed conversation, in a lifetime of failed conversations. But crying would be too great a luxury. Eric wanted this report on his desk by morning. She had to get it finished, and it had to be perfect, absolutely perfect, even if he didn't love her anymore. Especially because he didn't love her anymore.

• • •

Jessica woke, thirsty, around 3 am, in the spare room at the back of the old house, behind the upstairs bathroom. The bedroom was tiny, but she was grateful to Sophie for letting her sleep there until she found somewhere of her own. She padded barefoot down the two flights of stairs to the kitchen, and gulped down a giant glass of water. On the way back, her stomach now uncomfortably distended with liquid, she saw a door she'd never noticed before. It was bright apple-green, and it led off the half-landing just down from the bathroom door.

• • •

Jessica hardly saw the door at the time; she was still immersed in the dream she'd been having before thirst woke her. She'd been floating through the void between the stars with a dozen ancient god-beasts, horned and tentacled—or was she fleeing them? While she was at college, her mother had donated all Jessica's tatty paperbacks to charity, and she'd been too busy for fiction since— but the heavy-duty sleeping pills that the doctor had prescribed gave her strangely vivid dreams. At least they stopped the suicidal ideation, as the doctors called it, most of the time.

Afterwards, she lay back in bed despairing, remembering Eric's hair, as soft and pale as corn silk, and his blue eyes, cold as the south wind. But she was puzzled about that green door. She'd thought that she knew all the rooms in Sophie's old inner-Sydney terrace house. What room could possibly lie behind that door?

• • •

While Jessica was setting up her laptop in the family room after work the next evening, she saw the dried-up puddle of fluoro ice cream on the slate. She'd forgotten to mop it up for Sophie after all—too absorbed in the report for Eric, damn him. (*Why doesn't he love me anymore? Am I so old, so ugly, so fat?*) With a shock, she remembered Angela's lady on the stairs, and that green door she'd seen in the night. In her frenzy to get to work in the morning, Jessica had forgotten to check exactly where that door led.

• • •

It was time to get to the bottom of this door thing, Jessica decided, so that she could concentrate on editing Eric's new presentation. She left the clever silver machine to run a virus scan and walked up and down the stairs three times, looking for the door.

It wasn't there. The bathroom door was right next to the spare room door, on the back landing. The stairs went down from it to a half-landing, then up to the front landing, with Sophie's big bedroom next to Angela's smaller one. But there wasn't a door anywhere near the half-landing, let alone a bright green one. There was nothing but old bricks, stripped bare of their plaster back in the clueless 1970s. No green door, no nothing . . .

Jessica shrugged, and went downstairs to Eric's presentation. He had chewed up her heart and swallowed it, then decided he didn't want it anymore. It was a mangled mess now, and her life would never be the same, but he still *needed* her. She was the *best*. One day, he would realise what a fool he'd been.

She crossed her fingers, hoping that the day would come before despair sent her over the edge.

• • •

That night, music woke Jessica from her drugged sleep. Giant tripods straight out of *The War of the Worlds* had been hunting her through twisting lanes, their death rays coming closer and closer to her head. It was almost a relief to be awake—but what was Sophie doing, playing music in the middle of the night? Sophie was still miserable about James leaving her and the kids, and she wasn't exactly rational; but if the music woke Angie and Benji now, nobody would get back to sleep. She staggered to her door to investigate.

On the back landing outside her room, her eyes more than half-closed, Jessica listened for the source of the music.

The bathroom? Sophie was playing music in the *bathroom?*

Jessica swung the door wide open. There was the slightly grimy claw-footed bath crowded with plastic toys, the almost-clean sink with the grey slick of slime around the plug-hole, Sophie's thick paperback of short stories by H.G. Wells sitting dog-eared on the cane stool next to the toilet—but no Sophie, and no music.

The music had to be coming from *somewhere.*

Jessica stumbled sleepily off the back landing and down a few stairs to the half-landing. The music was louder now. She opened her eyes wide, and saw that door again. It was apple-green against the bricks of the wall, and it sounded as if there was a party going on behind it: music and loud voices, and the sharp, bright tinkle of ice in glasses.

What? Sophie wouldn't have a party without inviting her, would she? Her only sister?

Jessica grabbed the big brass handle at the centre of the door and tried to turn it, but the handle wouldn't move, no matter how hard Jessica tugged. Surely Sophie hadn't locked her out of a party. *Surely not.*

After pushing and pulling at the handle for ten minutes with no result, Jessica went back to bed, furious and baffled. She thought she'd never sleep, but all too soon the alarm clock dragged her out of the control room of a space-ship that was falling infinitely slowly towards the event horizon of a black hole.

As she woke up, she remembered the night. How could Sophie have held a party and not asked her? Not even *told* her? It was unimaginable.

But as she was stomping down the stairs, tears in her eyes yet again, she saw that the green door was gone. She put both hands out, touched the space where the door had been in the night. All that she could feel was gritty old hand-made bricks.

She shook her head to clear it, but it only made it hurt more.

"It must have been a dream," she said aloud. "Just a dream."

Angela's door at the top of the stairs creaked open, and the kid stepped out onto the front landing, in her blue-green dragon-scale pyjamas.

"Did you see the lady last night, Aunty Jessie?" Angela asked.

"What lady, chicken?" Jessica said warily.

"The lady on the stairs. She was playing music. She wanted me to go to her party."

Jessica just shook her head. This couldn't be happening. It was too much to deal with before she'd even had the first coffee of the day. Especially after the music in the night. But if there wasn't a door in the wall, how could there have been a party behind it, or music?

Too much thought too early. Jessica changed the subject to something more interesting. "Hey, Angie-pie, what does a durga-monster look like when it's not pretending to be a baby?"

Angela looked doubtful. "Well, it's got a lot of legs," she said slowly. "*Long* legs, like a spider. And long black wings. *Furry* wings, like a moth."

Over her muesli, in the family room, Jessica watched Sophie spoon pale sludge into Benji's mouth. Now and then, Jessica felt Sophie glance at her green snakeskin stilettos (too high) and the neckline of the black dress (too low), her sister's face creased with worry. Jessica couldn't possibly ask Sophie about what had happened during the night.

Jessie tried to imagine dropping it into the conversation casually: "Hey, sis, did you know that your house has a door that appears in the wall in the middle of the night? And that there was a party behind it last night? Loud music, and everything?"

No way. Sophie already thought Jessica was insane for moving in with Eric last year. Jessica couldn't possibly tell her sister that she'd seen a door that wasn't there.

Still, she had to say something. "Sleep well?" she asked, oh so casually.

"Like the dead," Sophie said, with a huge smile. Her eyes were clear and bright, without a trace of the dark circles that late nights always gave her.

"You didn't hear any noises in the night? Music?"

Sophie raised her eyebrows. "I keep telling you, you've been working too hard. You have to slow down, sweetie. Read a book. Fiction, not finance."

"I'm okay, don't worry about me. It must have been just another bad dream. I've been dreaming a lot lately." Too much, obviously.

Benji waved his anemone-like fist.

The baby, Jessica thought. Now, that was a thought to hold onto amongst the misery. He was *such* a sweet little nephew. And it was so sweet of Angela, too, making up the story about Benji being a durga-monster, whatever that was.

Jessica tried to smile, despite the night she'd had, and despite the day she was expecting in the office. There was Sophie, her adorable younger sister, being such a good mother, putting yet another spoonful of sludge into Benji's warm, wet, open maw.

The baby gazed at his aunt with dark, ageless eyes. He put a hand up in the air, and waved his fingers like an octopus's tentacles. Then he winked, very slowly. Jessica shuddered.

• • •

"Well, did you see the lady last night?" Angela demanded at half past six, kicking repeatedly at the leg of the table Jessica was trying to work on. "You didn't tell me. You have to tell me if you saw the lady."

"What lady, Angel-pie?" Jessica said. But she was only pretending. This thing with the door in the wall, and the lady, was starting to seem more important than the endless stream of urgent reports and presentations that Eric apparently needed her to work on until midnight every night. Perhaps he was just trying to drive her out of the firm with over-work, now that he didn't love her anymore.

Angela said, "The lady in the green dress, silly. The one who wants me to go to the party."

"Where does this lady live, chicken?"

"The second star to the right, and straight on till morning. That was what she said, one time."

"In the stars? Is she an alien, Angie-poo?"

Angela shrugged. "Maybe. I don't know. Do you want to go to her party with me tonight?"

None of this could possibly be real, but she might as well go along with Angela's fantasy—make her happy. The kid wasn't having an easy time any more than Jessica or Sophie was: her beloved father was off in Europe with his new wife, Sophie's younger and thinner replacement, and he hadn't seen Angela for months. No one mentioned his name, or even that he existed, anymore.

"Sure, why not?" she said. "I'll go to the party with you."

Angela nodded. "Good. She'll like that. She said she wants to meet you."

I can't imagine why, Jessica thought. *No one else wants to know me these days.* She said as breezily as she could, trying to be a good aunt, "Has your brother turned into a durga-monster lately?"

Angela picked up her favourite fluffy toy, an orange and gold dragon the size of a toddler, and held it over her head. "He's a durga-monster all the time, silly. He looks like a cute baby most of the time, to make people love him, but he's *always* a durga-monster."

Jessica tried again. "Um, has he changed into the thing that he looks like when he doesn't look like a baby, then?"

Angela threw the dragon into the corner. "He looks like a baby *now*. Mummy's in the front room with him. But he looked like the other thing *before*, while he was taking his nap and Mummy was watching Sesame Street with me. He looked like the bad thing, then."

"Oh, darling, I'm sure your baby brother never turns into a bad thing, really." *Even if grown men could turn out to be such bastards.* "Why don't we find a DVD for you to watch, just while I finish this presentation I've got to write?"

• • •

That night, Jessica woke gasping from a dream of sinister blood-sucking moths flying at her eyes and mouth. Angela was patting at her face and throat with small, sticky fingers.

"I want to go to the party, Aunty Jessie. The lady won't let me in unless you come with me. Wake up!"

What? Jessica blinked several times. But she might as well humour the kid, now she was awake. "Okay, Angel." It had to be better than dreaming about evil moths, or despairing over Eric.

Jessica got out of bed, feeling hazy, and walked behind Angela down to the half-landing. Eyes half-closed, she held Angela's hand while the kid knocked at that impossible green door in the wall, and saw a tall woman open it. Jessica blinked, and rubbed at her eyes.

The woman in the doorway wore silk the colour of green apples, with strings of pearls dripping from her neck and shining emeralds laced through her blonde hair. Behind her was a ballroom full of revellers. (That wasn't possible, of course. Jessica knew there wasn't any space behind the green door for a *ballroom*.)

This had to be another dream. One of the people behind the woman in the green dress had a curly pink tail poking through her blue velvet dress, and another's sleek body shone bright gold all over. On the floor near them there were two huge panthers, gloriously spotted, playing with a golden ball; and the man to the left, serving drinks, had long furry ears, and grey whiskers on his donkey muzzle.

"Come join the party, Angela, Jessica," the lady said, and smiled at them both. "The endless party."

Jessica was suspicious, even if this was just a dream. "Endless, like endless night, or endless sea?"

"Exactly. But this is an endless *party*."

Jessica didn't like the sound of that, any more than she liked the look of the green-silk woman. There was something not quite right about her.

Angela let go of Jessica's hand and rushed into the room. Jessica suddenly panicked. What if this *wasn't* a dream? Jessica could see her niece racing towards the corner of the room, where small people in silver space-suits were dancing around a table loaded with fairy-bread. Within seconds, a piece of fairy bread was in Angela's mouth, and another was on the way.

The woman in green smiled widely, and Jessica shivered. Her teeth looked very white, and very sharp. "You won't see your niece again, my dear," she said, "not unless you join us, but don't worry. She'll be happy with us. And everyone in your world will simply forget her. Even you will forget her, in time. In a week and a day, you won't even remember what colour her eyes were."

The door closed. Jessica just stood and looked at it, for a moment. "What? Let me in, you bitch! You've got my *niece* in there! Give her back to me!"

Jessica beat against the door, when the handle refused to turn, until her hands started to bleed. The door had gone, and there was nothing left but old handmade bricks.

"Shit," she muttered. "What am I going to do? I have to get Sophie. She's the kid's mother. That strange woman *has* to let Sophie in to the party, if Angela's there."

But no matter how long Jessica stood over Sophie's sleeping body, shaking her shoulder, Sophie just slept on, with Benji snuggled smugly against her side, his red mouth lolling open.

By dawn, Jessica was a snivelling mess. She was still sitting at the side of Sophie's bed, working her way through a large box of tissues, when Sophie finally stirred.

Jessica screamed at her drowsing sister, "Angela's gone. The woman on the stairs took her. The one who lives behind the green door."

Sophie grabbed Jessica's hand and stroked it. "No, darling. That wasn't real. You're just having a nightmare. Everything's all right." Beside her, Benji seemed to nod agreement.

"Angela's been kidnapped, I tell you—"

Sophie's voice had tears in it. "No, sweetie. I know you miss Angie. But she's still in Paris with her bastard of a father. It's just another nightmare, like when you were little. Go back to bed. I'll call your work, and tell that stupid bastard Eric that you're sick."

"Paris? But she was here last night!"

Sophie said, slowly, "You're still in your nightmare. It used happen to you when we were kids, remember? And it happens to Angela all the time. Just go back to bed, sweetie. Please."

"But Angela's—"

Sophie sighed. "Oh, darling, don't you remember the postcard I showed you yesterday? Go to the dressing table and have a look. Then you'll remember."

Too distraught to disobey, Jessica walked the three steps to the dressing table. Right in the middle was a postcard of the Eiffel Tower; on the reverse, Angela's wobbly writing and a French stamp. It was dated eight days earlier.

"Oh," Jessica said. "Angela's in Paris. You were right. I must have been dreaming. But . . . "

"Go back to bed, sweetie," Sophie said, and Benji gurgled happily beside her.

But when Jessica went downstairs for lunch, after a long, uncomfortable time of tossing and turning in the narrow spare bed, wondering whether she was having a nervous breakdown, the golden dragon was lying on its side in the corner where Angela had thrown it, and the dried-out fluoro ice cream was still puddled on the slate floor. She almost pointed them out to Sophie, but Benji looked at her with those deep, dark eyes, and she knew there was no point. What she had to do was to get in through that door and rescue Angela, no matter what.

For three days, Jessica let Sophie answer the phone whenever Eric rang to see when she was going to be well enough to finish the presentation for him. He didn't love her anymore, and probably he never had, and maybe she would never be truly happy again—but her misery about him was just a backdrop to her guilt and rage about Angela. Her only niece was *gone*, kidnapped and taken somewhere unimaginably strange in time and space. Jessica wanted to scream and cry, to rail against her fate, but that would do no good.

Instead, she babied herself by day: took afternoon naps, ate chicken soup and chocolate, read magazines in bed. But for those three nights, as soon as Sophie's bedroom light went out, Jessica sat on the landing and watched the wall.

Nothing happened: no door, no music, no party.

The fourth night Jessica slept, but woke in a panic. What colour were Angie's eyes? Brown? Green? She ran downstairs for Sophie's photo albums, and dragged them back to her bed. There were hundreds of photos of Benji, and even some of his father, but none of Angela. Jessica shook too hard after that to get back to sleep.

The next day, Jessica stayed in bed until Sophie went to the supermarket with Benji, then she rang Angela's school. They must have photos, records of her classes . . .

"Sorry," the school secretary said, "a girl of that name was enrolled with us last year, but she's never attended the school. Her father took her to Europe, I believe."

• • •

A week and a day after Angela had disappeared, when Jessica had almost given up, had almost decided that it was she who was deluded, not everyone else, she woke from a dream of matt-black spaceships hovering over the house's corrugated iron roof. Her mouth was dry as the vacuum of outer space. She started to walk downstairs for a glass of water—and there was that damned door again, bright apple green, the brass handle shining, and party music filtering out. The endless party.

Her heart pounding, Jessica knocked.

The woman in the green dress opened the door and smiled. Jessica looked past her, scanning for Angela. The room seemed to go on forever—where was the kid? Over to the left were five or six things with too many long legs, and furry dark wings trailing to the floor. *Durga-monsters*. They were dancing in a ring around Angela, who was singing at the top of her voice, and spinning around. She was still wearing her dragon pyjamas. Jessica squinted: did the monsters have claws at the end of those furry wings? Did they look hostile? She hadn't decided when one of them waved to her and winked, just like Benji had. *Shudder.*

"Give her back to me," Jessica said. "She's my niece."

"But she's happy here," the woman said. "You'd be happy here, too."

"Where is *here*? Where exactly *is* this party? It can't be inside the house. The room's too big—I can't see any walls—so where is it?"

"You should know that. You'd have known when you were twelve. You've spent too long reading the wrong books, Jessica."

What was she reading when she was twelve? Paperbacks with pictures of unicorns on the cover, or monsters—or aliens. "Angela said that you live in the stars."

The woman laughed. "Sometimes we do. Sometimes we live on an island of glass, or under the burial mound of a warrior-king. Our kingdom is a moveable feast. You stay here, and I'll find your niece and bring her to talk to you. Meanwhile, why don't you have a drink? What harm could it possibly do?"

The long-eared waiter came up to the doorway. On his tray was a bunch of white grapes and a single crystal glass full to the brim of wine the palest of yellow-greens. He held it out to Jessica. Automatically, she took the glass and lifted it to her nose. It smelled of spring. The shadow of a memory niggled at the back of her mind—but what harm could it possibly do to take a single sip?

• • •

Sophie answered the phone, Benji on her right hip.

• • •

"I've already told you, Eric," she snapped. "Jessica's in London. I have no idea what this presentation is that you're carrying on about. She's been there for weeks. And I don't care why you want to know, I'm *not* telling you what colour her eyes are. If you didn't bother to find out before you dumped her, you're a fool."

Sophie slammed the phone down. Jessica's eyes were brown, of course; dark chocolate brown.

Or were they apple green?

CROW AND CAPER, CAPER AND CROW

MARGO LANAGAN

Pen walked a long time back and forth, clacking the shells in her pocket. The light was harsh and yellowish, the clouds were like smoke off some disaster, and the sea had a nasty impatience about it, waves crossing one another and throwing their hands up. But now was the moment. All day its imminence had hummed in her skull; she had scratched at her head, stirring her hair up wilder than ever. The whole world had gone soft today and started shifting—it was time for Pen to do the little she could to nail it back into shape.

Four walnut-shell halves she had, all perfect, saved from Christmas. She herself was full to the brim. She had taken no strong drink in the year since the wedding. She had been eating well, was plump as a Christmas pig, in fact, for the voyage. And she had stretched and run and swum in the sea and climbed the hills; she was fitter than she'd ever been. She wouldn't have done this just for herself, but for a child, for a grandchild, she could turn herself into that machine, well oiled, well tuned, and with its battery charged to the full. She must, in fact, for there was no one else of her blood who could do this thing, who could make this journey, and bless the child as it should be blessed.

She readied her powers, admiring the powerful sea, the gathering darkness, the last yellow light leaking and sulking in the clouds. She felt ahead for the moment. It *eased* toward her, but she was too far gone into her plan to feel excited about it; she must be practical now and bring to bear all her eye and instinct and old, old skill.

She had stopped pacing without even noticing, had stood back from the water. Foamy wavelets raced up and reached for her toes. Now she took a shell and, bending down, laid it on a ripple. She uttered a Word and pulled from the shell an improbable boat—still walnut shell and no mistake, but with a mast to stand and cling to, and a seat athwart it to sit and croon upon when standing grew wearisome. There was a little flag from the top of the mast, a pennant, yellow, with a golden star; this would give her courage. The whole construction bobbed lightly as bubble-weed on the wavelets. It looked fragile and unbalanced, but it was made entirely of her own devotion and willfulness, and both those things, she knew, were strong and steady.

She stepped aboard, or the boatlet took her on—it was hard to tell and it did not matter, for the boat was part of her, after all. And she set out, first lifting and dropping and calculating a way through the waves, remembering how to balance, then moving faster and more smoothly across the less broken water, as much like flying as floating. Her boat had no sail, and the wind did not blow her; she was her own prevailing wind, and always the pennant flapped behind, pointing the way she had come. She had looped her mind around the arriving grandchild and now she was reeling herself in. The water had only the merest shading of green now, and the light was fading further. Soon there would be just these small scrolls and rolls of foam on the blackness. Then, if the clouds persisted, the foam would vanish, too, and she would only feel the tap and punch of wave tops against the shell-boat's breast in her feet and hands if she stood at the mast, in her spine if she sat against it—and the clamp and release of her magic, automatic as a sleeper's breathing, hurrying her through the night.

What did I do? she had asked Rowan. *Whatever did I do that you would go so far away?*

Nothing, Ma! He'd laughed and hugged her. *It's the job; it's the opportunity. And Sophie—*

And Sophie, she had said heavily.

No, all I meant was, Sophie says it's a great chance and we ought to go after it. She's going from her mum, too, you know, her mum and dad and her sisters and all her family. It's not all about you.

But some of it is. She dislikes me.

She's only frightened. Lots of people are; you know that.

Pen had looked up into his kind face. She was about to hurt him, but she must speak anyway. *I had hoped you would find a woman who wasn't one of the fearful.*

They must be very rare, he'd said. *Because I looked, Ma; you know I did. But I couldn't look forever.*

You are still so young—

Mum, I love Sophie for what she is. I can only care so much about what she's not.

She had admired him; he had seemed rather noble. But she had mocked him to herself, too: *He only doesn't mind because he's young,* she'd thought. *Give him time, and years catering to Sophie's limitations, and he will understand me, understand the mistake he is making.*

• • •

Morning climbed up behind her into the stars, and the streaky clouds grew gaudy with it. An albatross glided in angled flight low to the waves; some dolphins rose and fell past her as if they were fixed to some huge invisible merry-go-round. Tired, cold to the bone, Pen could no longer think; she had been pummeled all night by wind and water, and felt bruised from head to toe.

She came to land. The boat tipped her onto the beach, and she stamped about on the hard sand, waking herself, getting her land legs, watching the boat shrink back to walnut size and be overwhelmed by the next wavelet. Then she walked up the softer beach and followed a path through the dunes. On the far side lay a road, and a man was just opening the shop opposite. A line of houses stretched out either side of it, beach shacks, their lawns neatened for the summer.

Pen plucked a leaf from a hedge and used it to pay for a drink, for a packet of biscuits. She sat on the dew-damp iron seat outside the shop, and chewed three biscuits, and drank the drink; it was like eating mouthfuls of sand and washing them down with sweetened bilge water.

When she had eaten, she did her stretches. People came to the shop to buy their milk, their bread, their newspapers, and looked sidelong at her mad sea-blown hair, her dark, odd clothes, the strange postures she was taking up against the seat, against the shop wall. Families with small children, carrying bright towels and gaily colored floating toys, came walking along the road and turned down the path to the beach. "Good morning," said these mums and dads determinedly, and the children stared and reached for their parents' hands. Pen had no wish to frighten children, but if their parents raised them to be fearful there was not much she could do about it.

She chose a quiet moment and slipped in among the dunes. When she was all alone with the wind in the whistle-grass, she took out a walnut shell and with a Word and a sweeping gesture threw it into the careless sky. There it blossomed into a craft somewhere between a hawk and a microlight, but still keeping something of the woodenness and knobbliness of a walnut about it. She laughed with fondness for it and reached up her arms, and the thing swooped down and picked her up in its claws or its clamps or its breast, whatever it had, and carried her off over the country.

Pen looked ahead. The knowledge opened like a fat flower toward her from the middle of the continent. "She is born! She is born!" she cried, and already she was too high for people to hear her or to think her more than a distant bird. She felt a great joy, very pure—perhaps the purest she had ever felt. It was purer even than when she had carried Rowan inside her and brought him forth, for that joy had always been shadowed by fear, fear that she would fail him somehow, fear that he would hurt her by coming to harm himself. This granddaughter was at a safe remove from her; Pen could never do wrong by her. Nothing was required of Pen, not even love if she did not want to give it—but she did, of course; it flowed up and out of her like springwater, refreshing as it went.

There was still a good distance to be covered. Exulting, she flew on, over the land of her granddaughter's birthing. Oh, it was a beautiful thing, a country from above, like a masterpiece painting. You could see how it had come to be, piled and pushed up, and then blown and washed down, worn to plains and then through to gorges. It was subtly colorful and delicately patterned; everything that was so ugly when you were down among it seemed from this distance nicely worked, and human effort seemed rather dear and hopeless, even though it had cleared and scarred and excavated such great tracts of land, ruined them every which way. Dammed and channeled waters winked, traffic beetled along the many roads, cities hung in their shawls of smog. In between the clumps and blotches of smaller towns, crops lay golden and green, and dark plantations flowed over the hills. Only a few areas had been left raw, allowed to stay irregular in their forms and growths, and these gave up a thin power, which Pen drew on instead of her own store, much reduced from her night's paying out aboard the boat.

She was warm in the breast feathers of the walnut-hawk; they were like very thin roof shingles, and they rattled musically about her ears and stung her hands and arms with their flapping. If she pushed her face forward to crane after something she had just passed below, the cold went into her forehead like an ax blow, and pained right down her face to her teeth.

It was a very long day, because she traveled west. Midafternoon she began to seek out on the ground the features she had marked in her memory to tell her the way: the dogleg in the river, the three towns making a triangle, the cloverleaf where the highways crossed. When they came, she ticked them off one by one. She had not traveled a distance like this for a good while, not since she was in love as a girl—why not, when it was such a pleasure, the sensations and the sights, when it was so simple, really, if she prepared herself?

She dropped into an orchard of some kind; the fruits were hard and green, some kind of citrus. Her feet set down in sunny grass— that was nice, being in touch with the earth again. The walnut shell fell through the fruit-tree leaves behind her and patted to earth, too.

The hospital was not far away. She walked out to the highway, picking money from a tree as she went. She sat awhile at a bus stop, and then a bus came and took her to the edge of a car park, and on the other side the hospital loomed, enormous, white, and glassy, with somewhere inside it her granddaughter, and beside the girl, her mother.

The bus drove away and quiet fell, warm afternoon quiet in which things moved slowly, if at all. Half her strength, half the weight she had put on was gone now, merely from traveling here, with still the blessing to be done, and the traveling home. She walked slowly and kept a careful eye out for vehicles, for she felt a little dazed. She was also too warm in her dark clothing, now that she had thawed out from the flying; she would love a hot shower, or better, a bath with scented oils in it, and a candle and a glass of wine glowing on the rim.

In the hospital doors her sunlit reflection took fright, and tried to straighten her travel rags and tame her hair. It was no good; she was clearly a wild woman. Look at the claws in that hair, the bags under those red eyes! She hadn't calculated for this, but she pulled on a glamour of shining permed-and-set hair, neat jacket and skirt, stockings and well-kept shoes and handbag—all dark, as if she were in mourning, so that people would think twice about stopping her and asking what she was about. She was hungry; she pulled a few leaves from the plane tree nearest her, found a purse within the handbag, and slipped the leaves inside.

The glass doors slid open. She proceeded into the corridors and up the stairs toward the baby, not hurrying, not lingering where people might ask her her business. Reaching ahead for the little one, she was, and examining all around her, to see what would be necessary, how much delay, how much disguise.

The afternoon was drawing on; some patients had visitors, some lay alone and wakeful, some were asleep. Nurses conferred or chatted at their stations. An orderly with a drinks-and-snacks trolley trundled about; Pen immediately liked his manner, both hearty and gentle. The warm light through the sunlit blinds gave everything a sleepy-sickroom feel, only with more equipment—fire extinguishers, signage and warnings, phones and filing systems and computers. The floors that bore it all up shone and shone, polished right to the edges and into every corner.

Sophie shared a ward with three other women, each with a plastic cradle beside her high, narrow bed. Two of the women slept; one of these was Sophie—by the window there, on the right, behind that curtain. Of the two awake, one lay reading a gossip magazine; the other had visitors murmuring around her, taking turns with her baby. All heads turned to Pen in the doorway.

She put a finger to her lips and stepped in. Her sensible shoes made no noise on the gleaming floor. She crossed to the foot of Sophie's bed. Sophie lay on her back, her lovely lips a little parted in sleep, her hands folded on her still slightly rounded belly. Only now did Pen realize that the girl had been cut open to bring the baby out, as had two of the other mothers in this room—she looked around at them. What a pity. What they had missed out on. She had birthed Rowan in a crouch, catching him with her own hands. The whole earth had backed her up in doing that, the whole sky, the whole ungodly wonderful mess of the universe; she had laughed, surrendering to something else's power for a change.

The baby girl lay expertly wrapped, a saintly maggot, one hand at her chin to assist her in her sage thoughts. Pen leaned over and looked and laughed through her nose. To all other eyes this face would have seemed utterly still; to Pen, its tiny movements flashed out at her baby Rowan's face, her own face, her father's, her ex-husband Arsenio's in turn, as well as Sophie's, and others that must be Sophie's family's. This baby belonged to them all; she *was* them all in the future; she was Pen and the rest of them, carried forward.

Delicate pale reddish hair crowned the baby's head. Someone had tried to part it already, but it had sprung back over to the place it had been used to lying in, in the womb. Pen ventured to help it there. The hair itself was warm, and the skin with the skull beneath it was that miraculous combination of firm and soft that she remembered from her baby son.

Under cover of the visitors chatting, Pen whispered a welcome and a well-wishing. She planted a little seed so that the girl would recognize and accept her when they met again; she tweaked the fabric of things just slightly, so that circumstances would be kind to this girl and favorable. It was utter pleasure to make these murmurings; there was not the least trace of fear in what she did. She stroked the fine hair again, took hold of a tuft of it, and spoke it gently away from the child's head. From her handbag she brought a tiny ziplock bag, and she sealed the pale hairs into it. You never knew what work might be required for the girl in the future, from across the water.

The handbag closed with a *clop*. Pen's gaze leaped to Sophie's face, and she couldn't tell if the sound or the stab of her own fear fluttered the eyelids open. Sophie locked eyes with her mother-in-law, let out a little scream and started to sit up, but subsided under the pain of her wound. "You! What are you do—"

Pen put out a hand to subdue the girl, to erase this memory, to send her back to sleep.

But the hand flung back, as if she'd touched a hot stove. Sophie had resisted, thrown her off. Sophie *had known how to* throw her off—the gesture had been fast, smooth, practiced, quite invisible.

Pen took a step back. They stared at each other.

"I knew you'd come," said Sophie.

"You knew a whole lot more than you ever let on." Confused, a little stung, Pen decided to opt for being pleased. "At the wedding, even. At our little chat. That was a nice bit of concealment."

The girl began to blush. She checked her arm for a watch that wasn't there, consulted it on the side table. "Rowan will be here in half an hour. You don't want him to know you've visited." Maneuvering herself more upright in the bed, she spared a hand to wave Pen closer to the baby. "I need you to see, though," she said. "No one else will understand. Wake her up."

"Wake her? Are you mad?"

"Look in her eyes. Just for a second, but *properly,* you know." She reached over and gave the baby bundle a little shake. "Come on, Chrissy. Show Grandma." She looked sharply up at Pen. "Do you want to be Grandma, or Nan, or what? Now's the time to imprint it."

Pen balked. "She's as sensitive as *that*?" She met Sophie's level gaze. "I want to be Pen," she said breathlessly.

"Come on, Chris. Here we go. Just a glimpse is all Pen needs. Look right in," she said to Pen.

Baby Chrissy's face flitted through several expressions: Churchillesque stolidity, haughty surprise, crumpled on the point of crying. Her tiny bud-mouth tore itself open, her eyelids parted, and her slate-blue eyes swam nearly blind within. Pen bent to look in.

She did not show herself, the little one, so much as *throw* herself outward, not at Pen particularly, but furiously blasting in all directions, at all things and beings. It was not an event, a detonation, so much as a glimpse of a constant outpouring, outroaring state of being, snatched in a millisecond before the fragile eyelids closed again.

"Ah!" Pen clanged back against the foot of the far bed. The woman there woke with a cry; all the visitors turned, aghast, and saw Pen without her disguise. "What on *earth*?" came through the curtain from the next bed. A nurse appeared at the door as if Pen had magicked her up from the worst that could happen. "What's going on here?" The nurse stared at the madwoman intruder, her rags, her wide eyes, her wild hair.

"Nothing," said Pen, putting out hands to calm them all.

But it was Sophie who stroked down the air, turned the visitors' faces away, glued the woman opposite back down into sleep, threw a fuzz of forgetment through the curtain, snuffed out the nurse's alarm into boredom and sent her on her way. There was nothing left for Pen to do but to resume her mourning glamour.

Legs shaking, she crossed back to Sophie, took the chair against the wall beside the bedside cupboard, breathed.

Sophie was making the wryest mouth at her, beyond the watch and the water glass. Pen's own face had fallen open, cleansed of any expression by surprise.

"So you see," said Sophie.

A three-note run of cold laughter loosed itself from Pen's throat.

"I will need you," said the girl, eyeing the crib. "I was worried about letting you see what I was. I thought someone so powerful would scorn me, not think I was good enough for her son. But now?" She gave a helpless laugh. "Look what we've got on our hands. None of that matters—liking, not liking, who's greater than whom. Guarding this . . . *creature,* keeping her safe from herself—oh my God, Pen, I've hardly the first idea."

"Nor me," said Pen. "I only raised an ordinary boy, after all."

"There's nothing ordinary about Rowan."

Their gazes went from the crib to each other. Sophie was lit up from the inside; Pen allowed herself to glow somewhat with pride and love. "Does he know?"

"He begins to know, about me. He hasn't a clue about Chris. All he knows is that she's the most amazing baby that's ever lived—because she's his, not because of all that you and I see in her, not from anything in herself. Perhaps he'll never know more, if I bring her up right. She might only look like a genius of this world; he might not realize she has dominion in the other."

Dominion. The crib was misty with tiny scratches from nurses' use and cleaning, from countless previous babies being laid to sleep, being lifted out. Baby Chrissy lay motionless, her strengthless round fists beneath her sleeping chin. Pen stood and laid a hand on the tight-wrapped bundle, admiring the outer tininess, the harmless parcel containing the bomb flash, the shock, the star's worth of power she had seen in the beyond. Pen herself was pinhead-sized in that place, bright and hot and well-made but *small,* and her inflowings and her outgoings were like roots and tree branches either side of that pinhead, slow, established, spread wide, doggedly shunting the forces along themselves. This girl— oh, this girl!—she was a boiling-surfaced sun. She had put out few tendrils, and none of any great reach yet, but those few flickered their messages in, flashed them out, seethed, raced with light. Pen didn't know of anyone this powerful—now, or in history, or foretold. She didn't know what this meant for the world, whether it presaged disaster or glory. She only knew that she herself, with her nutshell work and her feeble blessings, she and Sophie here with whatever small talent Sophie had, had been laid down like paving stones in this time and place for this queen to tread as she walked forth into her fullness.

"I will give her my gift, still." So doubtfully did she say it, she was almost asking permission of the mother.

Sophie nodded. She looked immensely tired, shadows in her young face. Pen saw, as women do, ordinary women with no special talents, that Sophie would not age as well as she herself had, that she had no residual handsomeness that would allow her to go about wild-haired and pleasing herself. She would have harder work of it when her prettier days were done.

Pen stood over the crib, put her hands to the wrapped baby, closed her eyes, and cautiously entered the other world. Sideways she went this time, for her own protection, and she felt for one of the smaller outthrowings of her granddaughter's forceful self. She found no more than a thread. It petered out on the darkness yet pulled all of Pen askew with the force inside it, the baby's hunger, huge, unfocused, endless, its sucking of everything toward its light.

I have very little, she apologized. *I know hardly anything of what you'll need. But take it all, and use it as you wish.* She held on to her core and let the rest be taken. It was less a giving than a surrendering, but it pleased her immensely to be so emptied, to contribute as she could to whatever great things this granddaughter, this grand granddaughter, would accomplish.

She stayed a moment in that place, averted from the heat and light yet basking in it, a cautious small reveling and astonishment.

Then she withdrew into the ward, the accidental here, the arbitrary now, where all was flat and quiet and stayed in its place. She bent and kissed Chrissy's round cheek, then wiped away with her thumb the trace of crimson lipstick her disguise had left on the baby.

Sophie had a cowed look about her that Pen recognized: face tipped down, eyes turned up. Pen sensed how cruel she might let herself be toward this lesser witch, either directly or by many acts of benevolence, many offerings of advice, many withholdings and stagy ponderings of her own wisdom. She must not use Sophie to salve her own old wounds. She must try to keep her dealings with her straight and plain.

She laid her hand on the waffle-weave blanket over the girl's knee. "I'll go," she said. "You know where I am. Call me if you need me."

"Thank you for coming." Sophie strengthened, uttering the formality.

Pen patted her knee and left. Her son passed her on the stairs; he smiled at her, alight with father-love; he was bringing bright flowers in an ornamental box, fruit in a basket. How happy he was in this world, unconcerned with the workings moiling away behind the surface of things! The neat middle-aged woman, somebody's grandmother, smiled back at him. She had not much energy left. She would need food—ah, she was so hungry! She would need hours curled up in the sunny grass under the fruit trees before she could fly again.

Home's coast rose out of the kicking sea. Home's cove, home's beach rose out of the coast, headlands like arms, the sand blessedly still, blessedly soft-looking. The boat bottom skidded up the shelving sand. Pen took off her shoes, stepped out into the shallows, and waded to the beach. The boat shrank and sank behind her.

She walked up the path through the rocks and hardy wild plants, emptying her pockets of loose change, of spare leaves. The baby hair in its packet? She hadn't known what she was taking. She had thought to do favors for an earthly, ordinary child, using these pieces of her; instead she had an offcutting of a great power. How might she use it? Bind it into a ring, perhaps, and wield it, have her own way awhile as the new queen grew into her talents? She herself was one of the people Sophie sought to protect Chrissy from, the people who might take advantage. Pen dropped the packet, with the coins, into the toe of a shoe.

A paper flapped on the kitchen door of her little gray house, pressing out against the screen. "Ha." This would be from the people up at the store, who used phone and computer on her behalf.

It's a girl! their daughter had written in crimson and pink pencil, and she'd attached a sticker of a pink-wrapped baby, outlined in gold, and another sticker of three balloons, red, purple, blue, on golden strings. Pinned behind this paper was the email from Rowan, the general announcement, with a list at the top of all the people they had sent it to—that was showy, and possibly unwise, when she thought of it. The baby's name was Kristina Opal. (With a *K*! But she approved of the Opal.) And there was her weight, laughable next to her actual significance. Baby and mother, Rowan had typed, were "doing well"—she remembered the baby's pure clean skin, the mother's shadowed face, pained as she tried to move a body wounded, repaired, and only just beginning to knit itself back together.

Pen took down both papers and stuck the pin back in the door for whatever note might come next, whatever news—a death, new spring stock of clothes or garden tools, another baby, the newsletter she always read about people she didn't know and hoped never to meet. In the hall, she laid the papers on the shallow table, weighted them there with the shoes. The little bag with the tuft of hair she took from the shoe's toe. All through the house she went, opening everything she had shut before she left against possible wind and rain. Sea sound washed in, very gentle now that she was not on top of it taking the water's thumps and battings; the thin hiss of wind in the bent trees passed through and around the house. She loved these four rooms, their clutter and haphazardness, their comforts, the fact that everything was in easy reach, fitted to her own size and habits. She laid the witch-queen's hair on her night table and switched on the lamp above it like a ward-candle. There would be no binding, no wielding—she was beyond being tempted by such things. She would only keep the talisman here by her head, to see first thing when she woke in the morning, and last of all before she slept, every night.

· · · · · · · · · · ·

THE BLACK STAR KILLER

NICOLE MURPHY

Sinéad waved her hand over the candles and flames sparked to life. She smiled—the table looked perfect. The glass glimmered, the silverware gleamed and the red napkins provided a passionate splash of colour against the crisp white tablecloth.

Combined with the enticing smells wafting from the kitchen and the sultry jazz floating in the air, it added up to the perfect setting in which to welcome Dylan back home.

Her husband had been gone for two weeks—part of his role as the Heasimir, giving gadda worldwide their annual health check. She understood the dedication, just as he did when she was summoned away to deal with an errant incantation, but still she missed him.

A chime rang—someone was trying to contact her. Stifling a sigh, Sinéad walked through the loungeroom into her office.

A glowing orb hung over her desk. She touched it with a finger and it peeled open.

"Sabhamir? This is John O'Connor, from Boston. There is some reported trouble in Chicago that I think you should know about."

Sinéad took hold of her power and smiled as its warmth spread through her. Then she mentally contacted John.

"John, this is the Sabhamir. What is the problem?"

"I have been reading some newspaper reports of a murderer the police are chasing in Chicago. He has been leaving a calling-card, and it looks to me like the Star of Gulagh."

Sinéad frowned. The six-pointed star, with a heart at the centre, had been decreed the symbol of the gadda centuries ago. How could a human know about it?

"Can I come to see you?"

"Of course."

Sinéad broke the contact. She looked down at her silk evening gown and sighed, then flicked her wrist. The gown changed into the neck-to-ankle black robe of the Sabhamir. Her red hair cascaded over her shoulders. Mentally, she sought the pinpoint of essence that was her husband's. "Dylan?"

"Just a few more moments, my love. I do like your impatience to see me again."

Sinéad smiled. "It is not that. I have been summoned."

"Of course you have." She could picture his twisted smile. "I hope it will not take too long. I have plans." A vision of the two of them together hit her and with it, a pulse of lust.

"I love you." She broke the connection, focussed on John O'Connor and transferred. There was a moment of sliding through thickness, then a quick pop and she was standing in the other man's loungeroom.

He nodded. "Greetings, Sabhamir, and welcome to my home."

"Thank you, John. Do you have a copy of the newspaper?"

"Certainly." He handed it to her.

The article was titled 'The Search for the Black Star Killer'. Sinéad's eyes were drawn to the accompanying pictures. In one, a police officer was holding up a black card. The picture was not clear enough to see the star, as John had suggested.

She quickly read the article. Over the past month, five people had been killed—three men, two women, of varying ages. All had been taken from a speakeasy within an hour of a police raid. All were intoxicated. All had been strangled.

There was nothing to suggest that gadda power was being used. Except for the description of the card—a white, six pointed star with a heart in the centre printed on black.

Black was her colour. The colour of the Sabhamir, the protector of the gadda. The card was a message to her.

"Do you mind if I take this?" She waved the newspaper at O'Connor.

He shook his head. "Not at all. Is it important?"

"I do not know, but thank you for bringing it to my attention."

O'Connor smiled. "Always happy to serve the guardians."

Sinéad transferred back to her office. She sat down at her desk and stared at the newspaper. If a gadda was killing humans, why not use power? It would make their chances of being captured by the human authorities much less likely.

It would also make it easier for her to catch them.

A pulse of power came from the apartment. A shiver ran through her and a smile burst across her face. She put the paper down and ran across the room, throwing open the door.

"Dylan."

He spun around, grinning. Sinéad rushed into his arms and as his lips pressed against hers, power rushed through her body, igniting the passion.

Dylan's power responded with a roar and within seconds, she was wishing both their clothing away and groaning at the exquisite sensation of his skin against hers.

After two weeks apart, there was not time for finesse—they sated the first flush of lust on the loungeroom carpet.

Sinéad curled her body around Dylan's and kissed his chin. "Welcome home."

"Lovely to be back."

"You have been out in the sun." She traced the line on his waist where he had kept trunks on while swimming or sunbathing.

"I am not going to waste the opportunity to brown up where I can. It will die soon enough in the Irish drizzle."

Sinéad lifted herself onto her elbow to look down at him. It had been three years since they first met and still, the sight of him sizzled. His face was strong, with harsh lines and a hooked nose: overwhelmingly masculine. His brown hair now had blond streaks that made his pale blue eyes sparkle, although the tan detracted from the redness of his luscious lips.

"I thought you spent all your time indoors, talking to gadda."

"I cannot work all the time, Nady. That would make me sick myself." He pushed a strand of hair back behind her ear. "I am glad the call did not keep you away for too long."

Sinéad frowned. Although she was still aroused, and could also feel Dylan's mix of contentment and desire thanks to the sharing of their power, her mind flipped back to the mystery of the newspaper. "I have a feeling that it has potential to in the future."

"What do you mean?"

"I will show you." She got up, ignoring his groan and went into the office. She came back with the newspaper. "What do you think of this?"

Dylan sat up and read it quickly. "You have not felt anyone using power incorrectly in Chicago?"

"No, and there is nothing in this report to suggest power is being used." She sat next to him. "What do you think of the card?"

"Hard to tell, from either the picture or the description."

Sinéad took the paper back. "I have to get hold of one of those cards. Perhaps there will be an essence there that I can trace."

"It is still late afternoon in Chicago. We can go visit the police."

Sinéad nodded. "Find out which officer is handling the case, where his desk is, then at night, transfer in and get hold of the card."

• • •

That was exactly what she did, only to discover there was no essence on it. It felt as clean as though it belonged to a human.

"So is it a gadda, or is it just a human who has coincidentally devised the Star of Gulagh as their sign?" Sinéad paced up and down the loungeroom, tapping the card against her chin.

"It has to be gadda," Dylan said, lounging on the floral sofa. "It cannot be coincidence that they have used the colour of the protector. They have purposely designed it so black is prominent."

"Then we are going to have to flush him or her out somehow," Sinéad said. She stopped pacing and grinned at Dylan. "How would you like to run an illegal bar?"

• • •

The smooth sounds of the band floated around Sinéad's head as she stepped from her office onto the floor of her club. She stopped and watched the quartet—trumpet, piano, double bass and a sultry singer whose voice rippled through the air like the fine whiskey Sinéad sold.

Finding them was just one reason that the Lucky Clover had become one of the hottest gin joints in Chicago in just a couple of weeks. The other reason was the high quality alcohol that Sinéad transferred in directly from Ireland.

Right now, she did not have time to indulge in pride for her achievement. In a few moments, the police would arrive. She needed to make sure the Clover was still operating in an hour's time.

The speakeasy had to stay open, if she was to have any chance of catching the murderer.

She walked over to the bar, the beads at the bottom of her black dress snapping against her stockinged legs. She leant on the mahogany top and smiled at her barman.

"Now, John," she said.

He nodded, turned and pressed a button on the wall. The pockets of alcohol behind the bar spun around—a dozen small compartments—and on the other side were displayed sodas, cordials and juices.

The waiters started to move around the patrons, guiding them to finish the drinks in their glasses and fill them with the water provided in cut glass bottles. The band did not miss a beat.

A new song was beginning as the front door slammed open and a chill wind blew into the club, fluttering the candles that gave the tables a sought-after intimacy. Sinéad lifted her own glass of ginger beer and sipped at it while she watched a dozen men in dark suits and hats storm into the room.

She nodded at the band and the music stopped as the lead officer called out, "This is a raid! Everyone stay where they are."

Sinéad put her glass down and walked forward, the sound of the clacking beads on her gown drawing everyone's attention in the sudden silence. "Can I help you, officers?"

The lead man narrowed his eyes. "I am District Attorney Daryll Smith and I am here because of reports that this establishment sells liquor." He looked over his shoulder, nodded and the men started to move around the room. He turned back to Sinéad. "I want to speak to the manager."

"I am Sinéad Brennan. I own the Lucky Clover." She smiled.

"You are Irish."

"Yes, I am."

"Then perhaps you do not know the laws here, Ms Brennan."

"The eighteenth amendment? I am well aware of it, District Attorney Smith. It is one of the reasons that I came to America."

"Then you support prohibition?"

"I have seen alcohol cause great distress, sir. I think people should be encouraged to have a healthy lifestyle." All of which was true, although she did not support the laws—Sinéad believed people deserved freedom to make their own mistakes. But she would not tell Smith that.

The search was conducted and as expected, nothing was found. Sinéad struggled to hide a smile at the disappointment on DA Smith's face.

"Can I offer you and your hard working men a soda or cordial?" she crooned.

"No, thank you. We have other premises to visit." He spun around, gesturing for his men to follow as he exited.

"Half an hour," Sinéad said to the barman. "I do not want to be surprised by a sudden return."

She started to make her way through the crowded bar. This was the second time she had been raided—she hoped that this time the murderer would strike.

She loosened control on her power a little so she could feel if someone was human or gadda without touching them. She had an incantation resting on the door that should alert her if a gadda walked in, but she wanted to check herself.

It made sense that the murderer would not be here now—would be outside, waiting for the police to leave before he or she came in, but Sinéad was not prepared to assume anything.

Two weeks, and there had not been a sign of her quarry. Sinéad used the excuse of toying with the string of pearls to send a pulse of power across her shoulders to ease the tension. What would she do if the mystery gadda did not show up?

She stopped from time to time to chat with customers who had become regulars, stopping by every night for a drink or two and to listen to the music.

Dylan's voice slipped into her mind. "Sinéad?"

She rolled her eyes and headed back to the office. She was not going to speak mentally to Dylan in front of all these humans.

He was sitting in her chair, his feet up on the desk. He had taken off his sports jacket and rolled his sleeves up, revealing muscled forearms.

"I am bored," he said.

Sinéad shook her head. She did not want Dylan out in the club proper—his face was too recognisable. If their quarry saw him, they could be scared away. She, on the other hand, was not as well-known in the general gadda population. With her red curls cut off, her robe replaced by a fabulous beaded dress and her face painted, she felt she was disguised enough. "Then get a book to read. Better yet, go home and get some sleep. If I need you, I will call."

He smiled, his eyes twinkled and Sinéad's skin tingled. "I have got a better idea."

"If you are not going to behave yourself, I will make you go home."

"Oh, I will be very good. I promise." He held his hand out to her.

Sinéad gave the temptation half a moment's thought, but was forestalled by a rippling sensation in her power. Someone had triggered the incantation over the door. Dylan dropped his hand and she knew he had felt it, too.

"I think I need to check the club," she said.

Dylan nodded. "Keep in contact with me."

Sinéad slipped back into the main bar, now so packed with people it was hard to walk around. She started to wind her way toward the door.

As she skirted past a table where two men sat, her senses tingled. She glanced down as she walked behind them. One of the men was too drunk to sit straight, let alone stand. Sinéad frowned. She had directed John not to serve anyone obviously drunk—she did not believe a person's choice to drink should be taken from them, but she did not think overconsumption was a good thing either.

The other seemed unaffected by alcohol. He was leaning forward, talking earnestly while the drunken man nodded his head.

"I can help you with that," the sober man was saying. "Come with me, and I will give you a hand."

The drunk smiled and tried to stand, but fell back into his seat. His companion leapt up to help him and Sinéad also moved forward.

"Hello, can I help?" She put a hand on the drunk's shoulder. No power. She smiled at the gadda and her heart sank as she recognised him.

Ronan O'Sullivan. Second-order oman; he had been working as an odd-jobs man around Sclossin until he left a year earlier. She had briefly dated him during the terrible time that she and Dylan had separated.

Damn.

O'Sullivan smiled. "Oh yes, you can help, Sinéad." He turned and started to walk out of the club.

Sinéad signalled to John to look after the drunken patron, then followed O'Sullivan.

She lost sight of him in the crush and pushed her way through to the door, running up the three steps to street level.

O'Sullivan stood in the middle of the street. He looked at her, smiled, then disappeared.

Sinéad swore and strode forward to find his essence and follow it. She gathered her power to transfer, but a group of people came out of the club. They stood on the sidewalk, laughing and looking up and down the street.

She could not transfer in front of them, nor could she still them and do what she needed to—she did not know how long she would be gone, and someone else would be sure to notice a group of people frozen to the sidewalk. "Dylan?"

"Yes?"

She waved a hand and stilled the crowd. The silence was deep. "Come to me. Transfer."

He appeared in front of her. "What?"

"Feel this essence?" She took hold of the flimsy sensation and pressed it to Dylan's palm. He nodded. "Follow it. I will be with you as soon as I can."

He nodded and transferred. Sinéad released the crowd and walked toward them, hoping they had not noticed the few seconds that had passed. They laughed and jostled each other, and she breathed a sigh of relief.

A cut-off scream echoed through her mind and she swore. Dylan. Why had she thought it a good idea to send a healer to do the protector's job?

It took far too long to get through the club to her office, where she would have privacy to transfer. All the while, she hoped Dylan was all right. He was powerful, but he was not the Sabhamir.

Finally in the office, she reached for her husband's essence to transfer to his side. Nothing. Her heart skipped a beat as she tightened her grip on her power and sent more of it out, looking for the pulse that she knew so well.

Dylan was gone. Her first thought was that he was dead, but she pushed that aside. If he was, she would feel the spirit of the Heasimir, looking for its new home.

No, he was still alive—just hidden from her. How was that possible?

"Sinéad?" It took her a moment to place the originator of the mental message.

"O'Sullivan."

"Why did you send him after me? You know it is you I want."

"I am on my way." She focussed on him and transferred.

She was in the middle of a regular loungeroom—sofas, armchairs, bookcases, radio in one corner, bar in the other. O'Sullivan stood in the middle of the room, clad in the most ridiculous thing she had ever seen. His body was covered in stockings—he had pulled a pair on over his legs, another pair over his arms and a third over his face. His torso was wrapped in a patterned material that looked like silk and he wore shorts in the same material.

"O'Sullivan, what is going on here?"

"You took your time in finding me, Sinéad. I guess it just goes to show that you are not all that clever, are you?"

Star, he was not going to start with that again, was he? That had been his refrain when she had ended things with him—that she thought she was so much better than him, so much cleverer, just because she wore the black.

Sinéad decided the conversation was a waste of time. She lifted her hands and fired a stillness resolution at him. His body shuddered, and then he shook it off.

Beneath the stocking that flattened his facial features into a horrible rictus, he smiled. "Nice try. Now, here is what I can do." He lifted his hands and Sinéad saw the stockings had been cut away from his palms.

She threw up a shield to hold off his incantation. O'Sullivan's power, a pale blue, slammed into her shield and fizzled away quickly.

Only second-order, she remembered. She should be able to deal with him easily. Except—how had he managed to repulse her stillness resolution?

He put his hands down, hiding the hole in the stockings and sneered. "You think you are so good, Ms Sabhamir, so powerful; too good for the rest of us. Well, try this."

He whipped his hands up and fired another burst of power at her. Again, it exploded against her shield without causing her any concern.

His hands flipped back down. "You have got power, but I have got the smarts. I will get you. I can outlast you. There is nothing you can do."

After his next attack—each one just a quick pulse, not a sustained flurry—Sinéad realised he was hiding the break in the stockings over his hands from her.

She sent a flash pulse at him and it bounced off the silky material and sizzled into the floor by his feet. She nodded. There was something about what O'Sullivan was wearing that was repulsing power. He needed the cut at his hands to form his own incantations.

Sinéad noted there were some plants on the bar, and one of them was trailing across the floor and around O'Sullivan's ankle. She guessed the plant was replenishing his power, as the material that was protecting him from her power would also stop him replenishing his own from the world around him.

O'Sullivan laughed. "You see? Admit it—I have outsmarted you. I am better than you."

Sinéad recalled the other reason why she had ended things with O'Sullivan after a few dates—he had been determined to master her. He had told her that what she thought was wrong, what she ate was wrong, how she dressed was wrong. The one time they had kissed, his aggressiveness had turned her off.

After another disastrous attempt at a relationship, she had decided that men in general could not handle her being the Sabhamir. It was why Dylan had left her, soon after her elevation. She had put aside all thoughts of romantic happiness and had committed herself fully to her duty of protecting the gadda.

Then Dylan had come back, begged her forgiveness and castigated himself for feeling his masculinity threatened by her power. Over the next few months, he had proven he was more than able to be a supportive partner.

She had seen his elevation to the role of Heasimir—almost her equal—as the reward for his turn-around.

"Women should not be Sabhamir."

O'Sullivan's sneer pulled Sinéad back to the present.

"That is where you are wrong, O'Sullivan." She dropped her shield and gathered her power into a small, thin line. She watched him raise his hands and took her chance, firing her power out. It passed through the incantation racing toward her and struck O'Sullivan's palm.

His incantation hit—a power punch. She reeled backward, her head snapping to the rear with the force of the blow. She put a foot behind her to re-balance. Star, even from a second-order, there was enough there to hurt. But she was not going to let him know that. She straightened, checked that the pulse she had fired at him was still connected and smiled.

"Is that all?"

"No, not at all." He smiled, then frowned, his eyes darting to his hands.

"What is wrong? Can you not move your hands?" Slowly, Sinéad fed the stillness resolution along the thin strand of power between her and O'Sullivan's palm. "I wager that there is a lot more of your body that you cannot move now."

His body jerked and he gasped. "How are you doing that?"

"I am outsmarting you, O'Sullivan. That is how." She cut off her power and walked towards him. She touched his palm and nodded. It felt as though he would be able to talk and move his head, but the rest of his body was frozen. "Where is the Heasimir?"

O'Sullivan sneered. "You will never find him."

"We will see." Sinéad started to search the house.

In the front bedroom, a woman was sleeping. Sinéad touched her—she was human. There was a small child sleeping in another room—also human.

The third bedroom was just a storeroom and there was nothing in the kitchen or bathroom either. She came to another door and the moment she touched it, felt a curious deadness there.

She tried the handle—the door was locked. She called on her power and blasted it forward, but it bounced off the metal and she had to jump out of the way so it slammed into the wall behind her.

So this was impervious to power as well. She went back into the loungeroom, pleased to see that O'Sullivan had not moved.

"I guess you have got the key on you." Sinéad pulled at the stockings. She noted the material felt slippery, almost oily under her fingers. She found the key in one of O'Sullivan's shorts' pockets and opened the door with apprehension.

It was dark and still. She reached to flick the light switch but paused when she heard something like a moan. She turned the light on and gasped.

Dylan lay on the floor, at the bottom of a flight of stairs. One of his legs was twisted at an unnatural angle and blood seeped from a wound on his forehead.

"Darling." Sinéad rushed down the stairs and knelt by him, feeling the floor give spongily beneath her weight. A quick glance around showed the walls and floor had been covered in some sort of material—that must have been why she had not been able to feel Dylan and why her power had rebounded against the door.

She brushed her fingers across her husband's forehead. "Dylan?"

He moaned again. Alive, but badly hurt. She mentally connected with the healer on duty in Sclossin and after putting her hand on Dylan's shoulder, transferred him there, settling him on the bed.

The healer, a young woman with an overbite and stringy blonde hair, motioned Sinéad aside and bent over Dylan. She clicked her tongue.

"The leg is easily dealt with, the head wound less so. Power will not work to heal a brain injury. I will put him under the stillness resolution and we must hope he can heal himself."

Sinéad looked at Dylan, the colour of his tan leached from his skin, and tears pricked her eyes. "Please save him," she whispered.

"I will do what I can, Sabhamir." The healer pushed her away.

Sinéad stood in the corridor, fighting the fear. *Star above*, she thought. *Do not take him from me.* Please.

Slowly, the fear coalesced into anger and with rage flooding her system she transferred back to O'Sullivan.

The human woman was kneeling by his feet, taking the stockings off him. She looked at Sinéad, shock written on her face. "Who are you?" She jumped to her feet. "How did you get in here?"

Sinéad froze her and then stormed forward and slapped O'Sullivan across the face. The man screamed with more ferocity than her blow deserved.

"Coward," she sneered. "You killed all those people, have put the Heasimir in danger and for what? To pay me back for dumping you? Why not face me like a man?"

"You hide behind the black," he shouted. "Take off your robe and face me, woman to man. But you will not, because you know I am better than you."

"I have known rats that were better than you." She leant close. "You had better hope he lives, because I swear that if he does not, you will wish you were dead."

• • •

"Dyl?"

He groaned and opened his eyes. "What the hell happened?"

Sinéad squeezed his hand. Star, she wanted to dance and scream out her joy. "You seem to have taken a frying pan to the head, my darling. O'Sullivan's way of saying 'Welcome to my humble abode'."

Dylan closed his eyes. "Nice."

"You are going to be fine. There does not appear to be any major damage. You are going to feel a bit sore and sorry for yourself for a few days but otherwise, you will be fine." Thank the Star.

"So, did we defeat the bad guy?"

"I defeated the bad guy. He will face the bardria tomorrow and be banished, never to bother us again."

"Never doubted you would win, Nady."

She kissed his forehead. "You need to rest."

"I tried to reach you." His voice was hoarse. "I could not. My power would not leave the room."

She could hear frustration and fear in his tone. She touched his cheek. "It was covered in a man-made substance. So was O'Sullivan when I got there. It seems the humans have developed fibres and materials that appear to repel power. I have yet to work out how."

"Great. Just what we needed."

"Yet another reason to keep the secret of the gadda safe."

"So long as my failure does not repel you."

Sinéad smiled and pressed her lips to her husband's. "Not at all, my darling. Now, sleep."

The Sabhamir held the Heasimir's hand and watched over him until he slept.

....

THE LAST BOAT TO EDEN

JASON NAHRUNG

I look down the scope at Dougy. His denim shirt with the sleeves ripped off, hangen open over his flat, leathery gut. He scrambles outta the tent, takes a piss. I could put a slug through his cock at this range but I can't—I need to know where Blue is. It's still early, sunlight comin low through the trees around the hollow, birds whistlen and chirpen without a care in the world. Blue might still be in his cot; might be up and about, scroungen up whatever they can find to eat. The fire is barely smoken; no one's stoked it yet. Slack, boys. Real slack.

Dougy throws sticks on the fire—there's a puff of blue smoke and flame jumps up from behind the circle of rocks—and fills the billy from the jerry can on the fold-up table, but he doesn't go back to the fire. Me ears are ringen with the effort of listenen—I keep expecten Blue to turn up behind me with that big bloody leer he gets.

Dougy picks up a long, curved knife—a butcheren knife we've used on buffalo and goats in the past, back before it all went to shit—and I follow him as smooth as I can as he crosses the camp to an old, dead tree, its base all black with a hollow V where a fire had got in, however long ago. Two women in little more than rags cower in the dirt where they've roped 'em to the bulbar of the LandCruiser. And there's Chanda, tied to the tree, naked and shiveren. Hands over her head, the rope passed over a stub of branch. Ribs showen, gut hollow, thick black thatch between her legs. She turns her head as Dougy comes closer. He says somethun and she shakes her head and he gives a bark. Fucken hyena. Trust him to start with Chanda.

He holds up a steel I hadn't noticed him grab, and slowly runs it down the blade, worken both sides, and the rasp carries clear in the thin mornin air. Chanda struggles in her ropes and he's right up in her face, showen her the steel and the blade. He knows how to use a knife, Dougy. Him and Blue, they both worked at the meatworks.

Dougy jumps back with a howl, and I realise she's pissed on him. He grabs the tools in one hand and steps forward and slaps her one. The crack is loud. She gasps and her head hangs low. Must be hurten, hangen from them ropes. There's red marks on her wrists, lotsa bruises. Bruises everywhere.

Dougy puts the knife and steel down on a log, and then slowly undoes his shorts and steps outta them. His cock's already at half mast.

I wish I knew where Blue was. I should wait till I know. It's not like Chanda hasn't had this before, like one more time will matter. But of course it will. Every time matters. I feel sick at even havin had the thought.

I put a bullet through Dougy's brain.

Blood splatters Chanda's face and tits and she hangs on her rope, slack-jawed and stunned, as Dougy collapses at her feet. The sound of the shot rolls away through the trees. Ain't no goin back now. Not with Blue on the loose and a camp fulla prisoners.

I scan the camp. Where the fuck is Blue? I might not be worthy enough to inherit the Earth, but fucked if I'm leavin it for a cunt like him.

· · ·

Blue was tellen me about how he and Dougy had both shagged me ex on the night of the grand final, and that was why, the mornin after, she'd texted me to say we was over. I actually felt it was more'n likely she'd found out the reason I was so slow getten more beer was because her bestie was blowen me, me bein player of the season and all. Either way, I wasn't takin the bait. Blue was one of the biggest backs in the competition and he had the temper to go with that copper hair of his. He'd already laid inta Dougy for spillen the rum, I didn't want him takin a crack at me as well. I didn't care how Theresa liked to take it—she was as dead as the rest.

"Hey," Blue said, drawen me attention back from the fire I was stoken up. His eyes locked on mine, his hands poised over the barra fillet he was preparen. God, I never thought I could ever get sick of fish. "You reckon if there's no sheilahs around, it still makes you a faggot?" He leered, that short, sharp knife in his hand, and I felt the ground lurch under me. Is that what he'd been getten at, tellen me that Theresa had liked it up the—

"A boat!" Dougy burst inta the campsite, his face all flushed, his zip still undone. There was piss on his boots. "There's a motherfucken boat out there."

"A what?" I was still in a headspin—"boat" seemed like a foreign word. There were no boats, not any more.

"Like the Queen Mary?" Blue asked, putten the fish aside and wipen his hands on his bum as he stood. His whole body was tight, like he was about to hit some cunt who royally deserved it. Always good in a scrap, Blue.

"Don't be a goose. It's a reffo boat. Come and have a gander for yerself."

Blue grabbed his rifle from where it leaned against the side of the LandCruiser—liked to keep it handy, he said, though why I'd never understood. We was well away from the creek so the crocs weren't likely to give a shit, and we hadn't seen another person for four months, not since the shit had hit the fan. Not even a black fellah.

"Well?" Blue said, staren at us. He worked the bolt. Somethun about that metallic snick-clack broke us outta our freeze and we both pulled our rifles from the tailgate and followed him inta the scrub.

Blue led us past the designated crappen spot along a little ridge of hard ground, the smell of mud and ocean getten stronger as we neared the mangroves. Our tinnie sat in the mud, a coupla crab pots up above the high water line. In front of us was nuthen but the long curve of the shore, all mangrove and scrub and a narrow strip of dirty sand, and the blue water and blue sky with a line of grey-white clouds where they met—a storm comin, maybe, though the wet season was months away. Seagulls squawked overhead, their cries gratin like car alarms. There was a bit of chop on the water, a fresh breeze comin in. The sound of waves on the mud sounded kinda peaceful over the thudden of blood in me ears.

And there it was, and for a moment, I couldn't see or hear nuthen else.

"Fuck me," Blue swore under his breath.

"I told ya," Dougy said, as proud as if he'd made the fucken thing himself or maybe won it in a chook raffle.

The boat was like them ones in Darwin, the kind they take—took—rich pricks out deep sea fishen with. It wallowed in the bay, long and low, its front deck covered in boxes and crates and dirty white shirts and pants hangen off lines runnen from the prow to the cabin roof. I could hear its motor now, the sound comin in with the wind—a regular, asthmatic chug that sounded as if it was barely worken at all, as if pushen the boat across the Timor Sea had taken ev'rythun it had.

"There's people," Dougy said.

Observant cunt, Dougy.

Still, it took a while for it to sink in. They was all brown with black hair and loose pants and shirts, and they was all staren at us, lined up along the side. I had a momentary flash of one of them Viking boats, all the shields along the side. But this lot didn't look like they'd be up for much rapen and pillagen. They looked knackered, like the side of the boat was the only thing holden 'em up. And there was—

"Women," Blue said. "And kids. Look at 'em all. It's a fucken floaten kindy."

I counted two blokes, three sheilahs and five kids, though it was hard to tell who was what at that distance. Plus there'd be someone steeren, I guessed.

"Do ya reckon they seen us?" Dougy asked.

"They mighta seen the tinnie," Blue said, rubben his whiskery jaw. "Fuck, they prob'ly seen the tinnie."

"So?" I said.

"So they know we're here."

"That's a good thing, ain't it? Other people, I mean. We're not the only ones, dontcha see?"

Fuck me if I didn't feel like bawlen just then. If I didn't feel like swimmen out to that boat and huggen and kissen every last bloody one of 'em. *Welcome to Aussie, you beautiful brown bastards. Have ya got any beer?*

"They're reffos, Jimbo," Blue said, coolen off me excitement.

"Or maybe you hadn't noticed. It was the likes of them that did this to us."

"Huh?"

"Work it out, dickhead. We're an island, right? None of that shit coulda got to us excepten if some bastard brought it in." He pointed with his gun barrel at the boat as it chugged closer to land. We could see faces now, staren, grim, though a few of the kids looked excited, tuggen on the sleeves of adults. I wondered how long they'd been at sea. How long it'd been since they'd walked on land. Of all the places they coulda picked . . .

"It wasn't this lot, though, was it?" I said. "Prob'ly some blonde Swedish backpacker fresh off the plane."

"Nah, it woulda been someone like this lot. Sneaken in past quarantine, spreaden the shit before anyone realised."

"Well this lot don't look sick."

Dougy crouched, gun cradled in his arms. "Women," he said. I think there was tears in his eyes.

"I wonder why they come here," I said.

"Prob'ly dodged Darwin," Blue said. "Afraid of getten caught."

"Getten caught by who?"

"The navy," he said, and then added, "The likes of us."

We fell silent then, drinken in the sight of other people bobben on the sea. If they'd come in a UFO, they couldn't have surprised us more. Fascinated us. Maybe even scared us a little.

The engine stopped and an anchor rope splashed inta the water.

"Great," Blue said, and spit. "They're stayen. They *musta* seen the tinnie."

"Shit, eh," Dougy said. "What are we gonna do?" He didn't sound too rattled, his eyes glued on the shapes across the water as he chewed his bottom lip, prob'ly already rehearsen his come-on line. *So what's a pretty little darkie like you doin in a place like this . . .*

"No time to pull up stumps," Blue said. He brought his rifle to his shoulder and slipped the cover off the scope.

"What the fuck you doin?" I asked.

"Havin a closer look. That all right with you?"

"Jesus, we don't know nuthen about 'em."

"My point exactly."

Don't get me wrong. Blue and me, we was mates. Went back a long ways, back to high school footy. He'd got me outta a few scrapes, him and Dougy. Took me out when me old man died and got me totally shitfaced. They could be bastards sometimes but I always knew, when the chips were down, they'd be there for me. I just wished they weren't bein such pricks about this.

It was only luck we'd been out here on one of our fishen trips. Only luck we was still breathen. If these darkies had survived, then maybe there was some hope left. But Blue and Dougy weren't seein it. I think they was already scared of losen what little we had left.

Dougy squinted down his scope. "The birds are all right. That one on the left . . . "

I watched down me own scope as a dinghy hit the water and four people piled in: three blokes and a sheilah. They all had hair cut real short. Lice or fleas, maybe, or maybe that was how they wore it in their country. The only curry munchers I knew was in the kebab shop down the mall and them ones in the Indian restaurant. Blue couldn't handle curries, reckoned they made him shit hotter than hell, but I didn't mind a vindaloo. Gave the system a good workout, I always told him.

"Hey Blue," Dougy said with a dry cackle. "I bet they come to sell ya a mobile phone."

"Shut up, Dougy, this is serious. Who knows what they're carryin."

"They look okay to me," I said.

"Thanks for that, Doctor Jim. You given 'em a thorough examination, have ya?"

"I wouldn't half mind." Dougy gave a whistle under his breath, his usual sign that he'd acquired a target for his short-lived but energetic affection. "That bird on the left: nuthen wrong with her lungs, that's for sure. Wonder if she's wearen anythin under them PJs."

Blue kept his eye on the scope, the barrel tracken the dinghy. "Keep it in your pants, Dougy. You got no idea where this lot've been."

I lowered the rifle as the reffos paddled their way to shore. The dudes on the oars didn't look like they'd had much experience.

"I could pop 'em all, before they even hit the sand." Blue licked his lips, his tongue slug-like, leavin a glistenen string of saliva in the corner of his mouth as his finger tensed on the trigger. Me gut flipped and I tasted spew, choked it back down.

"We should at least see what they want," I said.

"We know what they want."

Dougy adjusted his pants without takin his eye off the scope. "I hope they want what I got."

"We should at least see where they're from," I said. "See what they know. Don't you get it—we aren't the last!"

"They got women," Dougy mumbled to himself. "Real, actual women."

"I guess we could just pop the blokes," Blue said.

"Jesus Christ," I said.

"Just joken. Fine, you get down there, Jimbo, roll out the red carpet for the ragheads. We'll cover ya."

"Rightio then."

Me legs felt wobbly as I scrambled to me feet. I could hear the oars slappen the water. A bit of chatter in whatever foreign lingo the reffos was talken. I imagined this swamp wasn't quite what they'd had in mind when they'd set out for Oz. The gulf is hardly Surfers Paradise. Part of its appeal, really.

"Leave ya gun," Blue told me.

I looked at him, wonderen, and he said, "You don't wanna look threatenin to the new neighbours, do ya?"

I thought about slippen the mag out, but that'd just piss him off. If he wanted to wipe out the landen party, he had enough bullets. He wasn't as good a shot as me—neither of them was—but at this range, they didn't need to be. They might even be able to chase down the boat. The tinnie's Mercury could prob'ly catch it before it got out of the bay, judgen by what we'd seen.

I left the rifle, tried to ignore the itch between me sweaty shoulder blades as I made me way down the slope to the beach. Mud sucked at me feet. I'd given up wearen shoes around camp once it'd become obvious there wasn't no point us goin anywhere else. Come the wet season, well, that might be a different story. Might be prepared to risk headen inta Borroloola full-time. We'd hit it twice for supplies—the first time there'd been bodies all over the place, and we wondered how the fuck anythin had found its way this far from civilisation. Mobile phones didn't even work, that was part of the reason we came campen here. Blue reckoned it was prob'ly them rich fly-in fly-out cunts who come in to land a few barra. The next time we'd gone into Borro, there'd been nuthen there at all, not even a black fellah's mangy dog. Fucken spooky, just how quiet it was. Crows, seagulls, a door bangin in the wind, a bit of a whistle through a piece of corrugated iron that'd come loose somewhere. But quiet. We'd grabbed booze and tucker and fuel for the Toyota and got the hell out before we caught whatever had wiped the joint out. So far, so good, but we couldn't go on like this. Tins weren't gonna last forever and we'd need more than barra to keep us goin. It'd been a bloody long time since I'd seen a buffalo—anythin with four legs. Birds and fish and crocs was about it.

I wasn't no green thumb—me mum had been pretty good at it (God, I was thinken of her as dead, but she had to be, right? There was no point looken, no point hopen; she and her carrots and lettuce and tomatoes was all gone). She'd had a good little patch out the back, and a big mango tree. But I guessed I'd have to learn, sooner or later.

I wondered if the new arrivals would be any good at growen veges. Anythin other than rice.

Fresh sweat broke out on me forehead and back, not just because it was hot and steamy in amongst the mangroves, but because that fucken moron Blue was talken about shooten the only other people we knew for a fact was left alive on the planet. The thought of losen 'em . . . fuck, I hoped they was healthy. I hoped they didn't have whatever it was that had been cruel enough to skip our little camp when everythin—*everythin*—on either side of the black stump had been wiped out. Everythin but us and these new fellahs.

I broke outta the mangroves and raised a hand in welcome-like. I musta looked a sight: hadn't shaved in months, me shorts and singlet were as filthy as, I'd lost a lotta weight. Prob'ly smelt like a dead dog, too. We'd nicked plenty of meds and tucker but had kinda forgot the shampoo and soap when we'd hit Borro. Couldn't smell each other over the stink of ourselves anyway, and we each had a tent to ourselves.

The four darkies had pulled their boat up onto the mud not far from our tinnie and stood around it, staren at me. They looked a bit unsteady, up to the ankles in mud, and one of 'em swatten at mossies. I barely noticed the little cunts these days. Maybe me stink was good for somethun. Or maybe they'd lost the taste for human blood. Maybe we was all diseased, but just didn't know it.

"Howdy," I said, me voice croaken out of a throat suddenly dry. I shivered, feelen Blue's eyes on me, peeren down that scope, the crosshair comin across me shoulder, prob'ly locked onto one of these blokes in front of me. Positively skinny they was, clothes hangen off 'em like they was fresh out of a prison camp, the material so thin I could see the bones sticken out underneath. "Any of you blokes speak English?"

"Hello," one fellah said. He took a good squiz around, then fixed his stare back on me. "This is Australia?" He looked a bit puzzled, like his car wasn't where he'd left it.

"Yep. Beautiful one day, fucken perfect the next."

"We were trying for Darwin," he said.

"Missed it by a mile," I told him, and pointed to the west. "It's about a thousand kay that way. But you ain't missed nuthen. As dead as a door nail, we reckon."

"We had hoped, despite the silence, that, given your isolation, maybe your country had been spared."

"Shoulda stuck with Indonesia," I said. "Or Fiji, maybe. Plenty of little islands there."

He nodded thoughtfully. "No one?"

"Not that we've heard. Radio's dead. No telly."

"Internet?"

"You seen where you are, mate?"

"Is there nowhere nearby? Could we get to Darwin?"

"Could try the café in Borro, I guess, if you could get the power up. You wanna bring your mates in from the boat, first?"

He looked over his shoulder as though he'd forgotten all about it. Then he cracked a big smile. His teeth were real white, and it made me wonder, just for a moment, when I'd last brushed me teeth. "A good idea. I am Baahir. We are very happy to meet you." He reeled off the others' names. Sounded like the openers for a Paki cricket team. I didn't take 'em in, except for the woman's. Chanda. Good looken noggin under the black stubble, with thick eyebrows, really dark brown eyes. Her figure was hidden under a loose top and baggy pants, kinda like pyjamas, but I reckoned a couple of steaks and she'd be good to go. Yeah, when I'd pretty much given up on ever seein a woman again, she looked pretty bloody good.

"I said, and you are?" Baahir asked.

"Huh?" They was all staren at me, maken me a bit flustered, given as how I'd been havin a good perv while they'd been asken me questions. "I'm Jimbo. Jim. Jimmy."

I shook his hand. He had a good grip. I wished he'd stopped smilen that smile at me. Made me think, maybe, he wasn't so much disappointed in Oz as in me. As though he'd been expecten to meet the fucken prime minister or somethun. Dougy wouldn't like that attitude; Blue neither. They'd knock it out of him quick smart.

"Are there others?" Baahir asked.

I hesitated, felt their stares boren inta me. "Yeah, just a couple. Man, we'd given up, you know? Where the fuck did youse come from?"

He laughed. "We will have time to tell each other our stories later. But now, you are right to say we should bring the others in. They have been on the boat since the world ended."

I looked at the boat, ridin low on the swell. Noah's Ark sure was a piece of shit.

• • •

"Quarantine, that's what the radio said. Remember? Don't go outside. Don't travel. And if you tried to, you'd be shot. That's what they said."

Dougy rubbed his face. He was clearly torn, but Blue didn't have any doubts. No way did he want the new arrivals in our camp. No fucken way.

"Well, they have to stay somewhere," I said.

"There's an entire town down the road if they want to clean it out," Blue said. "Otherwise, we aren't really lackin for space."

"The flat's too close to the river. The crocs . . . "

"Wouldn't worry 'em, long as they was careful. I don't want 'em up here with us. Keep 'em down there on the flat where we can keep an eye on 'em, or, like I said, they can have Borro if they want it. So long as we can still help ourselves to the tucker, of course. Shit, they're gonna scoff through that in no time flat."

It was his turn to rub his face.

"Maybe we should think about goin inta Darwin," I offered.

"We was gonna wait till just before the wet season. Give whatever it is a chance to play out. More chance of it bein around in town than out here."

"And more chance of us finden help. They'll look in the cities first."

"Who the fuck's 'they'? Another boatload of ragheads?"

We stood, glaren at each other for a bit, and I half expected Blue to lay inta me. He didn't like bein talked back to. Sometimes I wondered if that's why he was so inta the footy, playen all the time, or hangen out at the pub. No temper for bein a dad. Made me wonder if the reason he was so dead set against goin back to Darwin was not because his missus and kids was dead, but because he feared they wasn't.

Dougy spoke up: "So what are we gonna do with 'em?"

"Leave'em on the flat where we can keep an eye on 'em," Blue said. "We can talk about Darwin later. But we will have to work somethun out. Borro doesn't have a lot left."

We all went down—Dougy with his eyes hangen outta his head as soon as he saw his first reffo, and Blue, arms crossed, face in a scowl. You'd think the darkies had wanted to sleep in his tent, the way he was carryin on. As if we didn't have the entire fucken NT to share. Maybe the whole fucken country. Who knew?

"You guys got much tucker?" he asked Baahir after everyone had swapped names. Chanda hung at Baahir's shoulder. His girlfriend, wife maybe? The thought made me wonder if he'd share, if he'd have a choice. Aside from Baahir and Chanda, there was another couple their age, plus a much older pair, and the kids, one of which was a sheilah gettin close to rooten age. If this was all that was left, would anyone be content with missen out? Dougy sure wouldn't. He'd fuck a snake if someone held the head, and up till now, that had seemed like his best bet. Listenen to him jerk off over pornos had become a nightly routine. Almost asked him to move his tent further away, but none of us wanted to be too distant. Just in case.

"Chickens, eh?" Blue said, and I realised I'd missed a chunk of conversation. "Chooks is good. Ain't seen no chooks at Borro. Musta either got out or got eaten."

"I think birds are safe," Baahir said. "Birds and fish."

"We got fish all right," Dougy said, his eyes on Chanda. "Big fuckers, the best barra youse've ever seen. Mackerel. Snapper. You name it." He paused to scratch his scalp under his battered Lions cap. "You lot do eat fish, dontcha?"

Baahir nodded. "Our recent sailing trip has well prepared us."

"We done all right for buffalo for a bit, but we musta cleaned 'em out, 'cause I ain't seen none in months. If we roll one, though, you'd be welcome to some," I offered.

"I wouldn't recommend meat."

"In this country, we eat beef," Blue said. "Pigs, too."

"Fucken oath," Dougy said.

"I mean, I don't think mammals in general are a good idea. I think that might be how the contagion spread," Baahir said, real calm-like. "At least, in the beginning."

"Radio said airborne," Blue said. "Before it went quiet."

"A topic for discussion once we have established a camp. For now, we could use vitamins and medicine if you have any to spare. Our supplies have been severely depleted during the voyage."

"You people sick?" You could hear the panic in Blue's voice. Could feel him reachen for his rifle, though it was back in camp.

"Just from the voyage. We could use vitamin C, fresh fruit and vegetables."

"You can farm?" I asked.

"If we can't, we can learn," Baahir said.

And I felt meself smile, and the smile got wider as I saw Chanda smile, too. Stupidly, I was thinken that things might be okay. As if a fresh salad would make all the difference.

• • •

Blue paused at the door of the café, a rucksack over his shoulder as he prepared to join the looten "before the ragheads got the good stuff". He didn't care that Chanda was standen only feet away when he said it.

"There any more of your lot on the way?" he asked her.

She stuck her head up from the computer.

"My lot?"

"Yeah, reffos. Any more comin?"

She shrugged and kept diggen around at the computer. The generator was bangin away out the back, the noise kinda weird after we'd got so used to not havin any machines runnen at all. It didn't sound as if it belonged no more. We'd never bothered draggen a plant out to the camp; there wasn't no cold tucker to keep, and the beers stayed cool enough in the creek till we needed 'em. Besides, as Blue said, we'd run outta diesel soon enough. Might as well get used to it.

"Maybe this was the plan all along," Blue said. "Bomb us and then move in, ev'rythun still in one piece, just waiten to be turned back on."

"They got bombed, too, Blue; or sickened, at least. Or weren't you listenen last night? India, China, all of 'em: just the same as us."

"So they say."

"Fuck me, why would they come here on a piece of shit like that boat if it was some kind of conspiracy? Wouldn't their whole fucken navy just sail right inta Sydney Harbour and say thanks very much?"

"It's on the nose, I tell ya. Somethun ain't right."

"Ya noticed, have ya? Whatever happened, it ain't this lot's fault. They've lost ev'rythun, just the same as us."

"Then why come here?"

Chanda stuck her head up again. She reminded me of a prairie dog, or one of them kat-things outta *Madagascar*. Cute, but kinda determined. I got the sense that she was kinda tired of Blue's raggen.

"You were closest," she said. "Isolated, but modern. We hoped to find hospitals still working; hoped to be able to help find a cure."

"How could you find a cure if you couldn't even find Darwin?" he guffawed.

"We took the best boat we could find. All the cruise liners were taken."

"There's a point," I said, hopen to cool things down. "I bet there must be others out there. Boats. Submarines. Not infected, waiten for somewhere safe to pull in. We could do it, Blue. Set ourselves up in Darwin, find a cure. Get a radio goin."

"Jimbo, you're a fucken idiot."

And he left to make sure he got his share of beans and Spam.

"Your friend is an arsehole," Chanda said.

"He is, but he's the only one I got. Him and Dougy."

She looked at me, real hard, and I felt me legs go soft and me chest get real tight as she said, "Not any more."

• • •

Blue wrenched the radio button to off, bringen a sudden silence to the whistle and static of the past twenty minutes as he'd worked through the dial.

"Nuthen. And no internet." He looked at me as he put the radio down, as though he'd proved some kinda point.

"Just because the café's connection was down, doesn't mean there ain't no net out there somewhere. We should go to Darwin. Chanda says—"

" 'Chanda says'," Blue mimicked, his voice high-pitched and snarky, like he was a school girl. He stared at Dougy, then back at me. "You two are pathetic, fallen all over yourselves for a bit of pussy."

Dougy looked up from the tits 'n' arse mag he was readen by the firelight. "You seen that young one, with the short hair? Kala-somethun? She got tits on her like a jersey cow. You could suffocate between 'em. Not a bad way to go, eh." He cackled, sounden like a dog with flu.

"Cunt-struck, the both of youse."

"Chanda's a doctor, Blue," I said. "Her and Baahir. They might be able to do some good if we got 'em to Darwin."

"Some good for who? Who knows how many more are out there, just waiten."

"Waiten for what? Jesus wept, we're sitten up here like shags on a rock when we could be sitten around a fire sharen other people's company and a plate of tucker a damn sight more tasty than another barbecued fucken mackerel. Them and us is all we got, at least for now. We should make the most of it."

"That lot put me dad out of a job, you know," Blue said. "Ev'rythun goin offshore because the ragheads would do it all for cheaper. Didn't matter no one could understand a fucken word they said. As long as they was cheap."

"True or not, Blue, things've kinda changed."

"Do ya reckon they'll let us fuck 'em?" Dougy asked. "Reckon they'd mind havin a few half-castes runnen around?"

"I'm goin down there," I said.

"You ain't goin nowhere," Blue said. "Just forget about Darwin, forget about a cure. All we got is here, right here, and they're chewen it up faster than you can say."

"All the more reason to go to Darwin. More shops, more tucker, more ev'rythun."

"It's what they want. Like tryin to make us stop eaten meat."

"Eaten *red* meat. Mammals. You heard what Baahir said. They might be diseased."

"You really believe that? You really believe some kind of

fucken *red* meat disease wiped out the world? Then why aren't the vegetarians runnen the show, huh?"

"Because it spreads, dickhead. It don't care what you eat once you got it in you."

"I'm not goin vego," Dougy said. "I gotta keep me strength up." He rubbed his cock where it bulged under his shorts.

"We ain't seen many buffalo around lately anyway. Not much of nuthen, to be honest. Just birds."

"We need to find some cattle, some goats, somethun," Blue said. "If we're gonna make it. That's what we should be worryen about, not about finden some fucken lab so those monkeys can poke shit and study shit. Who the fuck are they gonna cure? Everyone's dead!"

"Might be nice to know that if we catch somethun, it ain't gonna kill us."

"We ain't gonna catch nuthen if we stay here. Stay here, and don't mix our spit with that lot."

"Spit was only me starten point," Dougy cackled.

"We'll need to breed if we're gonna continue," I said. "If the human race is gonna continue, we gotta breed."

"I don't care nuthen about that," Blue said. "I can spend the rest of me life with Mrs Palmer if I need to, as long as that life's a long one. The human race can go root its boot."

"Shit no," Dougy said. "I'm gettin blisters already. I don't see how it'd hurt to fuck that lot. They're not sick. I'm with Jimbo. Let's go down there and get us some action."

"That's not what I meant, Dougy," I said.

"It's sure as shit what I meant. If this is all we got, might as well get inta it. I got dibs on that big-titted one, Kanda-whatever. You can have first pop at your Shandy."

"It's Chanda, and it's not like that. She's a doctor, for fuck's sake, not some two-bit whore."

Blue laughed, and it was the kinda laugh that said someone was likely to get hurt. "She's a bird, ain't she? How many of rooten age do you figure, Dougy?" Blue added: "Just the girls."

"Counten that granny with no teeth, four I'd wet me wick in, if you don't mind 'em real giggly."

"With us makes six cocks for not enough holes. Do you really think they're gonna let us white fellahs fuck 'em? They'll be drawen lots as it is to see who gets the jailbait."

"Fuck." Dougy punched his palm. "Fuck!"

"Of course, it's the men who's the problem. They're the ones who'll make trouble. The birds, they'll fall inta line, once they see who's boss. Especially if there's a gun to a kid's head. But the men, they're the ones who'll fight for it. We got an advantage there, though. I ain't seen no guns down there, have youse?"

Dougy scratched his chin. "Not that I can think of."

"You?" Blue asked me.

He was watchen me real close as I stood by the fire. They were both still sitten in their camp chairs, Blue with his rifle and cleanen rod, Dougy with a troubled expression.

"They got an old double-barrel that I seen the granddad cleanen. But they ain't here to make trouble," I said. "They're just poor dumb bastards who got lucky. Like us."

"They ain't like us," Blue said. He turned to Dougy. "Get your rifle."

Dougy stared sat him, one hand frozen in the act of scratchen his crotch.

"I said get ya fucken rifle. If you wanna get laid."

Dougy got his rifle.

I ran.

• • •

Dougy used to play full forward at club level. He could run, the wiry little cunt. But the scrub was hard goin at night. Sticks and branches, logs, holes, rocks. Not much moon, either, so it was really pot luck whether you got smacked or not. I ran as hard as I could, feelen the pain in me feet as sticks bruised and cut me. Branches whipped me face. I almost took meself out on a tree trunk, dodged just in time, but took a hell of a thump in the shoulder that almost spun me inta the ground anyway. But I kept runnen, me lungs burnen, legs achen, arms up to protect me face. Stumblen along, headen for the fires of the reffos' camp.

I got close enough to hear their voices but didn't have breath to shout. Could see shapes, passen past the campfire. The pale patches of the canvas they'd brought off the boat and out of Bollo, the lean-tos and tents.

Could we run? I wondered. Get out to their boat? Take our tinnie and their dinghy and get out to the boat before Dougy and Blue flipped their lids completely?

I heard steps behind me, someone panten, branches cracken, someone swearen. And then I was nose-down in the dirt and me face was on fire and all the breath was knocked outta me. I was on me back, then, looken up at tree branches and the night sky, and then somethun hit me hard and it all went kinda dark and spin-wheelen. But I heard the shots. The shots and the screams. I heard all that just fine.

• • •

I'd felt it comin, since before we'd got back from Bollo and Blue had sat in his chair, sippen on a warm rum and Coke and cleanen his rifle. I'd underestimated his viciousness, though. Should've hidden me rifle along with the little pack of necessities I'd squirrelled away outside of camp when I'd gone for a slash. But he woulda noticed that.

I guess I'd had this notion that maybe me and Chanda would slip off in the dark, maybe grab the tinnie and motor our way off to a new life, Adam and Eve in the land of crocs and jabirus.

What a fucken idiot.

Lucky for me, Dougy and Blue had their hands full with the women and kids. Too many to spend too much time looken for me when they realised I'd crawled off inta the dark. Spent the night holleren and, I gathered at least for Dougy, fucken, and then packen up and moven out. I followed, slow and careful-like, knowen they'd be watchen. Watchen 'em run through the scrub, from camp to camp, kings of the fucken castle, haunted by the mate they'd left behind. Afraid to take a piss or a shit without me cutten off their nuts. The chicks and the kids all roped up and squeezed inta the LandCruiser, afraid to let 'em free in case they bolted. Squeezy, even in a troop carrier, and a whole lotta work for just two fellahs.

Takin out the truck really brought it to a head. Two nights ago, I snuck in and nicked their distributor cap. Wish I coulda maybe cut a coupla the women loose, but they was too close to the fire, too well lit. Too much chance of it bein a trap. So I settled for the truck, leavin me old mates inland with nuthen to shoot and very little to catch, and the tins runnen out, and all those mouths to feed.

Then last night I snuck in and flogged Dougy's Remington, a very handy thirty ought six, and watched the pair of 'em shout and swear at each other, and then shout and swear at me. They strung the women up but I didn't rise to the bait. I waited in the bush; waited for a chance to pop 'em both. And then this mornin Blue obviously sent Dougy out to push the issue.

Fuck one, slice one. Food was runnen low.

And so I shoot Dougy through the head, and then look for Blue, and find him a moment too late. He musta snuck out before sun-up, and picked a spot almost dead opposite me on the other side of the hollow.

I see the glint of his scope and we eyeball each other down the magnification, fingers itchen, prob'ly swearen at each other at the same time, like a shared breath.

The Remington kicks me in the right shoulder and somethun slams me in the left at much the same time, too close to call. I lie there for a bit, feelen the numbness turnen into a right fucken pain. Feel the weight in me chest and me guts, as if I've swallowed a hot bowlen ball. Can barely lift the rifle. But I can hold the Remington up long enough to see Blue. In through the cheek, and out, takin most of the back of his head with it.

I drop the rifle and look back down at the camp, the women and children strung around the trees, tied to the four-wheel-drive. Could tie a good knot, Blue.

I lay me head down, too tired to even breathe, and I wonder who's gonna cut the human race free.

• • • • • • • • • • •

KINDLING

KATHLEEN JENNINGS

Minke was hungry for a great story, but no-one who came to Ye Aulde Owle ever brought her one. She served stale sandwiches, glasses of wine and whisky and listened, discontent, to the idle tales customers told.

• • •

Ah yes. The call of the open road, the thrill of adventure.

Let me give you some advice.

Do you remember Ye Aulde Owle Café & Bar? A little before your time, perhaps. It was in that part of town—you're old enough to know the quarter I mean!—which was run by the arch-family in the days when they were the source of fear and order. It lay between the Royal Mechanical Gardens and the Crystal Valance, which even then was famed for its Ectoplasmic Peep Shows, though most of the ghosts were tricks back then.

A canal ran behind the Owle, a road in front. Omnibuses and wheel-horses rumbled by in dust and oil fumes. Little wind-up delivery boats and hand-punts slid along the greasy green canal. You could get the parts for them in those days, and curses were too expensive a fuel. Not like today. When we heard the grind of gears, no-one twitched and thought of war-machines. No-one listened for the whistling roar of spirit-eyed Steam Tigers.

If you were in that quarter already, you wouldn't have avoided the Owle, but you wouldn't have recommended it by name. It had a few apathetic regulars, an intermittent procession of visitors nursing their own distractions. It was, perhaps, as perfect a microcosm of life at the time as you could have hoped for. Dull, imperfectly gentrified, fraying at the hems. Little complaints. Little tragedies. Little ghosts. Little wants and hopes. All anonymous. None staying, all going nowhere much.

Looking back at it now, it's touched by the light of paradise.

• • •

Minke carried a box of empty cider bottles to the alley behind Ye Auld Owle Café & Bar. The brassy tendrils of the shopfront railings retreated into sooty stone, and the music of guitar, accordion, glasses and engines was muffled.

The boy was waiting in his boat in the canal, crestfallen, as ever. His twisting hair misted with rain.

"I'm going to sea, Minke," he said.

Minke met his gaze. This is what she saw:.

The boy did not want to go to sea. He wanted Minke. He was going to sea because she told him once that he would have to prove himself. He wanted her to think he was a hero.

It was hard to be a hero in that alley, in that city, in that world. Maybe heroes could still be made at sea. Perhaps great white ghosts endured beneath the oily waves. Maybe a giant, many-limbed curse could rise from unimaginable depths to pull down ships and crew, all alive-o.

Minke doubted it. There were no spectacular evils in the world, and so there could be no real heroes.

"I'll come back for you," he said, as he wound the boatspring. "You don't belong here."

"Where else is there to go?" said Minke.

She watched his vessel tick down the canal. She despised him for leaving on a fool's errand; but she envied him for still thinking the world might be big enough for adventures.

• • •

There was a waitress at the Owle in those days who had a talent. Not for waitressing—she dropped glasses, forgot menus, made change badly and kept her job only because her aunt owned the establishment. But she could light up that dingy room with a smile.

No, I don't mean she was pretty. I never worked out whether she was. It was that she could look at you and see what you wanted most in the world. Maybe it was a drink—she could guess an order without fail, even if she forgot the price.

She told me once that there were ghosts in the attic room where she slept, although in those days before the great wars began there were hardly enough ghosts in the world to really believe in. She said these ones had been drowned in the canals by the arch-family, but she could usually work out what they wanted, and so that kept the numbers down.

Could she tell what I wanted? Oh, when I went into the storeroom with a delivery she would smile at me like a twist of a knife, as if she did know and might just get it for me, if I pleased her. If anything in the world could please her. I'd have slain a dragon for her, if I could have found one.

Take it from me: don't go looking for adventure. Learn to be content with the cruel little dragons, like her, and the peace that comes before you get what you want. Before little dragons learn to grow.

• • •

The customers of the Owle didn't even pretend to believe in monsters for Minke's sake. She looked into their eyes, took their orders, saw their minuscule hopes, their little fears, and fretted.

"Hello," said Minke, leaning on the bar in front of the busker.

She could see what he wanted. He had written scurrilous songs and displeased someone great. His guitar was cursed—that meant he had made an enemy of the arch-family, since not many others could afford a real imprecation. Now he could only play true songs, and it cost him a career—he could have been someone, too. He didn't know how to lift the curse. He would never know. Nothing would come of him, there would be no grand adventure to follow from this beginning. Just slow decay.

"Let me guess your poison," said Minke.

• • •

I remember the light in Ye Aulde Owle was the reddish-yellow of gas and oil lamps, of street lamps through unwashed, uneven glass. It had sticky varnished tables with mismatched vases of wax flowers, undusted. There was a tarnished gilt-gambling machine in a side-room, but no-one ever won.

People walked in for no great reason, sat for a while in which nothing happened and walked out again into no particular story.

Maybe we can get back to that blessed boredom one day. After a few restless years, a body grows weary of adventure, of the world being all firelight, curse-light, the glitter of battle and glory. The sunshine through a whisky glass starts to look both more romantic and attainable. But there are promises to keep, roads which I still need to travel.

Don't start on journeys. You don't know where they'll take you.

• • •

Minke took a shandy to a girl in the farthest corner of the bar. The girl was dressed as a tradesman, but too clean. Minke could see what she was: a wealthy girl, a healthy girl, afraid of seeing the arch-family's livery in the doorway.

Minke noted the profile on both the girl and the coins she paid with, smiled at her and gave her back the money.

"Keep it," said Minke. "It may come in handy."

The girl looked abashed. Minke could see that she didn't want pity—she wanted the rough-and-tumble of the world.

Minke glanced towards the guitarist. "When he's drunk, he'll play," she said. "Well, when he's drunker. Give him the money then, and call us even."

Minke kept her eye on them, even when she should have been washing glasses. The guitarist played a song about giving everything up, going rambling, hitting the road and freedom, and people who'd treat you kind, treat you mean, until you hit the bottle and lost it all.

It was a true song, but the runaway with the shadows in her eyes only heard the first half: the dream of the romance of the road. Hope kindled in the girl's gaze. It shone there when she gave the money to the guitarist.

It would take time, Minke knew, but she thought this might be a long game. She saw the girl speak with the guitarist briefly, shyly. Their paths lay in the same direction. They would catch the same omnibus out of town. They would travel together, unmask each other. She would learn to lend a shoulder to someone else. He would learn that truth is powerful, but that sometimes lies are needed to temper it.

Given long enough, he would one day have to ask the girl to forgive him for something, and if she did, if she wanted to, with that blood in her veins, it would lift his curse. Until that happened, they would have adventures, however small. They would see the world.

"Minke! Bar!" said her aunt.

• • •

It's simpler now. The world is like a map drawn in spilled wine on a bar, with all the inaccuracy and convenience of that school of cartography. Here, world-sawing mountains. There, dark forest. The bird-foot marks of swamp. All that blank space in between—those are the stories, spilling out of the map like fat white grubs. The dirty marks where a finger lands on the paper: "Here be steel dragons. Here is the rendezvous. This is where our band was almost lost. Here is the poisoned river. Steer clear of that valley (heavily marked)—you won't be seen again. Here are all the ghosts of your nightmares".

The maps were more complicated back then, in the days of the Owle. People had time to draw them, and to invent the need. You could unreel a map across the bottom of a boat and see every shoal and all the endless empty places in between were filled with neat curving lines. They didn't leave enough room for stories to fill them. Perhaps there weren't enough stories.

Be a cartographer. You can probably take credit for reinventing the art. Fence the world in with lines, cage it with chicken-wire contours. You'll be doing us all a favour.

• • •

A gutter-sleuth arrived, looking for a girl, perhaps one disguised as a tradesman's apprentice. He sat at the bar and pretended nonchalance. He wore his hat low and tried to chat up Minke's aunt in a gravelly voice. Minke's aunt liked being chatted up, but she didn't know anything, and she had to break away to shout at Minke for spilling the suds bucket, to get back to the bar where she could do less damage.

The gutter-sleuth wanted whisky and lightening up. He wanted real crimes, real mysteries, not runaway brats, however much discretion they called for. He didn't want to die like his partner had, whittling his life down to nothing worth living, something so small and easily snuffed out. Not even a note left to explain.

The gutter-sleuth wanted an answer to how that happened. How to stop it happening to him. How not to get tangled up with the arch-family more than he already was.

• • •

I remember when people went on trips, not journeys. There's a difference—when people can go on a trip again, as a matter of course, we'll know things are mending.

We didn't have journeys, then—all those detailed maps had little wind-dragons drawn neatly in the corners, but no-one believed they still existed to be woken. Not even I, when I sailed off to find them. I was just going on a trip.

It's not a journey if you travel alone (and everybody was, then). It's just an itinerary. A quick tumble from one location into another. Might as well be asleep for it. People were just like cogs and wheels on lonely little paths, bumping elbows but not looking. Fitting in just as they ought, not trying something new just to throw everyone else off-course.

But a journey! Well, we have enough of those now. If you go out into the night brangling and singing, if you rub someone up the wrong way, or rub along well enough with them, if you can watch their back or know you have to watch yours—that's a Thing in its own right. It lights up a little bit of the world, like fire glowing on the edge of paper. Maybe it's a light in the darkness, maybe it will set off fireworks.

When enough of those sorts of journeys got going, they set the world alight.

• • •

The woman in red was looking for a ghost. It wasn't one Minke had met yet.

If the woman found the ghost, she would be able to stop seeing smears of blood on the wall. If she found the ghost, she could simply be afraid, she could forget the kick of the pistol in her hand, the shape of it under her fine silk handkerchief, the feel of the dead man's hand beneath her own as she had folded his fingers around the grip. She could remember simply how cool and careful she had been, for she had known the dead man had worked for the arch-family, and if they cared that he had died, they could afford to pay to have the smell of someone who had handled a weapon sniffed out. If she found his ghost, she could shut it up for good. She could forget the murder and remember the bruises.

She wore her diamonds discreetly. Her hair was bottle-blonde. She drank red wine. The makeup was heavy over her scars. Her lipstick, when she left it on the lip of the glass and reapplied it, was the colour of coals. Minke took the tube of it when the woman glanced away.

Minke was so careless, so clumsy. It was easy to bend down to sweep under the bar, to trip the woman up so that she fell into the welcoming arms of the gutter-sleuth. By the evening the woman in red would—against any good judgement—be his client. Neither would tell the other the full story, and they'd both find what they were looking for, eventually. They'd both get what they wanted.

Minke was satisfied with the first story she had started, but this she found more exciting. There was a salt-sour taste to deceit and murder, a gunpowder smell, that truth and music didn't hold for her.

• • •

Perhaps that's what she thought the world was missing, the waitress at the Owle—the one I was telling you about. Maybe she wanted stories to be big, with adventures that swept down in wind and fire and carried you off. That's what she wanted me to fetch for her.

I wasn't whole-hearted: I went over the seas for her but I never forgot that I loved the littleness of life—the fey and elusive moments that flitted across my path, as I puttered down the canals in my delivery-boat. A glimpse through windows at people laughing in a kitchen. Half-seen dim deeds of the arch-family's employees. The sounds of bar-room talk drifting out the back door. Polite morose customers who came in and went out, caught omnibuses and slept while the world rumbled by. The waitress with a tray and a laugh, both always for someone else—a girl who mopped the bar and didn't get out much more than I did.

Now she has what she wanted. Great and terrible rumours, gathering storms, things that chase you. And I have what she wanted, too: a storm warning, a world in turmoil and something to hunt down.

• • •

Minke's thoughts ran ahead of her.

"You're losing your touch," said the alchemist.

"Not your usual?" said Minke, surprised.

"This is a special occasion!" he said.

She looked into his bright, unsteady gaze. The alchemist, in his shabby striped suit, smelled of chemicals. His beard was patchy with burns. When he smiled, his eyes shifted and slid as if he watched a great and amusing secret scuttle across the walls.

He wanted everyone to know how clever he was, and Minke could see that he was clever. It was that as much as the smell of chemicals which took her breath away.

The alchemist thought he had invented a perpetual motion device, and he wanted someone to build it to his specifications, to prove it to the world. He was one of many customers with similar beliefs, and Minke had learned enough from watching mad scientists to see that the spinning wheels in his mind wouldn't do what he claimed.

But the truth of it would never be known—who would invest in a scheme proposed by such a man? He was mad. Yet although his device wouldn't provide endless energy, it was dangerous and—if only it could be constructed—completely and horrifyingly feasible. Minke knew the arch-family would have given lives to get it.

The alchemist thought about power in terms of combustion and friction, kinetics, reactions and catalysts. What he thought he had discovered for a machine with its cogs and vacuums and little explosions was merely a principle he had observed in the world: knowing what people are hungry for gives power. And to be powerful is to want more power and have the means to get it. It is a cycle of desire fulfilled.

Minke thought that was a beautiful thing.

• • •

We used to have stories, but in those all the puzzle-pieces would fall together, the good end happily, the bad less so. The travellers in those stories sang songs.

Our bad and benevolent governments alike were built to a modest scale—the arch-family with its conspiracies and quarrels, foreign kings with ceremony, mystery and human foibles. No great and terrible arts, no haunted air-breaking war machines.

To balance this, our stories had villains who wanted to hold the world to ransom, and green-black clouds gathering ominously in the west to spread their tendrils out over bright lands until brave hearts leapt to action. But we knew how those stories would end, and we kept them in books where they couldn't grow too large.

• • •

The tin-tinkerers were regular and irascible customers. They were short-sighted and their hands had been nicked by wires and burned by solder irons.

Minke's aunt did not like them, she said they lowered the tone, but they drank well and paid well. Sometimes they sang.

They looked at Minke over great bushy beards and wanted this: to make something worthy, something grand, something of fine gold wires and blown glass frail as a bubble, something with clockwork delicate as a heartbeat and riveting smooth as ice and a fire in its chest as slow-burning as a life—not factory engines or ship apparatus, nor gaudy necklets and tiaras, but something devastatingly beautiful in its function.

Minke flirted—she was good at that too—until they began to talk to her. She admired the twisted chain on which one of them wore his watch and wished aloud that she could have something so fine. He called it bread-and-butter work, and Minke wondered wistfully whether he took commissions?

"Not for trinkets and bagatelles," he growled. Minke was too tall—she wasn't his type at all. "There is no vision, no ambition in the world," he went on. "Give me an impossible contraption, an infernal device-" his hands gripped the air with frustration. "If someone designed it I could build a machine to take the pulse of the world to the accuracy of an eyelash, and they would weep to see it. And they want watch-chains."

Minke shrugged, but she had seen the alchemist look up, bleary with dreams and beer. He had enough courage by now—Minke had seen to that—to take himself over to the tin-tinkerers' table and introduce himself, enough stubborness to withstand their mockery, enough madness to intrigue them.

His hands, with their chemical stains, would trace delicate charts on the table and he would convince them. The tin-tinkerers and the alchemist would build something remarkable together, until they fell to quarreling about aesthetics, purpose, ownership. Then that marvellous machine would prove itself on the world, for better or ill. Built as it was for aggrandisement and born of dispute, it would most likely be for ill.

It occurred to Minke that someone who knew how to play on hearts could make use of that, if they placed themselves well.

• • •

What she gave the world, without being asked, without most people even noticing how she did it, was something to shake it up, a beat to dance to, a sun towards which to turn. Something to set the little stories in motion, and braid them together into one great tale. A common cause, a common destination.

• • •

Minke made matches in the bar, while her aunt grumbled and aspired to better, petty things.

Customers went out, not yet knowing their fates had been joined. Minke's heart ached. Not because she wished to find such a story for herself, or to know how each of these would end, but because she did know. She was doing no more than setting candles in paper boats and sending them out on the night tide—they would gleam beautifully, then burn out and sink while Minke stood watching in the shallows.

It wasn't enough. She wanted to join them all together into a brilliant light-show. She wanted to braid them into a great net of stories and fling it over the world. The cursed musician and the runaway, the gutter-sleuth and the murderess, the alchemist and the tin-tinkerers. Their mysteries and discoveries and inventions should not be allowed to fade gently into the night—they should set each other off, explode against each other like firecrackers, wake the ghosts of all the old stories and set them loose on the world.

I am piping on a penny-whistle, thought Minke, *when I should be conducting orchestras.*

She could not do that from Ye Olde Owle.

• • •

A common cause may start a hundred stories, but to weave them into one took a common enemy. Someone to throw a spanner in the works, to steal the inventions of quarrelling conspirators and spill blood for sleuths to sniff after, to cross the paths of young lovers with those of their pursuers. To tangle the threads, to take advantage of situations. Someone who wasn't tied into one little story, but could stand up and pull the strings of all of the characters. Someone to elbow out empty places on the map, stir up ghost-eyed dragons, set fire on the high mountains, raise storm clouds, start wars. Someone to take over the world.

Someone to call out a hero.

Here is my advice to you:

Don't start out to be a hero. If you must find a story, make it a little one, with someone content to stay near home. Find a cause and a goal which hardly anyone else shares. Don't add fuel to the fire. Dampen it. Turn your back on the flames. Starve them. Make a little light and let it die out when its time comes.

Set up petty, predictable bureaucratic villains as your government.

Be comfortable.

Make a difference.

Stay at home.

No, I can't stay any longer. I've been tangled in this story for too long. I have tigers to hunt, dragons to slay. An old friend to find.

• • •

There was an empty, sleepy world outside Ye Aulde Owle Café & Bar, and Minke had a gift she didn't want to waste.

"No-one will hire you!" said Minke's aunt. "Where else do you have to go?"

"I've everywhere else to go!" said Minke.

"What about that nice delivery boy who said he'd come back for you?"

But Minke had forgotten the nice delivery boy. She slung her bag over her shoulder and pulled on her boots.

The road lay before the door.

• • • • • • • • • • •

TIED TO THE WASTE

JOANNE ANDERTON

Leichhardt watched me as the waste rolled in. The ochre sky was heavy, and lights glinted within it. Not lightning—I couldn't remember the last thunderstorm we had, the kind with water-vapour clouds and rain—but metal polished by the sands, cleared by the wind of its ash layer and reflecting the close burning of the sun.

I struggled to prepare for the storm. The concrete ramp from my workshop ended at a tangle of wire that once fenced in the scrapyard, so I was forced to park my wheelchair and rely on crutches. My ankles didn't bear my weight so well any more, but I managed to grab the corner of an oiled-leather tarpaulin, drag it over the nearest scrapheap and secure it to a hook pinned into the dirt. The best I could do to protect the scrap collected in my yard.

"You could help," I wheezed to the cat.

Hidden against the oncoming darkness, only his eyes glowed back at me, catching the sun in their own cat way. He blinked. As much of an answer as I'd ever get, voice chip or none.

I struggled back into the wheelchair. Blood rushed to my feet with pins of fiercely tingling fire and the old ache set into my spine. By the time I'd wheeled myself up to the workshop door I was exhausted, arms shaking.

I paused on the threshold. "Coming in?"

He made no move to join me, just watched, two shining points much closer to earth.

Let him weather the storm on his own, then. When I gave them voices I gave them choice.

I rolled myself inside, bolted the door and barricaded it with steel beams set up on spring triggers. I drew water from an earthenware filter, swallowed a handful of painkillers and sleeping pills and made it to bed, just in time.

All I heard was the first knock, the hard crash of something small but solid against the iron roof. All I felt was the first pull, the tug of memory swirling in sand. Then the drugs took me away. Far from the pain of my device-riddled body and the scrap magic screaming in the rolling waste above.

• • •

I woke to the stink of cat piss and a taste in my mouth between acid and dust. The cats crowded at the workshop door—all but Leichhardt—glaring silent remonstrations at me.

How long had I slept?

Outside, the world was silent, the waste exhausted.

I eased myself from the bed. My ankles were swollen, the bulging skin darkened to a sickening red. So I stripped their bandages, fumbled syringe and vial from the drawer beside my bed and injected 5mls of a soup of my own creation: gangrene-eating and oxygen-feeding fused from waste dust and precious scrap. They were once jewels, the devices at work inside my deteriorating legs. Diamonds and gold, loved, treasured, now sand-scratched and tossed across the continent.

The devices buzzed their way up to my spine, to ride the network of nerves. Flashes of memory flickered across the back of my eyelids: proposals, birthdays, anniversaries. Small pockets of once-lives carried on minuscule, wiry legs to feed strength into my body.

I was forced to inject a second round and swallow painkillers before I could stand. Even the scrap I kept for myself, the strongest and cleanest of the waste's rubble, was stretched thin—*worn down*—compared to the power I had once known. Because even the most powerful memory loses its potential once it's been thrown around a continent for decades, and reduced to a spot of light in the heavy sky. As the memories weakened, so did my magic. And so did I.

I shuffled two, three short steps to half-fall, half-sit in the wheelchair. The cats wound around my ankles the whole slow way, rubbing against my fresh bandages and threatening to trip me up. I snapped at them, and brushed as much of their fur away as I could. I rolled to the door—released the unimpressed feline quintet—grabbed a canvas bag and balanced it in my lap.

The sky outside was gritty, the sun haloed by purple haze, and the ground littered. I wheeled myself to the edge of the ramp and took up the crutches again. Slowly, I hitched and lurched around the yard, the bag slung over my shoulder.

It must have been one hell of a storm. The tarps were shredded, fresh scrap had fallen everywhere. Most of it looked unusable: dead trees torn from the dry ground, and rocks. Lots of rocks. After all, the waste had stripped the world of most of its human layer. We were down to rocks.

But I still found some machine parts: pistons and crankshafts and fuses. A scattering of small, diecast toys that flickered faint yet playful memories against my fingers. Shapeless pieces of metal that once were cars, buildings, appliances, and all the small glories of an age now sandpapered down.

I stopped to wipe the sweat from my face and caught a fluttering of colour amidst all the iron-red and ash-grey. I dropped the bag and picked my way closer, fighting knees that refused to bend.

A bird, the most beautiful blue I had ever seen, unsullied and crisp. The very sight of it caught my breath, disrupted my faltering step and almost sent me face down into dirt and metal shards.

I stooped awkwardly to scoop it out of the sand.

It felt like air in my hands, like a breath of wind, like a cloud or, or, I didn't even have the words. No scrap called to me from within its fragile frame. No nano-threading in its wings, no pacer tied to its heart, no voice chip in its throat and brain.

The bird was not tied to the waste.

I stroked it, as gently as my twisted hands allowed, and it did not move, not even to breathe.

I carried the bird to my workbench inside.

I wiped away a heavy layer of cat fur from the bench, and the strip of heat-warped plastic and computer chips glowed like the faint curl of a misshapen moon. Once, it would have caught magic from my fingers. In a blaze of light it would have drawn memories from the scrap I laid on its uneven surface and filtered, enhanced, while I fused wire and gemstone and metal and glass.

Not any longer. Not with the quality of the scrap I brought it now.

Maybe, if I was still young, if I could walk on my own two legs, coterie of witches' cats in tow, and follow the song of the waste. Then, perhaps, I could bring my workbench the magic it required to fuse the kind of devices I needed, just to stay alive.

But no, not any longer. The world was old as I was old, and strung up on our lifelines of scrap, we would die slowly together.

I laid the bird out on my knees, spread its wings, and rested its head to the side. Its chest was white, beak long, half-lidded eyes dark. The blue of its feathers reminded me of a sky I had never seen, but knew from stolen memories.

The soft pads of cat feet and I glanced over my shoulder. The cats sat on the workshop floor. I was surprised to see Burke and Wills had dragged my scrap bag in after them.

I gestured, loosely, and they surprised me further by bringing the bag to my feet. Bending with a grunt and a popping in my back, I drew from the bag: a toy car, a fuse, a handful of copper wires stripped of their plastic coating and fraying to a rotten-metal colour.

The cats watched the dead bird on my lap with predator intensity. I rolled close to the bench, keeping it out of their reach, as I laid out my scrap. In the car was joy, hidden deep beneath its rust, stripped-down paint and decades of abandonment. It became the bird's torso. In the fuse was energy, indeterminate, ill-defined. The workbench shuddered against my knees, humming as it tried to drag something solid, something real out of the fuse. What had it been used for? Had that machine been named? Needed? Relied on? It became the head. The wings and legs I wound out of copper wire. They were soft, ungainly, and had none of the delicate strength of feather and bone.

The entire fusion was pathetic, but the best I could do.

I placed one hand on the bird in my lap, and one on the scrap toy on the bench. No balance there. The bird was freedom, it was fresh air. The device was a quiver of muted joy, a surge of directionless energy, and empty wire. Perhaps no device could ever encapsulate that freshness; perhaps the very weight of the waste robbed it of its freedom. Or maybe, in this worn-down world, there was simply nothing as powerful as dead, untethered bird?

Even if I had the strength to revive it, what kind of life could I give it? Plundered from a dead planet, fractured by alien emotion, eaten away slowly into powerlessness and madness?

Like me.

I considered the cats: Baxter's copper-plated skull, Bass's steel-mesh lungs, Kennedy's prismatic eyes. "Have I bound you here?" I whispered to them. What memories did those cats see, those familiars I had tied to the waste when I fused their bodies and saved their lives?

Slowly, walking with liquid smoothness and none of the heaviness he should have felt in his metallic legs, Leichhardt entered the workshop. Despite the storm and the shelter he had refused, his dark cat body was not sullied with even one grain of sand. He held me in his bright gaze as though he could speak to me, through that gaze alone, and not with the voice chip I had given him.

"What memories do you see?" I hissed. "Why won't you just tell me? What do you see?"

Nothing.

Whatever it was I had burdened them with, whatever memories they could not identify, whatever particle of a dying world dragged them down, down along with it, they would not speak. Perhaps they saw nothing? Perhaps they really had nothing to say.

I collected the scrap bird, held it out to them. As one, the cats twitched tails and flattened ears.

"It's not strong enough to give the bird back its life," I said, "but I think I can start the heart beating." I nodded, more to myself then the unreadable furry expressions. "Yes, energy and even the tiniest drop of joy can equal the beating of a heart. And maybe even breath. Won't be alive, but it will live." I held the device over my lap, wires drooping through my fingers, and tucked my free hand beneath the bird.

Did feathers carry memory? I hadn't thought of that. Perhaps, between us, the bench and I could draw enough out of the feathers to complement my unstable scrap and fuse the two—

Leichhardt leapt at my hand, and his hydraulic legs were strong. It was all I could do to swivel in my wheelchair and keep the bird away from the flashing of his claws and the snapping of his jaws. The scrap bird clattered to the floor and I lost track of it, beneath the shadow of the bench.

"No!" I snapped at him. "Not to eat!"

The cats refused to leave, and I was forced to keep vigilant, the bird on my knees, to protect it from their appetites.

• • •

The first customers since the storm arrived that evening, in wagons pulled by sullen donkeys and ringed by talkative dogs.

The cats disappeared in the face of the approaching lights. All but Leichhardt. I covered the bird in my lap with a patchwork quilt, and waited in my wheelchair at the bottom of the cement ramp.

The dogs breached the relic outline of my tattered fence in a defensive pack formation. The alpha approached, low to the ground, offering no aggression but ears pricked and nose working. Leichhardt made a show of ignoring him. The dog returned the favour.

"You smell most strongly of cat, witch," the dog said to me, voice chip set to a deep male tenor, calm and crackling faintly with age and use.

I did not smile. Dogs do not appreciate the baring of teeth. "And yet I am more dust than fur."

He paused, head tipped and his ears flattened. "Dust?"

"Devices," I said. "The memories and the waste." And for a moment, I was caught up in it. All that dust. The cursed devices hummed in my body, and the yard disappeared, the dog gone with it. I was holding a woman's hand, offering her a diamond ring. City lights on a night harbour bobbed and rippled below us. The wind was cool, and spoke of rain.

Then Leichhardt leaned his small dark body against my legs, and I returned. I sagged forward. "I'm sorry," I managed to say. "The dust, the devices, I am so full of them. Sometimes they take me away."

Can dogs pity? I did not know. "Do you wish to trade?"

"Of course," I said. He retreated to alert his masters.

The wagons pulled up close, people tumbled from their rickety wood and rusting iron. "Good evening, Tilda." I squinted at the young man who addressed me with such familiarity. I had no idea what his name was, or if I'd ever met him before.

He backed away to allow the women to approach me, heads all low, scarves wrapped around their hair and shoulders. They carried food, and their needs.

I traded a whole year's worth of abortion and birth control devices for a box of tinned tomatoes, beans and corn. Devices to ease infected wounds and chill fever, for bread only a few days old. Voice chips for dried apple and bone-setters for a large barrel of water—none too clean, but I had devices for that too.

Those devices were not as powerful as the ones inside me, though they were even older. I had made hundreds of them when the scrap was rich. They were, after all, my income. No amount of scrap-witchery can fuse food from memory, or water from the past. I relied on trade. And it almost seemed that they would be enough. Until the young man approached me again, hands clutching a tattered leather hat held close to his chest. "We have a gift for you," he said, and gestured to his men. My heart sunk as they unwrapped a whole leg of cured meat—pork, I thought. The dogs watched it with reverence. "And a request." More desperate gesturing, and another precious, carried package.

This one was a young boy. He sweated even in the cooling night, skin pallid and expression fearful. His leg had been crushed. It was splintered and bandaged poorly, and his body sung with the tangle of devices inside it, their struggling magic all that had kept him alive for so long.

"He is an oldest son," the young man pleaded. "To a father lost in the waste not three months ago. He cannot work, and soon, we fear, he will die. Leaving a mother, and three sisters."

"What do you want of me?" I asked, even though I knew.

"Please, Tilda. A leg for a leg." The entire caravan seemed to close in around me, all hope and desperation in the fading ochre sunset and the faint, device-powered wagon lights. "Fuse him a new leg, a scrap leg, or he will die."

"I can't." I felt smaller, weakened, by those words.

"Is he worth more? We can spare—"

"No!" I screeched, my voice rusting and inhuman. "Don't you understand? I cannot create anything worthy of a first son! Not any more."

"But—"

A scraping, dragging sound cut through his words. With a shudder, I turned in my chair to see Leichhardt dragging the useless scrap-bird I had fused out of the workshop. He dropped its limp and lifeless not-body at my feet and stood over it, his back arched, tail whipping fur against my legs, fierce and proud as though he had killed it himself.

"What is this?" the young man hissed, and the hackles on his alpha dog rose. Perhaps they took it as an insult. But Leichhardt stood his ground, and growled his own terrible wet-throat noise.

And in that terrible parody of life, that base imitation of the power of a lost world, I saw the dying boy. It would take powerful devices to correct the mangling of his limb, as powerful as those at work inside of me. More jewels, probably, for love. Something stronger than a fuse for energy—a battery, as stable as I could find—and a circuit board to channel it. But what could possibly equate to the potential of his young body? The life he had not led, the tasks he had not completed? No waste-tossed rubbish could do that, no matter how many of their stripped-down memories I cobbled together and forced beneath his skin.

"And I wouldn't, even if I could," I said, only realising it as the words escaped me. Because all I could make, all I had ever made, was just like Leichhardt's scrap-bird trophy. A terrible parody. A base imitation. Just like me. "I will not tie this child to a dying world, nor add him to the list of half-lives I have so wilfully created."

Leichhardt sat, arranged a neat tail and cleaned a casually hooked paw.

The young man seemed torn between anger and surprise. "How— how dare you? We suffer you because you are useful to us, witch. We trade, rather than take, because you have helped us in the past. If I were you, I would want this arrangement to continue."

"It doesn't matter what any of us want. The sands will scour us all, in time, and soon we will be nothing but scrap for the waste to play with. Don't bother with your threats, child. We will all end with the world." I kicked out with my bandaged feet, and ignored the stabs of pain that travelled from ankle to back. This unsettled Leichhardt again and he arched, hissing. "Just take your boy and go."

The boy screamed as they collected him, and carried him into the night to die. The young man and a few of his fellows stole scrap from my yard—useless junk, they were welcome to it, as far as I was concerned. The women refused to enter my workshop and steal devices. They, at least, maintained some residual respect. But I wondered how long that would last. What would they do when the devices they had just traded for ran out?

In my lap, the bird felt heavy.

As the wagons rattled away the alpha dog held back. "You smell of more than cat, witch," he said. "You smell of something I cannot name."

"Freedom," I told him. "And fresh air."

"No." His ears pricked forward and he panted. A moment of indecision, I thought, of contemplation. "Dead things," he said. "And new life." The dog stood, took deliberate steps backwards. A final glance at me, "Hope," and he disappeared into the night.

Sitting on the end of the ramp, I watched the wagon lights fade. The next time I saw them, there would be no trade.

"Is that what you wanted?" I asked Leichhardt. "No more magic, no more lives saved, and now, no more food. We will all starve, even while the devices keep us alive. We will be skin stretched over metal, and nothing more." He stared at the quilt in my lap as Bass and Kennedy dragged the scrap bird into the yard, and tore it back to rubbish.

I downed too many painkillers that night, with old water and beans. The cats knocked against my wheels, leapt across furniture, aiming for my knees. When I slept, I held the bird to my chest.

• • •

In my drugged haze, I had left the workshop door open. A fine layer of sand blew in to cover everything. As I sat up, and my ankles throbbed and my back jarred, I wondered how many painkillers I would have to take so I didn't wake up again. Then I realised the bird was gone.

I struggled into the wheelchair as quickly as I could and rolled out into the yard. The cats sat on the sand in a circle, the dead bird in the centre.

"What are you doing to it?" I cried.

As one, the cats drew back, opening the circle so I could approach. Only Leichhardt remained were he was. The bird seemed unharmed. It lay on a rag, wings outstretched, head to the side. Beside it in a neat pile lay claws shed before their time (edges still bloody, tips still sharp), hairballs (more than I had ever wanted to see in the one place) and whiskers (so many the cats were almost bald).

I glanced from the strange collection of cat-parts to Leichhardt. His face looked oddly lopsided with most of his whiskers missing. "What is this?"

Disdain articulated through the flip of a tail and the flinting of eyes.

I eased myself from the wheelchair, hissing at the pain. Leichhardt sat opposite me, Burke and Wills beside him, then Baxter, Bass and Kennedy.

I lifted a whisker: black, thick. Leichhardt's.

And it wound itself around my finger. I gasped, let it go, and it shimmied across the back of my hand to plunge needle-like into a vein. I felt it inside me, the way it coursed and wiggled. Up along my arm, across my shoulders and into my neck, then down through my spine, and along the nerves than ran to my leg.

"What—?"

Once there, it latched onto one of my scrap magic devices. It tied up the insect-like legs and dragged it through muscle, through skin and out of me entirely. The device was tiny, after all. Just a sparkle of diamond and wire. The whisker peeked out between my bandages and discarded it with an elastic flick.

And it took away a memory with it. The scent of pollution-heavy air and the bobbing of distant harbour lights vanished. In its place— I wasn't sure. But it wasn't the pain I expected, or the sudden resurgence of gangrenous rot. I felt clean, wherever the whisker had touched me. Scrubbed raw.

Then the whisker burrowed back inside, moving on to the next device. Where it wormed through me it left the promise of freedom.

"Leichhardt," I whispered.

He curled his tail around the bloodied tips of his paws and looked at me like I was a fool. The whisker tossed one, two more devices out of my body and left empty patches instead.

"There are no memories in your whisker, are there?" I asked. "No particles of a dead world. Where does this strength come from, then?"

Silence. Despite the voice chips I had given them the cats refused to speak. Or, perhaps, because of them. Those chips were but another chain tying them to the waste, to the memories and lives of the long dead. Did they even need the magic I had saddled them with? The waste I had tied them to?

"If I had not fused you, you would have died. I had to tie you, to save your life." But if that was true, then what were they doing to me?

Leichhardt looked at the dead bird, and I followed his gaze back to the pile of whiskers, claws and fur.

Cat scrap. Full not of memories and the past, but whatever it was the whisker was leaving inside of me. What the alpha dog had smelled. Dead things and new life.

"The future?" I asked the cats. Of course, they did not answer. But that was the point.

"But the future is fragile, it might not even be. The past, it is solid. It is trapped in rubbish, fed by the waste." But the past was also failing, tearing itself down, depleting as we used it for our own ends. I met the bright eyes of six cats; I stared at the delicate feathers of one dead bird. "I am used to working with memories." I closed my eyes. A flick of the whisker and I forgot the sound of waves crashing on a breach, overlaid by running feet and laughter. "I don't know how to work with possibilities instead."

Leichhardt sighed a cat sigh, the full-body type, dripping with scorn.

And I gave myself over to his whisker. "All right," I said. "I will try it your way."

I laid the bird in my lap, took up their scrap, and fused.

I wound wings out of whiskers and hair. A heart of claws. Fur for a body, more whiskers gave it shape. When it was done something was still missing, so I plucked a single silver hair of my own and wound it around the entire frame, hairball head to whisker pinion.

The device felt fragile, and yet very much alive. All the hairs along the back of my arms rose as I held it.

"Is that enough?" I asked the cats.

Their bright eyes lacked conviction. Bird in one hand, device in the other, I weighed them against each other as though I was a giant scale. They were uneven.

"Ah." The heart did not beat.

So I pricked my finger on the device's cat-claw heart and dripped blood into its lattice. This was a strange witchery. Cat magic, scrap skill and blood. But the semi-transparent network shuddered and clinked softly like countless cats running over tiles.

"Now what?"

The cats crouched low and tightened their circle, noses touching the back of my hand. They became my workbench. So I pressed the device to the bird, one hand over the other. And life—possibility— seemed to flow through us all, down from their six tense bodies and even, even from mine. Somehow, I found strength, not the kind that comes from drugs and devices, but the kind that survives out here, amidst the sand of a dying world, and lives. Just lives.

Then Leichhardt's ears twitched and feathers brushed against my palms. With one smooth movement the cats retreated. I opened my hands. The bird shuddered. For an instant I could still see the blood-splattered cage of his new heart beating around his old one, then the fusion completed, and the bird and the device were one.

He breathed, tested the length of his wings, then with a flutter and a hop he was perched on the nest of my fingers. He studied me, then the cats, and bobbed his head back and forward, his beak held high.

A single bright trill, an instant of song, then he opened his wings and darted up into the purple sky. A blue feather fell to my lap. When I touched it, it quivered, and threaded itself beneath my skin.

•••••••••••

THE DOG WHO WISHED HE'D NEVER HEARD OF LOVECRAFT

ANNA TAMBOUR

There was a man who had a dog who had—for the good part of every day—never heard of H. P. Lovecraft, though this dog enjoyed his Will Cuppy, always licking his chops over the line, "The nuthatch cannot sing and does not try."

Now this dog—and since we didn't catch his name, we'll just call him Ibsen—was a rough-haired, right-flop-eared bitser of no particular color except for the black patch around his left eye. Being a virile male of middle years whose chin badly needed a shave, one could easily have said he had a morbid cast but one would be wrong.

He could have been a cert in the movies, but if he'd ever wanted to sit at the drugstore counter to be discovered, he'd never have been allowed to, in that town—and besides, he probably would have preferred to work on the stage, though that is a speculation. The town's Players didn't tolerate children at performances and eschewed Little Orphan Annie because of Merrilee Fairweather's purported allergy.

Ibsen didn't feel the loss, and not because he was blissfully ignorant. He was self-employed, is all. And by that, we don't mistake busyness for work. He wasn't one of those dogs who spends his waking hours scratching his ears and falling over backwards after trying to bite the root of his tail, or whining to be noticed, or acting like a butler who never mentions the stench of slippers. And he certainly wasn't a dog who lives for chasing, or any purposeless expenditure.

Say Ibsen were famous and some dog were cast as him. That dog would have to learn how to sit in a loose-boned slump, tilt his head about 26 degrees, and quarter-close his eyes. As the script would direct, if a dairy farmer were to write it:

IBSEN. [*ruminating*]

For Ibsen was above all, a thinker. Sure, he read a lot (see ref. to Cuppy above), but in his limited way, he was an observer, and that limitation sometimes roiled. He often, as fall rain merrily ran down the windows, wistfully wondered whether Cuppy had been intentionally hurtful when he wrote "Hasn't everybody? [been to Ceylon]". The first time Ibsen read that unthoughtfully hurtful comment, he felt like he'd just swallowed a stone in his dogbowl, thinking he'd bolted a hardboiled egg. Though even with that provocation, Ibsen would most likely have jibed at the globetrotting life of a celebrity—all that interruption. His eyes, under that wild hedge of eyebrow, were deep wells into which his observations dropped. What did he make of all he learned? Who knows? His hairy face was as expressionless as a barber's floor.

The problem with not knowing his Lovecraft is that his master (we'll humor the man), Hylam P. Hector, lived and breathed the man *he* called 'the Master'.

It might be that Ibsen was, at heart, a contrarian, or possibly the strain of acting faithful when assaulted by the man (the 'P' stood for Pituitary, an attempt by Hylam's father, an internist, to infuse enthusiasm in the fruit of his loins, to take up his own adventurous practice)—the man who is Mr Hector to most of us and Hylam to some but who encouraged Ibsen to think of him as 'Daddy', to, where were we?

The strain, yes. Mr Hector had got in the habit, bad, of writing Lovecraft-influenced poetry. If only this disease had progressed silently, but it *would* out. Every evening, Ibsen was interrupted by a long portentous "Ahhh," followed by the dread Introduction:

"Daddy's finished."

And the poem would come out of Ibsen's master's mouth, the poem in all its rambling incoherent imperturbable interminability.

Ibsen didn't, in all honesty, consider himself capable of critical literary analysis. He would have been the last dog on earth to decry this drivel as mere pastiche. That it was as nonsensically dallying as the man who thoughtlessly tosses a ball in his hand while talking to a friend when his ball-besotted dog is at his feet, waiting, was as clear to Ibsen as the fanatic eyeglow of achievement in Hylam Hector's eyes upon finishing a reading.

So Ibsen humored the man, his master. But, like 'Pituitary', Hylam Hector's zealotic enthusiasm was inadvertently the One Surefire Method to turn Ibsen from anything Lovecraftian.

Indeed, these readings set Ibsen upon a new short course of learning, one clipped for purely pragmatic ends: Ibsen's Method of Self-hypnosis that Really Really Works, which he used to flush his mind after every reading, to convince himself that he'd never heard of Lovecraft. It worked until the next dread Introduction.

• • •

So the tragedy is set. On the left side of the stage, clutching a sheaf of pages, paces Hylam P. Hector, eyes bright, head thrown back in post-declamatorious rapture—a man who looks like the kind of bachelor to live in one of those dark-eyed apartments over the town's drugstore (but who in fact lives in a house too featureless to notice in one of those streets named after numbers).

Center-stage is the dog you know as 'Ibsen'. Luckily for Mr Hector, the pallid sea of light flowing from the green-shaded lamp laps not upon the shores of Ibsen's eyeballs. Yet if some foul fiend should, in a trice too quick for Ibsen to react, wipe from the dog's brow that rampant brush and shine upon the eyes of the hound, the unswerving gaze of a hundred-watt fluorescent bulb—if Hylam P. Hector had looked into his dog's eyes then, he would have been struck dumb.

For on that particular damp and gloomy evening indoors, Mr Hector's poem, Moon Something-or-other Someplace-else, must have had a dozen lines that in their hysterically romance-tinged paranoia, their frustrating inexactitude, made Ibsen itch as bad as if he'd been licked by a thousand fleas. But he was used to that from 'Daddy'.

No, what finally raised the hair on his spine and made him loll his tongue to keep himself from raising his lip and letting his canines glow, was, not that invidious use of the word that should only be heard in another context, the casually friendly 'hi'. Ibsen's sensitive hearing was bruised every time Hylam Hector read out *hie* (and two *hie*s made Ibsen want to bite). But that wasn't the snap of tragedy's jaw.

An observant master would have noticed the growing furrow under that hedge of brow, but Hylam P. Hector noticed nothing.

And Ibsen, never a demonstrative dog, showed as little emotion as the palace guard with heat rash. The hound was long inured to too many *moon*s, *hideous*es, not to mention the abomination *shewed*; Ibsen, toughened by countless *lurk*s, suffered silently also through too many exotic places celebrated (especially galling coming from this man who wouldn't even walk his dog); and still, Ibsen soldiered on, carrying out his duty, evening after evening after evening, and always interrupted, at that.

Ibsen, on the evening of evenings just ebbing into night, had managed dogfully to maintain composure, forgive his master's interruption (Ibsen had felt that evening, a whisker away from answering the age-old conundrum: Why, when you dig a hole, is the earth you toss out never enough to fill it?).

Anyone really observing Ibsen then would have known that if he were a human, the only interruption he might possibly appreciate: a stealthy refill of his tobacco pouch.

His eyebrows threw deep shadows, but they were twitching with deeper thought when, "Listen to this, Rover!" (*We sense a deep sense of outrage that Ibsen might feel at this common tag, but since he is middle-aged, and a dog at that, this tragedy is a burden that he must have borne so long that he hardly winces.*) "Daddy's most luscious poem of all!"

And forthwith, Hylam Pituitary Hector commenced to read.

While poetising, his eyes were always either fixed on his sheaf of pages or closed, so he never saw the moment when his dog's faithfulness turned from the tolerance of proprietal deference, to bitterly apathetic scorn.

It's a terrible thing to see in a dog, but ask yourself: Could YOU have withstood as much?—the one-and-ten-thousandth "*O!*"!

But for an 'h' . . .

And isn't that par for all our tragedies? If those two had shared a toothpaste tube, the rift would sundered them e'en before Ibsen was old enough to shave.

• • •

So

HYLAM P HECTOR. [*triumphantly brushing his fingertips over his chin that he tries in vain to unrecede*] What a treat that was for you, tonight, Rover. [*exits left. sounds of water running, toothbrushing as Mr Hector prepares for bed.*]

IBSEN. [*stands and shakes himself as vigorously as if he'd just been washed. walks off stage left. His steps down the wooden hall are abundantly clear. This dog doesn't get enough walking and has never had his nails clipped. Thuds and scrabble in the kitchen, as Ibsen opens the door and takes himself out, as usual, for his evening constitutional.*]

A nearby sash window opens with a creak, and an inarticulate but musical cry of pleasure is thrown from it by what sounds like a tiny bird, so must be a little old lady. In all modern theaters at this juncture, audiences are wafted with the Pavlovian smell of roast chicken.

• • •

ACT II

Outdoors, under the stars, on the lawn at the base of the neighbor's kitchen steps.

Ibsen is eating chicken out of the neighbor's right hand. She looks exactly like the little old lady who Tweetie Pie owns. Like all ladies of this type, she wears orthopaedic shoes that look as comfortable as a muzzle.

With her left hand she gives Ibsen's floppy ear a respectful fondle, so briefly that he almost nestles his head in her palm. She talks quietly to him of many things, but is either ignorant of H.P. Lovecraft or unusually sensitive to Ibsen's sensitivities. He knows she reads, because he of course, has checked out her house, though she wouldn't have dreamed of asking him to stay and he wouldn't have done so, partly for ignoble reasons (sometimes he wishes that his master and her could marry so that she might end Hylam P. Hector's poetising days with real romance, and their two libraries would, in combining, vanquish her collection of Readers' Digest Condensed books. Ibsen always thought the person who condenses a book to be quite as much a fiend as a person who clips a tail).

Tonight she talks of honeydew, how pretty the word it is, how extraordinarily ill-chosen by the ignorant compared to harsh reality, the black blight of aphids on roses. Ibsen understands her sentiments, if not the technicalities. He has always been a fine digger, but doesn't have a green thumb. He gives her fingernails a final wash and issues a complementary tail-wag. She stands with many creaks, but as many complaints as an old chair when someone sits in it. They part wordlessly and without looking back. He's off to explore the base of a birch tree or two before walking around the block pretending it's around the world, toward home.

• • •

ACT III

If only this were merely a play, but life is unfortunately, life. So the mundane must be reported along with the extraordinary abdication of Ibsen's responsibility for parting speeches, or at least a quip.

Ibsen lies asleep on an overstuffed chair in that same room that his master uttered the fatal O!—the room a real estate agent would call 'the living room', but Mr Hector calls 'the library'.

A large gasp, like that of a hot water bottle sucking down fluid, comes from the bedroom down the hall. This is followed by an annoyingly pendant silence. Then that gasp with perhaps a hint of shudder and a muffled scream, followed monotonously, by more silence.

Ibsen hears them all, and doesn't raise an eyebrow—all the sounds of normality to him who knows naught else but that all humans sleep as fitfully.

And now that we've ploughed our scene for action, we shall slip into the past-tense, the tense that dresses best bad memories.

• • •

Some things you should know about Hylam P Hector

In addition to his father wanting him to be an odontologist or something like that, or possibly because of that wish, little Hylam suffered from attacks of *pavor nocturnus* (night terror) so extreme that he used to sneak into his parents' bedroom when they went to sleep, simply to stay awake. He sat on the bare wood floor in his thin nightshirt, listening to them snore.

Never bold enough to wake them up, he ended this practice one night at age ten when he heard a team of robbers clean out his father's 'rooms' at the back of the house. The robbers had a horse with severe allergies to the flowers in the garden. It never stopped sneezing, and a horse who sneezes could wake a cemetery. But neither of his parents so much as turned over in bed.

He never told his parents about this incident, but it was only one of many that haunted him, before he met Lovecraft's works just after a failed love attempt in his first year of college.

His father was by this time, dead, and Hylam frittered away the rest of his inheritance on magazines that contained Lovecraft, notebooks in which to attempt to write stories like Lovecraft, and blank books with leather covers, in which he wrote his Lovecraftian poetry.

The problem with his taking up with Lovecraft, however, was not just that Hylam became a writer of insufferably frightful verse. He became an undocumented statistic in one of the most dreadful pandemics ever to hit humanity (and as a side-effect, other species).

He could have been the poster child for the disaster that until now has been nameless, but we shall break that code of silence and speak up. In that little upstate college in Horsenail, New York, Hylam P. Hector caught *Apnoea Pavorlovcraftis*, an anti-social disease.

Alone in his bed with his eyes tightly closed and his face turning purple from the effects of held breath, he'd inevitably break, issuing those antimacassar-shaking explosions of heretofore pent-up breath.

Every night come beddy-bye, he was so exhausted that he literally fell upon his gaping sheets, having barely had time to don his most beige pajamas. His eyes would close autonomically, and he would instantly be plunged into his first abyssal nightmare. And as everyone knows, now that we've revealed his disease, those nightmares were filled with grasping tentacled monsters and other women who were dangerously beautiful, strange gods with too many consonants to their names, things that lurk, hidden just out of view, more tentacles—and all the while he spent his sleep trying to hold his breath, so that he could not be seen (especially by the unseen). Then the air would blast out of his mouth and all those tentacles would reach out towards him till he made a pillbug of himself in the middle of his bed, holding his breath again . . . and so on, till his saviour, that he called affectionately and inaccurately, his 'alarum clock' rang at 8 o'clock a.m.

He never felt that he had slept a wink, yet he had nightmared loud as the Front all through the night.

Such a contrast to his day job. In his waking life, he was a writer, see—and not only that, but the celebrated enough never to reveal himself to his doctor: 'Augusta J. E. Wilson', author of AT THE MERCY OF TIBERIUS (*New.*), INFELICE; or, the Deserted Wife, ST. ELMO; or, Saved at Last, MACARIA; or, Altars of Sacrifice, VASHTI; or, Until Death us do Part, and INEZ: A Tale of the Alamo. (in cloth and paper covers at all good booksellers) "*Who has not read with delight the Works of AUGUSTA WILSON? Her strange wonderful and fascinating style; the profoundest depths to which she sinks the probe into human nature toughing the most sacred chords and springs; the intense interest thrown around her characters, and the very marked peculiarities of her principal figures, conspire to give an unusual interest to the Works of this eminent Southern Authoress.*" asks a back flyleaf of the "Intensely interesting" PRICE FIFTY CENTS D.M. Canright's THE MINISTRATION OF ANGELS, and the Origin, History, and Destiny of Satan.

So not only was he a secret Southern Authoress of intense 25-cent mysteries, but he wrote them without a single *O!*, and even at their most terrifying junctures, he bashed away at them with the coldness of a butcher tenderising steak. All day he wrote commercially, but something happened when the lights outside were low, or maybe it was that green-shaded lamp.

Luckily for him, after that failed one-sided love affair the week before he discovered Lovecraft, passion for another woman had been something he didn't feel the need of any more. Nor, fortunately for him, did he wish to have a dog in his bedroom at night. Ibsen had excellent hearing, but no wont to have his night disturbed by his master's commotions, since there was no cure he knew of for the disease.

Ibsen was able and quite ready to tear robbers to shredded meat, should they venture into the house. And Ibsen being a dog who was faithful to his master, was always ready to defend his master against anything a dog can sink teeth into. But short of peeing on his master's face, Ibsen couldn't think of what to do to break the nightmare/breath-hold/gasp explosion cycle.

• • •

Back to the Action

On this penultimate evening, the one in which Hylam Hector tried too far, the affections of his audience, Ibsen, as we have seen, had settled himself on the soft overstuffed chair in the library, as usual of an evening. We thought that he was asleep, and indeed, his eyebrows twitched as if he were dreaming, and his paws lightly pawed. A careful observer would have noticed, however, that only Ibsen's front paws pawed. His back legs were extended, and held quite rigid.

He was thinking out that problem of the hole, and being a dog who didn't believe solely in theory, was acting the problem out.

From the bedroom came a sound like the hot water heater blowing up. Then silence. Then another sound, like that of a giant eggbeater trying to turn a bedspread into butter. Then silence. The normal night noises. Ibsen pondered on.

In the contrast between the imitative heckle that Hylam P. Hector wrote and the professionally paced artificial hyde turned out by 'Augusta J. E. Wilson', we have forgotten to tell how fertile the man's imagination was, somewhere in his crowded brain.

On this particular night, that imagination had caught fire, perhaps lit by that one-and-ten thousandth *O!*.

Whatever, by the time he'd brushed his teeth, gargled, counted the hairs on his head, and done his chin exercises, his mind was still full of moon and exotic shores. He didn't fall into his gaping sheets, but lifted them up and inserted himself between them. And by this time, his thinking had spread to shadows. He laid his head on the pillow and glanced out through the diaphanous curtain, at the pale bright moon. He still wasn't sleepy. The curtain fluttered, and he thought to close the window, but the bed felt as delicious as the arms of a beautiful woman who is coming through the window now, her long hair flowing, and a tentacle reaching from behind her toward the bed.

His lungs closed, mid-suck.

The tentacle ran its tip over his left ear, then caressed his chin, what there was of it. And it seemed to find him good. Whether it was a part of her or some limb from another monster of polypous perversion, this diabolic limb was followed by a horde of silent others.

He knew the eyes of the beasts were upon him—beaks ready, maws opening, bodies smelling of reek from the farthest eaons—and with each new horror that inched forward, his lungs contracted and his throat clutched harder . . . then released enough to let him scream—that fine high wail of a boiling lobster.

And all that slink and drop and terror was just the first assault and reaction. That first woman and the tentacles, just the first of many creatures, gods, horrors—each freshly risen, driven, called from the unspeakable reaches of hauntingness, that visited him that night.

He held his breath, exploded, screamed, writhed till his sheets turned to cream cheese and his pillow to aged Parmesan—and *still* the dog we know as Ibsen but who Hylam Pituitary Hector called Rover when he called him a name at all, never lifted more than his floppy right ear in the bedroom's direction—and that, merely in a wishful surmise.

If only that fain poet had restrained, just one 'O!'—(or even drafted just the 'O' without also throwing in that perpendicular projectile strapped to its back) think what would have happened. Ibsen would have gone forth to grab and dispatch with a shake of his head, each and every thing that had flown, crept, emanated, and oozed in over that window-sill, even the Tentacled One. And who knows? He might have succeeded. His strong jaws might have made hamburger of even the most dread overconsonanted god.

For after all, he was a brave dog; and faithful to his duty—before the fall-out.

By 3:40 am, however, Ibsen was a changed beast. He felt he was on the cusp of solving the problem of the hole, and just needed to sleep on it.

At 8:04, Ibsen woke groggily. He had always hated that alarum. It was still ringing, an untoward that had never occurred.

Ibsen marched to the bedroom door, wrenched it open, and beheld what was left of his master—perhaps a spleen, and his pipe. Telltale sucker prints led out the window.

[*Ibsen walks down the hall, trying not to wag his tail, but the observant can see it sway slightly before he exits stage right, in the direction of the kitchen.*]

• • •

ACT, THE CLIMAX

In the next-door rose garden, sun shining brightly upon.

LITTLE OLD LADY. [*Her wrinkles look character-filled. She wears a pair of garden gloves and is throwing oaths at something we aren't privy to see on those gorgeous, big-headed blooms.*] Damn you to asphalt! [*She hears something coming up behind, puts a hand to her ear, and her face lights up. Suddenly she turns as if she forgets that she is not a young college girl. The object of her affections is the dog we know as Ibsen.*]

IBSEN. [*Drops bone at her feet. He gives her a wag-tail.*]

LITTLE OLD LADY. [*clasping hands in glee, and regarding the dog with upholsterer's eyes*] I wonder. How soft do you like your bed? [*She takes off her gloves and throws them and her secateurs into a trug, which she forgets as she trips up her kitchen stairs with Ibsen at her heel. They enter the kitchen triumphantly, and the door slams behind them, unattended.*]

[*A sound like a small bird singing in a shower wafts from the kitchen window.*]

LITTLE OLD LADY. [*still offstage, singing the words*] I'll put on the roast, but I never asked. Do you like stuffing?

IBSEN. [*also still offstage*] Tail-wag [*uttered with a slight dip of sadness. He already misses the library next door.*]

THE PLAY'S END

• • •

But that is why dogs don't appreciate plays.

Ibsen, being a dog, didn't waste time in Regret. He walked at the heels of the little old lady, through the kitchen and down the hall.

Ibsen's nose twitched. He realised that he'd never been in this part of the house, and a strange, exciting smell emanated from the closed door. The floor boards groaned and grizzled under the LOL's heels. It was *that* old a house. She reached out and tried to turn the china doorknob, but it didn't budge.

She gripped her hand, grimacing, and inadvertently looked down at Ibsen. He understood completely, suffering from a touch of lumbago himself. Up he leapt, and that doorknob didn't dare give his jaws trouble, not while the door itself was subject to his claws.

He'd looked back at the LOL, forgetting not to wag his tail. She went into the room ahead of him and . . . he didn't know what to think.

The walls and ceiling were hairy and scaled with many thought-provoking artefacts, and two walls were lined with bookcases so filled to bursting that Ibsen's tongue lolled. The LOL pulled out one oversize book, opened it and laid it on the floor beside Ibsen.

He'd never known a hole so wide and deep could exist.

Her laugh was a bit embarrassed. "I don't know why I'm showing you a tourist shot. But Frank took it the day we started that trip."

Ibsen nosed the book closed and read the words: Tectonic Geomorphies of the World's Five Grandest Canyons; an Introduction [and the author] Franklin G. Orpington.

A small thin book was placed briefly on the floor unopened and then snatched up again with an embarrassed giggle. But not before Ibsen had had a chance to read, "The Cavnericolous Fauna of the Dambool Region in Ceylon" and author: V. Patchoulevsky.

Then a large ball the size of a watermelon was lowered in her arms for Ibsen's inspection. It smelled like a mouse dipped in shaving soap.

"I picked up this in Trinkamalee. That's in Ceylon, you know."

She actually watched Ibsen when she talked, though he would have said that the strange ball was far more interesting than him.

"It was just upcountry from Trinkamalee that I was laid up with beriberi. I didn't want us to leave. After all, we were finding species of bats that no one had thought possible."

Ibsen was entranced. But why did she keep these treasures here? Of course! he blinked. *They're much too precious to expose to the unworthy.* Without realising it, he sat up straight. His right ear slightly rose.

"Oh!" the LOL said (Ibsen's eyes were misty by then, but not so much that he didn't surmise from a print of a young beautiful woman and a handsome man with a full chin, that her name was Violeta Patchoulevsky, *Dr* Patchoulevsky.)

"You must be suffering terribly!"

Ibsen hadn't noticed, but now that she had said so, he felt like a feather had been shoved up his nose, as the full effect of the camphor hit him.

His head wagged back and forth without him having the faintest control, and in shame and embarrassment, his nose shrunk till it was all wrinkles, and he stopped breathing and his eyes grew big enough that his eyebrow hedge parted . . . and he sneezed—all over the cover of that magnificent book that he had opened again and had been greedily reading surreptitiously.

"How thoughtless of me!" she cried. "If you're to live here, we must get rid of these."

This was all too much for Ibsen.

With every ounce of passion in him, the dog who was inexpressive as a barber's floor and as silent as the tomb, rested one paw on the edge of the book, the other paw in the Dr's lap, lifted his head, and *howled*.

Dr Patchoulevsky was not only *not* a dog, but *was* a zoologist. Even so, she understood.

• • •

A six o'clock she served dinner. Since the night was cold outside and sopping, she made him lamb shank stew and noodle pudding with raisins; and she had a bowl of tomato soup over crackers.

After an hour's silent companionable digesting, she put on her coat and a souwester hat, and picked up a large disorderly handbag, and they went for a walk. Not just around the block, no. This walk was a *dog's* walk. She waited at every tree that he needed to inspect and mark, didn't cluck when he squatted and took his time, and they walked past all the streets with houses till they got to the end of town and just past that, to a field.

Then she rummaged in her handbag and found a fresh bone that she gave to Ibsen.

He took it and dropped it solemnly. Then he dug its hole, savouring the pleasure of reaching in with both paws, flinging back the sticky mud, judging depth, slope, width of base. Barking sonarous soundings. By the time he dropped the bone into that hole, he'd never heard such a satisfying thud. And this time, when he filled the hole, he knew exactly why he had to cheat and dig another hole to top up the important one.

All the while, she waited patiently, in the rain. If he had been lesser than a dog, he might have looked back in time and Regretted that his master hadn't years earlier summoned his murderer.

They walked home in the drizzling rain in states of different but equal bliss. Both thoughtfully, of course.

This thoughtfulness was the reason both were unobservant, or they would have heard following them, something that sounded like the inexorable slink of a rotary carpet sweeper fitted with galoshes.

It was the giant tentacled Thing, the murderer Itself—its eyes big as watermelons, fixed upon *them*.

The giant tentacled thing was suffering mightily, having followed the Call all the way from the deeps of Chesapeake where the horseshoe crabs are feastly, up through beach towns rife with crab thieves and souvenir shops, out into the terrible wasteland of New England towns crawling with small but proud colleges, insane asylums hiding behind hedges, and poets.

Onwards the thing soldiered, till it reached the Caller. And though it dispatched Hylam Pituitary Hector as fast as it could gulp, the Thing remembered too late, that merely excising the spleen doesn't go far enough. One must never swallow a fevered brain.

It had suffered all day with dyspepsia. And to kill time till it could decamp, had peeping-tom'd thru the window and espied these now-boon companions, the dog and his mistress. It had watched them all day, traversing the outside of the house silently, its polka-dot sucker-prints washed off by the incorrigibly unsalty rain.

And it shadowed them now.

They reached her house and went in the door, totally wrapped in their world.

Ibsen shook himself in the front room (so violently did he shake off that hot steamy wetness, that the next day every volume of the Readers Digest Condensed books was nowhere to be found. They'd shrunk so tight that all that was left was a scattering of articles that had popped out onto the braided rug—*a*'s, *the*'s, and *an*'s. Useless as plots, Dr Patchoulevsky swept them up and boxed them for some purpose that would make itself known some day. About six months later, she wrapped a bow around the box and presented it as a welcome present to her new neighbor, the celebrated fly-tier Buff McInerny. He took them graciously and was touched that she had *tried* to give him a thoughtful gift, so he didn't look down on her ignorance. Trouts aren't smart, granted, but they're not dull. Clearly the woman didn't know fishing, or she'd not have thought anything less than a box of *peripatetically*'s would do.)

But the Thing with the tentacles was still outside and the woman and dog had now progressed to the room that had enchanted Ibsen. If they had been observant, they would have noticed a low regular squeak like that of windscreen wipers, and if they'd looked over at the window, they'd have seen, staring in upon them, an eye flattened across the expanse.

"I'm at least as intelligent as a dog," said the observer to itself. "And I've been to Ceylon."

And though it looked to some, as if it were of morbid personality, it was actually an optimist. So the Thing reached up to the second floor, where it found a crack in the bathroom window. It only needed an inch.

• • •

And to its delight, the dog and woman were as intelligent as it had hoped. The dog recognised the Thing's sucker-prints from the Deceased's bedroom, and welcomed the Tentacled One most heartily into the fold.

And the dog's mistress rustled up a bucket of clams.

• • •

LAST SCENE IN THE MOVIE

(although Ibsen insists he doesn't wish to play himself)

Full moon over the Grand Canyon silhouettes on its rim: one Winnebago; and the three companions—a paw, hand, and tentacle poised over each respective brow—the Dog, the Woman, and the Thing each gazing infinitely thoughtfully into the abyss.

CLOSING CREDITS

Music:

Craft My Lovethrob by the Arrhythmics

Galoshic Riff by Thing

• • • • • • • • • • •

TINY LIVES

ALAN BAXTER

I twist the tiny cog into place, my old-too-soon fingers gnarled, golden brown and cracked, but true. Complete, I turn the miniature dog over in my hands, the brass and copper of its construction shining in the late afternoon sun. I lift it to my lips, breathe softly into its mechanised heart and it stirs, shifts and wags.

The girl reaches out a greedy hand, eyes alight with wonder and I smile, place the wriggling clockwork puppy on her palm. She hugs it to herself, teeth white in a smile of innocence and immediate love.

"It'll never wind down, really?" the mother asks, eyes wide.

"Never," I reply, as the life draws through my chest like a thick needle through stubborn canvas. I wonder how many more I have in me. The breath is mere delivery, convenience. Something far deeper is taken every time.

"Thank you," she says, handing me so many grubby used notes, as weary as my hands and eyes.

"What do you say to the nice man?" the mother demands of the child.

"Thank you, mister!" the child enthuses and bounds away, her new pet dancing across her hands with tinny yips.

"Khob kun kub, little one," I whisper at her back.

The money goes into the leather satchel at my feet. I wonder when I'll have enough. Soon, I'm sure. I sit back in my tattered deck chair, let the sun bathe my wrinkled skin. My eyes roam the unsteady table before me. Boxes of parts glitter, cogs and tiny pistons, nuts, bolts, brackets and bars. But to me they are all limbs and muscles, nerves and hearts.

A man approaches, smiles unsteadily.

"Is it true?" he asks.

"Is what true, sir?"

"The toys you make. They act as if alive and never wind down?"

I smile. They never really believe, even when they see it. "They are alive, sir, and they will live forever. At least, until the parts wear out."

"Some old Chinese sorcery, is it?" he asks with a crooked smile. He has no idea how offensive he is.

"I'm Thai, sir."

"Ha! Well, there you go." He leans to inspect the compartmentalised case of parts, my neat row of tools in their leather wrap, looking anywhere but into my eyes where he would have to acknowledge the hurt of his words. "Can you make a bird?" he asks suddenly.

"Of course."

"And will it fly?"

"Certainly."

He points to the sign on my table, written when my hand was a lot younger, steadier. "Your price is *very* high."

America, where even the capitalism is subject to suspicion. I smile. "What you buy is absolutely unique, sir."

The chill of the Washington autumn lifts my wispy hair, chills across the back of my hands. The man pulls his jacket tighter. I wish I was back among the warm, humid days of my home, but it's foolish to pine for the past. Instead I am lost in the land of opportunity. But it wasn't for me that we came here. Always for the children. At the thought I smell disinfectant and bleach, see harsh fluorescents and white coats and quickly cast the thoughts away.

"Cash only, eh?" the man asks.

I nod, smile again. Where I come from this much smiling shows nerves, but the Americans seem to think it denotes honesty. Only sharks and the guilty smile this much, but I've learned it can save me a lot of conversation.

"All right, let's see it then!"

It takes nearly an hour to build the tiny hummingbird and test its wings. He's impressed, but scepticism still lives in his eyes. I put the tiny, fragile thing to my lips, breathe into its heart and it flutters up from my palm. The man staggers back and several people gathered to watch gasp and mutter. The bird alights on the man's shoulder and he looks ridiculous as he cranes to see.

"Amazing," he says.

I smile as the life drags again through my chest, snagging against my heart and lungs, adding a wrinkle to my eyes and another layer of weariness in my bones.

"Worth every dollar, buddy!" He hands me a folded wad of bills and I tuck them into the satchel.

Sumalee, my eldest daughter, comes to get me, her face pained at my appearance.

"How many today," she asks.

"Four."

"So we're nearly there?"

I hand her the satchel, its weight pulling against my shoulder like an anvil, though it only weighs a few pounds. "Nearly there."

"You must rest, father."

I nod, but the image of my youngest, Mali, in the hospital tears at me. *She needs rest.* That was how they started to tell us, to lead us to the truth that what she really needed was dollars. Tens of thousands of dollars for surgery. *No insurance*, they cried, aghast, and their interest drained.

• • •

It's colder again today, winter coming with relentless certainty. I'm surprised to realise I'm sad I won't see it. Sadder still that I'll never see another sunset in Chiang Mai. Never taste another of Chanarong's sticky rice rolls. But Mali will live, if I hold on a little longer.

Word must be getting around, several people stand impatiently near the spot where I've set up every day for the past month. Sumalee helps me as the people mill about.

"Father," she whispers, and I put a hand on hers to silence the question I know she will ask.

"For Mali," I say. "All of these people. It's enough."

"But can you . . . ?"

"I have to."

Another bird, then a kitten. An obnoxious boy demands a rhino of his fur- and jewel-clad mother and that tests my skills. I've never constructed one before. A puppy and another bird and the day grows old, the sun sinking low. With each enlivening breath I wither a little more. A subtle fears thrills through me. Not for myself, but for her. That I may not make it.

"Please, father," Sumalee says in Thai as I make another kitten. "Let me. Show me!"

"The gift is not something I know how to share," I say, though she already knows.

"Why's she crying," the new owner of the kitten asks as I put life into it. Hot rakes drag through my soul.

I hand over the mewling clockwork cat and smile as it curls in her palm, paws playfully at her fingers. The woman looks down at the tiny life in her hand, astonished, her concern for my eldest daughter forgotten. She hands me a thick stack of bills and I check, add it to the satchel beneath the table. One more and we'll have enough. Mali will get the operation she needs.

Blackness tickles in at the edge of my vision and I realise I'm not breathing. My heartbeat is a staccato throb in my head. Sumalee's face swims into view, her eyes wide, tears streak her cheeks. I was so close. I feel myself drifting away, as if carried like a dried-out leaf on a gentle stream.

"Father? Father, please." She speaks in Thai again and I see Mali in her eyes, stricken, pale. It halts my descent, so briefly, but for long enough. I can't fail.

I reach out, pull myself up with Sumalee's help, drag air reluctantly into my tired lungs. "One more," I whisper, my voice weaker than I expected.

"But, father, you can't . . . "

"For Mali. I must. Help me." I look up to the next in line, forcing a smile from my numbing lips. "What would you like?" I ask in English, ignoring the subtle slur in my words.

"A tiger, please," the man says, tousling the hair of the young boy grinning at his side.

My eyes hurt, throbbing with my irregular pulse. Sumalee holds onto her tears and assists me, steadying the fine tools, selecting the tiny pieces. I can't see by the end, my vision like smoke.

"It's ready?" I whisper to Sumalee.

"Yes, father."

I have one breath left. I'm sure I do. I must have. Suma holds the miniature tiger to me, I feel the copper coolness of it on my lips. I let my last breath go and feel the tiger twitch and stretch its tiny limbs as I sit back.

Sumalee hands it over, thanks the man for the money. My chest tightens, desperate for air I can't give it. The autumn cool gently caresses my face and I close my eyes against the swirling clouds of my vision.

Sumalee slips her hand into mine and I squeeze with the last of my strength. My body is a lead weight in the tattered deckchair. I feel as though I'm sinking through thick sand. Sumalee clears her throat, my tools rattle.

"My father needs to sleep," she says in perfect English, almost no accent from her schooling here. "I'm afraid that's all for today."

I can hear the tears in her voice. They will live for me now, my wife and *both* my beautiful girls.

"Tomorrow?" I hear Sumalee say as I fade. "I don't know, sir." But she does, of course.

ANVIL OF THE SUN

KAREN MARIC

"Move it, Songbird!" Osman the warden shouted at me, his voice muffled by the thickness of his sun-hood. "Next spot, now."

As I rose from my crouch, I automatically tugged the sleeves of my black robe down over my gloves to shield my weak flesh from the sun. My legs trembled from lack of food. Sweat poured between my tender breasts and over my swollen belly, yet I did my best to hide my discomfort from Osman. To be a model prisoner, obedient and repentant. Because unlike my fellow prisoners I stood a chance of being allowed off our island prison, and I did not intend to ruin that chance by complaining.

The Naked Isle blazed bone-white in the sun. Even with the black gauze of a sun-hood curtaining my eyes, I could scarcely bear to look up at its barren, shimmering outlines. The hunched black shapes of a hundred prisoners dotted the glaring ground. Hard-edged black shadows clung to every pebble and rock. I edged forward over the rubble. Two hundred feet below me, the ocean pounded against the island's white cliffs. Above me, the sky was an enormous blue bowl, so vast it was dizzying.

"Search!" Osman roared.

I sank to my knees again and sifted through the hot pebbles, searching for the pale, fleshy stems of the *liym* cactus. Rocks gouged into my knees. Hot air seared my throat with every breath. My unborn babe's tiny feet pummelled my insides as if in protest at his position, squeezed tight between my breasts and thighs. Yet if

I did not kneel, I could not spot the tiny *liym*. And if I did not find any *liym*, the guards would not let me eat.

I spotted a grey-green stem poking from beneath a boulder. I tore it free of the dust and dropped it into my sack.

Back on the mainland, in the candle-lit, subterranean safety of the Warrens, our Most Esteemed Leader, Potentate Rasif, would be sipping the delicate wine distilled from this cactus. I wondered if he would think of me, his former Songbird and lover, as he sipped it. Would he think of his babe, swelling in my womb while I toiled and sweltered beneath the deadly sun?

I spread one black-gloved palm on my belly and breathed, "Soon, my son." *Obedient. Repentant.* "Soon we'll be home."

Near sunset, the wardens herded me and my fellow prisoners back towards the prison complex. We trudged up the slope. The prison's crooked towers and white, winding walls squatted atop the hill like a jumble of bones, like further proof of the island's barrenness.

I heard the rasp of stone on stone. A thud. Ahead of me, someone had stumbled and fallen. The faintest whisper followed the thud: a word of encouragement, a gift from one prisoner to the fallen.

Osman snarled. "No talking."

His whip cracked through the heated air. It was a monstrous thing, a twelve-foot long strip of leather hung with shards of sharpened steel. It lashed the hooded, sexless form of the fallen prisoner, slicing through the protective layers of black. A scream tore through the hood. A spray of blood.

The faceless prisoner writhed, exposed flesh already blistering, melting, peeling off the bones beneath. Blood sizzled and skittered across the hot stones like oil in a cooking pan.

My breath snagged in my throat. I looked away, my arms instinctively fencing my belly.

I could imagine nothing worse than having my flesh caressed by the deadly, dying sun. I, who have seen so many terrible things . . .

Osman ordered us on, past the burnt prisoner. The screams receded behind us.

Inside the prison, the wardens chained us to the walls, twenty people to a cell. They chained us simply to torment us, I was certain, for there was nowhere to run to on the Naked Isle.

Obedient. Repentant.

Every night after our evening meal came the obligatory hours of singing and confessing. Every night, my voice rang out the sweetest and most fervent, no matter how badly my metal cuffs grated against my ankles and wrists, no matter how badly my back ached as I squatted in chains.

"One day that voice of yours will get you into trouble," my mother used to tease me, years ago when we had both still believed in a future that would be easier than our poverty-stricken past. And it had, because my voice had made me Rasif's.

"Sing for me, little one," Potentate Rasif had ordered me the first time we met.

I remembered the languorous ease with which he lay on his velvet divan. I remembered how, even though he was three times my age, I found him dauntingly beautiful: all long, curled, midnight-black hair and sharply sculpted features. I remembered how, as I rose from my knees to sing, I'd burned with the awareness that our beloved leader looked only at me.

I remembered his hazel eyes blazing like twin suns in the lamp-lit brilliance of his chamber.

That night, I clasped my hands in front of the silver-shot purple and vermilion robe that had cost my father and mother all their savings, and I sang. I used all the techniques my singing teacher had taught me: I used the bell, the rolling water, the warble and the trill. My high young voice reverberated around the cave.

When I finished, I sank to my knees again and pressed my brow to the Potentate's jewelled slippers.

His hand, warm and heavy with rings, stroked my hair.

"From now on you will stay with me, my pretty songbird, and sing for me every day." His beautiful face darkened. "And soon I will plant in your peasant womb the son my noble wives have denied me."

My heart sprinted as I smiled down at his feet. Rasif's Songbird? His lover? My elation was complete.

I was fifteen, a girl from Nadir in the Low Tunnels.

What a child I'd been back then.

• • •

By night in the prison, my fingertips mapped out the contours of the child I cradled in my womb. There were his tiny heels, hard round lumps just beneath my ribs. The bigger lump, down low on the bulge he made within me, his shoulder. The long curve his spine, curled snugly inside me.

Every night I wrapped my arms around my babe and breathed promises. "Soon, my little one," I would say. "Soon we'll be home."

I could no longer count the moons I had been on the Naked Isle. Rasif's soothsayers had said I would give birth in Bright-Fire Month, when the expanding sun was at its hottest. How far away was that?

It did not seem possible my babe could grow any bigger within me. Months of subsisting on nothing but boiled *liym* stems had left me so gaunt I could feel the outline of every bone in my body, much harder and sharper than the shape of my son. Even though the taste and smell of the gelid cactus stems turned my stomach, I licked my bowl clean every night and dabbed up and swallowed all the dusty droplets that had rolled down the side of my bowl and onto the ground.

Soon, I promised myself and my son.

Soon.

• • •

A shadow fell over my eyes, startling me: Osman the warden, rattling his key in the padlock that fastened my chains. I could not even recall falling asleep and yet here it was, daytime again.

A spear of sunlight stabbed through the darkness of the cell to stamp a white circle on the floor. Within that circle a pallid rock-grub writhed, caught unawares by the light and already too weakened to escape it. While I rubbed my thighs to restore circulation after a night spent crouched on my haunches, I watched the grub's movements grow ever slower, while all around me the stiff black shadows of the other prisoners slowly unfolded from the walls.

When I stood, a trickle of fluid spilled down my inner thighs.

I bit back my cry just before it escaped my lips.

No! I told myself and my child.

I clenched my fists.

No.

My babe would not be born here. I would *not* let it happen.

I waited for several sickening heartbeats, squeezing my legs together.

No more liquid escaped. I felt no pains.

I unfurled my fingers.

A false alarm. That was all. Because they'd free me soon: Rasif would not risk his only son dying here.

I wrapped my filthy cloak and hood about me and followed the warden and the prisoners out into the glare, obedient and repentant.

As I passed the grub, I saw that the sun had hardened it into something beautiful: a glassine, blue-black cylinder that glistened with every colour imaginable, like oil on a puddle of water. A prisoner trod on it, but when the booted foot lifted, the grub was still whole. Hard, lifeless, unbreakable.

I smiled.

• • •

Black-sailed ships appeared on the eastern horizon every day, all winging their way across the white-capped sea towards the Naked Isle. After docking, they disgorged more black-clad prisoners from their holds. But these were never common criminals, for the Sacker and his minions in the Warrens dealt with those. No, those sent to the Naked Isle were all political prisoners, like me.

One morning I was searching close to the barren, rocky shore when a new ship moored at the wharf. In the moments when the hold first opened, before the prisoners pulled hoods over their pale, vomit-flecked faces, I saw a man I recognised.

Lord Umair, younger brother of Lord Dayim, one of our Potentate's closest advisors.

Lord Umair's bony face was tight with pain beneath his long black hair. I remembered him as cautious, controlled, always carefully and excruciatingly polite—unlike his reckless older brother, Lord Dayim.

I recalled a night, soon after Rasif had begun his purges, when I had been standing next to our Potentate and Lord Dayim as they and the other nobles dined. Suddenly Rasif had lunged across the table piled high with roast lizards and baked voles, and sliced open Lord Khalil's belly with his meat knife.

I stopped singing. Every note of the song he'd ordered me to sing fled my mind.

Lord Khalil looked down at the wet purple coils filling his hands with an expression of shock and agony so extreme it tore a terrible, hysterical giggle from my lips, a giggle it still shames me to recall. Then I caught a whiff of the rich, faecal stink of his exposed viscera and my diamond and ruby headdress tinkled deafeningly in my ears as I bent and coughed and gagged.

The other nobles sat in terrified, motionless silence. Khalil's shrieks careened off the chamber's stone walls.

Rasif ordered his Yellow Guards to take the traitor Khalil to the Sacker.

Lord Khalil's shrieks intensified into desperate screams.

The yellow-clad guards dragged him out. The double doors slammed, cutting off his cries.

Rasif took a sip of *liym* wine. Firelight flashed off his crystal glass and the blood pooling beneath Khalil's velvet cushion. No one breathed. Above our heads, golden cages spun on chains riveted into the chamber's ceiling. Nightingales, canaries and doves perched silently within.

Rasif shot an irritated glance at the birds. At me. He reached out to fondle my breast with his free hand. I could not move.

"Look at this!" he complained to no one in particular. "My Songbirds have all gone silent. Why aren't they singing, eh? Why?"

Lord Dayim leaned forward and said, "Perhaps because they, like everyone else around you, are too afraid to open their mouths."

For an instant, I cringed, expecting our Potentate to open Lord Dayim's gut too. Instead, Rasif exploded into laughter.

"Too afraid!" he cackled, rocking back and forth as tears of mirth rolled down his cheeks. "Oh, Dayim, you are ever the jester, aren't you?"

When Lord Dayim dared give our leader a small, hateful smile, I thought him the bravest man I'd ever seen.

Later, I thought him braver still, while I had only ever been able to disappoint him.

I wondered if my refusal to help Lord Dayim when he'd first asked had led to Umair's banishment here now.

Of course it had, I told myself. Passivity is the twin of compliance. Wasn't that what Lord Dayim had warned me?

• • •

Every day there were more black ships. More prisoners.

The prison started to become crowded. At times, I overheard Osman and the other wardens cursing about the rapid influx of fresh meat. Sometimes at night, the new prisoners sung the songs of praise with such jeering savagery the only sweet notes I could hear came from me. Not even the wardens' whips could bring respect to their tones.

Obedient, repentant, I reminded myself, though my blood surged along with my fellow prisoners' harsh voices and I cringed at the black looks they shot me every time I added a trill or warble to my song.

One night a group of prisoners spilled forward, howling and shrieking, when the wardens moved to chain us in our cell. The wardens began slamming their iron truncheons into shoulders, knees and skulls. My babe kicked at my ribs, alarmed by the screams and shouts.

Still unchained, I dared to use the cover of the chaos to creep nearer to Lord Umair.

He was in chains in a corner, his black hair matted with sweat and oil. His dark eyes looked impossibly sad as he watched the prisoners attempt an uprising.

"My Lord Umair," I breathed. "Wh-why are you here?"

He looked sideways at me. "Does Rasif need a reason, Khidamun?" he said softly. "Why are *you* here?"

I shrugged, my bony shoulders stiff with pain, my eyes burning with unshed tears. "I don't know. The Yellow Guards bundled me onto a ship one night . . . " There they'd beaten me until I passed out, but I did not want to go into that. "I woke up here."

Lord Umair's gaze fell to my belly. He winced as if the sight of my belly hurt him, and then he grinned tightly and tried for a jesting tone, although he didn't carry it off with as much aplomb as his brother would have. "Well, rest assured everyone in the Warrens will know why we're here, little Khidamun. Our Esteemed Leader will have our crimes printed on a thousand posters and cried out by a hundred criers. *I* heard you were banished because the Great One had caught you in bed with your childhood sweetheart, Eijaz. *After* you became his Songbird. I heard that's why he had Eijaz drowned."

"Wh—" I was reeling. My lips and tongue had forgotten how to shape words. I swallowed. Tried again. "Th-that's not true. Eijaz . . . Eijaz never touched me. Not even when I begged him to. We . . . we grew up together, we were promised to each other when we were ten, but he always said we'd just have to wait till we were wed. But then Rasif—" I stopped.

We fell silent, twitching at every thunk and scream around us.

Finally, I said, "Rasif told me Eijaz had to be drowned because he was involved in an assassination plot. A plot to kill Rasif. He showed me a letter written by Eijaz—"

"A forgery," Umair said.

"I know that *now*." I touched my belly. "But back then . . . I was so scared I didn't know what to think."

I'd already been with child on the day I'd watched Eijaz die. On that day, Rasif had led me ahead of the nobles to the Sacker's vast, torch-lit cave beside the Sinkhole. All my life I'd heard tales of the place and the executioner who worked there; that was the first time I'd seen it. Massive and menacing, the Sacker stood in the centre of the cave. His grin bared yellow-brown teeth set in a long, ghost-pale face. Neat piles of folded sacks and coils of rope filled the shelves that lined one wall. Manacles dangled from the opposite wall. At the back of the cave, behind a long grille of iron bars, a wooden platform extended over the abyss of the Sinkhole. From behind the safety of the iron bars, raised viewing benches looked out over the platform and into the black void beyond.

I was wearing my finest gossamer and gold thread robes that day. I remember that, too. Rasif had ordered me to wear them. To mark the occasion, he'd said.

The day of Eijaz's death had also been the day I turned sixteen.

I watched the Sacker bundle Eijaz's bruised and bloodied form into the sack. Aware of Rasif's eyes on me, I fought to keep my face blank. The sobs and screams I dared not release made cramps tear through the muscles of my chest and back. Terrible, liquid gurgles churned my bowels. I clenched my buttocks for fear I'd empty myself.

Eijaz looked up at me once, just before the Sacker tied the sack above his head. His beautiful, bleeding lips parted in a trembling attempt at a smile. I did not smile back. To this day, I hated myself for that.

The Sacker dragged Eijaz across the platform and rolled him off. There were some faraway splashes, and then silence.

Eijaz was gone, drowned in the bottomless black waters of the Sinkhole.

Alone, sick with shame and horror and grief, I returned to my opulent bedchamber. The moment I shut the door, a silk-clad figure slid out from behind my bed-curtains.

Lord Dayim.

"If he discovers you here," I said, my voice so thick with anguish it was a stranger's, "he will kill us both."

Lord Dayim stepped towards me, his dark eyes burning with intensity. His palms were spread wide. Pleading. "Khidamun, we need your help."

Weeping, I shook my head. I knew who he meant by "we'. Rasif had whispered of them to me: those enemies that wanted to destroy the man who'd been born to rule them. Those fools that believed a council of the wise from tunnels high and low should rule us.

"No."

"But you are the only one who sees him alone these days. He suspects everyone—except you. His Yellow Guards search us all before we see him. We cannot—" He paused, tried a new, softer tack. "Understand, Khidamun, we would not ask you to do anything yourself. We simply want you to tell us his routines, his vulnerabilities, so that we might—"

I squeezed my wet eyes shut and clapped my hands over my ears. Lord Dayim caught my wrists and tugged my arms down to my sides.

"Khidamun, he's murdering innocents by the thousands. He killed Eijaz today simply because he knows you and Eijaz loved each other. *You* could be his next victim. Doesn't that make you want to stop him?"

I pictured Eijaz's beautiful, bundled body plummeting into the Sinkhole, and my legs gave out beneath me. With my brow pressed against the cold floor, I whispered, "My lord . . . I'm sorry . . . I can't."

I heard him sigh and curse softly. His footsteps retreated to the door.

Osman's furious shout tore me from my reverie:

"Everyone back against the walls! Now! Or tomorrow I'll have you all stripped and watch you fry in the sun!"

Bruised, sullen and seething, the prisoners in front of me began backing up.

In the seconds I had left before the wardens reached me, I blurted to Lord Umair the one question I scarcely dared to ask.

"My parents . . . Are they still exiled in Nadir, or—?"

He stared at me, appalled. "You don't know?"

I heard a whip crack near my head, but I could not seem to move. "*Know what?*"

"Khidamun . . . they're all dead. Even your brother, Yaghoub. Rasif had the Sacker kill them all. He said they were aiding you and Eijaz in your secret lovers' trysts. The trysts in which Eijaz planted the babe you carry now."

I could not take his words in. Stunned, I grasped my belly in both hands. "But my babe is not Eijaz's. He is Rasif's. Rasif knows that."

Then the wardens were upon me and hauling me away from Umair, and the sense of foreboding that fell over me swept all coherent thought from my mind . . .

• • •

When the pains started the following day, I knew full well what they signified. Yet I refused to admit it even to myself. All morning I worked on my hands and knees in the heat and light, sweat pouring down my brow and dripping from my eyelashes while agony tightened like a vice about my lower body.

Eventually, I could no longer kneel.

I staggered upright, biting back a scream.

Osman's hateful voice bounced off the rocks. "Back on your knees, Songbird."

Please, not yet, I begged my child.

I tried to kneel.

Pain pierced my lower spine like a sword-blade.

I shrieked. Straightened up again.

Pebbles rattled behind me as Osman stalked over. "You keen for a whipping today, Songbird?"

"Please." I reached one gloved hand out, stopping just short of his black-swathed arm. "I need help. The child is coming. Rasif's child."

I could not see his features behind his black hood. He faced me for an instant, then turned and walked away, back to his fellow wardens.

"Move the others on," I heard him say. "And leave her here. Potentate's orders. We're to come back for her tomorrow."

Potentate's orders.

The wardens' whips whistled out, herding the other prisoners on. Some of the prisoners risked looking back at me, their stiff frames radiating their unease, yet there was nothing they could do.

They stumbled over the hillock and out of sight, leaving me alone in the endless white glare.

The light was a scream made visible.

I gave birth alone, squatting on the hard ground, my shrieks echoing off the uncaring rocks. There was no shade. Even in the depths of my agony, I managed to stay lucid enough to keep my robes down over my legs so the light would not strike my child.

Potentate's orders.

My son slithered out of me in a warm, wet rush, onto the rocky ground.

I waited without drawing breath for a cry that did not come.

My throat tight, I leaned forward, curling my aching body to shade him. With my lungs burning for air I dared not breathe, I lifted the hem of my black robes.

He made a mewling sound. I sobbed and laughed all at once.

He was tiny. Perfect. Black-haired like his father, long-fingered like me. Hands trembling, I unfastened the front of my robe and carefully, carefully lifted his floppy body to my breast, making sure the sunlight did not strike him.

He sniffed without interest at my nipple. He would not suckle.

I murmured encouragements to him, stroked his squashed, blood-streaked head, kissed his brow where the black hair was plastered to his soft skull. Still, he would not suckle.

Were all newborns this small, I wondered queasily? This pale and mottled?

I held him to my breast. He stayed there, still and seemingly content, and did not make another sound. I told him I loved him, that I would love him forever.

He slipped so quietly and easily into death it was as if he had never truly lived.

When I realised his tiny heart no longer beat alongside mine, I lunged to my feet and screamed. I shook him, I breathed between his lips, I laid my head against his chest to listen—to will into existence—a heartbeat that was not there.

An abyss opened inside me. I clutched my child to my breast and shrieked and railed against Rasif until my prized voice became a rasp. I tore off my clothes: hood, gloves, robe, cloak, boots. I wrapped my son's perfect body in my black cloak, shielding him from the sun, while I let its ferocious heat lash and bubble across my skin.

Mad with grief and despair, I ran naked across the hot white rocks, burning, burning, courting death with the ardour of the damned . . .

Sunset was suddenly dusk. The fire in the sky was extinguished.

The sudden drop in temperature stilled my jerking limbs. I stood naked on the rocks, panting, shuddering, the night air like ice on my burnt skin.

I lived. I did not know how it was possible, but I lived. The sun's touch had not destroyed me—it had burnt away my frenzy. I welcomed the ashen numbness it left behind.

Alone in the Naked Isle's night, I crawled back to my son and dragged my robe and hood over my head. I lay on the rocks clutching my son's cooling body in my blistered arms, my sun-seared mind filled with the same stark clarity as the stars that shone so far above us.

Lord Dayim had tried to warn me of the price of refusing to act. Passivity is the twin of compliance, he'd said. But at the time, I had been so terrified I'd thought the only way to stay alive was to obey.

Such a foolish child I'd been.

As dawn bled across the sky, Osman and two other wardens walked across the rose-coloured rocks towards me. I did not try to flee. I imagined myself just another outcrop on the Naked Isle. Hard. Lifeless. Vitrified by the sun.

Osman tore my baby from my arms and strode forward to fling his tiny body over the cliff. I watched my child topple through the flaming sky, my heart its own fire in my breast, but I did not protest.

Potentate's orders.

I could still feign obedience. If I could survive the remainder of my time on the Naked Isle, perhaps I would see Rasif again.

If I did, I would do what I should have done the day Lord Dayim had asked me to help. I'd kill him.

Osman stood over me, his hands on his black-clad hips. "Ready to get back to work, Songbird?"

I stood, my burnt skin crackling and weeping beneath my robes, and I nodded.

"Good girl."

I followed him back to the other prisoners. Their hooded, featureless faces swung towards me and away. We searched on.

In the blank white moments that made up the days following my son's death, I pored tirelessly over the island's sunbaked surface. Sometimes as I worked my gloves slipped down, exposing a fragment of wrist and hand. Though my burnt flesh grew dark and mottled, I felt no physical pain. Only a welcome, crackling numbness.

I watched tiny fissures spread and widen across my charred skin. I thought of the rock-grub I had seen. How the sunlight had transformed it, stolen all weakness from its flesh.

For a time, my breasts throbbed and wet the front of my robe with milk that nurtured only my dreams of revenge. Then my milk also dried up, leaving me to mourn anew at that final passing of my child's transformation of my body.

I exposed my hands and wrists to the sun whenever the guards were not looking. Soon Osman ordered me to keep my hood and gloves on even in the cell. My blistered form, he said, was so ugly that not even the prisoners should be forced to look upon it. I did not protest.

One night, stalked by sleeplessness and terrible, tactile memories of a tiny body pressed against my breasts, I dug my fingernails into one of the fissures in my palm and tugged. As a child I'd done the same to the scabs on my knees until the blood ran freely again. This time, the skin on my palm broke off and transformed to dust in my fingers.

Beneath the dust, blackness glinted. There was no longer any blood.

In the glaring white light of day, I picked continuously at my burnt skin. Beneath my questing nails, my flesh fell away with faint crumbling sounds, and the hot wind snatched up its powdery ochre remains.

Underneath was blackness. Hardness. A substance as beautiful and shiny as the carapace of the rock-grub I'd seen transformed by the sun.

Our people wish on the moon, my old singing teacher had once told me, *but the sun has a power of its own, as do grief and love.* She'd told me that before teaching me *The Ballad of Mad Maysoon,* a difficult song, full of rolling water and bells. The song told the tale of a woman, Maysoon, whose beloved had been unjustly sentenced to death. In the days before the Sacker, criminals like Maysoon's man were tied up above ground and left to perish in the sun. Afterwards Maysoon had retrieved her beloved's blackened body. Like a statue he was, perfect black glass. Yet ever after, Maysoon had kept him with her—and in her cackling madness, she claimed that he lived still, that when alone with her in her chamber he could move and speak and even enter her . . .

I knew now that I had not died the day I'd run naked in the sun, because I'd needed its power to transform me. I needed to avenge the deaths of Eijaz, my family. My son. Of all the innocents.

When the guards were out of eyesight and earshot, I rasped my vitrified fingers across the rocks, sharpening them.

In the deadly sunlight, my blackened fingertips glistened like murderous jewels.

• • •

At night in my cell I listened to the prisoners packed around me plan their escapes. There were not enough manacles to chain everyone to the walls. The floors were covered with farting, snoring, fucking, fighting prisoners, and myriad plots were being hatched beneath the snores and grunts and groans.

Osman thought me broken. He never chained me now.

One night I crawled to Umair and touched him on the shoulder.

"Khidamun?" He sounded surprised.

"We should kill the wardens," I whispered to him and the prisoners he murmured with, "and wait for the next ship to come. If we can take it, we can sail it to the Warrens. There, your brother can help me get inside Rasif's chamber, and then—"

"We have no proper weapons," a young woman muttered. "Only rocks and—"

I tugged the glove from my right hand.

Starlight gleamed blue along my razor-sharp fingertips.

"*I* will be your weapon—" I said.

As one, the prisoners recoiled, and my lips peeled back from my teeth in a savage smile.

"—but Osman and Rasif are mine."

• • •

I killed Osman in front of the other prisoners in my work-squad by plunging my fingertips straight up into his throat. He stood for a moment teetering, coughing, spluttering, eyes wide with astonishment, before dropping to the barren white ground, dead.

Except for the howling of the wind, there was silence.

Then the voices of hundreds of prisoners screaming: "Khidamun! Khidamun!"

• • •

Armed with rocks and the desperate savagery of the condemned, we smashed through the remaining guards and swarmed aboard the next ship to dock at the Naked Isle.

"Fail to take us back to the mainland and I'll send you on a fast trip to the seabed with iron chains for company," Umair said to the captain and crew once we'd surrounded them.

Grim-faced, the captain bowed in surrender.

"Hold the surviving guards," Umair called down to the prisoners still on the island. "Don't let them sound the alarm. Fate willing, we'll return with more boats soon. And then we shall all be freed!"

As our ship skimmed away from the island, the prisoners screamed out both Umair's name and mine.

We moored the ship in a torch-lit cave that marked a smuggler's entrance into the Warrens.

Lord Umair led me and our forty fellow escapees through abandoned tunnels to his brother's chambers.

After Umair told him our plan, Lord Dayim turned to me. "Are you sure you are ready for this, Khidamun?"

In the dimness, I could scarcely make out his worn, bony face: my eyes were still accustomed to the Naked Isle's glare. But I could hear a great excitement tempering the concern in his tone.

"I am ready," I said.

"Then I will bring you to him as a prisoner, tell him you came here to me speaking of treachery, that the loss of your child has driven you mad . . . The rest is up to you."

I let him arrange the unlocked shackles about my wrists.

Outside Rasif's private chambers, Lord Dayim gestured at the pair of Yellow Guards on either side of the great, iron-bossed doors. The two guards shoved the doors open.

I stepped inside, my black robe snagging against my peeling legs.

"Here is the traitor Khidamun, Great One," Dayim said.

Rasif's black gaze skidded over my hooded face, my flat belly. He'd aged in the six moons since I'd last seen him. Deep lines inscribed his cheeks and brow. His hands shook. His eyelids shivered. He looked mad, surrounded by quaking nobles who seemed as unhinged as him.

Lord Dayim said, "She will confess to you alone, she says."

I could sense Dayim's tension. He feared Rasif would not allow this. But I knew it would shame our Esteemed Leader to admit to any fear of a broken girl-woman, hooded, shackled, and burnt.

Rasif ordered everyone to leave us. Dayim and the nobles exited. The four Yellow Guards did not.

"All of you," Rasif rasped.

If he'd said anything of the child we'd made together, I might have faltered or even frozen. But to Rasif, that life apparently meant as little as the countless other lives he'd taken, for he said nothing. Instead, the moment we were alone, he murmured, "I have missed your voice, little Songbird. Sing for me one last time, and I may show you some mercy."

I stepped towards him, head bowed, my sharpened fingers clasped in front of me and hidden by my sleeves.

"No," I said. "*You* sing."

And I drove my fingertips into the soft flesh beneath his ribs. His scream rose, higher and higher, a perfect warble.

• • •

Afterwards, Lord Dayim held me and patted me on Rasif's blood-spattered divan while I retched and sobbed and wailed. From the tunnels outside came the clangs and screams of Dayim's supporters overwhelming the last of the Yellow Guards.

I wept because, while I wanted to join my child in the Afterlife now Rasif was gone, I knew that it was not yet time for me to die.

First, there were prisoners to be freed. Wrongs to be righted. And perhaps someday, in a far-off future that was at this point as difficult to perceive as a face behind a veil, perhaps another babe to be loved.

• • • • • • • • • • •

TORCH SONG

ANDREW J. McKIERNAN

"That's him," Dee whispered in his ear between tunes. "That's the mook who slugged me, Joey."

Joe took a sip of whiskey, placed the glass back on the piano lid and looked to the bar's entrance. Through the blue haze of smoke he could see a guy checking his hat and coat. Young and suave. Dressed in a sharp suit, with a pencil-thin moustache. Hair slicked back and a cigarette tucked behind his ear. Joe didn't like the look of him at all.

The guy took a seat at the bar and ordered a drink. Pulled the cigarette from behind his ear and lit it. Blew smoke in the direction of the girl seated on the stool beside him. What a schmuck. Why did Dee always go for men like that? Joe's fingers twitched across the piano keys, aching to make fists and plant them on the guy's mug, smash his nose, make him bleed.

"Play me a song, Joey," Dee whispered again, her breath tickling the soft hairs on his neck. Like whiskey fumes, a little of his aggravation evaporated. How could he remain angry with her? That silky voice in his ear. Long lashes fluttering against his cheek. Still, he felt a need to make things right. To protect Dee from everyone and everything that did her wrong.

Tonight, he told himself. Tonight he would do something about it.

With newfound calm, Joe closed his eyes and played the opening bars of "Someone to Watch Over Me'. It wasn't long before Dee joined in, her voice filling him with the honeyed sweetness of unrequited desire.

• • •

Not long after he'd returned from the Pacific in '45, Joe stumbled into the Peacock Bar & Grill. Apart from killing Japs and patching up members of his platoon, playing piano was the only thing he knew how to do well. In Manila, between raging street battles and to the sound of low-strafing Zeroes, he tickled the ivories of an old upright liberated from a burnt-out church by some overly-enthusiastic GIs. The constant bombing had knocked the piano badly out of tune, but the men didn't seem to mind. They cheered and clapped and sung along to every song he played. Rewarded him with free beer whenever it could be smuggled in. A bright patch in the otherwise blood-and-scream-soaked years of the war.

Returning to New York had been something of a double-edged sword. Familiar sounds, familiar smells, a language he could understand. But all his friends were dead, or married, or moved out to the Midwest to try their hand at the lonesome art of farming. He wallowed in doubt and self-pity for the first month. Waking each night in a cold sweat, haunted by the faces of Japanese soldiers. Drinking away his discharge payment in a fruitless attempt to keep them at bay. Then, one night, he found himself drinking at the Peacock Bar & Grill. Walked up to the empty piano and rattled off a few tunes. Before he knew it, they offered him a job.

For six months he played solo, running through a repertoire of jazz standards seven nights a week. Making just enough money, after tips, to keep up the rent on his apartment. Invisible to the crowd. Solo and solitary.

Joe told himself that's how he liked it. That was until one afternoon, about an hour before opening, when Dee walked through the door.

• • •

Joe moved through a series of Cole Porter tunes and then onto Ellington's "In A Sentimental Mood'. His fingers danced across the keys. Caressed them. Coaxed the notes into something more than just a series of tones. They became an outward manifestation of the things he could never have put in words: his wants, his desires, his passions. And through it all, Dee's voice moved in him, filling the spaces the piano could not touch.

He remembered her walking into the bar. All red hair and swaying hips. Wide eyes and pouting lips. Cuter than a bug's ear. He'd stopped playing, stubbed out his cigarette and watched as she made her way to the man cleaning glasses behind the bar.

"I'm here for the job," she said.

"What job?"

"The one you're going to give me." Simple as that, and she stared the barman down until he smiled and shrugged.

"Sorry, we don't need no waitresses."

"I'm not here to serve drinks. I sing. Better than anyone you ever heard."

The barman looked up at Joe and nodded, impressed with her sass.

Joe ran his fingers across the keys, a simple scalar run he used to loosen up, and settled into the Gershwins' "Oh, Lady Be Good'. And good she most certainly was.

Dee's full lips parted and from between them emerged beauty in the form of song. Joe felt something tighten in his chest, an exquisite pain that would return to him each time she sang. Every word was soulful, heartfelt. She sounded exactly like the baddest of gals who desperately wanted to be good, and Joe believed it. Bought it hook, line and sinker.

The barman must have believed it too, because he nodded for them to continue. Joe segued into "I Fall in Love Too Easily'. It wasn't until he looked up, saw Dee watching him as she sang, that he realised how much his song choice revealed his feelings.

For the next two years, Dee sang accompaniment to Joe's piano at the Peacock Bar & Grill. Her voice and looks and feisty manner attracted the clients and she seduced, or was seduced by, many of them. All the while Joe played on, watching her bounce from man to man, totally smitten, his own affections ignored, wishing he could take her away from it all.

• • •

When the set finished, Joe looked up to see the man with the slicked hair and pencil-thin moustache retrieving his coat from the cloakroom. Joe closed the piano lid, swallowed the last of his whiskey, and excused himself to the dwindling late night crowd.

He grabbed his own coat, checked the pocket for his army issue .45 and followed the man into the night.

There were few cars on the street. Even less people. The smart-dressed man walked slowly, half a block ahead, weaving slightly with drunkenness. It didn't take Joe long to catch up, hand in his pocket, fingers stroking the handle of the Colt M1911A1 in much the same he caressed the piano keys. The way he yearned to caress Dee.

He waited until the man stepped out of the streetlight. Ran the last few yards to catch him just outside the entrance of a dark alley. Barrelled into him from behind. Heard a yelp of surprise and the breath leap from the man's lungs as he staggered, fell. Before the man could react, Joe seized him by the collar. Dragged him deeper into the alley. Kicked out and planted the toe of his shoe in the man's gut to keep him down. He took the .45 from his pocket and pointed it at the man's head.

"Scum!" he shouted. "You hurt Dee. Used her to get what you wanted. Beat her when you could get no more and then left her for dead."

The man looked up. In the pale light seeping into the alley from the street he looked scared, confused.

"I don't know what—"

"Scum! No more. No one's gonna hurt Dee no more."

"I don't know no Dee," the man said between gasps and sobs. "Please I never hurt no one."

"Yes, you did," Joe said, suddenly calm and unforgiving. Watching this slime grovel. Feeling the power he had over the man at his feet. The power in the cold steel he held in his hand. "The singer at the Peacock. She's a sweet gal and people like you take advantage. But it ain't gonna happen no more. I'm takin' a stand against low-lives like you."

"What? There ain't been no singer at the Peacock for years," the man said and, before he could say any more, Joe pulled the trigger.

• • •

Joe took a sip of whiskey and lit a cigarette. He started his set with Cole Porter's "I've Got You Under My Skin". As the night's crowd filled the Peacock, he moved to "There Will Never Be Another You" and then "You Stepped Out of a Dream".

The bar's clients ignored him. Drank their drinks and chatted amongst themselves. He watched as he played. Saw a man enter the bar alone. A man going to fat. Expensive suit too tight around his waist, lit cigar hanging from his mouth, sleazy eyes scanning the women at the bar.

"That's him," Dee whispered in his ear. "That's the mook who slugged me, Joey."

· · · · · · · · · · ·

JIMMY DEAN, JIMMY DEAN

ANGELA SLATTER

There's something weird about James Dean.

Apart from the fact he's dead.

This should mean he isn't moving.

But he is.

It's that woman's fault.

She started in a costume department—Lord knows how, she couldn't sew—but she was good at finding lost things, making luck happen. Next the B-girls were paying to get the crooked finger pointed at rivals, so their ankles broke or their diet pills went terribly wrong. She got invited to one party, then another. Soon, rich matrons became *patrons*, needing fortunes told. Then their studio boss husbands wanted opposing producers and backers hexed, things sent awry on sets, seamstresses finishing late-night cinches gone up in smoke from the L & Ms in their sleepy hands.

Money's thrown at her like candy, and she's doing horse like it's candy, too, to bring on the trances. Mickey Cohen, in spite of his Federal rest and respite program, set her up in a fine pink stucco Beverley Hills house. What gangster wouldn't want a woman like that beholden to him?

The studios she's working for got her on a steady income and flow of presents. Other studios, they're sending gifts, too. Hats, gloves, coats made of fur; necklaces and earrings royal as all get out; Chanel suits, Balenciaga dresses, Vivier shoes; scarves and handbags and shiny, shiny things.

Next, it's the boys, those who catch her eye. The pretty ones from the studio lots, the ones who might be something special one day, and the not-so-pretty ones who do stunts and still got some bounce in 'em. Even the Accounts clerks, the ones so homely you think no one else would look at 'em, just like my Tony.

Everything handed to her on a plate, all because she can pull some hocus-pocus.

And here's me, working my ass off, the only girl publicist in this mean old town. What do I get? Bupkis, that's what.

I haven't written a press release in months. I'm just the messenger, handing over votive offerings, rolls of cash, everything and anything you can imagine in return for a wide, white smile in a high yaller face. One day, turns out I'm a pimp too; I have to deliver Tony. There's no hesitation, no *Sorry, baby, I don't wanna do this*. There's only hot anticipation behind his coke bottle glasses, eyes sparkling like they never have for me, not even when I let him . . .

But then I got bigger things to worry about.

See, Mr Dean loves racing, can't get enough. More speed and more. That rod, it's silver and faster than anything else—except maybe a 1950 Ford Custom coupe. So, there's the star, not breathing and the studios with movies unmade and contracts broken.

Contracts they want *un*broken.

What won't they give the woman who can fix *that*? That's how I ended up with twenty kilos of heroin in my trunk, the finest golden brown money can buy, and promises of more and more and more. I sweat the whole trip, sure I'll get pulled over.

A day later, Jimmy Dean's back on set, looking Lana Turner up and down, being fed nothing but gruel by a minder, saying his lines a little stiff and moving the same, but hey it's Jimmy Dean, right? Box office gold.

Next thing, I have to pick up Tony, because she's bored with him. I take him, all glassy-eyed and wrung out, to his place (which smells like dust). My little numbers man, only now he's got new loves, the woman and the needle, and he whimpers and whispers, asking if I think she'll take him back? If she'll let him come *home* and sleep in her arms. That little chip of diamond on my left hand didn't weigh enough to hold memories of us in place.

So, one evening I go shopping. I find the man in a dive joint. He tells me how pure this sugar is, and I tell him, straight out, that

I'm not looking for quality. I'm looking to fix a pest problem. He stares, then gives me what I need. "Anybody asks," he says, "I ain't never seen you. You ain't never seen me."

I drop in at Tony's, parcelling a hit for my honey, watch him go down, down the long tunnel and not come out. Then I head over to the pink palace, those Enid Collins purses I souvenired last week still in my trunk.

"Evening, ma'am, a few new things for you."

She's swaying, singing under her breath, riding the golden brown. Just a pinch more. "And there's *this*, something special as a thank you for Mr Dean."

I wait a little while, watching as she ties her arm tight so the veins stand to attention, before letting myself out that flamingo-coloured door and driving home.

And I wonder what happens to all the spells she's got in place, once the spider's gone from the web.

Next day I'm watching Mr Dean led out on the set and I see right away that something's different, even more different than a walking dead guy should be.

And now Jimmy Dean, Jimmy Dean, he looks like a dog off the leash, like there's nothing holding him in check.

Oh, yeah, there's something weird about James Dean, as he lurches towards Lana Turner, determined and not in a good way.

•••••••••••

A SMALL BAD THING

PENELOPE LOVE

The Toyol was small and sly and meant no harm. He was not one of the *hantu raya*, the great ghosts. He was a petty thief who liked to steal coins and sweets. He could be scared away by mirrors, for he hated his own reflection. He could be distracted by a shiny scattering of dry beans.

He spied on the couple when they visited his apartment that night. He ran through the wall cavity, looking out through cracks in the plaster as they moved from the front door through the kitchen to the living room and then the bedroom. There he clung to the apartment's timber frame, inside the plaster, beside the long crack in the bedroom wall.

They were not like the folk he knew. They were big and pale. Their hair was wispy. They wore shoes indoors. They clattered on the tiled floors. They filled the space with the sound of unknown words.

The man was wide and tall. When he was excited he expanded to take up room. His shoulders broadened and he flailed his arms. He even breathed himself bigger, throwing out his chest.

The woman was thin, freckled, bony and intense.

"This place is not as old as I thought. It's the weather that makes it shabby," the woman said to the peeling paint and sagging plaster. "This horrible humidity." She stood with her back to the air-conditioning, her arms clamped to her sides.

"I like it," the man said. "These rooms are the largest we've seen. It's got character and it's cheap."

"Why is it cheap?" the woman asked. "The air-con cuts out at night? The elevator breaks?"

"I'm sure it only needs a lick of paint," the man said

"I don't like it," the woman said to the geckos crawling along the window frame.

The man drew a breath so deep that his head heaved up and down between his shoulders. He let out a long, slow hiss. "We must have looked at twenty places. You didn't like the last one because it was soulless and modern." His voice rose with every sentence. "This is old for Kuala Lumpur. Now you say you don't like this one either. I don't have time. I have to work. What do you want?"

"I don't know." The woman shrugged, not meeting his eye. She grimaced with distaste at the long crack in the bedroom wall. The Toyol quickly ducked out of sight.

"Will you just make up your mind!" the man shouted.

Shouting? The Toyol was so interested that he peeped through the crack again. He watched as the man stomped out before the woman could answer.

"I didn't want to come here," the woman said, low and sullen to the man's broad back. Her eyes sparked. She followed him slowly, with one last backwards look of disgust.

After they left, the Toyol mouthed their unknown words. "What do you want," he said, experimentally. "I didn't want," he replied. The words were not Malay or Hindi or Hokkein. They sat strangely between his sharp teeth.

The Toyol was small and grey. A *bomoh* had made him from a stillborn baby. His master had given him a cup of milk, morning and night, and an urn to live in. In return, the Toyol had stolen money for him. He was born of old, dark jungle gods of blood and vengeance.

When his master died old and alone in this apartment, no one came to claim the Toyol by giving him a cup of milk or to speak the words that released him. The Toyol was glad to be forgotten. Worse than anything he feared being trapped in his urn and thrown into the ocean, where slowly, slowly the waves would wash him away. The Toyol hated the sea worse than his own reflection. He shuddered at the thought of seeping into nothing.

Night after night and day after day he crouched on one of

the mould-furred windows of the tenantless rooms. He gazed at the lights of the city with red, wondering eyes and twitched his pointed ears at street noises, cars, motorbikes, music and hawkers' cries. The Petronas twin towers of metal and glass gleamed in the distance. He misunderstood their size. He thought they were baubles he could steal if he could only get outside. He watched and waited and dreamed of all the sweets and coins and shiny things he could not reach.

He had seen people come and go from these rooms before, but nothing ever came of these visits. Soon, he forgot that the pale people had come.

The Toyol was curled up in the wall cavity late one rainy day when the apartment door burst open and men hauled furniture into the kitchen. Men piled boxes and filled the rooms with scrapes and shouts. The Toyol peered out through the cracks. Sound and movement and shiny things, so many shiny things. He was beside himself with excitement.

"I thought you said the place would be replastered and repainted before we moved," the woman muttered as she walked in. Rain rattled against the windows.

"Yes but you know KL. Things get done in their own time," the man said.

The woman glared at the crack in the bedroom wall. "Don't think that I'm going to sleep with a dirty great draught at my back," she said.

"Hello sir, hello madam," there was a clap of hands at the door. A plump, middle-aged man stepped in. "Allow me to introduce myself. I am Mr Durajaya, your neighbour from downstairs. Welcome sir, welcome madam, to our happy home."

The men heartily shook hands. "I'm Andy. This is Meg."

"It is so wonderful to get new neighbours," Mr Durajaya beamed. "This place has been empty for too long."

"Why is that?" Meg spoke too sharply. The frail scaffolding of male camaraderie shuddered uneasily.

Andy scowled at her. Mr Durajaya hunched backwards with a nervous laugh, raising his hands. "No reason, no reason," he said. "What is the trouble?"

"There is a crack in the bedroom wall," Meg said with deep resentment.

"Let me have a look," Mr Durajaya bustled inside. He took in the problem at a glance. "A little plaster and paint and all will go well," he assured her.

"Let me do a quick fix for now," Andy shoved the headboard of the bed sideways with one big hand. "Ta-da," he said as the headboard covered almost the entire crack.

"Very good, very good sir, ha, ha, ha," Mr Durajaya applauded.

Aggrieved that his view was blocked just as it finally got interesting, the Toyol climbed out to peer over the headboard. His eyes met Meg's. She screeched. "What's that?"

The Toyol ran for cover, back into the crack and between the concrete wall and the plaster frame.

"I didn't see anything," Andy said.

"It was big as a rat," Meg said.

"Perhaps it was a rat," Andy suggested.

"Ugh. I should have known there would be rats in this horrible place." Meg whirled to confront their neighbour. "Mr Durajaya—" she stopped, disconcerted.

Mr Durajaya was in full retreat. He had taken out his wallet and was clutching it tight.

"I thought you said you liked this apartment," Andy said to Meg, with a quick gesture at Mr Durajaya and their audience of removalists.

Meg didn't take the hint. "I said I might like it if it was cleaned up a bit," she snapped back.

"You have to expect rats in KL," Andy said. "So much street food."

"So much *ghee* you mean. God I hate the stuff. It smells like popcorn gone off."

"Not one rat have I seen in this apartment building the whole time I have lived here," Mr Durajaya assured them both, and fled.

"Did he think we were going to mug him?" Meg asked.

"Perhaps he really doesn't like rats," Andy suggested.

Once safely downstairs, Mr Durajaya felt a twinge of remorse. "I can't tell them. They won't believe me," he told his wife, who was as plump as himself. His two glittering, bewildering, teenage daughters laughed over their phones on their way out.

Meg spent the evening cleaning. She scoured and mopped and dried with savage, compressed force. A horrible musty smell lay all over the place that she was determined to scrub out. Why had she said she hated *ghee*, she asked herself. Was it just to offend Mr Durajaya? She liked it, really. *Ghee* filled the food courts of the malls with the happy movie scent of hot butter. Once, she could be kind when she chose. Now, every time she opened her mouth something unpleasant spewed out.

It hadn't been like this before. Singapore had been fun. Brussels was great. She liked the expat lifestyle. She did. She had. There had been a long wearing down on her reserves until all at once, she could not cope. She said stupid things and alienated Andy's friends. Andy tried, he really tried, but he didn't understand.

She and KL had somehow not hit it off. The city felt too big, in a way which had nothing to do with its actual size. She could never orientate herself within it. She felt lost in a maze of glaring, intense heat, and humidity so high it made her eyeballs sweat, even when the rain pounded the pavement with brute, tropic fists. The city wouldn't slow down and it played by its rules, not hers, yet she felt she could be happy here if she could only seize the chance. She loved shopping, for a start. She loved the vibrancy, the colour, the chaotic traffic, the hordes of motor scooters, the dense crowds strolling, eating and chatting in the streets. She felt as if somewhere within this labyrinth of sweating concrete a warm heart beat, but she kept missing it.

She closed her eyes and drew a deep breath. She should treat this apartment as a fresh start. Things would be different, if she wasn't so angry. But it was no use to think on that. She got it from her mum; her mother was an angry woman. Always had been. Anything bad that had happened to her mum had been Meg's fault; she'd been locked in her room for hours without end. Now, her mind moved in circles when she was left alone. Only anger cleared her head.

She filled the crack behind the headboard with several tubes of builder's putty. The putty dried and shrank swiftly, leaving a large gap.

That night, the Toyol had no trouble wriggling through his crack as soon as the couple were asleep. He stole beneath their bed, listening to the reassuring sound of deep breathing. He climbed up the handles on the dresser drawers, one at a time, head cocked and ears straining for any disruption to the steady rhythm of their dreams. At the top of the dresser he found coins, ten, twenty and fifty sens, carelessly lying in a glittering heap. He carried them off to his stash behind the wall, then returned for more.

Andy's trousers lay discarded on the back of a chair. The Toyol rummaged in the pockets and found a wonderful shiny thing. It was red with a silver streak, as long as a man's thumb. There was a plastic clicker on the top and when he pressed with all his might, a spark shot out. Clutching his prize, he retreated behind the walls again.

The next morning Andy searched his pockets, checked the dresser, even stooped and peered under the bed. "Honey, have you seen my lighter?" he asked Meg.

She lay coiled beneath the sheets, reluctant to face the day. There was no reason for her to get up. "I thought you'd given up smoking," she said.

"Yeah, but you know sometimes when I go out with the boys," Andy said vaguely and retreated to the kitchen. "I've lost my change, too. Can I borrow some for the train?"

"You'd lose your head if it wasn't screwed on." Bitterly, vindictively, Meg rolled out of bed. She didn't need to get up. Andy knew where her purse was. She willed herself upright to make him feel bad. A simmer of rage bubbled. It was better to feel anger than emptiness. She found her handbag in the kitchen, got her purse, and slammed coins into his outstretched hand.

"There's no need for that," Andy said.

"I thought you'd given up smoking," she snapped.

"Look, I don't know what's eating you. Why don't you get out to a mall?"

"It's too hot."

"The malls are air-conditioned."

"Don't tell me where to go, all right?" The spark hit the tinder and ignited.

"No need to get snarky. I'm trying to help."

"How exactly are you trying to help? By telling me where to go; is that it? You want some trophy career wife?"

"You know that's not what I meant." Andy spoke quietly, but his frame swelled.

Meg stood before him, fists clenched, and dared him. "I saw you flirting with Stella and Imogen at that KLIA cocktail party. You thought I didn't? It made me sick. You know they were laughing at you behind your back?"

The rising tension fell flat. "Don't be ridiculous. You should get out more," Andy said. He turned and left, very quietly closing the front door.

Meg stood in the empty apartment. Her anger subsided into a dull throb of defeat. "I want to go back to Melbourne," she said aloud. No, she didn't. And yet . . . once upon a time, Andy would respond to her goad. He'd shout back. They'd have a fight and make-up sex. Now, she was a failure even at that. She couldn't make him mad anymore.

She had made a fool of herself at the KLIA party. One minute she was cool and collected, the next she was horribly aware that she was wearing the wrong dress. There she'd been, clutching a drink with shaking hands and blurting all to Stella and Imogen. Stella was Andy's manager, Imogen the vice-president's wife. And what had she been talking about? Her baby, born too early to survive. Miscarriage. What a stupid word. As if he hadn't truly been born in blood and pain, as though he hadn't lived when he was within her, and she'd wanted so desperately to give him everything good in all the world.

He would be a year old now and she would have had an instant circle of friends; mothers for coffee, shopping, movies and book club, all the little things about expat life that she really liked. Instead, she had blurted out an incomprehensible hurt in the wrong place and the wrong time, then cried in the toilets until Andy, with barely concealed annoyance, took her away in a cab.

"You should get counselling," he had said.

"I'm depressed, I know that," she had replied. "I can deal with this myself."

Her mother had tried counselling. It hadn't helped.

"I'm sorry," he had said. "I'm so sorry. I really am, but you have to move on."

She knew he was right. She had to get a grip on herself. She couldn't remain prey to this emotion. Was it truly grief? Grief was painful and sharp and stabbed when she least expected it, but it didn't speak. What burnt so long and loud? Could it be anger at that little, lost soul who hadn't tried hard enough to live?

Now she faced the empty apartment. The thought of going

outside hurt, the sheer futile effort of braving the crowds, the glare, the instant soaking sweat. She felt tired and defeated. She had better have a shower, she decided.

Brace up and face the day.

Be a trooper.

You'll be okay.

As she walked to the bathroom she heard behind her the patter of tiny, phantom feet.

Her back prickled with a cold shock. She rushed into the bathroom, slammed the door and shot the bolt. She looked around for a weapon then unscrewed the metal rod from the towel rack. She raised the rail threateningly, and sniffed incredulously as a horrible, musty smell flooded the room. Drains, she thought, before she remembered she was nine floors up.

She faced the door a long time, listening. The footsteps had stopped. An echo of her own, perhaps. Stupid, pathetic woman. Useless. Worse than useless. Couldn't even have children. She put the towel rail back with shaking hands and turned on the shower. She stood a long time before she realised she had forgotten the hot water. She was freezing cold and shivering.

• • •

Things continued to go missing. They couldn't understand it. Never anything large, never enough to call the police or lay a charge; never anything they could complain about to anyone except themselves; loose change, lone earrings, rings and keys. They spent their mornings searching through pockets, peering under the bed and lifting the sofa cushions. Andy kept running late as he rummaged for his train fare.

"This is getting old," he complained.

Bad feeling began to grow. It was small at first, but it swelled into a pall of ill will. It thickened in increments, with each lost coin and missing lighter, and every mismatched earring. It flooded the rooms, but they kept thinking they could live with it until it got too deep, suddenly, and spilled over their heads.

"All right, all right, I get it," a tired Andy said one morning to Meg, who was curled up in bed. "I shouldn't smoke. I'll give it up, but not right now, okay. You've made your point, but I need them. Just give them back."

"Give what back?" Meg asked without interest.

"My cigarette lighters. You must have a right stash," Andy said.

"I haven't got them," Meg rolled over to the other side of the bed.

"I don't see anyone else here," Andy said.

"Are you calling me a liar?" Meg scrambled out of bed.

"I'm calling you a thief," Andy said. "A klepto. A smoking vigilante. I don't know."

Meg strode right up to him, fearless. She glared at him. "I—didn't—take—anything." She punctuated each of her words with a strong shove to Andy's chest.

She drove him against the dresser. A musty smell choked him. His eyes watered and stung. "Jeez, what the hell is that?"

For an answer, Meg shoved him again.

He put his hand on the dresser to keep his balance. He looked down at the exact spot where he had left the change for his train fare. No coins were there. Frustration and rage stabbed home. "Quit shoving me," he shouted.

"I'm not a thief," Meg yelled, and shoved him harder.

"Stop it!" Andy hit her, hard and flat.

Meg reeled back, stunned and clutching her cheek.

"What, wait, I'm sorry," Andy cried. He half-lifted a hand to touch her cheek, then snatched it back.

Meg's eyes filled with tears. "You beast." Her cheek was a hot, ugly, appalling red. She ran to the bathroom and slammed the door.

"Meg, love, I'm sorry. I don't know what came over me." As Andy tried the handle, he heard her slam the bolt. "Don't shut me out!" he shouted. He raised both fists and hammered the door.

"Get out! Get out!" Meg cried, muffled.

"I didn't start this." Andy ran his hands through his hair. Then he slammed his fist into the wall by the door. The plaster broke. He cracked his knuckle on the stud beneath. "Christ!" He hunched over his hand as blood flowed.

Meg opened the bathroom door and came out clutching the towel rail. "Take that, you pig!" She hit him across the shoulders so hard that the rail bent. The musty stench flooded over everything, infuriating them more.

Andy grabbed her wrist and bent it, forcing her to drop the rail. Blood dripped onto the floor from his injured hand. "Meg, get hold of yourself," he shouted. Her eyes were glazed, her eyelids red, and her face streaked with tears and snot. "Stop it! Just stop it!"

Her eyes snapped back to the present. She dropped to the bed, crying hard.

He stood with his hand held out to her, uselessly, for he dared not touch. Then he went into the bathroom. He washed and bound his torn and throbbing knuckles. He moved very deliberately and carefully. When he came out, he spoke softly, "I've got to go to work. You should have a shower. Wash your face. Let's deal with this when I get back."

He realised in the elevator, with a surge of pure frustration, that he still didn't have any change. "Bugger it," he said, and waved down a cab.

Mr Durajaya and his wife and daughters heard the sound of the fight overhead.

"This cannot keep happening. It is getting worse. You have to tell them," Mrs Durajaya said.

"I can't." Mr Durajaya feared ridicule more than ghosts.

The girls texted their friends about it on their way out.

That evening, Mr Durajaya met Meg in the elevator on the way up. She had a bruised and puffy cheek, badly concealed beneath thick foundation.

"Dear me, that looks painful," said Mr Durajaya innocently.

"I ran into a wall." Meg stood in unhappy, fraught silence as the elevator rose.

It was her silence that tipped Mr Durajaya over into speaking. He felt so sorry for her and the strong, stern wave of pity washed away his fear of looking a fool. He clutched his briefcase tightly before him in self defence. "There is a Toyol in your apartment," he blurted out.

Meg just stared at him.

"Everyone knows. A Toyol is a thief," he said, then regretted ever opening his mouth. He was trapped in the elevator and the floor obstinately refused to swallow him. The silence drew on, scathing, disbelieving. He looked at his sweating reflection in the elevator mirrors. The door opened on his floor with a triumphant ring. He rushed out, happy to escape.

The doors hissed shut behind him then opened again. Meg had thrust her hand out. "A thief," she repeated.

"A little thief. It steals small things only. Keep it away with mirrors," he said.

"Thank you for letting me know," Meg said. Her strained face lit into a grateful smile. Then the elevator doors shut again. This time she did not stop them.

"There. I told her. You know, I actually think she believed me," Mr Durajaya told his wife that evening as they watched television. Relief made him feel light headed, and he went to bed content.

• • •

Meg went out that night and bought a large mirror. She set it on the dresser and put her small change and rings and earrings and keys before it.

• • •

Andy sent a text to say he was working late. He had not returned by the time she went to bed.

In the morning, Meg's little pile of treasure was still there, gazing placidly at its own reflection. "Andy, look!" she cried joyfully, turning to share.

But Andy wasn't there.

His side of the bed was cold and empty. There was no sign he had ever been in. She got up and dangled the earrings and rings with shaking hands. She jingled the keys, then poured the coins through her fingers, ten, twenty, fifty sens.

Andy texted later that day. He was staying at a friend's place for a bit.

Meg had breakfast at the hawker stall downstairs. She talked to the man making pancakes. He laughed off the Toyol. "It is an old story. It doesn't belong to modern Malaysia," he said.

She talked to the men playing chess in the street, the scooter riders, the taxi drivers, the girl at the durian stall, and the stall-holders at the market. She heard the old tale of the village miser who fed the Toyol with a cup of milk, morning and night, and how the Toyol stole from his neighbours until they chased the miser away. Story by story, she learned how to make a Toyol and dismiss it, and of the salt water that would slowly, slowly, wash a Toyol away.

Andy dropped by to collect some clothes. He had a white bandage wrapped around his knuckles. He could not even raise his eyes to hers.

"I'm better now," she said.

He didn't stay to listen.

That night, she poured milk into a cup and left it by her bed.

In the morning, the milk was gone.

Her coins and jewellery sat innocently by the mirror. Her keys stayed in place. She had not realised until now how much the constant petty pilfering had bothered her. She was filled with exquisite relief.

A plasterer and a painter finally arrived. They cut away the torn plaster next to the bathroom door to patch up the hole in the wall. She was in the kitchen when she heard them laughing. She returned to see them scooping glittering handfuls from the wall cavity. Coins were packed in a thick pile below. Afloat in the sea of small change was a flotsam of earrings, rings, keys and cigarette lighters.

"You must have a Toyol," the plasterer joked.

"Ha ha ha," she said.

The men patched and painted the hole. They promised to come back tomorrow to fix the crack by the bedstead.

That afternoon, she sat before her mirror and combed her hair. She regarded herself steadily over the heaped pile of loose change. The swelling had subsided and the bruise faded. The pain was gone.

She visited the Indian supermarket downstairs and bought a large glass jar with a screw-top lid, the kind used for pickling mangoes. She lugged it to her apartment and set it down on the bedroom floor.

She sat on the cool tiles as, outside, the sun set in a blaze of orange and blood red. Below the traffic blared and muttered. The evening darkened to night, until the street lights cast a pale glow against the walls. In the distance, the Petronas Towers wept great streams of glittering pearls.

"I know you're here," she said to the Toyol. "Come out."

Nothing stirred in the apartment.

She poured milk into a cup and set it before her. "You've drunk my milk. I am your master. Come out now," she ordered.

A shadow slipped from the crack behind the bedstead and stole beneath the bed. Its large head bobbed beneath the mattress. It peered at her with red eyes and reached with tiny fingers like the beloved dead. She breathed in the musty stench of jungles and blood.

The shadow stopped at the end of the bed.

"Drink the milk," she said.

It lifted the cup with both hands, drank, then licked its lips. It spoke to her, guttural and soft. She could not understand it.

"Get in the jar," Meg said.

The grey creature climbed inside. It was a large jar, but it was too small for the creature. The Toyol could only fit by squatting with its arms around its shins and resting its head on its knees.

Meg screwed the lid shut. She lifted the jar and shook it, so the thing inside flinched. Its red eyes blinked. "This is all your fault," she said.

She thrust the jar into the crack between the concrete and the plaster, as far and deep as she could reach.

The next morning, the painter and plasterer filled the crack and painted it over, then put the bedstead back. Meg sent a text to Andy. "I'll get counselling," it said.

He called later that day.

"I am so sorry about everything," she said.

"We'll go to counselling together," Andy promised her.

Meg told Andy that she didn't want to stay in that old apartment. They moved to a bright, modern tower surrounded by fellow expats. She found her lost rhythm. She made friends. Her days were filled with coffee, walks, lunches and shopping. She knew she had done a small, bad thing. But she did not dwell on it long. It was the choice she'd had to make to be happy again.

The Toyol crouched in darkness with his chin resting on his knees and his arms wrapped around his shins. He was not one of the *hantu raya*, the great ghosts. He could not free himself. There he sat, night after night and day after day, and the kind waves of the sea never came to wash him away.

• • • • • • • • • • •

TO WISH ON A CLOCKWORK HEART

FELICITY DOWKER

Marc met the clockwork fairy on his way home from the pub. That wasn't surprising, as he was always on his way home from the pub these days. The bitter wind reddened his cheeks and made his nose run. The dark street glistened, a blackened blister lanced by the moon and streetlights. Marc felt neither the wind's bite nor the night's gloom. He'd worked very hard for some time now on feeling as little as possible.

"Forget I ever had a wife and daughter. Maybe she was right. It hurts too much. But Mary . . . oh, Mary, my little girl . . . I'm so sorry. Daddy's sorry."

Tears blurred his already challenged vision. Marc staggered, leant on a telephone pole for support until the beer bees quietened their buzzing in his brain, and *clunk*, the clockwork fairy appeared on the footpath in front of him in a cloudburst of iron filings.

"I need oil," she said, her voice the shriek of rusty nails being dragged down a dented car door. Two huge wings rose like bridges above her shoulders, intricate spirals of metal laced with sluggishly turning brass cogs. Oversized brown aviator goggles dangled around her neck on a cracked leather strap.

"I'm drunk," Marc pointed out, somewhat redundantly, wiping his tears on the back of his sleeve.

The clockwork fairy tried to roll her eyes, but they made a sick whirring noise and refused to move, so she settled for hissing like a broken kettle instead.

"I don't have time for this. I need oil *now*. Do you live nearby?"

"I'm not really seeing you," Marc persisted. "It's the beer talking."

"Oh, for sobbing out loud." She stepped towards him, rattling audibly with each movement, and extended her hand. "I'm Pendula. Shake my hand," she instructed when Mark didn't move and, after a moment, he did as he was told. Her hand was dry and hard in his, and generated a rapidly dissipating superficial heat.

"Nice to meet you. I'm Marc." The inside of Marc's head gave itself an alarming twist, and the street tilted dangerously beneath him, threatening to pitch him to the ground. "Whoa," he muttered.

"Listen to me as carefully as your ale soaked senses will allow, Marc. Look at me!" Pendula screamed the last words, and Marc snapped to attention, one hand fluttering to his mouth in surprise. "See this?" Pendula stabbed a creaky finger at her forehead. A small heart-shaped clock-face hung there, suspended from a thin gold chain that hugged her forehead before disappearing into her frenzied russet curls. "Time is fleeting. If my heart stops ticking, I'm dead. That's true for humans and it's true for me, too. It's already running way too slow. Oil is the answer. I'll get you home, but you have to ask me for a ride. I can't give you one until you ask, or someone asks for you. Stupid rules."

"A—a ride?"

Pendula's glowing eyes—convex copper coins with lightning strikes of silver—narrowed, the movement making the heart-clock on her forehead drop and swing like a wrecking ball. Dreading that blood-curdling scream again, Marc waved his hands in a placatory gesture that almost cost him the last of his balance.

"Alright," he said. "I live three blocks from here. 30 Avondale Terrace. Could you give me a ride? But I gotta tell you, my place is kinda messy. I haven't had guests since . . . haven't had guests for a long time."

"I'll need oil as soon as we get there," Pendula said, pulling the goggles up from around her neck and snapping them in place over her eyes, managing to look both ridiculous and terrifying all at once. "But I'll make it worth your while. I have to. More stupid rules."

"Yeah, yeah, oil. Look, I'm about to pass out, and you're not real, so can we just get whatever it is you want over—"

Marc was swept off his feet, Pendula cradling him in her arms like a baby. He felt something cold and hard biting into his arm where it pressed against Pendula's torso. Turning his head, he saw a corset-like structure that appeared to also be Pendula's rib cage. It was made of bars of iron, and sat on the outside of her clothing. His arm was wedged in between two of her ribs.

Then they were in the air, rushing up toward the stars, Pendula's junkyard wings groaning and thrashing, cogs whirling. Marc's brain twisted again, too far this time, and he slipped gratefully into stupor.

• • •

He awoke supine on his bed, the wind toying with his naked body with thick icy-pole fingers.

Why is it windy in my bedroom?

Turning his head to the left—gently, gently, as greasy worms playing bongo drums filled with alcohol slopped queasily inside his skull—Marc saw the broken window, curtains flapping, moonlight glinting off glass shards scattered on the hardwood floor.

Ah. I didn't do that. Who did? Don't recall getting undressed, either. Don't recall much of anything. Good. That's good.

Something soft and wet caressed Marc's penis. He jerked as blood slammed into his groin with sudden force; gasped as the soft-wet-something lapped at him again. It slid up and down his length as he hardened beneath it, then he was enveloped, small sharp nubs adding an intense edge to the sucking, stroking, all-consuming bliss.

Who is that ooooooh don't care!

Marc orgasmed within moments. He cried out, spasming and twitching as he gushed inside the *something* that had an expert hold on him. It suckled him greedily as he spurted, his hot fluid gone the moment it left him.

Marc sighed, but the sucking didn't stop now his semen was spent; quite the opposite. It intensified, grew painful. The pull was irresistible, and darker fluid began to flow from him, deep crimson blood, salty and thick. Marc squirmed and moaned, the scorching, tugging pain in his groin quickly becoming unbearable, but he couldn't lift his limbs, couldn't fight, and soon, couldn't move at all. Could only lie there as the life—*oil*—was drained from him through his traitorously rigid cock.

After an eternity of silver bright agony, Pendula gave one last satisfied slurp and released Marc, her jaw moving smoothly, all creaks and rattles gone now. Marc was lost again, spinning unconscious through air filled with gold dust and industrial noise, his heart hammering in his throat.

• • •

. . . tickticktickticktickticktick . . .

A clock running fast as a hummingbird's wings thrummed near Marc's ear. He blinked his way back into the world, sleepily, cautiously. Sunlight illuminated the dancing dust motes in his bedroom. Pendula lay next to him, her face inches from his own, the hands of the heart-shaped timepiece on her forehead spinning in a perpetual blur. Her mouth curled at the corners, little fangs tipped with gold peeking through, her high cheekbones jutting as she smiled. The bongo drum worms in Marc's brain had downgraded now to millipedes playing rotten keyboards with their soft-shoed feet. It was bearable and he could move without needing to be sick. He wasn't in pain. He felt . . . well.

His daughter's face sprang immediately into his brain, and he pushed the image her along with the pain it brought down deep into his subconscious, with the practiced skill months of self-obliviating had given him. No use dwelling on things you couldn't change, and Marc couldn't change shit.

He pinched the bridge of his nose between thumb and forefinger, squeezed his eyes shut, frowning, cramming his brain with mundane thoughts *(milk, I need milk, better take some aspirin too, gonna have a headache later, feel great now but might not later, bread, need bread too)* to stop another image flashing behind his eyes.

Fiona. BELOVED WIFE TO MARC, DEVOTED MOTHER TO MARY. That was what her headstone said, and he didn't want to think about that, couldn't . . .

"Thank you," Pendula said. Marc opened his eyes, gazed at Pendula's pink tongue, nestled in her mouth like an ill kept secret. "You saved my life."

"Er . . . you're welcome?"

"I owe you a boon now." Pendula sat up and slid off the bed. Her wings were folded against her back like collapsed outdoor furniture, cogs still twirling in the complex structure. A steel bustle arced over her buttocks, attached to the ribcage corset around her chest and back. Beneath it she wore what looked like a black leotard, with a short striped tutu. Throwing daggers were lashed to her exposed thighs with leather straps. She wore chunky black boots with gold laces reaching to her knees. Her hair was a corona of red-brown double helixes, orbiting the planet of her head.

"What *are* you?" Marc propped himself up on an elbow. His eyes touched on his penis, wilted but otherwise unmarred and intact against his thigh, and then he gazed at Pendula. No matter how hard he looked, he couldn't take all of her in. New little details kept appearing. A dozen chunky wristwatches strapped to each of her forearms. A button pinned to her left breast—SUCK MY COG! A spanner, tucked inexplicably alongside the knives on her right thigh. A gust of steam, propelled from her magenta lips when she exhaled.

"A clockwork fairy. You get one wish." Pendula shook herself, and her wings clicked and popped into position, spread out behind her in a latticework of impossibility. "Do you want it now or later? I've got places to be."

"Later," Marc blurted, only wanting to stare at her some more. "How often do you do . . . this?"

She laughed, the sound like a knife being sharpened on a grindstone. "Typical man. I'd love to tell you that you were my first, Marc, but that would be fibbing. Rest assured that I only *need* oil once every so often, though I *want* it all the time. You're lucky I figured out a way that's at least partially pleasant for both of us, and that I was in a generous mood. Had I met you under different circumstances . . . " Pendula motioned to the knives strapped to her thighs. "Your experience would have been much different."

"What *is* a clockwork fairy, exactly?" Marc was stalling now, trying to keep her here, keep the thoughts and images behind his eyes at bay. She arched an eyebrow and smirked, then turned away from him. A large brass key, the handle shaped like a heart and styled in the same intricate patterns as her wings, jutted from the small of her back just above her iron bustle.

"Clockwork," Pendula said over her shoulder, reaching behind herself and running one long-nailed finger around the rim of the key. "Fairy," she added, flicking her finger upward, pointing at her wings. "And as for any other information about me, that's not for you to know. Unless that's your wish? I could show you . . . " Her voice was eager. Marc sensed danger.

"No," he said, and she hissed. She grasped the key in her back and pulled. It slid out of her with a sound like a tin can being grated into fine shreds, and Marc winced. *Oh yeah,* there's *that hangover I thought I'd skipped this time.* Golden blood dripped from the end of the key, falling to the wooden floor and solidifying into strange nuggets.

"When you're ready for your wish, you can call me with this," Pendula said, turning and flinging the heavy thing at Marc. He rolled, and it thudded onto the mattress beside him, denting it visibly. "But don't wait too long. Time is fleeting, and if you let it escape, it never returns. Call me soon."

"How? Wait, don't go," he said, biting back the *please* he wanted to add, but she'd already leapt through his shattered window and taken wing in the morning sky.

• • •

Marc had been at the pub to drown his sorrows, as always, but the bloody things refused to die. Now, in the wake of Pendula's bizarre entry and exit from his life, he found his sorrows had clawed their way to shore and, far from drowned, were invigorated by their time at sea. It was always this way. He had to drink more every time, and every time it wore off faster. He'd always loved the drink, and the drink had always loved him, but since Fiona . . . well, his flirtation with alcohol had gone from a casual affair to a devoted marriage.

He left the key on his bed untouched, slipped into pyjama pants, and headed to the kitchen to make coffee. A black lacy bra was tossed carelessly over the breakfast bar. It had been there, undisturbed, for a year. It was *hers.* Not Pendula's (did clockwork fairies wear bras?), but Fiona's. His wife—his *dead* wife. He couldn't move it, couldn't bring himself to pick it up and put it out of sight, let alone throw it away.

On that night a year ago, Fiona had left a note stuck to the pot of soup in the fridge: *love you, see you in the morning, remember to pick up Mary from after-school care, doofus!* She'd left her dirty bra on the counter in her rush, driven off to her shift at the Hospital, and had never come back. There'd been nothing exceptional about Fiona's accident, just crappy conditions and a tree waiting for her car to slam into it as she skidded off the slick road. But losing her was exceptional, very exceptional indeed, at least to Marc and six-year-old Mary.

Mary's face flashed into his memory again, scrunched into a red ball and made ugly with her screams, as Fiona's sister Helen dragged the little girl kicking and screaming down Marc's driveway.

Don't think about it don't think about it don't think about it!

Marc grabbed a handful of his crotch, shifting until he felt more comfortable. It was tender down there, but in a good way. He'd been dead a year himself, too, in a way—in *that* way. He wasn't used to the activity. Hell, who *was* used to having blood sucked out of their . . .

Grimacing, Marc swigged his coffee in two gulps and headed for the shower.

• • •

An agonising grind of days in the office talking to idiots about their gas accounts followed. Marc swung between contemplating the clockwork fairy, suicide, and murder as the months cycled by.

Yes, murder, there was a thought to keep him warm at night.

Helen. It was always Helen's throat he pictured his hands closing around. Helen, with her cold eyes, hard hands, and archaic views on "disciplining" children. How could anyone have thought her better able to care for Mary than he was?

"Forget you ever had a wife and daughter," Helen had hissed at him as she slammed her car door on his daughter's screams. Mary's little fists hammered on the car window and when that failed, the girl actually began to head butt the glass, her lips forming the word *daddy* over and over again. Helen ignored her, no doubt filing the "bad" behaviour in her mental catalogue of sins for harsh punishment with fist and rod later. "Mary's mine now. I knew the courts would see you for the louse you are. You're useless. You're nothing. Fiona probably drove into that tree on purpose. Killed herself, rather than have to face her pathetic excuse for a husband. I told her not to marry you, but oh no, she wouldn't listen to me, and now look what's happened. Well, you'll never see your daughter again. I'll see to that. Do you hear me? *I'll see to that!*"

At first he'd tried to fight, tried to see Mary, tried to get her back—all the more when he saw her bruised eyes and hollow cheeks in the glimpses he snatched of her before Helen slammed the door in his face and called the police—but it had been one brick wall after another. *An alcoholic with little hope of rehabilitation at this time*, the court shrinks had said. *Stuck in a time warp of losing his wife over and over again, and constantly trying to douse the memory rather than deal with it. A danger to himself and to others. Reports of threats against his sister in law, who is caring for the child. Sister in law confirms history of violence, leading to the child's current erratic behaviour, and flights of fancy about the villainy of her Aunt.* Lies, but that hadn't mattered. And the most damning two words he'd ever seen in print: *Not fit.*

Forget you ever had a wife and child.

Hating himself, Marc had eventually tried to do just that. To do otherwise—to dwell and agonise, to rage and regret—became just too much to bear. But a seed of hatred and rage planted itself in his heart, and it grew thick and deep in the fertile red soil.

And now every night, when he returned to his empty house, the golden key sat on his bedside table, a question waiting for him to answer it. He told himself there'd been no clockwork fairy, that it was a drunken hallucination, that he'd found the key on the ground somewhere as he'd staggered home after another bender, that it was all nothing, just like him. Nothing.

But.

In the end, it was the slow trudge of days that pushed him over the edge. It was all just finally . . . enough. He hated Helen, he grieved Fiona, he longed for his little daughter with an agony that was fresh each day, he raged against the injustice of it all, he struggled to live with himself, and it. Was. *Enough.*

He picked the key up, held it to his chest He needed both hands to grip it and his biceps quivered with the weight of the thing.

"Er . . . Pendula?" He said, feeling an utter idiot.

Nothing happened. Of *course* nothing happened.

He dropped the heavy key to the floor, and climbed into bed, sighing.

• • •

The immense weight of her woke him in the small hours of the night. That, and the clanking of her parts, the whirring of her cogs, the ticking of that cursed heart-clock—slower than last time he'd seen her, but still steady, and what had she said about it slowing down before? That was important, because it meant she'd be wanting . . . oil. Again.

She straddled him, her gold-tipped teeth glinting in the moonlight that washed his room ghostly grey-white. "You certainly took your time, didn't you, Marc?" She tapped one of the many wristwatches that competed for space on her arm. "Time is fleeting. Don't you know that? I keep telling you, but you don't get it. Nobody ever does." She shrugged, her wings grating against each other with a tortured metal scream that vibrated to the very roots of Marc's teeth.

"You're . . . "

"If you say "real", I swear to whatever pathetic deity you worship, it'll be the last word you ever utter." Pendula leaned down, adjusting her position, her thighs sliding against his until the knives and spanner strapped there dug into him painfully, her metal rib cage crushingly heavy atop his own fragile chest. Holding her face within kissing distance of his, she inhaled, copper-scented steam gusting from her mouth when she released the breath again, stinging his eyes and making them water.

"You're sober," she said. "Well, wonders will never cease."

"It's the day before payday. I can't afford to drink again until tomorrow." And didn't he know it. His body ached, his mouth was parched, and his thoughts capered uncontrolled like imps through his brain.

"Ah. I see. What a charming existence you lead. But don't their faces haunt you, Marc? How do you keep them at bay without your poison of choice?"

He gaped up at her, wanting to shove her away in outrage, but unable to move beneath her bulk. She kept on grinning, those strange teeth seeming ever sharper and more dangerous.

'But a wish will help you, won't it?" Her hand caressed his cheek, and then her finger traced a line down his torso, worming into the tiny space between their bodies and reaching for his groin. Marc bucked, the movement doing little to budge Pendula, but she chuckled and withdrew her hand with a melodramatic flourish.

"You already got all you're getting from me, and you already *owe* me a wish." Marc struggled to get the words out. Pendula's weight was making it difficult to breathe.

"Aw, not volunteering any more oil?" Pendula's coin-eyes twinkled, reminding Marc of pennies placed on the eyes of the dead, and he shook his head. "But you enjoyed yourself so much last time, Marc. Oh well. You're right, of course. I owe you a wish."

"I want—"

"Be careful." Pendula's voice was amused. "Time is—"

"Fleeting, bla bla, yeah, I got that part."

Pendula inclined her head slightly. "Go on," she said.

"I want my daughter back from that hag."

"Of course you do. But frankly, I find that wish boring. What's in it for me?"

Marc's eyes widened in indignation. "I don't give a shit what's in it for you! You said you owed me a wish!"

"I did say that, but did I say *what* wish I owed you? No. I owe you a wish, and I'll honour my debt, but guess what, kiddo? I get final say on whether your wish is suitable. And that one isn't. Try again."

"You fucking liar! You can't just play with words like that!"

"Never met a fairy before, have you?" Pendula stretched atop him, her wings spreading to their full formidable span, cogs turning sleepily. The little heart-clock on her forehead seemed even slower now, and her hand fluttered to it in an absent gesture. Marc's eyes fixed on it, and an idea began to form in his mind, which was a nice change from the usual parade of angst and self-loathing that marched there any other time.

"What if there *was* something in it for you?"

Pendula raised an eyebrow.

"I see your clock is slowing down again. What if there was a way for you to grant my wish and also secure yourself as much oil as you can consume, for the next, oh, I'd say thirty years or so?"

Pendula's flinty eyes regarded him suspiciously. "You can't trick me," she said. "Just so you know. Just in case you're thinking of being clever."

"No tricks," Marc said. "If you let me up so I can catch my breath, I'll explain. It's pretty hard to have a conversation with you crushing me."

Pendula regarded him a moment longer, then swung her leg over him with a metallic screech, and rose to her feet. The relief was immediate—air, sweet air, rushing into his lungs, and the blessed lack of weight on his body!—and Marc revelled in it for a moment.

"Hurry up," Pendula snapped. "Time." She didn't bother finishing her personal catchphrase, and Marc was grateful.

"So I'm thinking of something a little like this," Marc said, sitting upright.

Pendula listened as he spoke, and after a moment, she smiled fully, her teeth flashing and her face stretching into something truly terrifying.

• • •

Marc rapped on the wooden door, then, abandoning any pretence of politeness, he used both fists to hammer on it. He heard movement inside the house, hurried footsteps approaching behind the door. The outside light flickered into life, and the door was pulled open, just far enough for Helen to peer out, blinking sleepily, the chain still holding the door secure should anyone try to force their way in. She saw Marc and scowled.

"What are *you* doing here? The restraining order is still active, you know. Do you want a repeat of last time, with the police? You never learn, do you?"

A curtain twitched at an upstairs window. Mary, too frightened from a year of beatings to throw the curtain wide, but unable to resist the chance to catch a glimpse of her daddy. Marc's heart twisted with love and rage, and he smiled at Helen, who flinched as if he'd moved to strike her.

"Good evening, Helen. I just want you to remember that I tried for a year to do this peacefully. I tried to get my daughter back from you, you child-abusing cow, but you just enjoy torturing her and I too much, don't you? I've often wondered what's in this for you. Why do you *want* Mary? You clearly hate children. But I realised that's why you love this so much. You hate Mary, and you hate me, and this way, you get to take a daily hand in our misery, don't you?"

"I'm closing this door, then I'm calling the police, and then I'm going back to bed." Helen's voice was dull. "That's how little I care for anything you say. You're drunk, as usual."

"That's where you're wrong. I'm dead sober, and I'm glad of that, because it makes this moment *sharp*."

Two things happened simultaneously. Helen moved to close the door, and Pendula stepped out of the shadows that she'd so seamlessly merged with up to that moment, and halted the door with one hand. Helen's eyes widened at the sight of Pendula, and her mouth dropped open.

"Oh," Helen said. "Oh!"

"Open the door, or I'll tear it from its hinges." A hungry urgency had crept into Pendula's voice. Her double-helix hair flamed and bristled around her face. Her half-unfolded wings trembled and clinked. Her free hand lowered to the knives strapped to her thigh—not that she'd need them to harm Helen, but they were a solid threat the woman could grasp.

"No." Helen's innate mulishness overpowered her fear and wonder. "Move your hand or I'll close the door on it. I'm calling the police."

Pendula smiled. "I was hoping you'd say that." The fairy lunged forward, throwing her weight against the door. The wood groaned and splintered, and the door shot open, knocking Helen from her feet. She skidded backwards down the hardwood floor and landed hard on her side, her head hitting the wall with a *crack*, and lay blinking in shock.

Pendula and Marc entered the house, Pendula shoving the front door closed behind them with the edge of one of her wings.

Upstairs, a door squeaked open, and light footsteps scurried above their heads. Marc looked up, biting his bottom lip, and made to move for the stairs. Pendula clamped a hand on his shoulder, stopping him.

"No. I get mine, *then* you get yours." The hands on the clock-face dangling on her forehead were barely moving at all now. Marc sucked on his teeth in frustration, but nodded.

Helen hadn't moved, still lying dazed on the floor. Pendula crouched, rattling and squeaking. Her iron bustle nudged the floor, and her tutu-like skirt bunched up around her hips, baring her long striped legs. She reached for Helen, extending her arm to show the woman the wristwatches strapped there.

"See this?" Pendula gestured. Helen's eyes moved obediently to Pendula's arm. "Time is fleeting, Helen, especially stolen time. You stole Marc's time, and his daughter's. Not just their individual time, but their time together. That's a powerful transgression. Do you understand?"

Helen gave a weak smile, and nodded, her eyes rolling a little before refocusing on Pendula. She was obviously not herself—for one thing, she wasn't berating or striking out at anyone.

"Marc wants his time back, Helen. His time with his daughter. I'm going to give that to him. And do you know why?"

Helen struggled to speak, her lips puckering and twitching. "Trans . . . transgr-gr—"

"Oh, it's not because you've transgressed, Helen. I could give a shit about that. It's because I need some fucking oil. And you? You're a big ol' sack of it. You're, what, 40, 45? Yeah, I reckon you'll be good for a few decades, if I control myself, if I only take what I need when I need it."

Helen gave another idiot smile, and then, as Pendula reached for her, she gasped and her eyes closed. Her head flopped onto the floor and she lay still.

"She *would* pass out at the good bit," Marc muttered. Pendula looked over her shoulder at him, her eyes glittering through the latticework of the wing that partially obscured her face.

"This part wasn't your wish, was it, Marc? Unless you've changed your mind. Unless this part *is* for you rather than for me."

"No," Marc said. "No." And stepping around Pendula, he hurried to the staircase, tripping up the steps, heart pounding in his chest. He heard the sounds begin below, cracking and tearing and wet slurping, but then:

"Daddy?"

That one blessed sound obscured all else, defied all ugliness, and he fell onto the upstairs landing, grasping his little daughter's shoulders and pulling her to him, burying his face in her soft hair and wrapping his arms tightly around her. She clung to him with birdlike fingers, and they both cried, and time stood still for just one perfect moment, and that was enough.

• • •

There were no loose ends to clean up. Pendula made it so. First she took her key back from Marc. Then, as she slipped it back into her spine, sighing contentedly, things just . . . *shifted.*

There had never been a woman called Helen. Fiona had died, and that was terrible, almost too terrible to bear, but Mary had never gone away, had always been with Marc, and they grieved and loved *together.* At least, that was what the outside world—and Mary, it was kind of Pendula to add that touch—thought. Marc remembered all too well, but he would carry that burden. It was worth it for what he'd regained.

"Where is she?" Mark said, watching Pendula rub the spot where her key was reinserted, her fingers kneading and massaging.

"Who?" She smiled her sparky smile at Marc. He didn't return it.

"The Queen of England. Who do you fucking think? Helen, where is Helen?"

"She's with me now." Pendula ran her fingers over her ribcage corset, caressed her jutting hips, and patted her iron bustle. "My dimensions are misleading. She's in here, like a battery slotted into me. Alive. Suffering, Marc, oh yes, such suffering. And when I need oil, I'll simply take it from her. Symbiosis, of a sort, except it benefits me, and hurts her. It will hurt her more and more as I drain her in years to come. Does this please you?"

"Yes." Marc didn't hesitate. "Does it please *you*?"

"Oh, yes." Pendula beamed, all gold-tipped threat. "It was a good wish. Very practical. More symbiosis—you get something, as do I. And we get past those pesky little rules that would normally prevent me doing something like this."

Marc found Pendula's definition of symbiosis disturbing, but he didn't speak. He wanted her gone. Mary was in the kitchen, awaiting her cereal. He wanted to sit and stare at his daughter eat, just watch her for hours, soak in her proximity, memorise her every mannerism, every inflection and lilt of her voice. He thought maybe he might even move that old bra off the kitchen counter so he could use it to prepare Mary's breakfast. Maybe it was . . . time.

"Well, it's been swell, Marc, but I gotta go. Time is—"

"Fleeting. Yeah, I know. Look, uh . . . thanks." Marc extended his hand. Pendula looked at it, and shook her head.

"Don't thank me just yet. Haven't you ever read *The Monkey's Paw*? Wishes . . . they're sticky things."

"Yeah." Marc was only half-listening. He could hear Mary laughing at some cartoon on the TV, and he smiled, his heart full.

"You *really* don't know fairies." Pendula spread her wings, preparing to lift into the air. Marc waved at her, not listening at all now, his head already turned toward the kitchen and his daughter. His wish.

"I keep telling you humans, time is fleeting, but you never listen, you never hear. What you really should be thinking about is the fact that your sister in law still lives within me. She's giving me oil, and as you should know now better than most, I owe her for that."

Marc didn't hear a word. He moved inside the house, closing the door.

Pendula lifted into the sky with a deafening clatter, the heart-clock on her forehead ticking faster than it ever had before. She yelled her words to the wind, grinning. "What you should be wondering, Marc, my dear, is . . . what will your sister in law wish for?"

• • •

Many miles below, Marc entered the suddenly silent kitchen, and screamed.

• • • • • • • • • •

THE STONE WITCH

ISOBELLE CARMODY

Here's the thing. I hate kids. Always have.

I mean, I know the job of the race, biologically speaking, is to achieve immortality through reproduction, but the idea of getting impregnated and blowing up like a balloon as I serve as a carrier and service unit for this other person who will eventually burst out of me in the most terrifying way imaginable, then carry on using me one way or another for the rest of my life, is right up there with throwing myself off the top of a twenty-storey building. If I have a biological clock, it is digital and does not tick. Moreover, I am fine with being solo. I mean manless as well as kidless. Not everyone needs someone, no matter what the greeting cards say.

So it seemed like the height of unfairness that I should have a kid seated beside me for the trip. I mean, this was business class and I thought they banned children. Or was it just that adults with kids never got upgraded? Anyway, what was with spending all that money on a kid, given this one was easily small enough to curl up and sleep in an economy-class-size seat?

Seating the child next to me, the flight attendant gave me one of those hundred-watt beaming smiles that makes you want to squint or confess something, and asked me to keep an eye out. *For what?* I would have said, but I was speechless with indignation to have booked business class and find myself a designated child watcher. No doubt some of what was going through my mind showed because for a moment the honey-pie smile froze, but flight attendants are trained to cope with anything, and before I could marshal my objections, she looked at the kid and said reassuringly that she would come back after takeoff.

I watched her walk away twitching her ass in a perky way, wondering, *Why me?* I mean, I am not old enough to have a grandmumsy look, and I don't have that flowerlike eagerness that beautiful young women have precisely in order to entice a man to want to make them a mother. I am not curvy. I am skinny in some places and I have actual fat in other places, and the end result is not the sort of woman men gaze at in magazines with thunderstruck longing. I don't do vacuous smiles or friendly aimless chat. Especially I don't do it with a kid. Come to think of it, I have probably not spoken to a kid since I was one, and even then I didn't much like them.

I looked at the kid. I could not tell if it was male or female because it was a skinny, malnourished waif with jeans, a hooded jacket, and a choppy, chin-length bob that might have been a designer do but also could have been the result of someone having at it with the nail scissors in a dark room. The kid looked back at me. The disconcerting thing about this was that it did not smile. It just looked in that steady, slightly creepy unsmiling way little kids have. I wondered how old it was. Ten? Eleven? Seven?

I mean, how do you tell? I knew it wasn't a teen yet because it didn't sneer.

I could have asked but decided I didn't want to know badly enough to break my rule about never making conversation with anyone on a plane at the start of a long journey. No matter how interesting the stranger next to you is, you will not want to spend thirteen hours talking to them. Ergo, no conversation or eye contact until the last fifteen minutes of the flight, and then only the sort of fleeting friendliness you feel toward other survivors of a flight. The eye contact thing was already blown, of course, but the kid would not speak unless I spoke to it, I was sure, and I had no intention of doing that.

I fumed silently about having a kid next to me until the plane started taxiing down the runway, then I gave up fuming for imagining all the terrible things that could happen if the plane tilted and caught its wing on the ground, an engine burst into flames, or a terrorist leaped out brandishing a glass knife. I have always had a terrific imagination, and this was one of the occasions—like when you wake in the middle of the night and wonder in the pitch dark what woke you—when an imagination is not a good thing.

"You don't need to be scared," the kid said in this slightly raspy voice.

I glared at it. "I'm not scared," I said frostily, consciously loosening my white-knuckled grip on the armrests.

"You *look* scared," said the kid.

"I am *not* scared. I am *concentrating*," I said, enunciating carefully through clenched teeth.

The kid said nothing, and I looked at the back of the seat in front of me and concentrated on not looking scared or showing by any outward sign of how much I hate takeoffs, which is only a little less than how much I loathe landings and a little more than how much I hate flying. My irritation at the kid was swallowed up in a spurt of fear at the slight judder in the plane carriage as we took off. I wanted to ring for the flight attendant and point it out except she would be buckled in her seat, and if she came, everyone in the plane would know who had risked her life by selfishly summoning her while the seat belt sign was illuminated.

I listened to the clunk of the wheel carriage retracting and told myself that if there were anything wrong, the pilot would notice and land the plane. I looked out the window, but as far as I could tell we were not turning back. We were, however, tilted heavily to one side.

What if they had forgotten to put petrol in one of the tanks? But again, the pilot, or co-pilot, would notice and turn us around. If we were not turning around, nothing was wrong. The mantra had just started to calm the hysterical dialogue I always had with myself after takeoff when I noticed a faint knocking sound. I have extremely good hearing. It is a curse because I can always hear things no one else hears.

I said my mantra again: *Nothing is wrong if we are not turning around.* Even if the captain couldn't hear the things I could, he had all those instruments. They would tell him if something was wrong.

By this time, the plane had stopped climbing and banking and we had levelled out. The belt sign went off with a loud ping, and a smooth voice announced that we could get up and move around if we wanted but if we stayed sitting, we should keep our seat belts on. This seemed to me to be a barely disguised warning from the captain that leaving the seat was risking your life, in case we hit an air pocket or an unexpected hurricane, so I remained seated and buckled.

I closed my eyes and breathed slowly.

"Are you still concentrating?" asked the kid.

I stayed as I was and hoped it would think I had gone to sleep. I stayed that way for a long time, but when I opened my eyes a slit and looked sideways without turning my head, I encountered the kid's rapt dissective gaze, which clearly had been on me the whole time.

"Are you meditating?" the kid asked solemnly.

"I am minding my own business," I said coldly, and leaned forward to dig my book out of the pocket of the seat in front of me. I unlatched my tray table so I could rest the tome on it, and opened it up. It was a book on birds. The kid said nothing, and although reducing it to repressed silence had been my desire it was not long before I began to find its silence distracting. Surely it was unnatural for a child to be that quiet. I wanted to look at it but feared it was still staring at me. Indeed, the more I thought about it, the more I could feel its eyes boring into me. I licked my lips and pretended absorption. I read the same paragraph several times without taking it in, with growing irritation, knowing that if I did not soon turn the page, the kid would want to know why. I tried again to concentrate on the book, but to no avail. I closed the book and set it squarely on the tray table, just as the flight attendant bent over to pass the child a yellow plastic purse.

I turned to watch the kid accept it gravely. It did not smile, and it cheered me slightly that this seemed to disconcert the attendant. Her peachy pink smile dimmed, and she asked the kid if it was okay. She did not look at me, but I sensed that she suspected me of doing something to the kid. I felt the guilty heat glow in my cheeks. It was intolerable because I blush easily and noticeably, and when her eyes flickered over me, they seemed to harden slightly.

I did not know what to do. To say I was innocent would be like the man saying he no longer beat his wife. Silence would be the wiser course, given that the child had made no complaint. Even so, I noticed another flight attendant passing by a minute later giving me a hostile look, and imagined the first one telling the others to keep an eye on me. That infuriated me, but there was not a thing I could do about it.

I closed my eyes, reclined my seat as far as it would go, and willed myself to sleep.

The plane gave a frisky little buck, and my eyes flew open. The plane gave another buck and then a sideways lurch that had a hostess staggering hard sideways. The captain came on with a ping and told everyone to sit down, including the cabin crew, because we were flying into unexpected turbulence. I didn't like the word *unexpected*. Turbulence was seldom unexpected. What had probably happened was that some turbulence had gone where it was not expected to go. A hurricane sheered off from a coast at the last minute, sparing the people there the destruction they were battening down for, or rain somewhere fell unusually hard and long, causing a flood, which resulted in some sort of shift of air that pushed a fog bank inland. And the displaced turbulence had wound up in our flight path.

The plane lurched hard sideways and then dropped before rising again. I swallowed and found my throat unpleasantly dry. "Is the plane going to crash?" asked the kid. My head creaked around and I looked at it. It did not appear to be scared, and I was still trying to find some words to say when it added, "I've never been on a plane before."

My brain scrambled to do something with these two statements, but the plane now gave a series of playful little jumps and then suddenly banked viciously left. I heard a few gasps and a cry, and was amazed none of it had come from me. Then the plane reared up and my stomach did a slow queasy roll.

But then we levelled out and were flying smoothly, and it seemed the worst must be over. The only reason I didn't relax was because the flight attendants were still seated. I could see one of them a few rows forward, sitting on one of those seats that come from nowhere and blocks the aisle, facing back along the plane so he could watch over the herd. I could see that he was not smiling, but did he look scared? I noticed his lips were moving very, very slightly.

Is he praying? I thought incredulously. I wondered if the captain had told him and the others more than he had told us. Or maybe he was just running through the chores he would have to do when he was allowed to get up.

We flew for some time, everyone belted in and the plane giving the odd skittish lurch or tremble, but more or less moving smoothly, which made me wonder why I was so totally wound up.

But the body cannot sustain fear at a high level for very long, so after a while I relaxed and glanced at the kid, who was staring out the window. I felt a small twinge of conscience then.

"Are you okay?" I asked.

It turned and looked at me, the same grave, considering look in dark eyes too big for its face. Its mouth was a nice curly shape and it had very long lashes, like little black brushes. The chin was delicate and slightly pointed, the neck a thin white stalk. A girl, I thought.

"I think the plane is going to crash," she said.

My conscience shrivelled. "The plane's fine. If it wasn't, the captain would have turned us round and headed back to the airport."

"Not if it was too late," said the kid.

The plane jerked sideways and a shudder went through it that had people muttering curses and prayers. Then the plane began inexorably to tilt forward and speed up. There was a ping and the oxygen masks came snaking and bouncing down. People grabbed at them. I couldn't lift my hands. The speed of the plane was pressing me back into my seat. I felt heavy and weak. My body relaxed completely without my telling it to do anything. It had its own ideas. I stared at the oxygen mask tilting away from me. I saw that the kid's was swinging forward as well. I remembered the demonstration and the cartoon hostess telling me to fit my own mask before I helped anyone else.

I looked at the kid. "Do you need me to help you put on your mask?" My voice sounded as if I had my head underwater. The air was thrumming. Dimly I heard a woman sobbing. I looked forward and saw the flight attendant had his hands over his face. Somewhere outside the plane there was a terrific noise.

"You want to hold hands?" asked the kid solemnly.

I let go of the armrest and turned my hand up. The kid put hers in it, and I closed my hand loosely around it. The hand inside mine was small and warm and slightly damp, like a little hairless mouse.

I closed my eyes.

I must have fainted because all at once I was dreaming a dream I had had so many times in my life that I immediately knew I was dreaming.

I was walking over a flat, dark plain. I could not see far because a mist or a brownish murky-looking fog was billowing around me. A blighted light revealed pitted boulders here and there but no grass or trees. Not even dead ones. I had the feeling nothing had ever grown in that place. Nearby was the bed of what had once been a river, now bone dry and dusty. The air tasted dry, too.

It's the air in the plane, I thought. *I'm dehydrated. I can wake up and make that snotty smiling flight attendant bring me some water. I could even ask her for a cup of tea and she would have to make it for me.*

Usually, thinking about waking woke me, but not this time.

It seemed to me that I heard something where I had never heard anything before, and when I looked around I was startled to see the kid from the plane walking alongside me.

"Hey," I said.

She looked at me. Now that she was walking I was certain she was a she. Something in the delicacy of the way she put her feet down. Bare feet.

"Where are your shoes?" I asked.

"I took them off on the plane," she answered. "Are we dead?" I looked at her. Maybe it was an accusing look because she shrugged apologetically.

"This is a dream," I said firmly. "I am willing myself to wake."

"Is it your dream or mine?" asked the girl after a moment, when nothing happened.

I said nothing, feeling baffled and uneasy. And thirsty. Somehow anxiety always manifested as thirst for me.

"I'm thirsty," said the kid.

"It's just a dream," I said.

"How do you know?" she asked.

"Because I've dreamed this dream before," I said.

"Was I in it before?" asked the kid, sounding interested.

I stared at her. "No."

I don't know if she would have said anything to that, but we both heard the sound of footsteps approaching. That had never happened before, either. The kid was right beside me, and her hand crept into mine again as we waited. It seemed a long time before the fog stirred and a woman emerged. She was about sixty with iron-gray hair plaited and hanging over one shoulder to her waist. She wore a gray shift and cardigan and black gumboots, and she was carrying a broom of the sort you get from a craft market, made from a lot of little trimmed branch ends bound around the end of a pole. Padding along at her side was an enormous, ferocious-looking Doberman. It was big enough to have put its jaws around the kid's whole head. Its ears had not been cropped but otherwise it looked like the dogs that the young cloned Hitler in *Boys from Brazil* ordered to eat his interrogator.

The old woman and the Doberman stopped in front of us. I noticed that the dog's sleek, brutal head was level with the kid's.

"Don't be uneasy about Jasper," said the woman in a brisk, no nonsense voice. "He doesn't bite unless he has to. I'm Rose."

"Did you dream of *her* before?" asked the kid.

The old woman's gaze switched from my face to the kid's. "Who in the blazes is this? No one said anything about a child." "The hostess seated her next to me on the—" I began, then stopped.

"Why is she *here*?" the woman demanded with asperity. "How did she get here?"

"Where is here?" I asked, deciding I needed to take charge of my dream, which seemed to be getting out of hand. *Wake up,* I willed myself.

"Stop that," said the woman crossly, lifting her gaze from the kid to glare at me. "The point is that she is not supposed to be here. You ought not to have brought her with you, and she will have to be put back."

"Put back?" I echoed faintly.

"Back where she belongs," Rose snapped. "In the plane." "The plane was going to crash," said the kid.

"Of course it was," snapped the old woman. She looked at me again and added severely, "No one authorized you to bring a child."

"I didn't," I said. "I mean, I don't know what you are talking about."

"She thinks she's dreaming," said the kid.

Rose rolled her eyes and muttered, "God, just once give me a little originality."

"No," I said. "I have dreamed this dream before. Lots of times, and I always wake up."

"Not this time," said Rose impatiently. "Can we skip this part? It is unbelievably tedious how difficult adults find it to believe in anything but death and income tax. How about you pretend to believe this is not a dream for a bit, so I can get on with the introductory lecture. But before that, the child has to be returned to the plane."

"I want to stay with her," said the kid.

"You might survive," Rose told her. "Not everyone will die." "I don't care," said the kid mutinously. "I don't want to go back."

"I'm afraid it is not up to you," said the old woman repressively. She held out a hand to the dog. "Jasper?" He padded closer and she laid a hand on the back of his head. Then she let out a *tch* and looked annoyed. "Land sakes, I am so rattled by all of this that I am forgetting myself." She held out her hand to me. "Take my hand. Since you brought her here, I need to be in contact to send her back."

"No," I said. The kid and the woman and the dog stared at me. I would have stared at myself if I could have. I had not meant to speak the word aloud. But now that it was spoken, I felt stubborn. "No," I said again.

"You cannot proceed with this child," said Rose. "Proceed where?" I asked.

"With the testing," Rose snapped. She gave a huffy sigh. "Look, you have been brought here to be tested because you have a certain untapped potential and your life is about to end. A quest has been assigned you, which will reveal if you are able to make use of your abilities. If you are, you will become one of us.

If you fail, you will be returned to the plane. There is no place in any of this for a child."

"If this is real, then sending her back means she will die," I said, more for the sake of argument than because I was able to believe what I was saying.

"People die every day. Children die every day. Now, if you'd had the sense to bring an animal with you, it would have been a whole different thing. You could have taken it as your familiar. But there is no place for a child here."

"A familiar?" I said.

"As in a witch's familiar," said Rose brusquely. "A cat is traditional, but owls, snakes, and dogs are also common choices. Even a goat or the odd frog has been used. Your choice."

"All right, I choose the kid as my familiar," I said, thinking, *Did she say* witch?

For the first time Rose looked taken aback. "You cannot take a *child* as a familiar!" She sounded shocked. "A familiar is a resource to be drawn on to increase and focus power, and sometimes to be sacrificed. Would you use a child so?"

"Better than putting her back in a plane that is about to crash," I said.

"I want to stay with her," said the kid.

I looked at her and felt a moment of unease, but then sanity reasserted itself. This whole thing was a dream, and soon I would wake up from it. Insisting on not putting the kid back in the plane was just pigheadedness because I hated being told what to do.

"It is wrong," Rose insisted, an edge of worry creeping into her voice. "If you take this child as your familiar, there is a very high chance that you will fail your test, and if you do so, you will face a horrible death in the plane."

"Don't hold back," I said.

"This is no time for jokes," Rose told me severely.

"I'll take my chances," I said flippantly. I was getting thirsty again.

"You leave me no choice," Rose said very coldly. "I am afraid you will regret this. Both of you will regret it. The Desolation is no place for a child."

"The Desolation?" I echoed.

She spread her free hand in a gesture that made the mist swirl, and I noticed the tips of her fingers were stained green. "*This* is the Desolation, where you will undergo your test."

Rose drew herself up and again rested a hand on Jasper's head. The Doberman fixed me with its hot brown ravenous eyes as she announced in sepulchral tones, "Your quest is to wrest the amethyst egg from the demon king, Chagrin."

"You have to be kidding me!" I said. It sounded like the description of a bad role-playing game.

Rose gave me a reproving look. "Your levity is inappropriate. The amethyst egg was stolen from one of us long ago by the demon king. It has great power, and Chagrin will not easily give it up. Take the child's hands if you are truly resolved to bind her to you as your familiar."

Despite the gumboots and ink-stained fingers, the look on her face was so solemn that it gave me pause. I had to remind myself that Rose the witch and her familiar, Jasper the Doberman, had been jerry-built by my subconscious.

"Go for it," I told Rose, holding my other hand out to the kid. She took it, looking nervous but determined.

The witch pursed her lips and lifted her free hand. I was about to make some crack about a wand and a puff of purple smoke, but to my astonishment I saw that greenish gas was seeping from the green tips of her fingers. *Maybe not ink-stained after all,* I thought, trying for inward humour. I reminded myself that this was a dream, and in dreams all manner of weird stuff could happen. The trouble was, the longer the dream went on, the less it felt like a dream.

I watched the green gas detach itself from Rose's fingers and wind together in a sort of gauzy cord that snaked down to weave the sign of infinity around our clasped hands. I felt it as a cold wind around my wrist, and the kid, whose pointy little face was lit by a greenish glow that made her look sick, had her eyes fixed on the luminous bond.

"Will you bind this child to you?" Rose asked.

I could barely hear her over the sudden howling of a wind impossibly blowing up from the ground through the circle formed by our bodies and clasped hands, but I said I would and just like that the wind died. The fog about us billowed slowly, untouched by the freakish wind from the earth. The silence that followed felt hollow and portentous. I released the kid's hands and looked at the old woman.

"Until death do you part," she said grimly. Beside her, Jasper suddenly yawned hugely, giving me a gruesome view of his ivory fangs and red throat. Rose went on. "You had better get moving. The demon's keep is not far, but it will take you time to find the amethyst egg and deal with him. Here, you will need this." She held something out to me, and automatically I stretched out my hand. She put an eyeball into it. The eyeball stared at me. "It will enable us to keep an eye on your progress, excuse the pun. You have until the Dreadful Dawn. If you have not got the amethyst egg by then, you will be deemed to have failed."

"What's so dreadful about the dawn?" I asked, still staring down at the eyeball. It felt warm in my palm, and the thought of putting it into my pocket made me feel nauseous.

"I imagine it is because those who fail know they have done so when the sun rises over the Desolation. Or maybe it's because of the harpies that will come seeking meat when day dawns. *You* can't die here, of course, though you can suffer excruciating pain. Your familiar, however, can suffer pain and die, in which event you may request another. Now get moving."

Rose added brusquely, "My advice is not to waste time trying to decide if this is real or not. If you must do that, do it and walk at the same time. Try to learn how to draw on the energy of your familiar as you go."

"How do I know where to go?" I asked.

"Use your familiar," Rose said. "I linked her to the amethyst egg when I bound her to you." With that, Rose turned and marched away, Jasper at her heel.

"Hey!" I protested, but she neither turned nor responded. "Wonderful," I muttered after the murk had swallowed her and the dog up. "Welcome to the Twilight Zone."

"The amethyst egg is that way," said the kid, pointing with one hand and lifting the other to her heart as if she was making an oath. She set off eagerly, veering left from the direction taken by Rose and Jasper, and I followed her lead, trying to decide if

I was really starting to believe in what was happening and what this might mean in terms of my mental health. The only other alternative was that there had been a plane crash and I was in a coma, trapped in a new variation of a recurring dream, in which case it probably didn't matter much what I did. Just the same, I wished I had asked a few more questions about how I was to find the amethyst egg in the Demon's Keep, whatever a keep was, and steal it. Rose hadn't mentioned stealing, but they never call it that in those dumb fat fantasies geeks read, either, where a kitchen boy is sent to get a magic cup or sword from some wizard.

"I'm thirsty," said the kid. "Can you magic me an orange juice?"

I stared at her. "Are you nuts? I'm not a witch, and this is a dream."

"You could do what she did with the dog," the kid went on. "It must have been her familiar." She touched her shoulder.

I sighed. "I could try," I said, to shut her up. I rested a hand on her shoulder and visualized an orange juice. Nothing happened. I felt like an idiot.

"Maybe you have to chant what you want," suggested the kid after a minute. "Say some Words of Power." I swear there were capitals in her tone.

"I don't know any words of power, unless you mean swear words, and I don't say those aloud," I said through gritted teeth. I took a deep breath and intoned, "We want some fresh squeezed cold orange juice!" Just for good measure, I visualized the last glass of orange juice I had got from the juice bar in the food court near my apartment.

A tray appeared on the ground at the kid's feet, exactly as I had imagined, with a glass jug of orange juice cold enough to cause beads of water to form on the outside of the jug, and two glasses with the little curly crest of Juice Bar.

"Oh boy," said the kid.

I drew a long breath and then bent down and poured until both glasses were full to the brim. I stood up and handed one to the kid, my mouth watering in anticipation of my own juice. Then I saw she was white to the lips, her eyes wide and dark.

"What's the matter?" I asked.

"I . . . it hurt," she whispered in a thready voice. I noticed she was pressing her free hand to her heart again.

I set my own glass down and guided the glass of juice the kid held to her lips. I made her drink the lot and then I poured the contents of my glass into hers and handed it back to her. I watched her drink and was relieved to see that some of the colour had come back into her cheeks.

"You didn't have any," she said, pointing to the empty jug.

"I don't like orange juice," I lied. I was not sure what to do with the tray and the jug and glasses. It felt wrong just leaving them there, but it would be idiotic to carry them with us. I might have tried wishing them away, but I was uneasy at the thought of what that might do to the kid. Clearly summoning the juice had drained her, and it made me remember uneasily what Rose had said about her not being a good choice as a familiar. I had insisted because I had not liked the thought of consigning her to a crashing plane, even if it was just a dream, but now it struck me that Rose might have been telling the truth when she said the Desolation was no place for a kid.

"That way," she said, pointing. It seemed to me she was pointing in a different direction than before, and I said so. "I can feel it," she said wanly, and again her hand went to her chest.

"Okay," I said uneasily.

She set off and I followed, the feeling of unease beginning to edge into actual fear. What the hell had I got myself into? Was this really real?

The kid looked over her shoulder at me. "I can feel it when you have doubts," she said. "It makes it hard for me to feel where to go. It's like the buzzing on a radio when you can't get the station." She went on without waiting for me to respond.

That was downright creepy, I thought, but I forced myself to follow and tried not to think about anything, to avoid sending her white noise. We had walked maybe half an hour across a stony, broken terrain when the kid stopped, her eyes widening. The look on her face scared me, but I could see nothing in the thick murky fog.

Then the kid slipped her hand into mine.

Little by little the mist thinned, and I saw a grotesque edifice, part medieval dun, part oil refinery, surrounded by what looked for all the world like a moat. The tower had turrets and kill holes and a cupola and arched doors but also rows of round windows with metal rims and rivets and great wide metal chimneys banded in white, freckled with rust, and belching steam or blue-tinged flame. Several pipes ran flaccidly from the base of one of the towers to disgorge green sludge into the moat that surrounded the tower. The water was as black and greasy-looking as crankcase oil. There was a stone staircase that rose and arched high over the moat, but instead of going to the ground on the other side, the steps wove around and around in a coy spiral that ended in a little lookout above the castle like a crow's nest on a pirate ship. I could not see anything holding the thing up except spars of smaller steps, which arched like flying buttresses from the main stair to doors at different levels of the keep.

I drew my hand from the kid's grasp. "You'd better wait here," I said.

"But the witch said—"

"She said a lot of things," I agreed. "The question is, was she telling the truth about any of them? I mean, how many stories did you ever read where the witch is the good guy? Not too many, right? And maybe there's a reason for that. Maybe witches don't come in good."

"In stories, something bad always happens when people separate," she countered. "Besides, you need me to find the egg." I had forgotten that. As we set off again, the kid gave me the same sympathetic look she had given me when she had asked on the plane if I was afraid. Then she added. "I can feel it, but there is something with it, too. Something slimy and full of hate. Maybe it is the demon Chagrin."

"Maybe," I said, wondering why ordinary names were never good enough for the bad guys. They couldn't be Harold or Mr Jones, though at least Chagrin was better than Bloodsucker or Ripper. If its name defined it, then bad temper I could deal with. "So where is the egg?" I asked. "Up in the belfry or down in the dungeon?"

The kid knitted her smooth brow and then shrugged apologetically, saying she couldn't feel how the passages went inside the castle. "We need to get closer."

We went to the bottom of the steps. They were stone, solidly mortared together hundreds of years ago, but they were ancient and crumbling now and they would be on a condemned list if there were any sort of sensible authority here. They would probably crack and fall the first time anyone set foot on them. In fact, what if they had been designed to do exactly that? That would be a clever way for a demon to deal with unwanted visitors.

"We have to go in," said the kid.

"Fine," I snapped, humiliated that a perfectly reasonable response to this madness should feel like cowardice. I began to mount the steps, and the kid followed in my wake. When we passed over the moat, I saw that the gelid black liquid below was quivering and sending up hungry little wavelets. Bubbles broke the surface, and when one floated free and burst close by I heard the distinct sound of a belch.

"I think it's alive," the kid said.

I pretended not to hear, but I did not breathe again until we had cleared the moat.

"How are we supposed to steal this thing without the demon king stopping us?" I muttered.

"He might be asleep," said the kid, which made me think of Jack the giant-killer creeping around the sleeping giant until the smell of an Englishman woke him. *Fee-fi-fo-fum,* I thought cheerlessly, wishing I were American because then I would have a .44 Magnum or a Colt or even some sort of baby pistol in a clutch bag. Instead I didn't even have the can of pepper spray I usually had in my purse because you were not allowed to carry any sort of aerosol onto a plane. I didn't even have nail scissors. What I did have was a sudden wild desire to laugh hysterically.

By the time we reached the first spar of steps leading to the keep, I was panting hard and seeing little bursts of light before my eyes. *I have to get more exercise when this is over,* I thought, and then winced at my idiocy. I looked back at the kid, who was not even breathing hard, and asked if she could feel where the amethyst egg was now. I had no idea what we were going to do when we found it. I kept hoping a brilliant plan would occur to me, but so far all I could imagine was racing in, grabbing the thing, and running out.

"I think something is watching us," the kid said. "Out of those windows." She nodded toward a row of portholes on the level of the steps. The first spar of narrow steps ran down to a heavy looking door of dark wood just above them. I took a quick look at the windows but saw only darkness behind dusty glass. I told myself the kid had got spooked and had imagined eyes the way kids do.

As we approached the hinged wooden door at the end of the spar of step, it swung open to reveal darkness so complete it looked like a solid wall. *Maybe it is,* I thought. I licked my lips and stepped into the darkness.

I found myself in my own kitchen, only the furnishings and crockery sitting on the benches and in the dish drainer were those my mother had used when I had been a child. I heard a footfall and turned to find her coming toward me. It startled me how obese she was. She had a baking tray loaded with freshly baked muffins.

"Yummy muffins for my baby," she sang in her wheedling little-girl voice.

"I'm not hungry," I said. The words were out before I could stop myself, because all of a sudden I was remembering this day.

Tears filled her eyes, and the smile, painted in shiny coral-pink lipstick to match her coral-pink fingernails, wobbled. "So Mama made these all for nothing, did she? She might as well throw them in the rubbish, then. Doesn't matter that the ingredients cost money, does it? Mama's little girl doesn't have to eat them if she doesn't want."

"Please, Mama, I just meant I have to go to the library now," I said. "I can have one later."

"Maybe they won't be here then!" she snarled, and she slammed down the tray and began stuffing muffins in her mouth. Her cheeks and her eyes bulged as she tried to chew. Then she started choking, spraying chocolate crumbs all over the spotless floor, dribbling chocolate drool down her apron front. Her face was purple and terror shot through me. I pounded her on her back, terrified she might die. But she gave some explosive coughs and then collapsed heavily into a chair, burying her face in her hands.

"I'm sorry! I'm sorry!" she wailed. "I try so hard but it's never enough and never the right thing. It was the same with your father. You can't wait to grow up and get away, and then I'll be all alone. I could die and no one would know or care."

"Mama, I won't leave you! I won't ever," I promised hysterically. I grabbed a muffin and shoved it into my own mouth, chewing frantically, tasting the sticky, rich sweetness.

"Did you keep your promise?" asked the kid, and I realized she was holding my hand again. My mother and the kitchen had disappeared, and we were standing in a little round room with dusty black and white paving stones laid out in an eye-watering geometric configuration on the floor.

"I . . . you saw that?" I said, reeling from the vividness of the memory or vision. She nodded. "Was I a kid again?" I asked. She nodded again. I blew out a breath of air, the fright and emotions sinking into a strange heavy feeling of sadness that I always felt whenever I thought about my mother and her life. Slowly I said, "It was real. I mean, it happened. But why did I remember it? What was the point?"

"Maybe it was to make you forget about finding the egg," the kid said. "It's not here."

We went back out and mounted some more steps. "I did," I said. She looked back at me. "I kept my promise, and I'm still keeping it, even though my mother died years ago. I never left home. I lived there until she died, and I still live in the same house. I never moved out." I said the words, wondering if it could really be true, that this incident in the kitchen had been the moment I had decided never to leave home.

The kid said nothing, the way kids can and adults can't, and I was grateful. We went on till we came to another spar of steps that brought us to the next door. This one was lacquered red and shiny like a Chinese puzzle box. I hesitated, wondering if there was another memory behind it waiting to ambush me. The door swung open with a whisper, and this time there was a muddle of light and noise coming through it. I entered and found myself at a party. People were standing around talking and laughing. There were servants with little trays of canapés and others with trays of half-filled champagne glasses.

"Hey there!" said a voice, and I turned to find myself looking at Emily, the wife of my first employer. She was a small, rounded, very pretty woman with a soft voice and straw-pale straight hair, cut with a perfectly straight fringe à la Alice in Wonderland. She was wearing a neat blue apron over a blue dress, and her pale glossed lips were curved into a smile, but her eyes were anxious, urgent. "Is Mike with you?"

"He's . . . he is coming along later in his own car. He got caught up in a meeting," I said. I didn't say he had gone off to play golf, sending me in his place to his eldest daughter's thirteenth-birthday party.

The anxiety in his wife's eyes turned to weary disappointment and for a moment the smile faltered, but she sucked it up and asked me brightly if I would like a drink.

"I'll just put Mr Willot's gift in with the rest, shall I? He didn't want it not to be here if the present opening happened before he got here, so he asked me to bring it with me." I was gabbling because I could see she knew her husband had ordered me to get something appropriate and had sent me, knowing that he would not arrive before the party was over. She knew that she and his kids were window dressing for his life as a banker. I wished I'd had the courage to refuse him so that I could have avoided seeing the pain and humiliation in her eyes as she turned away.

"My father isn't coming, is he?" asked a familiar voice in a clear grammar school accent. I turned from the gift table to face Amanda Willot. She was tall and slender like her father, pretty like her mother, but with a sharp cleverness that showed in her eyes and manner and that made her more striking than them both.

"Hello, Amanda," I said. "Happy birthday. You father got caught up, but he says he'll try to be here before it ends."

She gave me a look of cool dislike. "Does he pay you to tell lies for him?"

I swallowed and thought, *I will never let this happen to me. I will never be that wife being lied to or the mother who has to watch her daughter learning to hate her father. Better to be alone. Better never to trust anyone.*

"Is it?" the kid asked, and we were standing in a vast empty ballroom with two cobweb-draped chandelier. The kid had laid her hand on my arm, and it struck me that her touch had ended both visions.

"Is it what?" I asked.

"Better to be alone? Better not to trust anyone?"

I looked at her. "You can hear what I am thinking?" "Only when you're remembering," she said.

I shifted away from the kid, unsettled at the thought of her having access to my inner monologue, unsettled by the visions I had experienced, both of which seemed to show me making decisions I had not realized at the time I was making. I had always felt as if I had been sidelined by life, cheated out of the things other people seemed to get as a matter of course. Was it possible I had chosen the course of my life? And what did any of this have to do with the demon and an amethyst egg? Unless the kid was right and the whole point was to get me caught up in analysing the past.

"Let's go," I said. Outside there was a red blush on the horizon; if that was east, and if this place obeyed at least some of the laws of the known universe, it meant the Dreadful Dawn

was approaching. I looked at the kid. "Can you feel yet where the egg is?"

"Up," she said.

We got almost the whole way to the top before she pointed to a glass door at the end of a short set of steps running down from the main stair. Once again the door swung open as we approached, but this time when we stepped inside, I reached out to take the kid's hand. I thought I had figured out that it would stop me having a vision, but instead I found myself in a kitchen I didn't recognize. There was a small child with a shaggy mop of hair playing with a rag doll under the table. I realized I was under the table with the kid. Suddenly two sets of legs came in, one after the other. Both wore suit trousers and shiny black shoes.

"What about the kid?" one man said.

"Welfare will take charge until they sort it out with the relatives. They're not keen on getting involved. Can't hardly blame them for thinking twice about taking on the kid of two drug addicts."

"Some kids got no luck."

"You never know," the other said. "Maybe the parents taking off and leaving it is the best thing that could have happened. Sounds cold, but who knows what would have happened if they'd stayed around. I mean, parents that would leave a kid like a sack of clothes they didn't want."

"Pity the relatives won't step up," said the other man.

The kid sitting beside me looked at me with eyes that were a pale honey yellow at the centre, running to butterscotch at the edges. It was the kid from the plane. Her eyes were so sad it made my chest ache. I reached out to rest a hand on her shoulder, and the kitchen vanished, leaving me standing in a cramped sitting room with two dusty mismatched sofas pushed against the walls to form an L.

"I was under the table playing with Rosa when the men came in," the kid said. "They were from the government. One of them took me to the home and I stayed there for a long time because I was too old for anyone to want. Then one day the man came back. He told me my mother's sister had decided to take me after all. He said she and her husband felt it was their duty to take me. I said I didn't want to go, but the man said I was a kid and kids have to do what adults decide is for the best. Then he put me on the plane."

"What a prince," I muttered.

"It's close," she said in a voice so soft it was almost a whisper. She went back outside, and we both stopped dead to see what we had been too intent on our purpose to see before. We had finally climbed high enough to rise above the roiling murk. It lay below like a blanket of dark clouds seen from a plane window. All around were high mountain peaks, and above them the sky was a very clear and dark blue on one side, running to red and purple on the other side.

"The Dreadful Dawn," said the kid.

"Not quite," I said. I turned to her. "Where now?"

The kid pressed a skinny hand to her heart again, and then she pointed down. Only then did I see there were metal rungs set into the side of the building, going down to a gaping hole of the kind you see in bombed-out buildings. There was fear in her eyes, but it was not fear of harpies and the Dreadful Dawn. It was the greater fear of abandonment; of being left behind. I knew I ought to leave her because whatever lay in the hole below was nothing good, and every bone in my body said you didn't take a kid with you into a thing like that. Nor did I subscribe to her view that staying together was safer than being alone. Hadn't I built a life out of being alone because that was better than being eaten alive by someone else's needs? And wasn't it the kid's need that was sucking at me now like quicksand?

But somehow I found myself saying, "I'll go first."

The gratitude in the kid's face was so intense it pained me. I forced myself to concentrate on climbing because it was a lot of years since I had done it and the rungs were coated in a greasy slick that made me afraid of slipping. There were fifteen rungs down to the level of the hole blasted in the side of the wall. I stepped into the rubble gingerly. A second later the kid swung in like a monkey and beamed at me. I turned to squint into the murky darkness, all too conscious that if the witch had meant it about the harpies coming at dawn, we would be sitting ducks.

"I'll show you," said the kid eagerly, and before I could stop her, she had darted ahead. Cursing, I followed, stumbling over the broken stone underfoot and wrenching an ankle painfully. Limping on, I opened my mouth to hiss at her to slow down but then saw that she had entered a cavern rather than a room. There was a great hole in the floor, and rising from the near edge was a plinth of white marble cradling an oval of amethyst as small as a regular egg but faceted. The kid reached out to take the egg, and immediately the facets began to pulse delicate flashes of violet and lavender. The colour was so beautiful it ravished my senses, and I felt a jealous hunger for the egg take hold of me.

I looked into the kid's face expecting to see my own possessiveness reflected there, but there was a different sort of hunger in her face. Her eyes were bright with pride as she came toward me, holding the egg out to me reverently.

"I am sorry to interrupt this touching little scene, but I am afraid that belongs to me, ladies, and I suggest you put it back where you got it," said an urbane masculine voice with just a hint of laughter.

We both turned to see a form rising from a brown armchair with the stuffing boiling from a slash in one arm. The demon king, I thought, and my heart gave a great salmon leap of fear. But when the form stepped into the light cast by the amethyst, it was a tall and extremely handsome man clad in a charcoal sports jacket, a Neo Tokyo T-shirt with a Japanese motif, gray jeans, and loafers. His hair was very short and he was clean-shaven, but when he smiled again I saw the flash of a black stud on his tongue.

"You are the demon king," I said.

He smiled. "I am, and you are yet another thief sent by the hags."

"I have come to take back something you stole," I said evenly.

His brows lifted and his smile widened. "Just like that?"

I drew a shaky breath and reached out to scoop the egg from the kid's hands. I looked down at it and that was a mistake, because when I managed to look up again the demon had the kid, and although he was still handsome, there was an ugly look in his eyes.

"Let her go," I said.

"The hags lied to you. They will never turn you into one of them. That is witchkind for you. They are all about themselves."

"The witch said—" I began.

"Yes, yes, that you were chosen because you had special abilities, yada yada. You didn't fall for that, did you? I mean, no offense, but look at you. They offered power to a weak, powerless woman, and they backed it up with a threat. A terrible death versus magic powers. Hmmm, tough choice."

"You are lying," I said.

"I lie often and well, but I can also tell the truth if it suits me. Did the hags tell you the witch I took the stone from had originally stolen it from me?"

"You'd say anything to get your hands on this."

He laughed, revealing perfect white teeth. "My dear woman, do you really imagine I can't simply take it from you, even using this weak human form? You are middle-aged and fat, and you were never fit. And this form you see is only the form your mind has cloaked me in, because it is too weak to see the truth. But you are correct, of course. I would lie and cheat and murder to possess the egg. Indeed, I have done all of those things for far lesser prizes. But in this case, the truth should do nicely. The witches are using you, and when you bring this to them, you will be returned to the plane crash. End of story. Literally."

"In the movies, the bad guys always talk too much," the kid said suddenly.

The demon king smiled down at her, but I saw her wince and realized he was digging his fingers into her shoulders. Only for a moment his fingertips looked like claws. The egg pulsed in my fingers, but I managed not to look down. I looked instead at the plinth on the edge of the hole and wondered why the demon had asked me to set the egg back on the plinth. Surely he should desire to have it safe in his hands.

"Do as I have said, while there is time," the demon said, and this time there was the hint of a snarl in his pleasant voice. I looked up to see that his brown eyes had gone red, and his smooth hair had lost its sleekness. He smiled, and my blood ran cold to see that his white teeth were now pointed and the dark stud on his tongue looked bigger.

"Okay. Maybe you are telling the truth. Let the kid go and let us get to the ground on the other side of the moat, and I'll give it to you," I said. "But you have to promise to return us to the airport before the plane takes off."

The demon's eyes flared. "I will return you, but first replace the egg on the plinth. Do it now, or forfeit the child." He nodded to the hole. "That goes directly into the void."

I saw acceptance on the kid's face and knew she was thinking, as I was, that Rose had said a familiar could be sacrificed. As I looked back at the demon it suddenly struck me that I didn't like kids because their vulnerability scared the crap out of me.

"What makes you think I would exchange a kid whose name I don't even know for this?" I held up the egg in one hand. "I hate kids. And what makes you think I will give it to the witches, either? That is what I told them, but once I can figure out what to do with this, I will deal with the witchfolk."

I had been moving closer to the demon as I spoke, and now, without warning, I tossed the egg at his face. He threw up his hands, gave a guttural scream that had more bird than human in it, and reeled back, only to stumble into the hole. The kid overbalanced and fell backward, too, but I was already diving forward. I caught one of her flailing hands in mine. She was slight, but there was enough weight in her to bring me thumping painfully to my knees at the edge of the hole.

"Take my wrist with your other hand," I cried, for her small hand was slipping from my grasp.

She shook her head, and I saw that she was holding the amethyst egg in her free hand. "Take it," she said, holding it up, eyes shining with triumph.

"I can't. If I let go of one hand, you'll fall. Throw it up and take my hands, quickly!"

"What if it breaks!" she said.

"Better it than you. Now come on!" I screamed.

She threw it, and it gave a great blinding pulse of light as she caught hold of my hands. Immediately I adjusted my grip and hauled her up laboriously until she could scramble the rest of the way. We both lay on the edge of the void for a second, panting and gasping. Then the kid's expression changed, and I knew from her stricken face what I would see when I turned.

The amethyst egg lay in small pieces, all of them dull. "That's that, then," I said as red light speared into the grotto.

• • •

Rose was waiting for us at the foot of the steps. On the other side of the moat, Jasper stretched out on the ground with his massive head resting on his paws. The fog had long gone, and the plain stretched out dead and black in all directions, the early morning light giving it a reddish brown tinge that reminded me unpleasantly of congealed blood.

"I failed," I said.

"No," said Rose. "You got the amethyst egg from Chagrin before the Dreadful Dawn."

"But I broke it," I said.

"The child broke it," Rose said mildly. "We saw what happened because of the eye you carried."

"How could it see anything in my pocket?" I asked.

"It is a metaphorical eye," the witch said impatiently, as if I ought to have known that. "You were clever to work out that the demon could not bear to touch the egg. Chagrin defeated those who came before because they did not reach the egg. But instead of walking away when you had it, you chose the child over it."

I glared at her and asked, "So what happens now?" She chuckled.

"Now you go back to the real world and learn to see it through the eyes of a witch. Then the real work will begin." Rose dropped her hand to Jasper's head, and just like that, we were all standing on the little path leading to my front door. The cottage, bathed in golden morning light with its little garden full of roses and lavender and the twisted lilac bush, humming with bees and glistening with spider threads, had never looked lovelier.

"It's perfect," said the kid, looking past me at the house wistfully.

"The bond of witch and familiar cannot be broken unless the familiar dies," Rose said, looking at me. "However, she can be taken to her original destination, if you prefer."

I glanced at the kid, who was carefully not looking at me. "Maybe we'll stick together for the time being," I said gruffly

"Very well," said Rose. A black crow appeared and landed on the edge of the verandah roof. It uttered a drab croak, and the witch sighed. "I am summoned, but I will return in due course. In the meantime, see what you can figure out for yourself. Just one tip: when you summon an orange juice, try not to be so specific. Calling up anything from a specific moment in the past consumes a lot of energy."

She set her hand on Jasper's head, and they both vanished. The crow uttered a croak and launched itself into the air, too. I watched it until it had flown out of sight, then I looked down at the kid and said brusquely, "I am Hester Hallow."

She gave me a glimmering smile and said shyly, "My name is Katya, but you can call me Kat."

• • • • • • • • • •

SLEEPING BEAUTY

THORAIYA DYER

It's time for me to go into the earth.

I feel that imaginary, frigid wind blowing across my skin, even though I'm protected by dozens of metres of steel and double-glazed, bulletproof glass. Before I go, I want to finish my chocolate pudding. Cream slides down its steep sides like the doomed terminal face of a melting glacier turning to forked streams over volcanic soil. My mouth waters.

"It hurts me to see you like this," Pete says, his buttoned overcoat, grey cuffs and gunmetal timepiece swimming into my peripheral view. I don't ask him to sit at my table but he sits. His grey eyes fasten pitifully onto my face over the football-sized pudding that waits on my plate.

If only that were true, I think, irritated. *It would make me happy to see you hurt.*

"Like what?" I say innocently, carving into the pudding with my spoon. Steam and liquid chocolate erupt from its centre.

"Like this. There was a time I thought you were smart enough, strong enough, to be in the parliament instead of on the sidelines. But look at you. One setback and you've gone to hell. You're going to give yourself a heart attack."

"You care about my heart, Pete? That's so sweet."

Not as sweet as this sweet, sweet pudding.

His pity is gone now. Only anger is left in his eyes. Pure, white hot anger. He's heard what he expected to hear, confirmation that I've tripled my body weight over the past six months to punish him for rejecting me. Even though I've admitted to nothing of the sort.

He stands.

"Eat yourself to death, then. You're only hurting yourself."

"That's not what you just said."

I smile at him as he walks away. People in the food court watch him go. *He's on television*, they whisper to one another. *The new anchorman. He must have been pumping that woman for information. She's one of the Minister's science advisers. She knows about the meteor, the one that's coming close enough to cast a shadow over us.*

That woman, they say, or sometimes, *that fat woman*. Despite decades of experience, I can't say exactly where the tipping point is between *that woman* and *that fat woman*. A certain amount of extra weight is expected in a desk job. Obesity becomes ever more common. But there is a point where the invisibility of the unattractive woman becomes the behemoth impossible to ignore. Instead of skimming over you, the eyes stop, and they ask themselves, *Where does she buy those enormous jeans? What size underpants does she wear? How does she get out of bed?*

It is my bedtime. I can't even taste the pudding, now; it's just a floury pressure in my mouth; in my gut. My gorge is rising. Only a few more spoonfuls to go.

When I go to the front counter to pay for my pudding, the waitress says,

"See you tomorrow, Miss Mennin?"

"No," I say. "I'm going overseas on an assignment."

"Oh, how long will you be away?"

"Six months."

"Smart move! You'll be missing the Canberra winter."

I have always missed it. Sometimes, when I wake, there's still enough snow, and I'm slight enough, to go skiing for a week. More often than not, though, what's left is a thin, transparent crust of ice, split by the scarlet lignotubers of snow gums, their yawning and stretching already begun.

• • •

The basement holds the smell of apples.

Apples haven't been stored here for twenty years, but the earthen walls won't let the aroma fade; they're passing judgement on me for replacing the apples. I am no autumnal keeper of seeds, sun-warmed slice of the seasons, but a sleeping infertile abomination; unnatural accident; hidden shame.

Despite that, after all these years I've attained a kind of rapport with the apple seeds in jars and the sacks of old grain. It used to be a game with my mother, to guess which seeds were still alive. We'd split them to see the green inside or the ashy layers of the dead ones.

Back then, I used to cheat by feeling the weight of them in my palm. Life is heavy.

But now I can tell without touching them. Somehow, I can smell the life in them.

My mother bought the orchard, and with it, the barn, when I was six years old. I told her I couldn't sleep properly in my bed. I felt cold. I wanted darkness and dirt all around me.

She cried, that first time. Stayed beside me and cried and waited for me to wake. She cries a lot, since it happened. I should phone her laboratory, now, to let her know I'm tucking myself in for the long sleep, but she'll only cry and apologise, and there's no point in it.

It's done.

She was trying to invent a cure for obesity, a one-off hibernation that would melt the fat away. When she couldn't get approval, she decided to test it on herself. It was her own DNA that she used to make the virus target-specific; to make it safe, she thought.

Only, her DNA is in me, too. It's these little unintended consequences that always catch them out. Why is that? When any normal, not-smart person could have picked the fatal flaw? Her immune system fought the virus off, much to her dismay.

But I was only six years old.

The apple press and the copper still are long gone. No more bottles of cider rest on the racks. If I live long enough, maybe my essence will seep into these walls.

Maybe the basement will smell of me, long after I am gone.

• • •

I dream of fire.

• • •

When I wake, for a moment I believe that a forest of mushrooms has grown up around me. I can't see them, in the dark, but I smell them.

Why is it so dark?

When I open the trapdoor, there's no longer a barn to block out the sky. Only fetid, rotting humus. And the sky is grey, grainy, like an old black and white television set refusing to tune.

The city is gone. I stare down from my hilltop at a plain devoid of anything green or growing.

I can think of only one explanation. The meteor did not pass by. Dust from the impact has blocked solar radiation and caused the death of all plants. The death of animals that feed on plants. The death of animals that feed on animals that feed on plants.

Hunger rises in me. I am awake. I need food.

There are mushrooms. Valleys of edible fungi. I pluck them; suck them from wooden surfaces. I dig for them in the soil. My clawed fingers emerge, triumphant, tangled with worms. I swallow the worms whole, unwilling to taste them, but unable to discard them. My choices are few.

The sky brightens and darkens and brightens again. I don't see the sun. I don't feel its warmth. For an instant, I don't want to obey my disgusting urge to eat; what is the point of living when everyone else is dead?

My life was always lonely. I had my mother's love, but that was all. I loved them, though. All those unique and imperfect people. I showed my love by writing the best reports I knew how to write; doing the best research I knew how to do. My warnings didn't protect them.

It turns out there was no point to me then, and no point to me, now, but perhaps I am more animal than I know, because my rational mind is not able to override my instincts.

I use the worms to bait snares for carrion-eating birds. Their meat is dark. I eat it raw. The spring is colder than any spring I've ever known. The bird skins with their glossy black feathers, I make into a blanket to keep warm, stitching them together with wooden slivers; a blanket of blunt needles.

My mother is dead. She must be dead. Everyone is dead.

I can't stop eating, even when I'm bawling my eyes out.

• • •

The next time I wake, the world is a little brighter.

"I miss you," I say to the smell of my mother that lingers even after my eyes are all the way open.

If she hadn't done this to me, I'd be dead, too. But I know I'm not able to reproduce. I'm no saviour of the human race. I wouldn't be, even if there was a man hibernating beside me. I loved Pete because he seemed like an uncaring husk, but I could sense the seed of compassion inside him. It never got a chance to grow. His corpse is here, somewhere. Worms, mushrooms. Perhaps I have eaten organic material that was once part of him.

"Peter Samford," I say to the clear sky, "I wouldn't sleep with you if you were the last man on Earth."

Sunlight warms my skin. Immediately I feel optimistic.

Are there others?

There are always others.

We're like cockroaches.

Once the worst of my hunger is sated, I set off to find them.

I walk down the hillside, wrapped in my raven cloak. Underfoot, ferns are busy uncurling. Moss is beginning to spread. My clothes, my shoes, are too big, but I'll grow into them.

I stop to eat. Worms, mushrooms. Like knowing which seeds are viable, I know which mushrooms are safe. It wasn't always the way; I'm like a human pig, now, sniffing for truffles. Have my cells been instructed to manufacture pig proteins as well as grizzly bear ones? Only my mother would know.

My mother's gift; the gift that keeps on giving. She used to pick the mushrooms off her pizza. It was the texture, like slugs, she said.

I have eaten slugs and I disagree.

I eat dandelion shoots and pigweed. I gobble sour, under-pollinated blackberries and the sweet heads of kangaroo grasses. I catch birds and the now abundant frogs. There are streams of clear water. I drink from them.

There's nobody in the scorched, flattened remnant of the city. No secret tunnels. No footprints in the ash.

Cold catches me before I can walk to the coast, to the next, bigger, second city. I dig a tunnel and reinforce it. I sleep.

• • •

It takes most of my waking months to walk the rest of the way.

I smell the snow-in-waiting, think: *It's three years since I sat at the parliament house cafeteria, eating chocolate pudding.*

The second city, too, is burned to the ground, but roofs of rubble have been erected over entrances to underground car parks.

Footprints mark the ground between the cracked, patchwork concrete slab that the city once stood on and the freshwater sources that slide curious fingers around it.

When I see the dark silhouettes moving, I stay low. What bestial depths have these people sunk to? I don't care to know. Not now.

Not when snow is coming to old Sydney Town, too early and too deep. If I don't dig a shelter now, it will be too late, too difficult to break through the ice.

I take a last, deep drink from a subzero stream, and hear a voice that belongs to memory.

"Kate," says Peter Samford, aghast, stumbling back from the water's edge, upsetting his wheelbarrow full of water bottles. "Kate Mennin?"

His head is a skull. His eyes are sunken. I see his ribs at the open collar of his shirt.

"You're not real," he shouts at me. "You're not real."

He is starving. Yet he has survived. In my pre-hibernation condition, I am four times his mass, though he remains taller than me, a shivering skeleton.

"One more winter," I say. "Make it through one more winter and the earth will be returned to you, Peter Samford."

He runs away, leaving his wheelbarrow behind.

• • •

Deciding to leave it hidden, I gently fold my raven-feather cloak.

My clothes? I can't take them off. They're the only ones I have. Four years in the same clothes. The abandonment of my normal hormonal cycles to the grizzly's fat storage and hibernation mechanisms has meant no menstrual blood to musk them, but they reek, all the same, of soil and sweat and sorrow.

They are ten sizes too big, hanging like a collapsed tent over the bones of my shoulders. I could steal from the starving stick-people, but they might die. Stealing seems more serious when there are lives at stake.

At the same time, it seems entirely more necessary. It's how this country was made, I suppose, before it was blasted clean.

The footprints connecting the city to its fresh water have become well-trodden paths. Men and women in army uniforms take note of my arrival. My stomach is audible. I'm as skinny as they are. They direct me to a kind of refugee camp that overlooks a harbour littered with steel wrecks. A grey-bearded man with watery eyes gets up from an old piece of carpet. He's winding the ends of bits of wire together to make a longer spool.

"I'm Ted," he says. "I'll show you where to go."

The bridge is rusted, but it still stands. I spot another refugee camp on the north side of the harbour. There are no gulls. Nor are there people fishing.

"What is your name?" an old woman asks me in a soft voice when we reach the main building. It's made of salvage, its supports of different materials, different lengths, but it's well-made; it doesn't rattle in the chill salt wind.

"Kate," I say. I haven't said it aloud for so long, I barely recognise it as mine.

"Surname?"

"Mennin," I say, and she laughs as she records it in the yellowed pages of a spiral-bound book.

"You don't want to tell me? That's fine. Mennin is as good a name as any. Ted can show you where to shower, eat and rest. We'll assign work tomorrow morning."

I ask her to look for my mother's name. It's why I've come. It's what I'm there for.

"No," the old woman says at last, after skimming the pages of the book. "No record of her."

"Please, let me look," I say. Her eyesight is probably hopeless.

Reluctantly, she passes over the book.

It's not her eyesight. My mother's name is not there.

Peter Samford's name is.

"Pete Samford," I mutter as Ted leads me to the cold showers.

"You mean the Priest," Ted says, his furry eyebrows shooting up. "Have you come to worship? Of course, that's why you've taken that name."

"Worship who? What?"

"Mennin," he says. "She's the earth goddess. The Priest saw her in a vision last winter. She told him the earth would be returned to him. Do you wish to attend the ceremony?"

"No," I say. I don't want to see Pete, crazy or not. And I don't feel any urge at all to correct Ted when it comes to the supposed vision. If belief in the earth goddess kept Samford from dying over winter, who am I to set him straight?

Besides, nobody can know what I am. Not now, not when there isn't enough food to go around. *They'd despise me more than ever,* I think.

Just then, I glimpse colourful pictures on the walls of the bunkrooms. The rooms are terrible, claustrophobic spaces, each with a dozen pair of men's boots lined up outside the door. Bundled shapes of sleeping adults lie on some of the simple, shelf-like bunks, but it's the gleaming posters that catch my eye through the open doors of the rooms.

It's fat porn. All of it. Naked women rolling in calorific wealth.

I stop still in the doorway and stare at it, astounded.

Ted retraces his steps to see what I'm looking at. He grunts, takes my sleeve and leads me away, to the mess at the very end of the corridor. I am given a small bowl of porridge and a vitamin C drink. My raucous stomach refuses to be silenced.

In the night, I leave the little settlement. I walk down to the shoreline and stuff my face with seaweed and jellyfish off the sand. In the morning, I climb the sandstone cliffs to find eggs and snakes to eat.

Then I eat mushrooms. It occurs to me that there were no mushrooms in the settlement. No wild greens. I have no time to spare for them at first, but as the months pass and I grow fatter and sleeker than I have since the impact, with more and more plant sugars to feed on, I realise I have a little time to spare.

A little time to gather mushrooms and leave them in baskets outside the rubble houses of the settlers.

A little time to take their sacks of grain and sort them into viable and non-viable seeds.

The children who are supposed to watch the grain are always napping. They are thin and short on energy. I can't blame them for falling into exhausted sleep. One moonlit night, a little girl opens her bleary eyes and catches me cross-legged on her tarpaulin, pawing through a sack of barley. The time when I could spring lightly to my feet and dash into the trees is months behind me. I'm wearing my full weight and my raven cloak, and my skeleton is groaning with it in the chill.

I take a single seed from the sack.

"This one," I whisper to her. "This one is the only one that will grow."

She takes it reverently, her eyes popping.

"Thank you, Mennin," she whispers back.

"I'm going now. Please don't wake the others."

• • •

Years later, it is they who leave offerings for me.

Baskets of tomatoes, sugar cane and kiwi fruit. All pollinated by the wind. Bottles of strawberry cider. I am an autumn goddess. That's the season when they see me walking at the edges of their new civilisation, hands outstretched to catch falling yellow leaves, wishing they were butterflies, straining for the sound of honeybees. There is no apple harvest; never will be again. Children will find the basement one day, and crawl into it, and how will they describe the smell?

I can't say where the tipping point is between skinny, wandering woman and Mennin, the Earth Mother. But there is a point where they can't ignore me any longer. Though I keep myself hidden as best I can, they spot me, sometimes. I hear them shouting to one another and realise I've been seen.

Sometimes, I stop so they can talk to me. I still get lonely. I still talk to my mother's ghost.

"Mennin," a bony, black-haired girl cries. "Mennin, will you bless my fields?"

I turn in a circle of ebony feathers, a circle of early morning mist. My face is dirty. My eyes are wide.

"Yes," I call back to her. "I will bless them."

The girl drops to her knees. Her brothers, her mother and her father kneel beside her. Their bare knees are in rich soil. I have eaten worms here before.

"Will you grant me a child, Mennin?" the girl begs.

"Soon," I say.

I wrench myself away. The air is still, but I am windswept.

It is time for me to go into the earth.

• • • • • • • • • • •

PIGROOT FLAT

JASON FISCHER

The flies should have given fair warning to Hazel. That, or Codger straining at his leash and barking like an idiot. But the dog was asleep, his feet twitching in a dream. Hazel was wool-gathering in the garden, turning pigshit into the red earth and wondering if anything would grow. A dozen flies became a hundred, then the tin-cans began to rattle.

Dropping the shovel, Hazel ran.

Swearing at the useless dog, she knocked him in the ribs with her boot. Codger barked then, barked for all he was worth. Hazel hauled him along by the collar, and the stupid mutt yipped excitedly, doing his best to wriggle out of her grip.

Hazel had done a turn or two as a roustabout, and years spent throwing sheep and feed gave her ropy arms strength. More cans rattled, and she dragged the pig-dog up the ladder, even as he yipped and gagged and choked on his collar.

Early on she'd spent a whole day on the roof, and nightfall saw her sunburnt and thirsty. She had a camp up there now, slept there most nights. A beach umbrella, food and water, a swag and some chairs. The old rifle and the CB, for all either were worth. Codger couldn't be trusted not to fall off the bloody roof, and so he was tied to the TV antenna.

He barked enough to do himself an injury. Hazel sighed, and watched as her visitors ran around the yard, buggering everything up. Dozens of them today, tripping over the ankle-high fencing wire, rattling the tin cans and cowbells she'd attached every few feet.

They were in the garden now, knocking over stakes and squashing the seedlings. The sound of breaking glass came from the green-house, and they even tried the doors on the four-wheel drive, chattering excitedly as they pounded on the windows.

"Ba Ba Ba!" they shouted gleefully. HAZEL'S ECO TOURS, a dusty decal read on the driver's side door. The tires were flat, the engine out and in pieces.

"Stupid bastards," Hazel said, wincing as they clattered around on the porch, ran through the house underneath her. It got that it wasn't even worth fixing up the doors and windows, so she just left everything open now. That way, they'd go through the house with a minimum of damage, and pour out into the backyard when they got bored.

Hazel had set up a playground to draw them out. Toys, bikes, footballs, even a swing-set. She'd visited the Halletts recently, her neighbours from ten clicks up the road. They'd had kids, probably all dead now. Their farm was silent, and she never cared to linger long.

The ladder scraped along the guttering, and Hazel swore. She dropped her half-rolled cigarette, and slid across the hot tiles, grabbing at the top rung. There was resistance at the other end, and she peered over the side. A rotten face stared up at her.

A woman, a few days on the wrong side of dead. She should have been so much rotten meat, but here she was, smiling up at Hazel, hauling on the ladder for all she was worth. The stink was enough to make Hazel gag, and almost every inch of the walking corpse was covered in flies.

"Play?" the dead woman said, rotten slug of a tongue still working in her mouth. In time, she would become like her idiot friends, speaking in an autistic babble, finally communicating with nothing but the click of teeth, the excited wheeze of maggoty lungs. The fresh ones liked to have a chat.

Hazel let go of the ladder, watched as it clattered to the red earth. The dead woman tried to raise it up again, couldn't quite work out the angle. She gave up the attempt to reach the roof and stood underneath Hazel, waving cheerfully. Fetching up another cigarette with shaking hands, Hazel looked down at the corpse, tried to recognize who it was. Probably someone from town, or hiding out on one of the stations. Underneath the shroud of flies, the dead woman wore dusty jeans and a flanno, torn to strips now.

Near as she could tell, the dead woman had been beautiful once. Maybe a tourist, or some fool from the coast, looking to snag a rich farmer. Hazel felt angry at the thought, and then weird, the way she remembered when she saw someone prettier than her. Jealous, wanting to belong to their world.

Now, the pretty girl was just dead meat. Hazel shook her head, vanished the dark thoughts. Everything was different now, and Hazel needed to get used to it.

Codger was going nuts. He stretched out as far as the leash would allow, snarling along the gutter's edge. The TV antennae strained, and bent with a worrying creak.

"Doggy!" the dead woman shrieked with delight, pointing. "Dog doggy. Doggy. Play."

Hazel looked over at her campsite, wondered if it was worth fetching Gilbo's gun. A big .303, it would drop anything worth dropping. As he'd often reminded her after a few beers.

"Play!" the dead woman insisted, reaching upwards as if in benediction. Codger yipped and hauled at his collar till he was bug-eyed, teeth and scrap of tongue dancing along the edge of the gutter.

They were like something out of the old science-fiction movies, like at the picture theatre when Gilbo was courting her. The recently deceased, risen from death and come for the living. But in none of the b-grade horror flicks had the ghouls been like this.

Idiots. Cheerful monsters, who came calling like the Sandlot Kids. When they caught something living, they'd swarm in, babbling and chatting, smearing their rotten fingers all over the poor bugger, slobbering and kissing them.

That was all it took. You'd be dead in an hour, and up and walking by sunset. They didn't need to bite you, not these idiot dead things. They killed you with love, doomed you with a toddler's affection.

Hazel considered their affliction, and decided that she understood them all too well. She had a grudging respect for these lost souls, exasperation rather than anger as they wrecked the place. Turned out it was hard to hate something that loved you back.

The dead woman was caught up in a stream of corpses that poured out of the house. A man who was almost rotted down to bone carried Hazel's toaster. Another an old record. The walking corpses made for the impromptu playground, and the dead woman waved at Hazel.

"Bye!" she called. "Bye doggy!"

Hazel watched the corpses at play, and realised that her distraction worked too well. They clamboured over the swingset, and lined up patiently behind the slippery dip. Normally, they'd have lost interest and moved on by now.

There was a pattern to these visits—gangs of the friendly dead visited all these old holdings at least once a month, and back again on their way to town. She'd seen groups heading north to Darwin, others south and maybe all the way down to Alice.

She picked up the rifle. Grimaced. Set it down by the water container. Codger looked up from his paws, whimpered with something that might have been boredom or frustration.

Only a dozen or so of the idiot dead, but she couldn't bring herself to shoot them. They were dangerous, she reasoned, the way that a snake or a dingo could be dangerous. Just part of their nature, and they couldn't help the way they were put together.

They were dead once, but the rules for death had changed.

Even as she watched the joyful corpses, she found her eyes drawn to the dam. A broken tractor lurked by the water, jerry-rigged with a digging bucket. The metal teeth rested on a bank of cracked earth, mud once.

Across the bank, she'd laid out sheets of tin, weighed them down with cinder blocks. Empty beer bottles, anything that would make noise. The beginnings of a concrete slab; a mixer standing idle, cement bags split and gone bad from neglect. Gravel was scattered everywhere. Cursing and crying, she had quit halfway through, tossing the shovel out into the middle of the dam.

Something buried once was buried good enough.

Next to this, the trunk of a long-dead iron gum, bound with chain. Old iron, red from decades in the weather. The links ran down the trunk, ran across the clay-pan until they ended in a single shackle.

The meat chain.

Hazel took her crossword book out of her back pocket, and attacked the squares with a stub of pencil. There was nothing left to do but put her feet up and wait for the pigs.

• • •

Pigroot Flat belonged to Gilbo's dad, until lung cancer ate him inside out. Young Gilbo didn't have anyone else, and so he spent five years in a boy's home down in Adelaide. On his eighteenth birthday he came back, moved into the old shanty. Now Gilbo was gone too, and Hazel supposed that made it her place now.

Ten acres of scrub, an hour's drive west of Katherine. Gilbo had spent twenty years on this block, trying to turn his old man's leavings into cash. He put up a dormitory for the backpackers who never visited, and bought riding horses that grew fat and lazy in their yard.

"We're too far from town," Hazel said to Gilbo, back when she still had hope of a ring on her finger. "Should look into guided tours. A boat on the Gorge. Take tourists pig shooting."

Gilbo did none of these things. He drank, broke Hazel with his words, then his fists. Introduced her to the meat chain.

• • •

That old fear tickled through her belly. Hazel bit at her nails as the sun drifted through the scrub, watched as her dead visitors organized a simple ball-game.

She gave up on the crossword. Opening a tin of dog-food for Codger, she heard grunting, the thump of many feet, an excited squeal that echoed through the bush. Codger danced about on the roof, torn between his dinner and the sudden stink of pig.

They came pouring out of the bush, a big hunting pack. Razorbacks with nasty tusks, their fat sows bouncing along behind them. Piglets jumped around, struggling to keep up.

The end of the world meant nothing but good times and fine dining to these residents of the Northern Territory. Hazel watched as the pigs bolted through the playground, knocking the dead over. They squealed and squabbled amongst themselves, stripping the rotten meat from still twitching skeletons. Whatever fear they'd had of people was long gone.

The dead girl had enough sense to climb the slippery dip, but a young boar clambered after her, snapping and slavering. It reached her foot, and tore it loose. Three more pigs joined the first, fighting to get at the freshest corpse.

Hazel wasn't scared of the idiot dead, and the pigs were just a fact of life around here. But that old anxiety still danced around in Hazel, until her gut felt like it was full of bitter coffee. Gilbo taught this feeling to her, even as he showed her how to take it away. There was a process to follow, but now the bloody pigs were ruining things.

Fear. Amplified by the simple fact that she was completely alone. Last woman standing. She trembled all over, moved her dry lips in a silent litany.

Meat chain.

It had to be now. The rules had changed, but it was do this, or lose her mind.

"You bloody well leave her alone," Hazel muttered. She rested the .303 on an old esky, lining up the sights on the next leaping pig.

"Keep away from her."

A thunderous crack, and then the first pig ran in a confused circle, bleeding and screaming. Codger barked fit to burst, as Hazel sent round after round into the pack. Finally they fled, some dragging their rotten meals back into the bush.

She let Codger off the chain, and the pig-dog fought out of her hands, leapt off the roof with no hesitation. He was off, barking and bounding through the scrub like madness on legs.

Gripping the gutter, Hazel lowered herself down, dropping almost a metre to the ground. Wincing, she limped across the yard. The last light of dusk painted the carnage in shades of grey.

The idiot dead never stood a chance. Rotten meat lay strewn across the yard, guts and bones spread wide by the feral pigs. Some of the bodies were still twitching and trying to move. Hazel coughed up a little vomit into her mouth, fought the rest back down. *This is not the time to lose it, love.*

A razorback lay slumped across the slippery dip. Its life-blood ran down the plastic chute, pooling at the bottom. A fat pig, well-fed and fresh, but Hazel wasn't game enough to eat it. Who knew what the zombie-meat did to its insides? She missed bacon and pork chops, but it wasn't worth the risk.

"Piggy?" the forlorn voice came. Still perched at the top of the slippery dip, the dead woman looked down at Hazel with some confusion.

"Piggy's gone," she replied, and crooked a finger. "Come on, love. We can play now if you want."

The dead woman smiled then, lips sliding across a slimy jag of teeth. She slid awkwardly down the slide, clambering across the barrel chest of the dead pig. Hazel moved backwards, beckoned. The dead woman fell to the ground, tried to rise on the shattered bone where her leg ended now.

"It's okay," Hazel said, making sure to stay clear of those reaching hands. Even in the gloom, she could see the rapture in the corpse's face, the joy of friendship, even love. The dead woman rose, crawled forward when walking failed her.

"We can be friends now," Hazel called out, and meant it. "Let's play over here."

She led the dead woman on, past the house. There was a toolshed by the silent dormitory, and Hazel reached into the gloom, found the old school bag just inside the door. Dusty now, wreathed in cobwebs. A familiar weight, and it felt good.

"Keep coming," she said.

Codger came back from his fruitless pursuit of the pigs, trotting through the yard with a human femur in his mouth. When he spotted the dead woman crawling towards his mistress, he dropped the bone, hackles rising. Lips slid away from bared fangs, and a snarl came from deep down in his chest.

"Leave off!" Hazel shouted. When Codger began growling and edging closer, she fetched up a stone and skipped it across the dust. The dog shied away from the bouncing rock. Fetching up the bone, Codger retreated underneath the house pilings, sulking and whining.

"Idiot dog," Hazel said, shuffling backwards. The dead girl crawled closer, beaming, reaching for Hazel's feet almost shyly. This close, the mortal stink almost overcame her. Hazel fought the urge to vomit.

"Play?"

"Over here."

Slow backwards shuffle, ever aware of the disease on those lips, knowing that a single scratch would doom her. She'd fought off this moment as long as she could, held those old feelings at bay.

There were ways to cope with life on Pigroot Flat.

Living woman and dead obscenity inched across the dusty yard, past the four-wheel drive, around the brooding hulk of the tractor. Hazel led the monster towards the dam, beckoning her on.

"You're beautiful. Pretty girl," Hazel said, wondering who she was trying to convince. The dead woman preened at the compliment, the slimy crack of her mouth turned up at the corners.

"Pretty," the cadaver agreed.

"This way," Hazel said with false cheer, beckoning as if to a puppy. She felt her boots crunch into gravel, lead the dead woman across the corrugated iron. Clattering across the iron, the corpse wheezed with excitement, moving faster now.

"Come and play, pretty girl," Hazel said, kneeling in the cracked clay. Behind her, thousands of mosquitos made an airfield on the dam water, dancing on the murky film. On the water's edge, the cracked clay gave way to pig shit and algae. She wouldn't let an animal drink from it, but that was the point of the whole thing, an element of Gilbo's infamous script.

Hazel tensed, held ready. Opening the school bag, she tipped out her tools, checked that everything was there. She'd need to be quick.

When bruise-coloured fingers brushed against her boots, Hazel ran around the iron gum. With reflexes born of farm-life, she snatched up the rusting snake that was the meat chain. Dove upon the dead woman like a calf in need of hog-tying.

She clapped the shackle around the corpse's ankle, just above its remaining foot. Even as it turned and grabbed at her, screaming like a terrified toddler, Hazel dodged the reaching hands. She pushed it face first into the clay, knelt in the small of the corpse's back. Something gave beneath her with a sickening crack. Hazel's whole world seemed like a miasma of rot and flies.

In seconds she had the muzzle on. A wire frame, much like what the greyhounds wore. Next came the oven mitts, strapped onto the corpse's hands with duct tape.

"Yes, that's it," Hazel exulted, looking down on her handywork. A moment later she staggered over to the dam, and vomited up everything she'd ever eaten.

• • •

Gilbo vanished for a week once, took the house-keeping money and the only car that worked. He came back in the middle of the night, and Hazel woke to a furious beating. He was blind drunk, stank of booze and vomit. She begged, pleaded, crawled across the bed. He hauled her in with no effort, dragged her out of bed by an ankle. Boxed her almost into that sweet darkness.

From a dim place in her mind, she noted how he broke her nose, cracked a rib, and snapped several of her teeth. She'd been beaten before, but never this bad. *He's going to kill me.*

"It's time, bitch!" he shouted. Gilbo carried her out of the house, across the yard. Towards the dam, the iron gum stump, the old chain that he refused to speak of. She wriggled and fought, but Gilbo was built like a brick shithouse.

He threw her to the ground, kicked her in the gut for good measure. Winded, she tried to crawl away, tried to call for help. *Stupid.* Even if she had an air-raid siren, the neighbours wouldn't hear. Gilbo knelt on her back, an implacable force. Something fastened around her ankle, a tight pinch.

Next came a muzzle, and she cried out as the steel jammed against her broken face. He placed something around each hand, binding it up tight with tape.

Then Gilbo left her alone, to sob and shake in the dark.

Terror wouldn't let Hazel sleep. She saw the sun rise over the dam as she shivered in her dirty nightie. The house was silent and still, and she strained her ears, heard Gilbo's snoring.

Every movement brought a wave of pain. Hazel worked herself up to a sitting position, tried to tear off the tape. She couldn't do anything with the mittens on, and the muzzle prevented her from tearing at the tape with her teeth.

Heart sinking, she examined the shackle, noted how the rough metal already wore at her skin. The iron was weathered but strong, almost a half-inch thick. Even if she had a hammer and chisel, Hazel doubted she could hack through this. The other end of the chain fed through a bracket, hammered deep into the tree.

Planting both feet against the stump, Hazel strained, pulled the chain as hard as she could. After several minutes, she slumped to the ground, defeated. She wouldn't be leaving until Gilbo unlocked it. Or killed her.

The sun climbed into the sky, and burnt the last of the night chill. Hazel started to roast in the sun, and by the time noon rolled around, she was burnt from tip to toe. Gilbo snored through the day. The sweat poured out of Hazel, and she circled the stump, trying to hide in a sliver of shade.

She licked her lips, wincing as her dried tongue danced across the skin Gilbo had split with his fists. Her whole mouth and throat were as dry as leather, and she ached with thirst.

When he'd had a skinful, Gilbo was known to sleep till dusk. Hazel realized that she might die of thirst before he bothered to see to her.

Crawling across the clay, Hazel inched towards the old dam. Her hands slid around in the greasy pig shit, but she picked herself up, reached towards the foul water.

A tug at her ankle. She looked back to see the chain at full stretch. The water's edge was just beyond her reach. She strained, winced as the shackle rubbed her ankle raw.

Curled around the stump and dozing, Hazel was later woken by the slam of the screen door. She looked up in terror as Gilbo stepped off the porch, a dusty old school bag in one hand.

"Richie, please," she whimpered, daring to use his first name. He crossed the yard like a man with a purpose, and Hazel couldn't remember the last time she'd seen him stand so tall.

He looked at her indifferently, all the anger of last night gone. This dead stare was far more terrifying than the drunken rage, and she trembled, tried to back away from this stranger.

"This is the meat chain," he told her, placing the school bag on the ground. KATHERINE AREA SCHOOL, the faded old legend read. The leather straps were busted, and a canvas flap hung loose. He flipped it open, and Hazel moaned with fear.

Knives. A hacksaw. Hammers and even an old hand-drill.

"My great grand-dad brought this over from Mount Isa," he said, rattling the chain idly. "He had a claim there, ran a thousand head of sheep. Black fellas ran wild over there once, killing stock, spearing folks in their huts."

He tested a big knife against his thumb, found the edge wanting. Even as Hazel moved her lips in a silent plea, Gilbo worked a whet-stone over the blade.

"An army of savages, real cowboys and Indians stuff. Their land, and they fought for it tooth and nail. So, my great grand-dad lost one sheep too many, and saw red. Fixed this here chain into a stump, much like this one. Went out on his horse, sent a mob of blacks running. Killed three or four, dragged an old woman back by the hair."

Tested the edge, drew blood. Smiled, but it was just a quick twitch of the lips, his eyes set in a cold lizard stare.

"Kept her in the chain for a week, shot every black face that came to save her. In the end her mob were just trying to bring food and water, but he shot 'em just the same."

He ran the blade along her leg, little steel kisses that parted her skin, sent a trickle of blood into the red clay. She screamed, and her curses echoed through the lonely scrub.

"Turns out the meat chain was good fun. Character building. This here is a family heirloom. I've worn it too, and now it's your turn."

Gilbo brought her into the family tradition, a long and bloody lesson. He did not kill her that day, or the next. He promised that one day she would die in the meat chain, but only when she begged him for it, and only when he had a kid to pass this dark legacy onto.

Eventually Hazel agreed to these conditions, and she meant it too. Then he let her go. The visible wounds healed in time, and Gilbo never laid a hand on her from that day.

He had another outlet.

Hazel found a new role as Gilbo's apprentice. Lost waifs, hitchhikers and tourists, they all took a turn in the meat chain. Hazel was part lure, part caddy, and she handed over the knives, watched happily as her man carved up the women she'd befriended.

One night, Hazel put sleeping pills in Gilbo's curried prawns, concerned that he was going about things wrong. Quite simply, he didn't love them. Everything Gilbo did to the girls in the meat-chain was hateful, an act of violence, dominance. It was his legacy, and he didn't even understand it.

The true secret of the meat-chain was intimacy, a love that transcended all common sense. She saw glimmers of it, lurking around her man's shoulders as he went to work.

Even as the life rattled out of them, the girls always loved him. Friendship stripped down to a bare honesty, even as their skin parted from flesh and their flesh parted from bone. They shared confidences with their hulking killer, more than even Stockholm's Syndrome could explain.

These girls needed to be treated properly. With respect.

Gilbo woke in the meat chain, and died slowly. Hazel did her best to make him proud. About a week later she put him in the ground with all the others, and took over the family business.

Beautiful backpackers from Europe, leggy blondes with light smiles. They came to stay at her block, lured by the cheap rates. Green-friendly tours, run by a female owner-operator. A safe destination. It was hardly a success, but she got by.

Some came alone or in twos, and these were the tourists she sometimes introduced to the meat chain. Over days she befriended them, learnt their innermost secrets. They grew to love her, as she loved them, even as she ran Gilbo's tools over their bodies.

She wasn't deaf, knew that the tourists giggled at her crooked nose, her gappy smile. Teased her in their Nordic tongues, even as the four-wheel drive bounced their pert bodies around. Time was not kind to Hazel's looks, and no-one kissed her anymore. Still, she gave these girls new kisses, in all the places that the handsome men kissed them.

Hazel's circle of friends grew year by year. In the times that the chain was empty, she'd sit by the dam, reliving these brief friendships. She remembered them fondly, and mourned them with kindness.

Then one day, the world ended. New friends were hard to come by.

• • •

"This is the meat chain," Hazel told the dead girl. The corpse smiled up at her, reaching for her with mitten hands. She brushed aside the reaching hands, continued with the script.

"Chain," the dead woman echoed.

Apparently Gilbo's dad introduced the oven-mitts into the ritual; this was about the time that law-men took to scraping dead women's fingernails, to see who they scratched at in their last moments. Hazel figured a mass grave was damning enough, but praised her dead father-in-law today. The resurrected girl could do little to infect her.

Hazel wore a butcher's apron, rubber gloves that reached almost to her elbows. A bandana, soaked in vinegar to keep out the stink, and thick safety goggles from the shed. No sense risking a bit of spit or blood landing in her eyes.

She ran through the history of the chain, told her new friend all about her part in its legacy. She'd always found the initial begging and screaming a little annoying, so it was a pleasant surprise that the dead woman went along so cheerfully. She even echoed the words as best she could, and Hazel had never laughed so much.

But then it all went wrong. The woman happily let her peel off the rotten skin, take off layer after layer of meat. But the pain was missing. There was no communion to this, no intimacy. The dead woman did nothing but gurgle happily, even after Hazel took her slimy tongue out by the roots.

"It doesn't work!" Hazel cried. Wielding knife and saw, she broke the woman down into her individual parts, left with a neat stack of rank meat that continued to writhe. Normally this was a meditative time, a goodbye to a new friend. Hazel was shaken to the core, and hacked away messily. She'd never been lonelier, or more frustrated.

Empty.

Safe or not, it was time to leave Pigroot Flat.

She left the dead woman by the side of the dam. The stack of severed limbs continued to twitch and shiver. When Hazel limped back to the house, an arm rolled onto the ground, kept rolling until it was thrashing around in the dam.

Only then did Codger deem it safe enough to come out of hiding. He was canny enough to know that the pigs would be back, and they'd make short work of all that meat. He stole across the yard, wary of his mistress. In seconds he was back under the verandah, dragging the dead woman's head by a hank of hair. Her jaw still worked, and the remaining eye regarded the half-starved dog with love.

"Doggy," she mouthed, her blue lips curving up into a radiant smile.

• • •

Hazel spent a long time by the dam, bidding her friends goodbye. She made her final peace with Gilbo, and left Pigroot Flat, left her history slumbering beneath the earth. Codger trotted behind her but she threw stones and curses, drove him into the scrub. The dog had tasted people flesh now, would probably turn on her if she got too weak.

The township of Katherine was an open-aired graveyard, full of playful corpses. They splashed around in the Gorge, others wheezing rotten laughter as they kicked the footy. One even had a fishing line out, the hook dangling a good foot above the water.

The cars all sat on flats, batteries long dead. Gilbo might have got one working, but Hazel was no bush mechanic. Snatching a bicycle from a dead man's hands, she ignored the invitations to play, dodged their skeletal fingers.

She pointed the bicycle down the cracked highway, and rode.

Every place was the same. The apocalypse had rolled over every farmhouse, every roadhouse, every sheep station and shit-shack. Numb, burnt to leather by the sun, Hazel passed through Tennant Creek, Davenport, Alice Springs. The dead, red heart of Australia.

By now the idiot dead were little more than skeletons in the sun, sinew holding bones together, skin drawn taut. They waved enthusiastically, shuffling after her bicycle.

On the day she saw the crude fort, she was walking like a dead thing herself. The chain on her bicycle had snapped, but she pushed it mindlessly, useless pedals clicking, busted tire dragging. An enclave, set almost a mile from the highway. Behind the barricades, a stand of trees. *Perhaps a waterhole?*

The gate opened. Figures rushed towards her. Hazel dropped the bicycle to the red earth, and shook with silent sobs.

People embraced her. Someone pressed a water bottle against her lips, and she gulped it gratefully, water running down her filthy face.

They led her into their compound, and she gazed around in wonder. Buildings, green gardens, livestock. Kids, playing in the street.

People, dozens of people.

The first she'd seen in years.

They closed the gate behind her, and Hazel clutched the old schoolbag close, the one marked KATHERINE AREA SCHOOL. Dangling from the open canvas flap, a loop of rusty old chain.

"You're amongst friends now," someone said to her, and she smiled.

•••••••••••

THE FALL

STEPHEN DEDMAN

The flight to Tokyo had taken more than nine hours, without a chance for a cigarette, and the bus ride from the airport to the hotel took another two through a mostly grey landscape under a low grey sky. Wilson had to walk the last few blocks in the rain because the shuttle didn't go to his hotel, only to a more expensive one nearby. The lift groaned and shuddered as it took him up to his room, and the ride up to the thirteenth floor seemed to take as long as his flight. After shutting the door behind him and dropping his pack on the floor of the tiny room, he prised off his shoes and collapsed on the bed, face up. He drew a deep breath, then lit a cigarette and lay there for a few minutes, just reminding himself how it felt to be horizontal and motionless. Days like this convinced him that man was never meant to fly—or at least, he told himself wryly, never meant to fly economy class from Australia to Japan. He was too tired even to take any pleasure from the thought of finally being here.

It was already dark at six, when he finally found the energy to pick up the phone and call Kyoko and tell her he'd arrived safely.

• • •

Kyoko met him in the lobby. They recognized each other instantly, despite never having actually met: he was the only Westerner around, she the only person dressed in Lolita-Punk. She rushed up to him, then stopped just short of flinging her arms around him, and they stood almost nose-to-nose for a moment. Years of smoking had all but destroyed his sense of smell, but he was faintly aware of an elusive, exotic, enticing fragrance.

"How are you?" she asked, a little awkwardly. "Jet lag?"

"I'm okay, though my body clock's a little off. I didn't think it was night-time already."

"It gets dark early here, at this time of year. It's fall,nearly winter. Short days, long nights," she replied. "What is it in Australia? Spring? But it's spring in Australia, isn't it?"

Wilson nodded. "Where are we meeting Yoshi?"

"Ahh." Kyoko looked even more embarrassed. "Yoshi won't be coming with us."

"Will he be at the meeting tomorrow?" The three of them had been working together for years on an irregular web-based comic, *The Conqueror Worm*. Wilson had written most of the story, Kyoko had translated it into Japanese and drawn the human characters, but Yoshi had designed the distinctive steampunk hardware, the elaborate deathtraps, the architecture of Hell, and most of the dreaming demons. Though he was unable to draw a living being that didn't seem to be in constant agony, his mechanical plans were so painstakingly detailed that Wilson found it easy to imagine the devices working—which, he suspected, had played a major role in attracting the attention of a publisher.

"I don't think so," said Kyoko, uneasily. "He's . . . can we get out of here? There's a good sushi place around the corner."

• • •

The little restaurant was nestled between apartment buildings, and obviously catered to locals rather than tourists: Kyoko ordered for him, as Wilson's Japanese was rudimentary and no-one else in the place spoke any English. "Have you ever heard of hikikomori?" Kyoko asked, once the waitress was out of earshot.

"No."

"They're mostly boys, or young men, who don't get into university and can't find good jobs, so they stay at home, more and more, until they finally stop leaving their bedrooms completely unless there's no-one around. Yoshi's been like that for a few months."

Wilson stared into his green tea. "This happens often enough that you need a word for it?"

"Yes. I'm sure there are other cities where the unemployed find it hard to leave home, and are ashamed and withdraw to some degree . . . but the hikikomori are extreme cases. Yoshi still communicates in other ways—e-mail, mostly, or online chat with people he trusts—but he will not see anyone else or let them see him."

"You knew him before we started working on the comics, right?"

"Yes, in high school. He was doing well until the exams, but after that . . . " She paused, as the waitress returned with their miso soup, then lowered her eyes and stared into the bowl for a moment.. "He has headaches," she continued, when they were alone again, "sees things strangely, out of proportion, I don't know the English word . . . "

"Migraines?"

"Thank you. I know he's suffered from those for years, but they didn't stop him going to school. I think he was depressed, too, but it became much worse after his father died . . . which happened just after Yoshi failed the exams. I don't think there was any connection—Ushiba-san had been sick with cancer for some time—but Yoshi may not believe that."

Wilson swore softly under his breath. "What about selling *Worm*? Hasn't that helped him? I know the advance wouldn't have been enough to let him move out, but it must have made him feel better . . . "

Kyoko bit her lip, then looked at her watch. "It did, but not in a way that brought him out of the room . . . or out of himself. Please, I'll take you to the Ushibas' house. That might be easier than trying to explain any more."

• • •

Yoshi and his mother lived on the top floor of a narrow grey-walled apartment building that had been hastily and unlovingly built soon after World War II, and overlooked a murky canal. Kyoko pointed out the dull, dark, somehow eye-like window of Yoshi's room, then led the way up a stairwell that smelled of mildew and fish sauce.

Yoshi's mother answered the intercom, and seemed glad enough to see Kyoko, but warned them that Yoshi seemed still to be asleep. "I hear him moving about some nights after I've gone to bed," she said quietly in Japanese, as they removed their shoes and winter jackets. After the chill of the night, the apartment—heated by a small gas fire—seemed almost oppressively hot. "Not often: I think he waits until he's sure I'm asleep."

Wilson decided to let Kyoko translate for him, rather than trust to his own Japanese. "Does he speak to you at all?" he asked Mrs Ushiba, as they sat down at the kitchen table.

"He leaves notes, sometimes."

"Do you know if he ever leaves the building?"

"I don't think he ever does."

"Do you ever go into his room?"

"I tried. He put a latch on the door after that. He buys things on the internet and has them delivered here." She covered her mouth, hiding an embarrassed smile. Wilson looked at her, and said softly, in English, "Would it be a really bad idea to ask what sort of things?"

Kyoko thought about this for a second. "Probably," she replied; then, in Japanese, "Can we stay until he wakes up?"

Mrs Ushiba looked uncertain, then nodded. Kyoko took out her phone, and quickly keyed in a short message. "If he's awake, he'll probably answer, even if he doesn't actually get out of bed."

A few seconds later, the phone miaowed. "Tell him I'm here," suggested Wilson.

"He says Hi," said Kyoko, after another exchange of messages, "and he asks if you have a phone."

"No; my service provider doesn't work here."

"What about your computer?"

"I left it back at the hotel. Can you ask if he can come out?"

Kyoko hesitated, then did as she was asked."Yoshi says no, not while there are so many people here," she relayed, with a slight quirk of her lips. "He knows you've come a long way to see him, and he says he'll try to come out later . . . which means after I leave." She drummed her black fingernails on the shabby table, then looked at her watch. "There's a store around the corner; Mrs Ushiba and I can go there for a few minutes and have a coffee or something."

"We can't ask her to leave her own home!"

"It's a little early for her to go to bed," replied Kyoko. "If we go out for, say, twenty minutes, that gives him time to get dressed and come out to see you. I'll text him when we're about to come back. Do you have a better idea?"

• • •

When the women had gone, locking the door behind them, Wilson waited in the unnervingly quiet apartment for several minutes. He stared at Yoshi's bedroom door, noticing the faint zigzag cracks in the grey walls around it—souvenirs of a few earthquakes and many minor tremors—and despite his best efforts, found himself remembering how, in Dr *Jekyll and Mr Hyde*, Jekyll had also communicated by notes slipped under a door, unwilling to let anyone see that he'd transformed into Hyde . . . then, Dracula warning Jonathan Harker not to explore his half-ruined castle . . . then to "The Monkey's Paw", then Bluebeard . . . By the time he heard the bolt slide back, he half-expected to see Yoshi transformed into a Lovecraftian Deep One or a similar monstrosity. Instead, he saw a plump, weak-chinned, eerily pale Japanese teenager wearing black sweat pants and a T-shirt emblazoned with a portrait of Edgar Allan Poe.

Unlike the bare-walled living room, Yoshi's refuge was lined with posters, artwork, and unstable-looking bookshelves. Reproductions of Goya woodcuts and Giger grotesques, as well as tattered and much-annotated printouts of Yoshi's own designs for weapons, framed the desk; a scroll depicting the seven hells of Japanese mythology ran above the blackout curtains and around one corner; a full-sized picture of Elvira in an open coffin was taped to the ceiling directly above the unmade bed. "Excuse me for a moment," said Yoshi, speaking English so quickly he was barely coherent and brushing past him as he hurried towards the apartment's bathroom. "Go in, sit down, I'll be back."

Wilson hesitated, then ventured inside and sat in the only chair, at the desk. He looked around at Yoshi's library, the works apparently shelved at random, non-fiction mixed with novels and manga, English with Japanese, books and DVDs with figurines. A copy of *Tales of Mystery and Imagination,* bound in fake scarlet leather, lay open, spine up, on the pillow; Wilson glanced at it, then noticed strands of black—thread? hair? protruding from beneath the rumpled quilt. Uneasily, he lifted the covers and saw dark eyes in an ivory-pale face framed by ebon hair. A faint smile played about dark crimson lips, showing a hint of white teeth.

Wilson sucked in a lungful of air and stared for a moment, waiting for a sign of life or movement; none came. He heard the toilet flush, and dropped the covers and sat down hastily in the chair.

Yoshi returned to the room a few seconds later. "Sorry," he said. He picked up the volume of Poe, placed it on the floor, and sat on the pillow. "I've been re-reading this, and thinking of including some of his characters in *Worm*. General Smith, the Man Who Was Used Up, might still be alive; the old men from "A Descent into the Maelstrom"; maybe have them find Fortunato in the vaults . . . "

Wilson realized that he was holding his breath, and let it out. Yoshi mistook this for disapproval, and his shoulders slumped slightly. "Of course, you're the writers," he said gloomily, "it was just an idea . . . "

"I'll think about it," said Wilson, trying not to think about what might be underneath the hills and valleys of the quilt. He suddenly remembered another Poe story, "The Oblong Box", in which the central character travels with his wife's corpse in his cabin. He dismissed *that* thought—the room, and Yoshi, had a sour shut-in smell, but not so oppressive that it could have disguised the rank odour of a decaying body. "Right now, though, the main thing on my mind is meeting with Mr Tanaka tomorrow."

"Oh."

"He wants to meet all three of us." No reply. "We're equal partners in this."

Yoshi looked away, and was silent for a moment. "You and Kyoko do all the words, though." His voice, which had been animated, now seemed leaden, as though he was reading a spell in an unknown language phonetically and feared that an error in pronunciation might summon up the wrong demon.

"He's interested in your artwork, too—just as much as the words, or Kyoko's drawing."

"But you are better with words. I can send him as much artwork as you want, but talking to him . . . I dread it. I dread the events of the future, not in themselves, but in their results. I'm scared I'd say the wrong thing."

"I don't think you would."

"I would. I can't be in a room where there are other people talking; it confuses me. It's not so bad when I read, but I can't even stand music any more; I can't always tell what other people are singing or saying and what I'm only thinking. I don't think I can go," he said, shaking slightly. "Not yet. I have to study for my exams. I failed last time. I failed badly. I don't want to fail again." With a visible effort, he looked Wilson in the face again. "Not so soon. Please. This is at best but a harmless, and by no means an unnatural, precaution."

Wilson blinked. The phrase sounded familiar, but in his jet-lagged and weary condition, he couldn't remember where he might have heard or read it before. "What should I tell Mr Tanaka?"

"Tell him I'm not well. Tell him . . . " He shrugged. "You and Kyoko are writers. You will think of something. Do you want some sushi?"

• • •

When he left the building an hour later, hurrying through the rain towards the subway with Kyoko, Wilson could barely remember one word of the often incoherent conversations he'd had with either Yoshi or his mother: the vision of the strange face staring out from the shadows in Yoshi's room was still impossible to shake. He'd tried to convince himself that the 'hair' had been nothing but the fringe of some garment, and that he'd only imagined the face, as humans often did when they glimpsed an arrangement of spots and curves that might have been eyes and a mouth . . .

"I see you've met Midori," said Kyoko, when they finally reached shelter.

Wilson turned and stared at her. "Midori?" he spluttered.

"It's what he calls her."

"I wasn't imagining her, then?"

"Not the way I think Yoshi does. Do you remember asking if he was feeling better since he received the advance from Tanaka? I gather that's how he spent it."

"What is she? A mannequin?" Wilson blinked. "Well, that's not quite as scary as some of the other possibilities that had occurred to me. I knew she couldn't be dead, and I didn't think she could be alive . . . "

"You thought he was dating a vampire?" said Kyoko, amused. "Or a zombie?"

"No. Well, they crossed my mind, along with cataleptics and the Bride of Frankenstein, but I thought it was much more likely that I was just hallucinating the whole thing. But her face looked so real . . . I could have sworn I saw teeth . . . "

"Very likely. She's a sex doll—a top of the range one, not one of those blow-up things." She shrugged. "There are places in Akihabara where you can rent them by the hour, but I don't think they deliver, so he probably bought his with the advance."

"Fuck."

"Probably the only sort he's ever had," Kyoko agreed, "though that's just a guess. I almost envy him, in a way."

"You can't be serious."

"Not completely, though there *have* been times when my life would've been easier if I could've put my lovers in boxes when I didn't need them. But some people might say he has everything he needs."

Wilson snorted, and fumbled in his pockets for his lighter. "Only as long as his mother keeps enough ramen in the house."

"He can get food delivered."

"What if their money runs out?"

She shrugged. "They own the building, and rent out the other two floors. It's not much—the place is a dump, as you probably noticed—but they live frugally."

"They'll be able to live a whole lot better if we do this deal!"

"True. I guess we'll just have to hope Tanaka doesn't insist on meeting him."

• • •

They caught the subway back to Wilson's hotel, neither of them speaking until they were alone in the grumbling lift, when Kyoko suddenly threw her arms around her co-writer and gushed, "A TV series!"

Wilson grinned back at her; her joy seemed to flow through him, intoxicating as sake and tasting much better. "It's really going to happen?"

"I think so. Tanaka has a good reputation, and even if it doesn't, the money for the rights alone . . . "

"I know. Even converted into dollars, it sounds like a mountain of cash." The lift doors opened at last, and they walked to his tiny but well-equipped rooms, still holding onto each other as though scared of being pulled out of a dream. They both sat on the bed, then fell over, lying on it face to face. Kyoko wriggled up the bed until her face was level with his; then, suddenly at a loss for words, grabbed her smartphone.

Wilson's disappointment couldn't be hidden, but he tried, "Do you think Tanaka bought the story about the migraine?"

"With that much money, he could buy my firstborn," she replied, but with a slight downward quirk of her lips.

"Yoshi hasn't replied?"

"No. But yes, I think Tanaka bought it—for now. But he's going to want to meet him, and more importantly, he wants the animators to meet him." She shrugged.

"Can you think of any way to get Yoshi . . . "

"Out of his room? This might. And the exams start next week—I hope he can make it to the exam hall, because if he doesn't, the next lot isn't until June."

Wilson bit his lip. "We have to do something. Not just because of *Worm*, not even just because we owe him; he's—"

"No-one's ever come up with a reliable way of treating the hikikomori," cautioned Kyoko, "and there's been at least one case of one who was sent to a mental hospital, hijacking a bus and running over a crossing guard when he was released."

"Somehow, I can't see Yoshi doing anything like that."

"Me neither, but . . . I know that being hikikomori may seem strange and scary, but that doesn't mean that we can't make things even worse. Do you know the Poe story, "The Premature Burial"? The narrator is cataleptic, but this stops when he stops obsessing about death, gets rid of his medical texts, and thinks and reads about other things instead, travels . . . and lives. The macabre thoughts became a self-fulfilling prophecy—and the reverse."

"You want to stop doing *Worm*? Maybe I'm rationalizing, but I don't see that making him happier."

"I don't know. It's just . . . maybe he dreams he's the artist starving in a garret, like his heroes Poe and Lovecraft. Maybe he thinks you have to suffer like that, to feel everything and nothing, to make the lasting art. But you're right, we just have to wait and hope. What else can we do?"

• • •

Wilson woke the next morning, to find Kyoko gone. He lay there, feeling completely disoriented, for more than a minute before fumbling for the light switch. He stared at the depression in the pillow next to his, then buried his face in it for a moment. That was when the idea hit him.

• • •

Yoshi opened the bedroom door when he was sure that his mother and Kyoko had gone. "Thank you for letting me know about the anime," he said. Though clearly excited, he also seemed nervous to be outside his bedroom.

Wilson nodded. "Tanaka wants you to meet the animators," he said, without preamble. "Can you do that?"

Yoshi seemed to turn even more pale, something Wilson hadn't thought possible. "I don't . . . excuse me," he said, rushing off towards the bathroom. Wilson waited until he'd heard the bolt slide home, then hurried into Yoshi's bedroom and raised the covers. The life-size doll lay there, face down: Wilson grabbed it, surprised more at its weight than its lingering smile, and carried it over his shoulder to the apartment's front door. Kyoko was waiting on the landing with a large empty suitcase; she raised an eyebrow slightly when she saw the doll, but helped him fold her up until she fit inside the case. "I hadn't expected her to be quite this big," she admitted.

"They make small ones?"

"You don't want to know," she assured him. "I'm glad I thought of the case, though; I'd hate to have to stuff her into a taxi while she's naked like this."

"She?"

"You'd better hope Yoshi thinks of her as 'she', not 'it'," said Kyoko. "This isn't likely to work if he doesn't—not that I like the chances of it working, anyway." She brushed Midori's hair out of the way of the zip, then closed the crimson suitcase. Together, they carried it down to street level, dropped it once, and wheeled it out of the alley, and stood there for a moment until Kyoko had recovered her breath enough to phone for a taxi. "Okay," she said, as she returned the phone to her bat-winged handbag, "you'd better go up and tell Yoshi what happened, before he decides to leave the place by the window. I'll see you back at the hotel."

Yoshi had retreated into his bedroom by the time Wilson returned to the apartment, and when the Australian knocked on the door and identified himself, the reply came in the form of a note slipped under the door: *Where is Midori?*

"Midori's good."

I want her back.

Wilson considered telling him that he had playmate, in the hope that Yoshi would open the door and speak to him directly, but didn't want to risk being caught in a lie. "You'll have to leave the building."

A pause, then: *Why?*

"Tanaka and his animators want to meet you."

I can't. Not yet.

"When, then?"

No answer.

"What about your exams?"

Wilson waited, but there was no reply. Ten silent minutes later, Mrs Ushiba knocked on the front door, and Wilson let her in. Not knowing what else to say, he said thank you and good night, and left.

• • •

Kyoko phoned him the next morning, waking him. "Ushiba-san called," she said. "She didn't sleep much last night: Yoshi nearly tore the house apart looking for Midori, in case we'd hidden her there. She got some sleep after she made sure he couldn't open her bedroom door. She says she's scared to stay there with him, but she's also scared to leave."

Wilson rubbed his eyes, opened his laptop, and lit a cigarette. "He hasn't e-mailed me," he said, a moment later.

"He messaged me last night, and asked if I had anything to do with this 'somewhat childish experiment', as he called it. I don't think he wants to talk to you."

"I keep expecting him to demand to speak to the doll," Wilson replied, with a glance at the suitcase. He'd resisted the urge to open it for a closer look at the toy, but its presence had made him feel weirdly nervous. "He does know she can't talk, doesn't he?"

"I think that's what he likes about her," said Kyoko dryly. "One of the things, anyway. What do we do now—apart from stalling Tanaka?"

"Tell him that if he wants to see Midori again, he's going to have to talk to me."

"Okay. What about his mother?"

"I don't know. I forgot to ask: does she go out during the day?"

"Some days. She doesn't have a job, if that's what you mean."

"Uh-huh. What about someone she can stay with?"

"No other family . . . but she knows my parents, and they know about Yoshi, I think they'd let her stay in my room for a while . . . "

"Ask. If they say yes, let her know." When Kyoko didn't reply, he asked, "You both know Yoshi better than I do—"

"I'm not sure about that—"

"— and I'd never *heard* of hikikomori before. If you think this is too risky, tell me."

"I don't think Yoshi would hurt his mother," said Kyoko. "Not knowingly—not physically, anyway. She means too much to him, even if no-one else does. I don't think he'd hurt anyone else, except maybe himself . . . but I think he's too scared of pain for that. Did you see any weapons in his room?"

"Not real ones. Only drawings."

Kyoko nodded. "He can design them—he's been doing that as long as I've known him—but I don't think he's ever used one, even if he is a ronin."

"He's a *what*? I mean, I've heard the story of the forty-seven ronin, I know they're masterless samurai, but I —"

"Sorry. It's slang—what we call students who fail to get into uni. What do you think we should do now?"

"I guess if he doesn't come out, we'll have to tell Tanaka the truth. Do you think he'll pull the plug?"

"If he thinks Yoshi's unreliable, he might . . . and I think Yoshi will blame himself if he does."

""I dread the events of the future, not in themselves, but in their results.""

"What?"

"Something Yoshi said."

• • •

They spent the day in Akihabara and Harajuku, window-shopping and admiring the cosplayers, then found a small restaurant that served inexpensive tendon and tempura. Kyoko's phone miaowed while they were ordering, sending the waitress into a fit of head-lowering giggles. "It's Yoshi," said Kyoko, after a quick glance at the screen. "He says he wants to see Midori, to be sure she's okay."

"Tell him where my hotel is."

"He says he's not leaving the house until he sees her."

"There's a webcam in my laptop. If he'll chat with me, I'll let him see her."

Kyoko keyed that in. "He says okay; call him tonight."

"Tell him I will."

• • •

Wilson unfolded the doll and sat her in the room's only chair. There was something disturbing about her immobile face and unblinking stare, and he had to resist the urge to close her eyes—or to cover them, as they apparently lacked lids. Instead, he grabbed the white bathrobe from the closet and dressed her in that, suspecting that Yoshi might become jealous if he saw her naked with another man in the room.

He logged on to g-chat and pinged Yoshi, who replied instantly.

LET ME SEE MIDORI NOW

Wilson turned the laptop around so that the doll was staring over his shoulder.

CLOSER

The Australian shrugged, wishing that he had a cell phone that worked in Japan, then picked up the computer and placed it on the table in front of the doll. He tilted the screen to give Yoshi a full-length view, then positioned the laptop so that Midori was staring over his shoulder as he typed.

ok?

BRING HER BACK TO ME

will you meet Tanaka?

A moment's hesitation, then IF YOU BRING HER BACK AND SHE'S NOT HURT

tomorrow?

No hesitation this time. IF YOU BRING HER NOW

Wilson looked at the wan face on the screen, and decided to trust him. *I'll be right there*, he typed, then shut down the computer, stubbed out his cigarette, and packed Midori into the crimson suitcase. He wheeled the case to the lift, and pressed the button for the lobby. The lift shuddered, descended—and then the lights went out as it jerked to a halt, halfway between two floors.

• • •

Yoshi sat at his desk, trying hard to concentrate on something other than the digital clock in the corner of the laptop screen, not to think that if they were going to come, they'd be here by now. His need to see Midori had become so urgent that, despite the risk of his mother coming home unexpectedly, he'd left his bedroom door open so that he'd hear Wilson walking up the stairs or knocking on the door just a few seconds sooner, and could let them in a moment earlier. He glanced at the clock again—11.49—and tried telling himself not to worry. Wilson had come here before, he knew the subway system and wouldn't get lost, he . . .

so where is he? Wilson spoke enough Japanese to give directions to a taxi driver if he didn't want to haul the suitcase to the subway . . .

maybe he decided to keep her

He wouldn't do that! He's my friend!

then why did he steal her?

Yoshi gritted his teeth, and reloaded the news headlines. Nothing about a disaster in Tokyo that would explain Wilson's tardiness. His hands shaking, he picked up his copy of *Tales of Mystery and Imagination* in the hope of losing himself in a story. The book fell open to the first page of "The Tell-Tale Heart", and he read "TRUE!—nervous—very, very dreadfully nervous I had been and am; but why *will* you say that I am mad?"

He closed his eyes for a moment, then opened the book to the story that most spoke to him. I won't do anything until I finish this, he told himself. Or midnight, whichever comes later. Not before then.

• • •

Every few minutes, Wilson pressed the button on his solar-powered watch to provide a little light in the oblong box, until eventually the battery ran so flat that the watch refused to glow. By the time the doors were prised open, he'd long since lost track of time, and would not have been astonished to see daylight.

He hauled the suitcase out of the lift and hurried down the stairs to the lobby, barking out a request for a taxi. He lit a cigarette as he waited, and stubbed it out as soon as the cab pulled up outside. He stared at the blank face of his watch, then smiled wryly. He knew he'd have to apologize profusely to Yoshi for his lateness, but at least he felt sure that his friend would still be home when he arrived.

• • •

Kyoko was sitting up at her computer, translating dialogue for the next page of *The Conqueror Worm* by turning Wilson's English into appropriately nuanced Japanese. As she positioned the speech bubbles so that they didn't obscure the elaborate steampunk architecture of Yoshi's backdrop, something niggled at her, preventing her from concentrating fully . . . something Wilson had said that Yoshi had said . . .

She closed her eyes for a moment, trying to remember the exact words, then googled the phrase "somewhat childish experiment'. All of the hits linked to a Poe story, "The Fall of the House of Usher".

She glanced at the clock—12.14—and realized that she hadn't heard from Wilson since he'd said he was taking the doll back to Yoshi's home, about four hours ago. She checked her phone for messages, but there was nothing. She opened g-chat, but neither Wilson nor Yoshi were online.

She tried to tell herself that she was worrying unnecessarily, but knew that she'd never be able to sleep until she was sure that both of them were okay, so she called for a taxi.

• • •

Yoshi had spent many hours designing deathtraps and dungeons for *The Conqueror Worm*, and he did a thorough job of sealing the apartment's doors and windows with duct tape before turning on the gas. Once that was done, he sat back in his chair wondering what to write as an epitaph. A quotation from Poe—"Should you ever be drowned or hung, be sure and make a note of your sensations"—came to him, and he deliberately typed that out and hit *save*.

• • •

Wilson paid the taxi driver, then hauled the crimson suitcase out of the trunk and carried it up the stairs. There was no answer when he knocked on the door, so he deposited his burden on the landing, sat down, lit a cigarette, took a deep drag to try and soothe his nerves, and tried to think. He knocked on the door again, harder and harder each time. "Yoshi!" he yelled. "I'm sorry I'm late, but the lift in the hotel broke down. I'm here now, and I have her with me!" He unzipped the suitcase, and lifted the white-shrouded doll free, holding the manga-eyed girl up with an arm around her waist, her face on a level with his, almost cheek to cheek, He felt strangely light-headed, and short of breath. . "I'm not leaving until you open the door, so you may as well let me in!"

• • •

Yoshi had slumped over the keyboard, but even in his oxygen-deprived stupor, he became aware of a distinct, hollow, apparently muffled, reverberation. Unsteadily, he tried to stand, then, swaying gently, he slowly staggered towards the source of the noise, his footsteps leaden. Wilson continued to pound, until his fist smashed through the dry and hollow-sounding wood.

For an instant, Yoshi saw Midori standing outside the door, and the redly gleaming tip of Wilson's cigarette..

A taxi stopped on the other side of the street, and Kyoko stepped out just as the explosion blew out the windows. She watched aghast as the once barely-discernible fissures in the cancer-ridden concrete walls burst asunder, and the top floor crumbled into the murky waters of the sullen canal.

• • • • • • • • • • •

YOU AIN'T HEARD NOTHIN' YET!

MARTIN LIVINGS

IRIS FADE IN

It all changed in '28, didn't it? One little man, five simple words, and the whole fuckin' world came down around me.

You know that, though, don't you Morty? You were there at the beginning. Not the very beginning, of course; back in Ireland, or New York after that. But you were there when I climbed off the train in the spring of 1921, so goddamn certain I'd make my fortune in Hollywood. You were there, and you saw me, and that was that. You made me change my name from Ryan Murphy to Randolph Murray; to make it more sophisticated, you told me. I knew the truth. It was to make it less Irish. I didn't give a fuck, though; Ryan Murphy wasn't even my real name. Shit, I've changed my name so many times over the years, I barely remember the one my mam gave me.

So, Randolph Murray it was, and boy, did Randolph Murray make some money, for you and me both, hey Morty? Eight years of feature films for Paramour Studios, for that slick fucker Bill Morrison, the studio exec who produced them, one after another. They were golden years, my friend, for everyone. The people couldn't get enough of Randolph Murray, romantic star of, god, I don't know how many movies. I've lost count, we churned them out so fuckin' fast. I was a good actor, had to be in my previous life, so I could pull off the debonair toff easy enough. The films blur into one another, the plots basically the same over and over again—handsome rich man meets beautiful but poor woman, love at first sight, cruel forces conspire to keep them apart, but in the end they embrace, together forever. Iris fade out. The End. And once you've made one like that, well, the audience just wants another, and another, and another. It was the easiest money I've ever made, that's a fact.

I missed the easy booze, mind you—Prohibition was a pain in the arse for a whisky-drinking son-of-a-bitch from the streets of Belfast—but the great thing about being a movie star was that the law didn't apply to you the same way. If I wanted liquor, I could get it. And the good stuff too, not that fuck-awful home-made hooch that was selling to the normal folks from under the counter at the speakeasies. I could get a table in any damn restaurant I wanted, any time I wanted, day or night. Everyone called me "sir", unless they were pretending to be my friend, then they called me "Randy". You and Bill Morrison both called me "Randy", didn't you? Yeah, thought as much. To my face, at any rate. Fuck knows what you called me behind my back.

Never the women, though. I know you were dipping your wick in as many starlets as you could get your tongue around, and I heard the stories about Morrison as well, saw the girls with bruised eyes and bloodied lips, but I didn't want any of that, no matter how much they threw themselves at me. The actresses were so damn selfish that I swear they'd just watch themselves reflected in my eyes if we fucked, lost in their own beauty. And average women, man, there was just this desperation in their advances, as if I was a prize to be won, a mountain to be climbed. I was Randolph Murray, movie star, not a human being at all. So I kept to myself, mainly. I know you thought I was a queer, Morty, but it wasn't that, not at all. It was just a single red-headed girl back home, one whose face I could never get out of my mind, no matter how hard I tried, how much I drank. Still, all in all, it was a pretty fuckin' spectacularly good life, especially compared to the one I'd had before it.

And then, in '28, those five damn words, and it was all over.

It seems like more than a year ago, doesn't it Morty? When Jolson stood up in front of the world in his blackface makeup and told them to listen? That little kike ruined it for us all. Talmadge and Jannings, gone. Lillian Gish, back to the boards. Hell, even

Doug Fairbanks and Mary Pickford packed up and left, goddamn it. And then, of course, there was matinee idol Randolph Murray. I knew it was over the moment Jolson opened his mouth on screen. I knew it was over, but I didn't believe it until Bill Morrison called us into his office. You remember that, Morty? Five months ago? After half a year in limbo, barely a peep from anyone about the next film, the next lead, the next role. Oh, the paychecks kept coming in, of course—I was under a nice, iron-clad contract with Paramour, thanks to you—but no film bonuses, nothing, just the basic stipend. And bad news spreads fuckin' fast in this town. The drinks became harder to get, the tables at restaurants were suddenly busy—could I wait an hour, maybe two, come back tomorrow? But I told myself it was just a bad patch, that it'd all be okay.

And I almost believed it, until that day we went to see Morrison at Paramour. That fuckin' office, where I always felt like a star, a hero, a god amongst men, all of a sudden made me feel small and insignificant. I'd never noticed how huge the overstuffed leather chairs were that faced Morrison's equally-oversized desk. Definitely compensating for something. He smiled at us both, told us everything was going to be fine. Told me I wasn't fired. Told me this talkie thing, it was just a fad, it'd die out soon enough. Told me I was one of his most valuable stars. Then you joined in, Morty, repeating the words like a damn parrot. And I knew I was royally screwed. Morrison was so crooked, he made a lightning bolt look like a yard stick; I knew that, and so did you, and damn it, I *knew* you knew. My contract was nearly up, and it wasn't going to be renewed. And why? Because Randolph Murray shouldn't sound like a shitkicker from Belfast when he opens his goddamn mouth. Or maybe Morrison was just sweeping clean with a new broom, using the talkies as an excuse to get rid of his expensive stable of stars and replacing them with new blood—young, pretty, stupid, and cheap. And with respectable accents to boot.

Afterwards, in Rudy Valentino's speakeasy on Hollywood Boulevard, enjoying a quiet glass of bathtub gin and a couple of Cubans, you touched my elbow and told me I'd be okay, that we'd had a good run. *We had some laughs, hey Randy?* you asked me, with that little breathy laugh-gasp that I've always hated. Seriously, Morty, you have no idea how close I came to punching you in the face, right there and then. It took all my willpower to keep my fists by my sides, nails digging into my palms. *Blood, sweat and tears,* you told me, *that's what I've given to your movies. Blood, sweat and fucking tears.* Then you said it, the last nail in my career's coffin.

You can always go back to what you did before, right?

Morty, you have no fuckin' idea what I did before this. Eighteen months hauling girders in New York City, breaking my back, keeping my head low and my eyes open, certain to my bones that one day someone would tap me on the shoulder, a gun hard against my back, ready to ship me back to Ireland to face trial. And before that? Jesus, I was goddamn IRA before there even *was* an IRA, in the Irish Volunteers. Travelled down to Dublin and stood alongside my fellow patriots in '16 at the Easter uprising. Even killed some Brits there, before twelve thousand fuckin' troops came down on us like the hammer of God itself. I got away with my skin, though, and continued the good fight for three more years. I was a soldier, Morty, not in the so-called Great War, but in a much less glamorous battle, the battle to keep my country free and independent. You should understand that, living here, a country with a history like yours; all we wanted was what you already had. So I killed people, yeah, a lot of people, and hurt a lot more besides, but all enemies or collaborators. And never women or children, I made that a rule. Never women or children.

Until 1919, and the damned tobacconists' on Church Lane.

We knew the British commander of the local garrison bought his tobacco there. He came by every Friday at closing time, and the tobacconist, a fat sweaty cunt with eyes that darted like moths around a lantern, he'd let him in, flick his sign to "CLOSED", and they'd be in there for twenty minutes at least. Every Friday, without fail. Stupid bastards, should have known better than to be predictable. So that Friday, late in the afternoon, I went in and bought some cigarettes. And while I was browsing, I slipped a present under one of the counters, a bomb with a thirty minute clockwork timer on it. I walked out, went to my parked car across the street, lit up a cigarette, and waited.

Nearly half an hour passed, and the commander didn't show. He was late for the first damn time in the three months we'd observed the shop. I was sweating like a pig, even though it was cold as hell—typical fuckin' Belfast autumn—and had smoked almost all the cigarettes I'd bought earlier from the same man I was planning to blow to kingdom come. Then the official military car pulled up, and the commander got out. Straightened his uniform, walked around to the other side of the car, and opened the door.

His teenage daughter climbed out. She couldn't have been more than sixteen, gorgeous red hair and freckles. Even from across the street, the girl's blue eyes were startling, the same blue as her pretty dress, way too light for the chill in the air. My heart felt like it had stopped in my chest. She spotted me staring at her, gave me a bright, innocent smile and a happy wave. Then they both walked into the shop.

I tried to get out of the car, tried to run across the street, tried to warn them, but I was frozen in my seat, the cigarette in my hand burning down to my knuckles unnoticed. All I could do was watch, and pray that, like so many times before, the bomb failed.

It didn't. God forgive me, this time, this one time, it didn't.

That night, I mugged some poor Protestant bastard who'd been drunkenly bragging about emigrating to America in the pub earlier, took his papers, his boat ticket and his name. I hit him pretty hard, maybe too hard. Probably killed him. But at that stage I didn't care, and the next morning I left my home as Ryan Murphy, bound for the home of the brave and, god willing, the land of the free.

And you sat there, in Valentino's up-market speakeasy, in your expensive suit and your cheap cologne, chomping down on a cigar and grinning like you just shit your pants, and you told me I could just go *back*?

You left soon after that, which was a good lifestyle decision on your part, and I stayed and drank as much as I could. Some flapper took pity on me—my age, maybe even older, but pretty enough. She drank with me, danced with me. Maybe she was nostalgic for the good old days, the days when her heroes were the strong, silent types. None of this talkie shit. It used to be about the acting, expressing everything in the raised eyebrow, the lowered shoulder, the quivering lip. This new stuff, it's not acting, it's just . . . *narration*.

I drank, and she drank. Then she leaned in to kiss me, and I looked at her face, and saw those damn blue eyes, the young full lips, the red hair. I panicked and lashed out drunkenly, catching her across the cheek with the back of my hand. She screamed and fell to the floor of the speakeasy, hit the floorboards pretty badly. Blood spattered from the corner of her mouth. And I just sat there on my stool and looked down at her, frozen all over again as she writhed there, just an aging flapper again, sobbing and moaning in pain. Then something shifted in my head, a tiny twinge somewhere deep inside me, and I found myself listening to her, just . . . *listening*.

By the time the speakeasy's goons grabbed me by my arms and carried me up the stairs and into the street, tossing me in the gutter, I knew what I could do, what I *needed* to do. It took me a few days to straighten up from my bender, get myself together. I wanted to be professional about this, the same way I'd always been. I still had some savings—my mam had taught me well, told me to always put money away whenever you can, save for a rainy day; living in poverty will do that to you—so I went out and bought the equipment I needed. I had contacts in the industry still, people who'd talk to me. I always made friends with the crew wherever I could; they're the ones that make you look good, not the fuckin' directors. They pointed me in the right direction, though they seemed understandably dubious. Of course, I didn't tell the whole story. How could I? Other gear I got from the hardware store.

The talkies had made me an invisible man, *persona non gratis*. Until that moment, that had seemed like a bad thing. But now I could walk right up to Paramour Studios and find out where Bill Morrison lived, from his secretary. I could wait near his home in the hills without worrying about the police. I was known, sure, but no longer relevant or important. It was the perfect state to not be seen in. I grabbed Morrison as he parked his fancy car in his driveway, dragged him back into the bushes, hit him over the head a few times until he stopped struggling.

He woke up in my studio. It was actually an old shack I'd found in the hills overlooking Hollywood. If I hadn't boarded up the windows, you could have caught a glimpse of the "HOLLYWOODLAND" sign out of it, back to front mind you. But I *had* boarded them, and put mattresses against the walls as well, just for good measure. Morrison was in the middle of the room, sprawled on the dirt floor. I was kneeling next to him, waiting for him to come to. When he did, I got up and walked over to the camera. It wasn't anything too flash, just the cheapest piece of shit

I could get, but it was hooked up to a Vitaphone disc recorder, and that wasn't cheap, not even a little. I wanted the best sound I could manage. The camera would be fixed, so the cinematography wasn't exactly going to be groundbreaking. Hell with the picture, though, that's not what it was about.

Once the camera was running, I pulled the black woollen balaclava down over my face, the same one I'd worn so many times back home, and returned to Morrison's side.

And . . . action.

I got eleven minutes of footage. It wasn't the first time I'd tortured a man, though I hadn't done it in over a decade. And I'd never done it like this before. Not for show. I didn't want Morrison to talk, to give up his secrets, his compatriots, his alliances. I wasn't looking for answers to any questions, never even spoke a word myself. All I wanted was to make him scream.

I timed it pretty well. He didn't go quiet until the last minute of footage, when I ran the razorblade across his exposed throat and turned his screams into wet garbled nonsense. He sounded like he was drowning, which he basically was. And, as he gasped his last burbling breath and slumped forward, the film ran out. It was beautiful. I burst into tears, amazed and humbled by what I'd achieved.

I did what you suggested, Morty. I went back to what I did before, but I also kept doing what I've done for all these years, what I love. Being in front of a camera, that's a bigger rush, a bigger addiction than booze or drugs or women. This is what I did it for. What I'll always do it for. And now? Now it's your turn to be in front of the camera for once, here in my crappy makeshift studio. Not quite the quality facilities you're accustomed to, I know, but if it's any consolation, you won't be here that long. Eleven minutes, tops. Blood, sweat and tears, Morty, like you said. Blood, sweat and fucking tears.

I . . . *we* . . . have a much smaller audience now, of course, much more . . . specialised. And discerning, too. *You ain't heard nothin' yet*, that's what Jolson told us in '28, and he was so right, more right than he could ever have imagined. To be able to see what I do, well, that's something of course, but to be able to *hear* it, listen to every groan, every gasp, every slice and crunch, every sob and scream . . . well, that's something else entirely.

You see, like any audience, once you give them a taste, well, they're fuckin' insatiable. They want *more*.

IRIS FADE OUT

• • • • • • • • • • •

BEAUTIFUL

JAY CASELBERG

They said it started in Northern Europe somewhere, though nobody really knows. At first, it was a small footnote article in the web press, but then it spread, grew viral in the media, in the hushed and slightly panicked conversation around dinner tables. It gave hell to the cat population for a while, but that was then. They gave it a label too—*necrotising something-or-other.* It's just a label, and in a way, it only serves to sanitise the true nature of that particular, peculiar beast.

I read all I could at the beginning, tried to comprehend what was happening, but I only got so far, immersed in all that medical jargon. What I did understand were the bacteria. Cartilage and flesh and bone. They were hungry little buggers. You shake your head, read on, know deep inside that it can never happen to you. That's the other thing about the media; it puts things right there in front of your face, but keeps them at a distance. For all of the reportage, it's like watching a movie, always at an acceptable distance, that extra step removed. It could never happen to us. Nothing could ever happen to us. Nothing like that.

That first night, a heavy sticky evening, not a breath of air, I was standing out on the porch watching the bug light, as we used to call it, fanning myself with an old hat, feeling the sweat trickles crawling down between my shoulder blades. A hazy white corona encircled the porch light, small insects and moths darting in and out, fading into darkness and back again. I remember the smell of damp earth and vegetation filling the surrounding atmosphere with extra weight. At one end of the porch sat a pile of stacked chairs, covered with an old blanket. From time to time, we'd pull them out and sit around at the back of the house, sharing drinks or simply reading, but the rest of the time, they were stacked there out of the way of our comings or goings. Our cat had decided that was in ideal spot to curl up and sleep in comfort. Most of the time, he seemed to do little else. As I stood there, I was tempted to go over and disturb his feline reveries. What right did he have to sleep while we stood around and sweltered? Good luck to him that he actually could. I turned away to watch the insect dance for a while, still fanning myself before heading back inside, my hopes for a little relief in the evening air already faded. At least we had a fan in there.

Just as I was about to reach for the back door, a movement in the corner of my eye caught my attention. At first, I thought it was merely Angus, turning and stretching on his accustomed perch, and I was tempted to go over and give him a scratch anyway, but it was something else. Nuzzling up against him, licking at his exposed pale belly fur was Cashew, the neighbour's cat, a friendly, stocky, black and white, easily recognisable by her burglar-mask facial markings. I crouched down to call her over. She was fond of bumping up against your legs and sliding in an out.

"Hey, Cashew," I called. "Here puss."

She halted her ministrations and jumped down from the stack of chairs, quickly padding across to my outstretched hand with a faint miaow. There was something funny about the sound, something different, but I didn't register it immediately. I was still looking up at Angus when Cashew butted against my leg and miaowed again. At that point, I looked down, preparing to scratch the top of her head.

"Shit," I said and scuttled backwards. There was something wrong with her face. The burglar mask was still in place, but all around it and below, the fur was gone. No, not only the fur. It was just hollow, missing. Where there should have been white fur, where there should have been flesh and more, there was nothing. Just deep incised hollows, and at the bottom of them, it looked like bone. It was hard to tell in the shadowed light, but it was enough. I shot to my feet, scrabbled with my free hand at the back door behind me and stumbled back into the house. I stood panting there, like that, for a couple of seconds, shaking my head, something cold working inside me. Then, I headed further back into the house to find Anna.

"Christ," I said to her, standing in the doorway to the lounge. "I don't know what's happened to the neighbour's cat, but it's dreadful."

She looked up from her place on the couch, lifting her gaze from the magazine she was reading and gave me a frown. "What do you mean?"

"Cashew. The neighbour's cat. You know." I proceeded to describe what I'd just seen.

"Oh God," she said. "Really?"

"Yeah. It didn't seem to be bothering it though."

"I wonder what happened. Maybe it got hit by a car or something."

"No," I said. "It didn't look like that. It was something different. Oh shit, I touched it." I dropped the hat and quickly strode over to the kitchen sink and started scrubbing my hands. "I touched it," I said.

"John, you don't know. It didn't sound as if it was something like that," said Anna from the lounge.

"No, I *don't* know," I snapped back, but by then, it was probably too late anyway.

We weren't aware of the growing tide then.

Angus was the first to get it, our Blue Burmese with his beautiful face, his silky sealskin fur. The first sign was that he started to look patchy around his eyes, like mange, but it was too even for that, too regular. Thin lines of bare skin appeared beneath his eyes and down the sides of his nose. Apart from the missing hair, he seemed completely unaffected. We took him to the vet, who gave as some ointment to apply and told us about this new mutant strain of *streptococcus*. He'd seen more than a few cases recently and there was very little he could do about it. What was peculiar about it was that it was so targeted, so *specific* about the regions that it attacked. He told us to expect further degeneration in the affected areas. As he said, there was very little he could do about it until they understood more. Angus grew steadily worse. The skin along the affected areas just seemed to withdraw, the flesh beneath drawing back and collapsing into itself till it revealed bare bone beneath, and then it kept going.

We were worried of course, but he didn't seem to be experiencing any real discomfort. He was still hungry, affectionate, his usual cat-like self.

"But it's so ugly," said Anna.

"I know," I told her. "There's nothing I can do about that. He's still Angus. Perhaps it will grow back."

The first human cases appeared a couple of days after we had taken Angus to the vet. It wasn't until it broke the press in full force that the words "flesh-eating bacteria' appeared. Anna and I were already nervous. That first experience with the neighbour's cat had been enough, but after the press got hold of it, we didn't know what we were going to do. By then, there was nothing we actually could do. It was far too late. And anyway, perhaps we'd be okay. It's funny how you always live with that vain hope.

I was the first to exhibit the symptoms. Deep lines appeared below my eyes like grooves in the skin. There was no real discomfort, more a sort of numbness. At first I didn't believe it. I poked and prodded at my face, but they didn't go away. I tried smoothing them with my fingers, but that did nothing other than making the numbness around the area more apparent. For a while, I simply ignored the fact that they were there, but I could see them in Anna's expression when she looked at me. The lines started to grow deeper, and two days later, they appeared on Anna's face as well. We raced to the emergency room, but the hospitals were already overflowing, the panic was on the streets. Even the medical staff looked at us askance, apparently reluctant to approach too close. Pills and ointments and salves, they provided in abundance, but the truth was that they didn't really know what to do at all. They didn't understand it, and that soon became painfully apparent. I shouted at them. I yelled and I ranted. There had to be something they could do. What sort of medical facility was it anyway? Did we live in the Dark Ages?

By the time Anna started exhibiting the full-blown symptoms, we knew, it was firmly on its path. We didn't bother calling the doctor. We didn't bother heading back to the hospital. We stayed locked behind our front door, hidden, drawing back from our own images in the hall mirror, from the unfamiliar ruined faces, from the hollows where our noses had gradually dissolved away, from the deep grooves across the tops of our cheeks. I couldn't look at myself. I couldn't look at Anna without turning away despite myself. We weren't sick. We didn't feel sick, but the thing continued regardless and dragged us down with it. I even considered drastic action for a while, but my mother used to say to me that that was the coward's way out. Those words had stuck with me for some reason.

One day, it simply stopped. Angus was Angus, and he continued on with his cat life as if nothing had ever happened. Anna and I didn't believe it, looking, waiting, hoping that there would not be any more, but it had really stopped. The gradual deterioration slowed, then crawled to a halt and went away as if it had never been there, leaving us with nothing but our ruined images and our . . . shame . . . yes, that was the best way to describe it. We felt ashamed. We were embarrassed about our own faces. We could not look at ourselves, let alone each other. How could we carry on like that?

Each day, we peered at Angus, hopefully, praying that there'd be some sort of improvement, that he'd regain some of the parts that had simply shrunk away to expose the ugliness, but there was nothing. We saw Cashew a few times too, but it was the same, and she had had it longer.

We had to venture out eventually, from sheer necessity. We had to eat, we had other things to attend to, and we weren't really sick, were we? We decided on hats and scarves, despite the weather. At least it would do something to conceal a part of our humiliation and if we didn't look at people directly, if we kept our exposure to the outside world to a minimum . . . . We simply had to hide what we had become, that was clear. Work, social interaction, other things, we could deal with those in due course, but in the meantime, we had to live. We still had to live. All around us, the plague continued, passing from cat to human to country to country, across oceans and mountains, around the globe, as more and more became afflicted, but to us, that no longer mattered. We were too busy dealing with our own little microcosm to pay any real attention. It was still hard to look at each other, to look at ourselves, but we were learning to cope. Outside, and we had started to think of it as that, the outside, things were more difficult. I know that look. We've all done it. You look at something or someone, register, and then your gaze simply slides away pretending that you hadn't seen.

The maimed, the disfigured, the unusual, I'd done it myself. You don't want to be caught staring, do you? It was strange being on the receiving end instead.

"There might be options, things we could do . . . " I said to Anna a few days later.

"Like what?" she said. There was still resentment in her voice. I couldn't work out whether it was directed at me or at the circumstance. We were learning to accept how the disease had left us, but it was not enough.

"I don't know. Surgery? Prosthetics? I'm sure there's something they can do."

"And where are we going to find the money for that?"

"What about masks? We can get those medical masks. You know, like the ones they always seem to wear in Asia. I'm sure they're easy enough to get."

Anna narrowed her eyes at me, processing the image, but at least she was considering.

"Maybe," she said, resignedly and turned away.

My shoulders slumped and I let out an involuntary sigh. I was trying. Why couldn't she see that?

For a while, we were so bound up in dealing with our affliction that we hadn't really been paying attention to what was really going on outside in the big bad world. It consumed us, just as the bacteria had consumed our cartilage and flesh. Every time we thought about the future, a cold hollowness grew inside. The road ahead was bleak, but gradually, some sort of acceptance had started to come with it. I don't know whether it was displacement or simple resignation, but after a few more days locked in our self-imposed social quarantine, we turned back to the television. It was another reminder, but we felt there was nothing more we could see that could make us feel any the worse about our condition. There was the vague hope, perhaps, that we might even see something about some potential cure. It was not to be. The Eater, as they called it now, continued its spread. Some seemed to be immune, but mostly, it was indiscriminate. At least they'd passed beyond the cat culling that had taken place in the early stages.

The funny thing was that I hadn't been too far off the mark with my suggestions. Things had moved on in other ways whilst we'd been locked away. Masks are all the rage now. Even the newsreaders are wearing them. And the weather girl. It won't be long before they're appearing on the sitcoms too. The designer labels have started with their own lines of specialist fashion masks and, of course, they cost and arm and a leg, well beyond our reach. The aesthetic of what is desirable has always been defined by its context. The culture, the social media, the fashions of the age, all of them delineate the boundaries of what is attractive or acceptable. It doesn't matter if it's the dimensions of the Rubinesque or the frame of Heroin Chic, the use of labrets in the Amazon and Africa, the stretching of the necks. I understand that better now, or think I do and Anna too. We have discussed it at length. Together though, finally, we have come to a decision. In the end, perhaps, we won't be too alone. But then again, perhaps it's just our way of coping.

We built a fire in the back yard last night and burned our masks. We stood there, hand in hand, watching the sparks float up into the night sky, a symbol of our transformation. Tomorrow, we plan to venture in to town, together, our heads held high. We don't need the masks any more. Nobody really needs them any more. After all, why would we? We're beautiful.

•••••••••••

STALEMATE

NARRELLE M. HARRIS

It takes Helen several moments to register that her mother has entered the kitchen. This may be because Olivia has no right to be in Helen's kitchen, under any circumstances.

As Olivia grumbles about her arthritis, Helen stares into space. Her hair straggles over her sallow skin. Her nightie and shabby slippers are pale and washed out, like Helen.

The kitchen is spotless and not in any need of Olivia's bustling attention. She thinks making tea will keep her useful. Twice she asks Helen where to find the cups. Still Helen doesn't notice her.

But when Helen finally rises, sighing, to go to the sink, that's when she sees her mother. She gasps, her hand jerking upwards to cover the shocked "Oh!", then freezing part way through the movement.

"Stop staring at me like that," says Olivia crossly, "the wind will change direction and you'll get stuck like that."

Helen swallows. "Sorry."

"So you should be. You've been ignoring me since I came in."

"Sorry," repeats Helen.

"You're always in such a bad mood in the morning. And you don't suffer the way I do, with my arthritis."

Helen can almost hear the snap of her surprise breaking into pieces. "I've been sick too."

"I know you've been sick. Why else have I been here?" Olivia is peevishly annoyed. "But *you're* getting better. That's more than I've been doing. I've woken up in pain every day for the last ten years."

That rankles. "I didn't know it was a competition." It comes out even more waspishly than Helen means it to.

Olivia dislikes her daughter's tone. "Young lady, you can get to your room if you can't be civilised."

"For God's sake, Mum, I'm thirty years old. And it's *my* house."

"Well act your age. And don't blaspheme. You know I don't like it."

Helen doesn't have the energy for yet another fight, just like all the other fights. "Sorry."

"That's better. Did you take your pills this morning?"

"Of course I did."

"All of them?"

"Of course all of them." Helen resents being treated like a child, but not half as much as she resents being ill. "Not that they're helping much. I feel worse every day. I should call Dr Palmer and ask him about them. Check out the dosages."

"I'm sure you're just a little tired, sweetheart. I'll make you some soup for lunch today. Why don't you give your mother a love." Olivia holds out her arms, lips half-puckered for a kiss, her expression a postcard picture of a doting mama. Helen fails to run into her open arms as expected. Instead, she gives her mother an unsettled look.

Olivia's unkissed mouth pulls into a severe frown. "Don't stare at me like I just asked for something awful."

Helen is suddenly flustered. "I just . . . "

"Is it too much for a mother to expect a kiss good morning?"

Helen doesn't want to answer that. "Did you sleep well last night?"

Olivia folds her arms. "It's funny. I usually sleep so badly, but last night I slept all the way through. I hadn't expected to. That cup of tea I had last night tasted off. You need to stop buying that funny tea of yours. No knowing what it can do to a person, especially someone with my angina."

"You drank the tea? All of it?" Helen looks at her mother from under her lashes, her expression strangely guilty.

"Most of it," confirms Olivia. "It had a funny taste, but I thought that might be my new heart or blood pills. Some of my medicines make things taste strange."

"Oh." Helen looks relieved. "It's a sencha tea. Japanese." She regrets the clarification almost instantly.

"Those Asians like some strange things, don't they?" says Olivia brightly, as though such tastes are both peculiar and comical. "The church committee went to one of the new Korean restaurants after the last meeting. Margaret is always dragging us off to some new place or other. I don't know what's wrong with the sandwich shop at Garden City. A nice sandwich and a cappuccino at the café near the food hall is just fine, and only six dollars for seniors. I've heard the Koreans eat dog in their restaurants. It shouldn't be allowed. The Health Department . . . "

Helen takes a deep breath. Then another. A third. "What are you doing here?" she asks at last.

Olivia scowls. "That's the thanks I get for coming to nurse you through your illness. I suppose I shouldn't expect gratitude. I'm only your mother."

Another guilty flush steals over Helen's features. "I'm sorry. I didn't mean that. I'm a bit confused."

Her mother softens. "My poor baby girl. You've been so ill. Come and give me a kiss."

This time Helen responds to the command. She cautiously kisses the air just above the offered cheek. Her lips brush against the fine hairs of her mother's soft, aged skin.

"There, that wasn't so hard, was it?"

"No," says Helen meekly.

"Are you sorry you snapped at your mum?"

"Yes."

"There's my good girl. My sweet Helen. My little Nellie Bly." Olivia sing-songs this last in a baby voice.

Helen is immediately on edge again. "Mum . . . "

"Nelly Bly, caught a fly, tied it to a string," sings Olivia.

"Mum, don't."

"String broke . . . "

"Stop it."

" . . . Cut its throat, poor little thing."

Helen's hands claw the air before her, like she's trying to throttle the song. "Why do you do that? I don't know how many times I've told you how much I hate that."

Olivia's frown is defensive. "I used to sing it to you all the time when you were a little girl."

"And I always hated it. It's cruel. It's horrible. I'm not like that."

"It's just a nursery rhyme." Olivia's tone is hurt and puzzled.

"It's hateful," snaps Helen. "I've told you and told you. Why don't you ever listen to me? Why are you here, if . . . if . . . " she trails off, dismayed, confused.

"If what?" prompts Olivia.

Helen's jaw sets in a determined line. "If this is our last chance to finally talk about everything."

Olivia shakes her head. "I don't understand you, Helen."

"No. No, I'm sure you don't." Helen's shoulders sag.

"There's no need for you to be so rude to me, no matter how sick you've been," Olivia berates her daughter. "I can see you're feeling much better now, so if you don't want me here, I'll go." She heads for the door, her body language haughty, the tilt of her head and clip to her step saying "no one appreciates me'. When Helen does this sort of thing, her mother calls it a huff. When Olivia does it, she calls it a dignified exit.

Helen stumbles into her mother's path, her hands held up to halt the departure. "No. Don't go. Not yet. Please."

Olivia crosses her arms. "Make up your mind, Helen."

"Isn't there something you want to talk about first? Something you want to tell me?" Helen's tone is pleading now.

"What's got into you Helen?"

"I just thought . . . I thought you might want to . . . apologise." A shrug, hands spread in helpless entreaty.

This annoys Olivia. "Apologise? I've come all the way here, spent all these weeks looking after you, even though my own health hasn't been anything to talk about . . . "

"It doesn't stop you from doing it. Constantly," mutters Helen.

"I'm sorry if I bore you."

"Come off it, Mum. I know the only reason you came down to look after me was so that you could revel in knowing how I couldn't cope without you."

"That's . . . "

"It's got nothing to do with my needing help. You just wanted to feel in control. How often have I had to listen to you in the last two months? "There, see, you still need your mother." You made it sound like you were enjoying the fact I was sick. You got to treat me like a six year old and be my mummy-wummikins again."

Olivia's face grows pinched in her fury. "You ungrateful bitch."

STALEMATE • NARRELLE M. HARRIS

"You know it's true."

"You were so sick when I came here that you couldn't sit up in bed without help." Olivia's arms fold tighter around herself, forming a shield against the accusation. "I fed you and cleaned up when you were sick all over the bed and yourself. I held you when you were frightened. You cried yourself to sleep in my arms every night for the first week."

Helen wants to glare back, but the truth trumps her own anger and frustration. Curdling guilt floods back, souring her gut, and she has to stare at her feet.

"I came to look after you because I love you, and you needed me," Olivia declares triumphantly.

"I know," says Helen softly, "I was glad you were here."

"Then why are you being so cruel?"

Helen blinks at tears that burn but refuse to fall. "Because when I started feeling better, you kept smothering me." Her voice is quiet but firm. "It felt like you preferred it when I was helpless. You didn't let me even try to do things for myself when I was stronger."

"You were too sick," says Olivia. "You still are."

Helen takes another breath. Deep. She needs it because what she has to say is important and it must come from a dark place, deep inside and under her heart, where she has hidden the thought for weeks. "It feels like don't want me to get fully well, because you want to keep on being needed."

Olivia is very, very still. After a moment she says: "You're an evil girl."

"It's what it feels like," Helen says it gently, but with conviction. She doesn't know if it's true, but now she has said it aloud, it feels like it is.

"How can you talk to me like that?"

Helen shakes her head slowly. A tear scalds its way into the corner of her eye. It doesn't burn away the feeling. "If I can't say it now, when can I?" she asks, her voice rough, "I thought . . . if you were here now . . . we could finally . . . finally say all the things we've avoided . . . all the things we need to say . . . "

"You don't make a word of sense," Olivia snaps, but then the stiffness vanishes and the look she gives Helen is pitying. "You poor thing. You're so pale. Have you got a fever again?" She holds the back of her hand to Helen's forehead. Helen flinches.

"Heavens," cries Olivia, "you're as cold as ice."

"It's your hands. They're freezing," Helen counters.

Olivia places her hand briefly against her own cheek. "Well," she concedes, "they're always a little cold, with my circulation. Maybe you should get back to bed, if you're not feeling well. I can get you some tea."

"I don't want any tea!" Helen's voice is an aborted screech.

"Or some soup. I'll bring it to you in bed."

"I don't want to go to bed. I want to talk to you."

"If our conversation so far is anything to go by, I don't want to hear anything else you have to say to me."

"Stop blocking me, Mum. I want to talk to you. Properly."

Olivia's arms are tightly folded again, arms of kevlar. Her eyes are hard like a mask. "I don't see why you're so keen for us to talk now. You've never wanted to before."

"That was. .. before. I just think this could be our last chance."

Olivia's stance of armour does not change. "So what do you want me to say?"

Long moments pass before Helen says: "The truth."

"I always tell the truth,"

"You don't lie exactly." admits Helen, "You just *reinvent* the truth."

"I don't know what you're talking about," says Olivia, not entirely convincingly.

"How about last Easter, when you told Auntie Hazel you didn't have room for them to stay with you."

"I didn't."

"Except you then told Robby there was plenty of room for him and Dhanya—but when they got there, you told them they had to stay in separate rooms."

"They're not married . . . "

"They've been living together for seven years, Mum. I think Dhanya is here to stay, whether you approve of her or not."

"They shouldn't have expected to sleep together in my house."

"Except that Rob said he asked and you seemed okay, until he got there. So you weren't honest with him and then it was too late for them to book a room somewhere else."

"So you came to the rescue and Rob stayed with you instead." This is an old sore spot, which they still gnaw at from time to time.

Olivia always sounds like she is accusing Helen of theft when it comes up.

"I don't have a problem with Rob and Dhanya living together, Mum, or staying in the same room when they visit me."

"I didn't want my son staying somewhere else. I wanted him at home with me. Where he belongs."

"So you fudged the truth to trick him into staying with you?"

"I have never tried to trick anyone. Though certainly it might be what it takes to get either you or Robby to visit me these days. I get more attention from strangers than from my own children."

Helen can't help herself. "Well, strangers don't know what you're like yet."

Olivia strides towards the door leading to the hallway. Helen curses her own lack of discipline as she leaps between her mother and the exit. "Mum! No! You can't!"

Olivia glares. "What on earth's the matter with you?"

"Are you s-s-sure you slept well?" Helen's hands are shaking.

"The sleep of the just," sniffs Olivia.

"And you drank the whole cup of tea?"

"Most of it. I told you." Puzzlement changes the lines of Olivia's angry scowl. "What's got into you?"

"It's just . . . " Helen hesitates then decides to brazen it out. "I put something in your tea last night."

"Something to help me sleep? That was silly of you, Helen," Olivia scolds. "It might have clashed with one of my other pills. What was it?"

"It wasn't . . . " Helen's tongue hovers on the word "poisonous'. "It was something herbal a friend gave me. You're only supposed to have it in really tiny amounts. But I was so . . . you spent all night fussing and smothering me. Going on and on and on about your veins and your arthritis and your angina . . . I only wanted a morning's peace and quiet really. Just some quiet."

"What you are raving about, Helen?" Alarm creeps into Olivia's face. "What did you put in my tea?"

"It was only for some peace and quiet," continues Helen, her tone calm and confessional. "I just wanted a morning with the newspaper and a cup of chamomile without you fussing around me like a demented mother hen. Making stupid comments about the news and ethnic groups and herbal tea. And your fucking health."

Olivia shakes her daughter by the shoulders, demanding to know now what has been put into her tea, but Helen cannot be shaken out of her calmness.

"And when I got up and looked in on you this morning . . . there you were. You were . . . blue. I didn't know anyone could really turn blue. Blue and cold and stiff as a board."

"Helen, stop it, you're frightening me."

"I felt so dizzy. So sick. So I went to my room and took my pills."

"Helen . . . "

"It was so strange. Because I was so sorry I'd done it. I didn't mean to put so much of it in. But I did. And there you were, all stiff and dead . . . "

"Stop it." Olivia is shouting.

"But it was so nice, too. So quiet. No incessant talking. No fussing. No suffocating me. I think I fell asleep then, for a while."

"I don't want to hear it." Olivia covers her ears with her hands to emphasise the point, but it doesn't stop Helen speaking.

"But here you are," she continues, wonder in her gaze now as well as her voice, "and I saw your body myself. So you must be here to say something to me. You must be. I know what I saw."

Olivia slaps Helen. Slaps her again. The stinging sound falls, dead, into the kitchen.

They stare at each other.

Those burning unshed tears glisten in Helen's eyes. "I'm sorry. And I'm not. How did it come to this?"

"I'm not dead," says Olivia angrily, "What a stupid thing to say."

"I saw you this morning with my own eyes," says Helen, sorrow overtaking the wonder. "If you go down the hall, you'll see it too."

"I can't be a ghost," says Olivia, "I'm going to heaven."

"Maybe this is our chance to clear everything up at last." Underneath Helen's sorrow, the pleading note rises again.

"Maybe it's *your* last chance," sneers Olivia. "You've always been hateful to me. I'm just your stupid old mum. Your father couldn't do a thing wrong, and I could never do anything right."

"It was never like that," protests Helen.

"Oh yes it was." Olivia draws away. Her arms no longer folded like armour, are now wrapped around herself, in a terrified hug, as though it will keep her loved as well as safe. "You always ran to the door to hug him hello. It was a fight just to get you to talk to me. You adored him. I adored him. He was the whole world to me. And you kids were the whole world to him. I was always on the outside."

This shocks Helen. "He cared about you."

Olivia's anger dissolves. The despair, the need, rises up. "I wanted him to *love* me, the way I loved him. I wanted you and Robby to love me the way I loved you. The way you did when you were little. But you never did. I wasn't clever, like your dad. I had to be the one who punished you when he was at work. I had to cope with the two of you all alone when he was away on business. And when I was sick. And I *was* sick. You think I made all that up, but it was true. But I managed. I looked after you and Robby and made a home for your dad, even when I was hardly well enough to move . . . "

"You didn't have to be a martyr," Helen says impatiently, "No one asked you to be."

"I didn't want to be!" Olivia's denial is plaintive, "but I wanted to look after my family. I loved you all so much, and you hardly loved me back at all."

"It wasn't like that."

"That's how it felt."

"Of course we loved you," says Helen, but she doesn't look sure of it.

"You loved your dad more."

"He was just easier to talk to." And that is true. Dad was always so easy to tell things to.

"What did I do that was so wrong?" She sounds like a child now. "Why wasn't *I* easier to talk to?"

Helen thinks about it. "Because you never really listened."

Olivia dismisses the argument. "What was the point? You never listened to anything I had to say either. My advice was never any good. My ideas were never any good." She glares at Helen. "I was never good enough for any of you."

And Helen realises that this isn't news to her. She has known that this is how her mother has felt all of her life, but she has never known what to do about it. For the first time, she wonders if it is true. Does she think her mother isn't good enough?

"All I ever wanted was to be loved," Olivia's tears stream down her face, gathering on her pale chin before disappearing, ghostly tears falling to the places where ghosts go, after the haunting. "All I wanted was to love you and be loved back. That was all."

"I'm sorry." And she is.

The tears abruptly end and Olivia snarls: "You should be. You should be. You poisoned me. My own daughter. My own flesh and blood."

Helen feels sick because it is true and she still doesn't know if she is really sorry. "I just couldn't take it any more."

"You could have told me to go."

"I *did*." The frustration flares up again. "Every day I did. And you wouldn't go."

"You needed me," insists Olivia. "You were still sick. Your pills weren't helping you like they should. You needed me."

"I . . . " Helen closes her mouth to block the retort. She closes her eyes so she's not tempted by the look on mother's face to say something else cruel. Instead, she says: "Yes Mum. I did. I needed you." And that's true too.

She opens her eyes again to look at her mother. For the first time in a long time, she sees the person standing there. Her mother. Not the complaints or the manipulation or the irritating habits. Just her mother. What a mess. Oh God, what has she done?

Helen has no idea how to begin to apologise. She opens her mouth to try.

The sound of a key in the door stops her. Helen is momentarily puzzled before she remembers that Robby has a key. Her little brother Robby, who she trusts and loves and . . . how is she ever going to tell him what she's done?

Footsteps in the front room, and then Robby walks into the kitchen. Robby is tall and handsome, dressed in jeans and t-shirt and a worn leather jacket. He looks like he hasn't slept in days.

Olivia whirls away from Helen and waves her hands in front of Robby's eyes. "Robby? Honey? Can you see me?"

Robby walks past her, past Helen, through the door to the hall. The hall that leads to his mother's body. Helen presses her hands to her mouth, swallowing her cry down. She can't confess yet. Let him see and then she will explain. Try to, anyway.

Olivia lifts her hand in supplication at the space where he passed by. "Robby?!"

"He can't hear you Mum," Helen says apologetically. "Maybe it's just me that can see you."

"I don't want you to see me," Olivia cries. "You poisoned me! Robby would never have done anything like that to his Mum. Robby!!"

Robby returns looking pale and sad, but not shocked. Not like he'd just seen his mother's body lying blue and motionless. Olivia hovers a step behind him as he walks around the kitchen, running his finger over surfaces, nervously checking that the room is tidy. He doesn't react to her at all.

"Leave it Mum," Helen says gently, trying to be kind. "He can't see you."

Olivia turns on her. "Well he can't see you either. Can he?! *Can he?!* You're as invisible as I am."

Helen's heart lurches. "Don't be ridiculous. Rob . . . ?" She reaches out to her brother, and he ignores her.

Rob's mobile phone rings and he answers it. Helen stands forlornly in front of him, her hand in front of his face, ignored, like the rest of her.

"Robert McConchie speaking," His voice sounds heavy. "Hey babe. No, I'm just having a final look. Everything's tidied up now . . . . The estate agent is coming around tomorrow. The sooner we get the estate all . . . all . . . "

He can't continue. His face scrunches up, like he's holding back a sob. A gentle voice buzzes from the earpiece. "Thanks Dhanya, baby. I'm gonna be fine. Really. It's just hard. Both of them at once. Mum was always so tough, no matter how much she moaned about her health. And Helen had been getting so much better . . . "

"I am better Rob," Helen tries to tug on his sleeve, but her fingers skim above the leather, repelled. "I'm right here, Robby. Right here."

"I can't believe what the coroner said." Rob's voice shakes as he speaks into the phone, "Mum wouldn't do something like that. She took so many pills herself, she knew better than to muck around with Helen's."

The words are like an electric shock. Helen snatches her fingers back, like they've been stung.

"Baby, I need to go now. I'll see you soon. I love you. I love you so much." Rob hangs up, and when his hands shake too hard for him to put the phone back in his pocket, he puts it on the table. Hands either side of the phone, he leans and draws deep ragged breaths that do not seem to give him enough oxygen.

"What do you mean?" Helen asks him, but then she remembers he can't hear her and turns to her mother. "Mum, what does he mean?"

Olivia has backed away from them both, and will not meet Helen's gaze. "He doesn't mean anything, sweetheart. It's a mistake."

"No it isn't." Helen feels the horrible certainty swelling in her chest. "You did something to me."

"Don't be silly." There is something sinister in her denial, "It wasn't important. I just gave you some of my pills. Yours didn't seem to be working."

"You . . . ?" Helen tries to fold this into her understanding. "Why would you want to . . . ?"

"I wouldn't," Olivia says, a little frantically. "I never . . . "

"Oh God." Helen stares at her mother. "I was right, wasn't I? You didn't want me to get well. You wanted to keep me sick, to keep me needing you."

Olivia's mouth is a thin hard line, and her eyes are anguish. And anger. And fear.

Helen and Olivia looked at each other, and Helen keeps thinking *Ohgodohgodohgod, to have this much in common. To be so alike and so unable to speak or listen or learn or make anything different now, not ever again. What have we done to ourselves? To each other? What have we done?*

She looks at her hands, turning them over to see the lines and the hairs and how three dimensional and solid they seem. "I don't feel like a ghost."

Robby takes another ragged breath and as it shudders out of him, his body decides that this is enough grief for now. His hands are calm enough to shove the phone into a pocket. He fishes the keys from his jacket and, after a final glance around the kitchen, he leaves. Helen and Olivia stand very still as they listen to the door close, very finally. They hear the key turn in the lock, and his footsteps as he leaves them to their fate.

Then they stare at each other.

STALEMATE • NARRELLE M. HARRIS

"Were we happy, once?" asks Helen, her voice very small.

"Very happy." Olivia sounds just as timid, just as reduced. "Your father loved me. And you and Robby loved me. And I loved you all back so much."

"What went wrong?"

"You grew up," says Olivia. "You didn't need me any more."

This answer is not enough. "Kids grow up," says Helen. "But other families . . . " She considers the problem. "You just didn't know how to be a mum to grown ups," she decides. "To you, we were always ten years old."

"I always loved you," says Olivia with feeling.

"Of course you did," replies Helen. "But you never *knew* us."

Olivia bristles. "Any more than you knew me."

Helen bridles in return. "You never *wanted* to know me. You wanted to see me as the daughter you thought I should be—not the person I am."

"You're no different," Olivia snaps back, "I was never good enough for you. You always thought I was stupid."

"I never thought that," Helen knows it is a lie as she says it. "I thought you didn't try hard enough."

"Nothing I did was good enough. No matter how hard I tried."

"Well, it's too late now!" Helen shouts. "We're both dead now. We can't learn, we can't change. That's what being dead means."

"I just wanted you to need me," Olivia flings at her.

"You couldn't stop treating me like a little kid," Helen flings back.

"I'm not listening to any more of this," Olivia turns her back on her and marches towards the hall door.

"You always walk away in the end!" Helen shouts after her. "You never talk!"

"You don't want to talk," Olivia's voice is like ice. "You just want to blame me."

She walks through the firmly closed hall door.

"We've got to finish this!" cries out Helen, but there's no reply.

The kitchen is very, very quiet.

The light fades. Helen sits in her nightgown and shabby slippers at the kitchen table.

After a long, long time, her mother appears, bustling around, looking for something to tidy. Grumbling about her arthritis.

It takes Helen several moments to register that her mother has entered the kitchen. This may be because Olivia has no right to be in Helen's kitchen, under any circumstances.

• • • • • • • • • • •

POPULATION MANAGEMENT

TOM DULLEMOND

Formless formless formless!

Brandon scrabbled at his desk, knocking over his foot-wide fossil Ammonite paperweight as he pulled drawers open and dug through their contents—blank sheets, sticky notes, stationery.

Not the right forms. He needed the right *form!*

His Death stood motionlessly beside him, oval head at waist height, humanoid plastiform face serene.

Half a minute or so passed over that stoic translucent face while Brandon continued to sift through his desk.

"My condolences," Death repeated, assuming Brandon hadn't heard it the first time. "On your death."

"Listen, I . . . uhm . . . I need to requisition the *Intent to Confirm Death Notice* form."

"That is form D-12, and any 'intent to confirm' form requires four working days to process. I am afraid you are dying this Friday morning, so there is not enough time to acquire the form."

"I need to post the *Expedited Request* at the same time, that will give me a—"

"Congratulations!" Brandon's Death stood a little straighter, and its eye LEDs glowed greener. "I have expedited your request for the *Expedited Request* and the requirement has been waived!"

Before Brandon's expression had time to shift from panic to relief it added, "Your *Intent to Confirm* has been expedited and your Death has been confirmed. My condolences on your death!"

Something in its simplistic logic circuits tripped on that non sequitur and its green eyes faded apologetically back to sorrowful orange.

Brandon wasn't consoled. "I'm twenty-four! And I process death forms, I'm supposed to—" But it didn't matter. The confirmation had come through so there wasn't much point in filing a counter notice of intent to reconfirm the confirmation of the *Intent to Confirm Death Notice.*

He sank back into his thousand dollar ergonomic chair and closed his eyes, struggling for some of the inner peace he achieved each morning on the commute in his little one-person cablet.

"My condolences on your death, but I'm pleased to tell you that the department is actively recruiting a replacement bureaucrat as of this morning. I'm told they're having some trouble finding a person with your experience and dedication. You're quite a unique individua—" it hiccupped briefly "— Brandon Somerset."

Brandon held up a hand, stared off past the Death's rounded plastic shoulder and beyond his small cubicle across the otherwise empty office.

"Is this because I wouldn't take the job down-state?"

"Oh, I'm not privy to HR decisions, Brandon."

"I emailed them this morning that I wouldn't take the job, and now I'm being served with a Death. This is bullshit."

"I'm sorry you feel that way Brandon, but the lottery doesn't discriminate or favor. I'm simply here to help you through this difficult time. I have a list of affairs the department thinks you need to tidy up. They've taken the liberty of updating your public PeoplePage status to 'Dying'. You should probably prepare some replies. Your mother is very worried about you."

"Gah!" Brandon spun in his chair to face the terminal and flicked virtual windows aside until he saw his profile page.

Condolence notices clogged his inbox. He pulled a few apart then realized most of them were just templates.

Sorry to hear about your loss. That was from an ex.

Damn, sucks to be you right now. Four of those from various acquaintances and from friends he'd lost real-life track of over the years.

His mother seemed the most upset, but even her handful of

grieving paragraphs held an overtone of restrained effort, like she wasn't sure how much grief was appropriate.

He dashed off an *I'll sort this out* blanket response, but the reality was there wasn't much to sort out. His Death would help him wrap up his earthly affairs, accompany him to the government hospital on Friday morning, and pat him on the head while they gave him his lethal injection or whatever. Maybe they'd drop a piano on his head on the way, to give the newsies some filler.

"Is this some kind of trick?" he asked the robot. "Are they teaching me a lesson?"

"I wouldn't know about such things, Brandon. I'm your personal Death, ready to help you finalize your affairs. You should take a break and let yourself get used to the idea."

Brandon didn't need to get used to the idea. He'd seen this plenty of times. Most of his work involved allocating appropriate resources to the dying. He just figured that that gave him some kind of special immunity, so he'd grow old like in the movies, live his life out on a grassy hill somewhere. Not that he'd ever seen a genuine grassy hill with his own eyes.

Dammit! He was twenty-four! He only had twenty-four tickets in the lottery.

"What do I die of?" he ventured.

"Heart failure, in your sleep," the Death said. "It won't be any trouble. Thousands of people die of this every day."

"And you're sure this isn't some kind of elaborate prank? I have two notices on my file about being obstructive."

Notice one was the old lady who'd died of a heart attack when Brandon had messaged her that her husband had died of a heart attack. That little fiasco ended up costing the department a kidney transplant, after they had to account for the unexpected death and tweak the statistics back. He still got an email from that kid every year, on the anniversary of his free life-saving operation. Very messy business. Lots of accusations.

Notice two was from trying to tweak a Death for personal reasons. That hadn't worked out so well. But Brandon thought the department would have moved past that now, since the lady in question was dead despite his best efforts.

He made a sudden decision and grabbed his phone, stabbing a finger at his mother's number.

She picked up and . . . it was the answering bot. Somehow it was always the answering bot.

"Hey . . . hi. I was just wondering . . . Can you guys make it to the hospital on Friday morning? I'd really appreciate it. No . . . no, I just need to talk to ma. No, I'm not ready to talk to her shrink about it. I'm fine . . . yes . . . yes. No. No I don't have time right now. I'm dying. Bye." He slammed down the phone. Roboassists were getting far too personal.

"I'd be happy to listen to anything you might want to talk about, Brandon," the Death said.

"Well I really think we ought to—"

"But first, I have a suggested list of people with whom you need to make amends, drawn up by the department to maximize your well-being."

"Uh . . . o . . . kay, then. Sure, what's on the list?"

"The lottery distributes death fairly, but it is always a shock for the winners. As part of your winding down, the department ensures that you attempt to make amends with those you have upset in your life. For you, Brandon, the list is longer than average."

"Yeah, well I grew up around a lot of jerks."

The Death paused and blinked its tiny LED eyes.

"It's why you aren't dying until the day after tomorrow, Brandon. You have a lot of relationships to mend."

"Well, first maybe you should mend this," said Brandon, and he put the spiral Ammonite paperweight through Death's faceplate.

• • •

He was still sitting in his chair, staring, when the new Death rolled in. The lift dinged and when he looked up, there it was, pretty much identical to the first, which still lay in pieces at his feet. It had been about five minutes. Not bad.

Brandon sighed.

"Alright, let's get started, Death." He began packing up his belongings. The Ammonite was barely scratched by the broken Death's head. He placed it flat on top and paused with the cool stone under his fingers.

"The very first person on your list is Bettina Grayling, a young girl who—"

"Seriously? I didn't ask her out after Junior High. That's it."

"She was very upset and remained single for three whole years. She bears you a grudge, and we'd like to cheer up her life."

"Oh, man, this is ridiculous. That's *her* issue. It was a kid's promise."

"Since it's my job to ensure each lottery death is a net gain for societal happiness, I would like you to contact Bettina and apologize for disappointing her."

"You're joking, right? Is my piano teacher Mrs Andrews next? I remember I skipped out on a few classes my mom paid for." He laughed.

"Mrs Andrews is third on the list. You also need to apologise to your brother for taking credit for his creative writing assignment in the eighth grade."

Brandon blinked at the Death, speechless.

"And it would be a nice personal touch if you handwrote each letter." Death handed him a gold-filigreed fountain pen.

• • •

By the time his Death explained that they had completed enough apologies for the first day, Brandon was emotionally exhausted and his concerns about how petty and ridiculous each offence was had been drowned out by the cramping pain in his hand. Who still wrote things by *hand?* In the end he had nine painfully handwritten apologies, black ink on marbled grey paper. The Death provided matching gray envelopes, addressed in machine-perfect cursive.

"That's lovely work, Brandon. Shall we go home?"

"Uhm, well . . . "

"I've requisitioned a two-person cab, so you'll have some company for a change."

"Suuure . . . Thanks, but—"

"Let me accompany you."

"Yeah, I was going to go to a bar instead. Just on a whim. Just the kind of day it's been, you know?" He lifted the box of work possessions and headed for the door.

The Death didn't notice his sarcasm. "I will accompany you, Brandon."

• • •

Brandon stared at his whiskey. He'd not been in this particular bar before but this was as good a time as any to establish new habits.

The other booths were empty. Quiet Muzak trickled through concealed speakers.

The autobar next to their table waited politely for him to hold out his drink. Two perfect, chilled ice cubes landed in the glass and the autobar rolled silently out of sight.

Brandon turned to his Death. "So . . . so I can't have my job back?"

"That's right!" Death said. "I'm glad to report HR found someone with the right skills to replace you. It was close, you certainly are a unique individual."

"But I'm not dying today."

"It would be cruel to expect you to complete your apology letters as well as turn up to work in the last days of your life."

"This is all a big joke, isn't it? You're making me a better person, and if I pass the test I get to take that job down-state." He paused.

"Does this count as bullying? Is this some kind of departmental bullying?"

"Not that I've seen," said Death.

That didn't make much sense but Brandon let it slide and sipped at his scotch. He could afford to try the more expensive single malts. Maybe he'd down a whole bottle.

He thought of the cramping in his writing hand and how utterly unpleasant that would be with a hangover. *Or maybe I'll just stay drunk until Friday morning.*

• • •

The twincab ride back home was deadly silent. The Death said nothing, staring into space. Brandon looked out his window at the other opaque bubbles moving alongside through dark sleet and had the oddest sensation that he was the only person left alive. When was the last time he'd spoken to someone in person?

He thought about it for a moment, realized he'd had an almost real-time conversation over email with his supervisor, and felt a little better. Maybe next week he might—

Brandon stopped. That's right, there was nothing to look forward to. He'd always defined his life by having things to look forward to: finishing his studies so he could leave the damn boarding school and get a job, the holiday he was going to have when he finished accruing leave at work, the next episode of *Darius Grey: Resource Pirate*. And how was he going to watch all those classic episodes of

Arcblazer he'd bought last week? Was even a single episode worth watching, given how little time he had left?

"The odds of me winning the lottery were pretty small," he said into the silent cab.

"It's unfortunate, but that's the reality of a lottery, Brandon."

"But how many tickets could there be, realistically? What's the average human age these days?"

"In the low 50s. The lottery program has helped ease the midcentury population pressures significantly, but with birth rates under control we expect the global average age to trend higher for another decade or so."

"Sure, uh . . . Okay." He'd never really understood statistics.

"But basically that means most people have at least twice as many tickets as I do."

Death didn't reply.

"So there must be a billion tickets in there just in this sector, maybe even two." That was forty million people in the entire country, though, which seemed high. He thought maybe the Indian sub-continent and New China were allowed that many. Maybe.

"The lottery ticket count is obviously confidential, but there are thousands of draws a day. It's just bad luck, Brandon. If it makes you feel better, I'm personally very sorry. You are a good person. We're just making sure you leave behind the legacy you deserve."

The cab pulled off the road near his house, and Brandon flipped his wallet over the charge-pad. It blipped denial at him.

Death put a gentle plastic hand on his, pushing it back. "The department pays for your transport in this trying time, Brandon. It's the least we can do."

Brandon stepped out of the car, his box of possessions under his arm. "You're not coming in with me, that's for sure."

Death was already outside, on the cold permacrete. "I need to make sure you don't do anything drastic, Brandon."

"Right . . . " Brandon looked out over the road. Cabs flitted over the sidewalk, mostly singles but with the occasional double cab shooting past. Was there a lottery winner with a personal Death in one of those twin cabbers, too?

"Well you can stay in the laundry room while I sleep."

He collapsed onto his bed five minutes later then spent another hour staring at the ceiling, trying to hear the sounds of life from his neighbors' apartments and failing. From his kitchen he heard the occasional tap of metal or plastic on wood as Death positioned itself amidst the laundry soaps and fabric softeners.

Eventually the silence around him faded away and he slept.

• • •

"Good morning, Brandon."

"I told you to stay in the laundry!" he said crankily. This was the last full day of his life.

"We have to spend the morning finishing your list, Brandon. There are only a few more letters to write, and I think you did a marvellous job already."

"And then?"

"Then you need to think about what you want to do with all . . . this." Death looked around the bedroom, waving blunt articulated fingers at the handful of movie posters, his clumsy bookshelf, not quite top-of-the-line chip equipment.

Brandon's stomach flipped for the briefest moment, but then he managed to latch back onto his suspicion that this was all a part of the department's efforts to improve his attitude and ship him down-state. The world refocused enough to let him climb out of bed and stumble into the shower.

"Go wait in the kitchen!" he shouted through steam. The hot spray clarified the world. Brandon pressed barely trembling hands flat against the tiled wall and scalded himself awake.

Death was waiting calmly beside the breakfast table when he walked out, refreshed and calm. It had laid out the fountain pen and several sheets of paper beside a bowl of breakfast flakes soaking in milk. Brandon was too polite to explain he didn't take his cereal with milk, and prodded the limp flakes half-heartedly while he looked over his list of grievances.

"Michele from *payroll?* Because I muted her PeoplePage account?" He'd never spoken to anyone at the office directly. The local department offices were mostly empty during the day and inter-office comms came through email.

"It's an unfortunate case. She heard about your efforts on the Sandra Cunningham Death lottery case and began to idolize you. When you stopped following her status updates she became depressed and tried to embezzle money from the department. Eventually she needed to be medicated."

"I knew you'd bring Sandra back into this."

"Sandra never knew you. There was no reason to try to fake her death."

"I saw it on the news. She was gorgeous, and she had a little daughter. If we can't make exceptions, what's the point of working in population control?" It didn't matter, because Sandra was dead anyway, and his current between-jobs-predicament might very well be related to his attempts to game the system on her behalf.

The Death paused for a few seconds, some sort of pre-programmed social affectation. "It's important that we keep human intervention out of the death lottery, Brandon. That's why robots manage lottery entries and why robots carry out the draw and robots help lottery winners like you. Robots like me, Brandon. We're the friendliest sort. I like what you did with your hair, by the way."

"You . . . What?"

"Please write that letter to Michele; she'll appreciate it."

At noon, Death folded the last of his letters and slipped them into their named envelopes. Brandon cracked a beer can from his fridge in lieu of lunch and stared at his hands for a while.

Were they really monitoring world citizens in case a few of them died and needed a list of aggrieved people to apologize to? Really? Monitoring the whole world like that?

"No need to dwell, Brandon," Death said. "You did a great job. Now we should go through your possessions. The department doesn't have a Will on record but you have some savings, as well as accrued departmental benefits. I happen to have a list of recorded assets here. It won't take long, and afterwards we can have the rest of the day off together."

"Sure. I have a pretty tight schedule. Let's see . . . Last day today . . . Tomorrow is Friday. We're going to the hospital where I die but instead you're going to tell me the truth about what's happening?"

"That sounds perfect, Brandon."

Just hearing that from Death made him feel a little more in control.

"Hey, actually I do have something to say."

"I'm here to help. If there's anything you need to talk about, I'm here for you."

"I'm . . . I'm sorry I took you out before. You know . . . back in the office yesterday. I knew it wouldn't matter but I guess it was just my nature, fighting back."

"That's understandable, Brandon. These days when people die, they know they're doing so for the greater good, but even knowing this isn't always enough to overcome base human instincts of survival. For what it's worth, I forgive you."

"Uhm, sure. So . . . "

Death slid his list of assets across the table.

"You're a child of the new world, Brandon. The resource crunch is a thing of the past and you have no grandiose wasteful assets, and most of your wealth is in your bank account."

"I guess—" He ran his finger down the itemized list. "—these books can just go to charity. My clothes . . . well, sure, the same. Make things better for the rest of us, right?"

Death did not respond.

"And then I suppose the furniture can go to . . . Screw it! It can all go to charity. My mother doesn't need any of it."

"Personal items?"

Brandon looked at the list. A few drawings he'd done in early college art classes. Lots of digital music and films that anyone with a half-decent job could afford to buy for themselves. He was about to shrug it all into the recycle bin when he saw, "Personal note—Mother' and stopped. What was that? He *remembered* that. It was a letter ma had sent him in high school, so where would it be?

Somewhere in the shoebox, of course.

"Are you alright, Brandon?" Death had noticed him jolt.

"Oh yes, of course. Just remembering." That feeling curled back in his guts again. He hadn't thought of his mother's letter for years. Sixteen-year-old lonely Brandon had really appreciated it, the old world charm of handwriting a letter when email would've reached him quicker . . .

He stood up suddenly and rushed to his desk, where his box of personal items from work sat forgotten. The spiral of his stone Ammonite felt like a glaring, accusing eye. In a desk drawer, underneath old magazines and bills, he found his shoebox, flipped it open, dug through some old digital camera chips from his youth. He stopped at an actual print photo someone had created of little

Brandon and ma at a kids' birthday party in the city park. When had he last gone to a park?

He found his mother's letter at the bottom, flattened and smudged a little, still in the original torn marbled gray envelope.

Death rolled closer behind him, where he crouched over the little treasure.

"Did you find what you were looking for?" Death said.

"It's . . . yeah, I just remembered it. I was having a tough time, you know how it goes for . . . actually, I guess you don't. Ma really helped, I don't even think she knew what was going on with me. Just apologizing for stuff, little things I barely remembered but, yeah, I guess they just sat inside me for . . . "

He paused as he folded open the letter, skimming the neat cursive writing. "You know, if it wasn't for this letter I would have killed myself. It arrived at just the right time and . . . Wait a second!" He bit his lip, looked up at the robot. "This is the same kind of paper I've been writing on. And . . . and the envelopes . . . ? This is a five year old letter! Is ma dead?"

Death said nothing. "You're very attached to your mother, Brandon. I wouldn't try to over think these things. Remember you spoke to your mother last week?"

"But that was via email. I . . . I'm not sure the last time I actually spoke to her. We keep missing each other, leaving voice messages . . . " His voice cracked. "What kind of sick game is this?"

Brandon stood up and placed the letter onto his desk. "I need a moment."

He walked back to his living area, found where he'd left his wallet and access card, and took a step towards the kitchen just as Death rolled into sight, then sprinted towards the front door.

"Brandon? Where—?"

He swiped the door open and threw himself through the gap and didn't pause as his eyes adjusted to the gloom of the stairwell and—

Ten small white cleaner bots crowded at his feet, all leaning backwards in surprise as he ploughed into them, felt his foot hook on a smooth plastic scrubbing brush and lost his balance.

His wallet and keys went flying, and Brandon crashed headfirst down the stairs, spinning in a cloud of plastic shrapnel and tiny wheels, the plaintive cry of Death following behind and up and around and—

Permacrete punched him into the black.

• • •

The blackness split into bright sunlight and Brandon blinked his eyes, gathering his wits. Something tight wrapped around his head and he tentatively explored bandages with his fingers.

He was lying in a hospital bed.

Death stood beside him, plastic face at eye-height.

"What . . . what happened?"

"You tried to fly down the stairwell, Brandon. You hit your head. I was worried it might be a skull fracture."

"I . . . Hey, is that . . . ? It's bright outside. Is it Friday?"

"Yes, unfortunately. I brought you to the hospital just in case. It seemed efficient."

"Uhm, thanks, I guess."

"That's what I do."

Brandon said nothing for a little while, blinking at the white wall.

"I was trying to escape."

Death waited patiently.

"But . . . I think it was all part of this whole test, right? It was that letter from ma, reminding me how those few words just at the right time convinced me to hang on to life. I was really depressed."

"I know, Brandon, I saw it in your file. All the signs were there in your correspondence to your peers."

"I didn't kill myself back then. Life had promises still and ma showed me that, and then last night . . . I thought if I keep following you around, isn't that just like killing myself? So I decided I wouldn't go quietly. I . . . I was running away." He looked around, shrugged. "So . . . Yeah . . . That didn't work out so well."

Death remained politely still.

"Why were all those cleaner bots outside my apartment?"

"They don't see lottery winners often, Brandon. I wouldn't worry about those things. It won't matter soon."

"What did the doctor say?"

"The autodoctor says you are concussed, but you've been provided with anti-emetics and there should be no further problems."

"Except I'm supposed to be dying today."

"That's a separate issue. I'm very sorry about that."

Brandon paused again then grinned.

"Okay, okay. So are we done now? This was all just to mess with me, wasn't it?"

"Oh." That artificial pause again. "Oh! Oh yes, of course."

"Ha, I knew it!" A brief flicker of doubt, then, "Are you sure?"

"Yes, I am sure, Brandon. You were right all along, it was all a clever plan to motivate you, so that you would become a better person."

Brandon lay back in his bed, sighing. "That's such a relief, Death. I'm only twenty-four. I'm too young to die."

"I know."

"When will I see my mother?"

"Your mother is outside, in the waiting room. There are just some formalities to complete." Death rolled a little closer, placing a smooth hand on his shoulder.

"You've had a long day, Brandon. You should rest."

"When do I see my mother?"

"Soon. After you've settled in a little. Here, drink this to calm your nerves." Death handed him a cool glass of water.

Tired, Brandon pulled himself up a little and sipped at it.

"Thanks. I'm so relieved. I really thought it was the end."

"It'll be fine, Brandon. Everything is fine now. Finish your drink. Just close your eyes and rest."

"All that talk about lottery numbers, that was just to keep me guessing, right? Ha ha!"

"Just a part of the . . . exercise, Brandon. You were very clever to work it all out. I'm very proud of you."

"Right . . . well . . . We'll talk about that later, okay? When I look into that new job. But first I'll rest, and . . . then I'll see some visitors?"

"Yes. Trust me. And we'll talk about it all later. I promise. But first . . . Just . . . close . . . your . . . eyes . . . "

And Brandon did.

• • • • • • • • • • •

SWEET SUBTLETIES

LISA L. HANNETT

Javier calls me Una, though I'm not the first. There are leftovers all around his studio. Evidence of other, more perishable versions. Two white chocolate legs on a Grecian plinth in the corner, drained of their caramel filling. A banquet of fondant hands, some of which I've worn, amputated on trays next to the stove. Butter-dipped petals crumbled on plates, lips that have failed to hold a pucker. Butterscotch ears, taffy lashes, glacé cherry nipples. Nougat breasts, pre-used, fondled shapeless. Beside them, tools are scattered on wooden tables. Mixing bowls, whisks, chisels, flame-bottles. Needles, toothpicks, sickle probes, pliers. Pastry brushes hardening in dishes of glycerine. In alphabetical rows on the baker's rack, there are macadamias, marshmallows, mignardises. Shards of rock candies, brown, yellow and green, that Javier uses to tint our irises. Gumdrop kidneys, red-hot livers, gelatine lungs. So many treats crammed into clear jars, ready to be pressed into cavities, tissue-wrapped and stuffed into limbs. Swallowed by throats that aren't always mine.

"Delicious," I say as Javier jams grenadine capsules into my sinuses, a surprise for clients with a taste for fizz. "Delicious." The word bubbles, vowels thick and popping in all the wrong places. Gently frowning, Javier crushes my larynx with his thumbs. He fiddles with the broken musk-sticks, tweaking and poking, then binds the voice box anew with liquorice cords. I try again.

"Delicious."

Still not right. The tone is off. The timbre. It's phlegmatic, not alluring. Hoary, not whorish. It will put people off their meals, not whet appetites. It doesn't sound like me.

Javier's palm on my half-open mouth is salty. His long fingers gully my cheeks. I wait in silence as he breaks and rebuilds, breaks and rebuilds. Concentrating on my lungs, my throat. Clearing them. Making sure they are dry. I don't mind being hushed. Not really. Not at the moment. If anything goes wrong, if I collapse this instant, if I crack or dissolve, at least my last words will have been pleasant. Something sweet to remember me by.

It won't be like before, he said. There will be no weeping. No throttling chest-rattle. No thick, unbreathable air.

• • •

On Monday, I made my latest debut—I make so many. Served after the soup but before the viande at the *Salon Indien du Grand Café*. My striptease was an enormous success. Fresh and unmarked, clad in edible cellophane, my marzipan dusted with peach velvet. Even the stuffiest top-hat couldn't resist. Javier had contrived a device to drop sugared cherries onto every tongue that probed between my legs. Dozens of gentlemen laughed and slurped, delighted I was a virgin for each of them.

"Marvellous," they shouted, licking slick chops. "Belle Una, tonight you're more divine than ever!"

• • •

"Marvellous," I say, calm and mostly clear. Mostly. Close enough.

Sugar-spun wigs line a window ledge above Javier's workbench. Faceless heads, all of them. Now visible, now obscured, as he bobs over me, intent on his work. The hairdos are exquisite. Some pinned up in elaborate curls, some plaited, some styled after Godiva. Glinting honey strands. Carmine. Deep ganache. Exquisite, all of them, despite showing signs of wear.

Between soot-streaked portraits on the walls, wooden shelves support a horde of glass moulds. As one, they gape at me from across the room. Their faces as like to each other as I am to them. High brows and cheekbones, pert mouths, strong jaws, noses so straight we'd be ugly if it weren't for our delicate nostrils. Javier insists we are identical, indistinguishable, impeccable casts of the original. We must be the same, he tells us. We must be. We *must*.

Once people have well and truly fallen in love, he said, *they do not want variety.* They want the same Una they enjoyed yesterday, last week, last month. They want the same Una, now and always. The same Una that Javier, confectioner gourmand, is forever recreating.

• • •

For the *hauts bohème* on Wednesday evening, I played the role of limonadière. Stationed behind the bar counter, I wept pomegranate jewels while spouting absinthe verses. Odes to beauty, freedom, love. Javier encouraged this crowd unreservedly. "They've loose clothes, loose hair, loose morals," he said. "And loose purse-strings." Under his guidance, the bohèmes tickled my limbs with the bows of gypsy violins. Scratched me with pen nibs. Trailed paintbrushes along my soft places. With each stroke, swirls of hippocras bled to my surface. Ale, brandy, champagne, rum. One by one, the lushes lapped it all up. They prefer drink to desserts, Javier said. Those with maudlin constitutions cannot keep anything substantial down.

"Una, chère Una," the bohos cried, slurring into their cups. "Promise never to leave us again."

Emotional drunks, I thought. *Glutting themselves into confusion. Muddled on passion and wine. Can't they see I'm here? I am forever here.*

• • •

"I feel—" I begin. Javier traps my jaw. Holds it still. Wary of what, I wonder? That it will fall off with talk, no doubt. That I'll run out of things to say before tonight's performance.

I feel solid, I want to assure him. I feel settled. Take it easy now. Easy. I'm going nowhere. I'm right here.

• • •

Friday's connoisseurs ate with torturous restraint.

"Pace yourselves," the women said, cracking knuckles with the sharp edges of their fans.

"Sugar is a mere distraction for the palate," said the men. "It will never satiate."

As centrepiece on their ruby tablecloth, I sat with legs pretzelled into Sadean poses. Wearing garters of hardened molasses, nothing more. By the second remove of sorbet, my contorted ankles and wrists had crumbled. I couldn't stand for all the gold in the world.

My paralysis thrilled our hosts no end—as did Javier's copper blades. Two daggers per guest. Honed to ravage goodies from my thighs, rump, belly. Tantalised, the feasters took turns at fossicking. At knifing currant ants and blackberry spiders from my innards.

"What an illusion," they moaned, crunching aniseed antennae. "So convincing, so real . . . And not even a splash of blood! When did you learn such tricks, *chère fille*? Why have you not beguiled us this way before? No matter, no matter. Bravo, chère Una, *et encore!*"

Tips are highest when egos are stroked, my confectioner says. When pomposity is rewarded with flirtation. So Javier slapped their bony backs. He stooped and kowtowed. I bowed as best I could. Waggling my fingers and toes. Letting them caress me long after the coins had rolled.

Rigged with peanut-brittle bones, my digits made such a gratifying snap when the party finally succumbed. When they gave into temptation. Indulged in wounding and breaking.

• • •

Javier ribbons my chin with silk to hold it in place for a few minutes. My neck needs patching; he's made quite the mess of it. He spritzes rosewater to keep me malleable, then shuffles to the stove. Bent over hotplates, he sings quietly as he stirs. His plainchant quickens the pots' ingredients. Sifted flour, hen-milk, vanilla essence. A sprinkling of salty eye-dew to bring his subtleties to life. Over and over, mournfully low, he garnishes the mixture with tears and base notes of my name.

Una, Una, he whispers, adding a pinch of cardamom to freckle my skin. *Una, this time you'll be just right.*

• • •

For tonight's outcall, Javier embeds a diadem of Jordan almonds into my curls. "The candied treasure of Priam," he says, chiselling them into my scalp. Content, he moves on to my hazel eyes. Sets them with a stony stare, like Helen's transfixed by the sight of her city ablaze. She's a favourite of Javier's. Peerless Helen. Unforgettable Helen. With that legendary face. All those ships sailing after it. Lately, while assembling and reassembling me, he's worn grooves into her story, worn it thin with retelling. The affair. The abduction. The hoopla and heartbreak. His sunken cheeks gain a healthy sheen as he talks of truces made and broken. Gifts offered, shunned, accepted. The permanence, the stubbornness of young lovers. The tale spills from him like powdered ginger, spicy and sharp, as he presses buttercream icing into my moist gaps.

While he pokes and prods, I make predictable observations. Repeating comments he himself once made. Repeating threadbare conversations. Repeating things he'll smile to hear.

From the shelf, the moulds watch us, unblinking.

"Ignore them," I say, repeating, repeating. "It's just the two of us now."

• • •

Javier rubs the scowl from my forehead. Heats a spoon and melts saffron into my eyebrows. Sunshine lilts through the studio's crescent windows as he works. The deep gold of late afternoon adds fire to his story. Promises broken, omens ignored, the grief and wrath of Achilles. Every word igniting, ablaze. But when he reaches the sack of Troy, Javier pauses. Unwilling to narrate the ending, he backtracks. As always, to Helen.

Concentrating, he plunges a series of long plaits into my scalp without letting even a drop of custard ooze out. Carefully, precisely, he stretches them down my spine. I'm half-bowed under the weight of so much hair. He fusses with the braids, fusses.

"Menelaus is furious when his wife returns," he eventually says. "Can you imagine? Almost as furious as when she first left. How dare she have survived so much without him? How dare he remain such a fool in her presence."

I shrug. Javier pushes my shoulders back down, checks for wrinkles. Checks the portrait above the assembly table. Nodding, he reaches up to drape an icing chiton over my nakedness. I am taller than him by a hand, but he is clever as a monkey when it comes to climbing. Hopping from footstool to bench and back, he manoeuvres around me, the long tube of material bunched in his arms. Though the gauze is thinner than faith, the strength of his recipe keeps it together.

That, and his devilish fingers.

• • •

They dart in and out, gathering, smoothing, fluffing my garment until it blouses in wondrous folds. Pins appear, disappear. Puncturing, piercing, holding the fabric in place. Javier's lips smack as he thinks, as he tucks. He steps back to take me all in. Steps up, tugs a pleat. Steps back, cocks his head. Steps up, fidgets a cord around my waist. Steps back, smacks, annoyed. Up and back, up and back. Step-ball-change, once more from the top. Up and back in the perfectionist's dance.

At last, he is satisfied. A pendant is the final touch, a mille-feuille heart on a string of rarified gold. "You are a feast," he says, coiling the cold thing around my throat. "You are a picture." Overcome, he smacks lips and hands—and his cufflink catches on my neckline. Catches, and tears.

The robes sigh apart, exposing me from gullet to gut. Javier rushes to fix it. He flaps and gouges, making it worse. Up and back, up and back, he flaps, gouges, wrecks and ruins. Up and back, the necklace snaps. The silver bonbons he'd spent hours spiralling around my cinnamon aureoles are scraped loose. Part of my ribcage concaves. Tiny candies plink to the floor.

But there is air in my chest. There is breath. Surely, this is good?

"And he is ever at mercy of the gods," Javier mutters, smudging my marzipan to keep the custard from seeping out. "We'll have to cancel, Una. Reschedule for another time. We can't arrive with you in this state—what will they think?"

"You underestimate—" I almost say *yourself*, but taste the error before it's spoken. A confectioner does not reach Javier's standing without resolve. Without ego. Instead, I reassure him with a familiar wink. "Tonight, I'll play the mystic. You know the routine. Smoke, mirrors, communing with spirits. It's only fitting." I look down at my Hellenistic garb. The ragged flaps of material lift easily and, thankfully, with minimal debris. I fasten them on my left shoulder, covering the worst of the mess. Leaving my heart and one flawless breast bare.

Holding his gaze, I curtsey. "A seer should ever reveal as much as she obscures. *N'est-ce pas?*"

His laugh is a sad little bark.

"And you are a vision," he says.

• • •

I am ready to go, but Javier is nervous.

I don't tell him he's being silly. Don't remind him I've survived three vigorous outings this week, mostly intact. He doesn't need to hear it. There's no limit to his talent, no damage he can't reverse. I'm living proof, I could tell him. I'm here because of him. I'm here. But he's heard it all before.

Everything will be fine, I could say. Three faultless soirées in the space of a week. Three journeys, survived. As many trips as Helen made, or more, depending Javier's mood when telling stories. And only a few pieces lost, despite the Sadeans. Nothing important. I'm still together—*we're* still together. Everything is fine.

Even so, Javier is nervous.

"They want to see you, Una. That's all, so they say. After so long. Only to see you." He is speaking to me, but his back is turned. Facing the faded oil painting. "They've got countless portraits, cameos, ambrotypes. Countless memories. *Insufficient*, they say. *It's just not the same*." Javier snorts. "So now, finally, they want to see *you*."

Vacant glass eyes gaze down from the shelves. The moulds sneer at me. Waiting their turn.

"I'll give it my all," I say, the phrase stale on my tongue.

"Yes, of course, *ma chère*," Javier replies to the wall. "You always have."

• • •

In the mansion's grand dining hall, dinner is imminent. The sideboard is weighed down with a hoard of gold dishes. Steaming tureens, saucières, bain-maries. The room suffocates with aromas of the meal to come. Fine claret is decanted. Muscat and champagne are chilling for later. Legions of silverware are arranged in ranks beside plates. Crystal stemware gleams. Footmen stand at the ready. Carafes of ice-water dripping condensation onto their white gloves. Poised to begin service, they look out over the room. Vigilant, unblinking.

As always, Madame dominates the table's head while Monsieur commands the foot. Eight rigid people occupy the seats between. Men sporting versions of the same black-and-white suits. Women in lustreless monochrome. All posturing, variations with the same facial features. To my left, Javier folds and refolds his napkin. A cue, perhaps? I await further signals—but like the hors d'oeuvres and drinks, none are forthcoming. For all his anxiety, my confectioner has neglected to give me instructions. Am I the centrepiece this evening? Am I the dessert? Our hosts have offered no guidance.

Made no requests. The moment we entered, they simply invited me to sit. To join them at table, like a guest.

They want to see you, Javier said.

They all do, don't they? They want the same Una, over and over. I am always her. Over and over.

But tonight I am also sibyl, oracle, prophetess. Tonight I am breathless from seeing so much. Seeing and being seen.

• • •

"A striking resemblance," Maman says at last.

"We had heard," says Papa, moustache bristling. "But, you understand, we needed to see for ourselves."

"Of course," replies Javier. "Of course. Remarkable, *n'est-ce pas?*"

I shiver under their scrutiny.

"How many of these—" says the youngest Demoiselle, *la sœur*, jewelled hand fluttering. Grasping for an explanation. "How long has it been—? How did you reconstruct—? I mean, look at her. Just, *look*. Please tell me this isn't her death mask . . . "

They look and look and look away.

"Absolutely not," whispers Javier. "Does she look dead to you?"

Of course, I repeat silently. Of course. Remarkable, *n'est-ce pas?*

I reach down. Pull my legs up one at a time. Twist until I'm perched like a swami on the mahogany chair. Mousse leaks from my hips. Cream swills in my guts. I exhale and collect my thoughts. Prepare my premonitions. Summon my ghosts.

"Shall we begin?"

One of the black-ties glares at me. "Una was much more lithe," he says. "Much more vibrant. Such an exquisite dancer, such a beautiful singer. To have wasted her life on vulgar cabaret . . . "

"Slinking in alleys . . . "

"Scuffling for coin in dank, decrepit places . . . "

"Cafés and *folies*." Top-hat shakes, spits. "Damp, even in summer. Small wonder the wheeze got her—"

My joints stiffen as he speaks. Vein-syrup coagulates. Grenadine clogs my nostrils. I exaggerate a cough, swallow fizz. Use spittle and phlegm to demand their attention. "Shall we begin?"

"Heartbreaking," says another. "Clearly, a wife cannot survive on sugar, liquor, and promises alone . . . "

"A husband should provide more—"

"*Ça suffit*," says Maman. "My daughter made her own choices. What's done is done."

"But this," says Papa, crossing himself. Expression doughy. "She has had no say in *this*."

"Open your eyes," I intone with all the gravitas of Helen on the ramparts. Fire flickers in my gaze. "Open your eyes. Una is here."

• • •

Give them what they desire, my confectioner once told me, *and the audience will never forget you.*

Cardamom flakes from my cheeks as I grin, enigmatic. Remember me? Peppermint auras smoke from my mouth, sweet and pervasive. What a show we've planned! What a performance. There will be no weeping this time. No throttling chest-rattle. No thick, unbreathable air. It won't be like before.

Remember?

I am weightless, seeing them here, being seen. I am buoyant.

A fairy-floss spirit spins out of my fingertips. She clouds up to the ceiling, floats down the walls. Shrouds the gallery of portraits hung there. "Una," I say, louder now. At my command, the spectre coalesces. Straight nose, high brows, Helen's fixed stare. She is the mould, the paintings, replicated in floating skeins of cotton candy. "Una is here."

My eyeballs roll back in their sockets. The undersides are concave. Hollow, but not void. Diamond-shaped dragées trickle out. Dry-tears. My pupils turn skullward, but I am not blind. I am Delphic. Past, present, future. All-knowing. All-seeing.

I look and look and don't look away.

Chairs screech back from the table. Heels chatter their exit, but not mouths. Mouths are black lines, firm-clenched or drooping. Mouths are hidden behind satin-gloved fingers, closed behind handkerchiefs. Mouths are quivering disgust. There will be no licks, no nibbles from these. No kisses.

Maman's handmaiden swats the apparition, clearing a path so her mistress can leave. Papa sniffs. Dabs his lowered eyes. Orders servants back to the kitchens. Follows them out. Javier sits rigid as meringue beside me. Will he add this story to his repertoire? Will he tell the next Una what he's told us already, over and over, so many times?

Give them what they desire, he said.

Spectres, spirits, sweet subtleties.

"Wait," Javier says as his in-laws retreat from the room. Indecorous penguins, making their excuses before the entrée. "Stay! You wanted to see—"

New memories to replace the old.

Pulling, pulling, the ghost unspools from my heart. She spills. She aches.

"Is this not her face?" he says, leaning close enough to kiss. "Is Una not right here? Is she not perfect?"

"This is not her face," I repeat. Wrong, try again. My thoughts are muddled, drunk on passion and time. "You wanted to see." Musk falls from my gums. *Bohèmes break brittle bones*. No, wait. Not quite. That's not alphabetical—macadamias, marshmallows, mignardises. Better. My fingers snap, one by one. *Bohèmes bones break brittle*. Sherbet foams from my mouth, grenadine from my nostrils. Custard seeps, melts my delicate robes. My hands find, flail, flounder in Javier's warm grip. Cream gluts from my sternum, splattering the Wedgwood. Shaking, my head teeters. Throbs. Tilts.

"She is not perfect," says the ghost.

Forced skyward, Helen's stony gaze comes to rest on the ceiling rose.

"This is not her face."

Will Javier tell the next Una this story?

Give them what they desire, he said.

New memories.

Remember?

My chest heaves, drowning in buttercream. The ghost breaks its tether, unmoors, dissolves. "This is not her face," she says. Not quite. The tone is off. The thick-glugging timbre. "Javier."

Try again and again.

"Una is not right here."

• • • • • • • • • • •

THE BULL IN WINTER

DIRK FLINTHART

The dingy room was spattered with blood and feathers. Bull flared his nostrils and snuffed deeply. The place stank of old sweat, stale piss and black mould. Only the faintest, fading trace of frankincense clung to the tattered corpse nailed to the lath-and-plaster wall.

"They took his wings," Kaia observed, her voice a gutted whisper. "There's nothing left."

"*Someone* took 'em," Bull rumbled. "Didn't gotta be the killers. Plenty of mojo in those wings, for somebody as knows how." He picked his way across the room, through the litter of empty bottles, pizza boxes, and Chinese take-away containers until he stood below the sagging, half-flensed mess. He sniffed again. Up close, the frankincense was strong, cloying. No mistaking it. "Help me get him down. Hold him so's I can get the nails out."

Kaia took a step, then stopped and looked away. "Can't," she said. "I can't touch . . . that."

Bull grunted. "Do it myself, then. Look around. See what you can find. Maybe something to show us what happened." He sidled into position, sliding one powerful arm behind the corpse, under its flabby arse, and hauled it up until it rested messily on his hip. The blood had stopped flowing long since, but it was still moist and sticky. He'd have to throw away his jeans after this. With his free hand, he pinched the head of the big nail that stuck out of one wrist. It was slippery with blood; he had to rub it a bit before he could get a decent grip, but once he got it tight between his finger and thumb, all it took was a good, strong pull. The nail came out of the wood and plaster with an ugly screech, and the arm fell to hang uselessly by the side of the corpse. Bull shifted his grip a little, and gave the second nail the same treatment, then lay the maimed body on the stained brown corduroy couch. As an afterthought, he dragged a dirty sheet over it. "Anything?" he called out.

"Nuh . . . no," said Kaia. She sniffed and wiped her nose on the sleeve of her threadbare sweater. "Doesn't matter, anyway. Nobody can help him now."

"It matters," growled Bull, still looking down at the sad, shapeless lump under the stained cloth. "He was good. He was my friend. He thought I was . . . good. Someone shouldn't oughta done this."

Kaia moved against him then, sliding herself in under his elbow, wrapping her arms around his waist. The blood didn't seem to bother her. "What are we going to do, Bull? He was strong, but they came for him. What can we do?"

Bull shook his head. "I'm stronger'n him. They won't come for us. If they do, I'll smash 'em. They know it." He growled deep in his chest and hugged Kaia close. She felt thin and brittle in the circle of his arms. He wanted to hold her closer still, squeeze her, protect her, but she felt so small he thought she might break.

She coughed, her thin body quaking against his. "I'm cold, Bull," she said. "Can we go? There's nothing we can do here now."

He looked around the squalid little apartment. How long had Angel lived here, among the junkies and the filth, the stink of his own decay? Yet the place was lifeless. Nothing of Angel to be seen anywhere; no photos, no keepsakes. Not even a potted plant. "Like he wasn't never here," Bull said. "Just nobody."

"What are you talking about?" Kaia looked up at him. "There's stuff everywhere. He left a mess."

"Yup," agreed Bull. Gently, he uncoiled her arms from about his waist, and propelled her towards the scarred wooden door that hung slightly askew on rusted hinges. "You get goin'. I can catch you up, eh? Got somethin' still to do."

She hesitated in the doorway, watching him from beneath the straggling green curtain of her hair. "Don't be long?"

He waved her away, and watched until he couldn't hear her footsteps in the hall outside, nor pick up her clean, fresh scent in the general reek of the place. Only then did he turn his attention to the corpse on the sagging, foldaway bed. Clasping his big, scarred hands, he lowered his head, and closed his eyes. "Sorry, buddy," he said. "I weren't there when it mighta helped. Ain't much I can do about it now. I don't even know what kinda words is right. But you'da done right by me, if it was me lyin' there, so I'm gonna do the best I can, okay?"

He opened his eyes and waited, but nothing happened. The corpse didn't move. The stink didn't go away. There were no signs or wonders. Bull hitched his shoulders wearily, and smiled to himself. Signs and wonders. Been a long time since any of that kind of thing had happened. He fumbled in the pockets of his old jacket until he found what he needed, and then he set about doing what ought to be done, near as he knew how.

Tucked into the street-light shadow of a bus stop, Kaia was waiting for him when he came out. Most couldn't have spotted her there, still and small in the dark like that, but Bull knew her ways, and anyhow, he could smell her; all woodland-soft and fresh in the rough, harsh stink of the city. She pulled herself out of the dark as he came close, looking past him to the rotting red-brick building he had left behind.

"You did it, then?" She licked her lips nervously. Kaia never did like fire.

He glanced back over his shoulder at the flames leaping high from the solitary window of Angel's apartment. They'd spread some already, since he came down. The flickery orange-red light showed at the end of the hallway, and as he watched, the window burst, and thick smoke poured out. Somebody shouted, a string of choppy, angry curses echoing round the high walls. In the distance, a siren yowled like a cat somebody had stepped on.

Bull turned away, and dragged at Kaia's coat until she stumbled after him, protesting. "There's people inside," she said. "Someone ought to help."

"They coulda helped Angel," he said. "They didn't." On the sidewalk in front of him, Bull's shadow wavered and twisted as the flames behind rose into the night sky. For an instant, it almost looked like he had horns again. He raised a hand, touched one of the rough spots on his scalp, but no—they hadn't come back. Not yet, anyhow.

They kept walking through the wintry darkness until the city swallowed them up.

• • •

Kaia woke him in the night with her thrashing. That wasn't so bad, but nights where she did that, she sometimes talked in her sleep, too. Snatches of the Old Tongue. Bull had forgotten most of it by now. Couldn't remember more than a few words, mostly swearing. But the sound of it still gave him sweats and bad dreams; nightmares full of twisting stone passages and the smell of rotting meat. He couldn't sleep, nights when the Old Tongue came to her like that.

• • •

By the cold light of the moon through the window, Bull sat up and watched her for a while. He liked to watch her sleep. Her face relaxed, and she turned soft, like she'd been when they met, such a long time back. She was still beautiful, of course. Always would be. It was the nature of her kind. But lately, it was a hard, brittle kind of beauty, like a tree under winter ice.

After a while, he got up and padded naked to the kitchen to get a beer. When he came back, she was awake, looking around in confusion. "Bull," she said, as he approached the bed. "When is it?"

"About three," he said, settling next to her, so that the bed creaked under his weight. "Hours yet 'fore sun-up."

"No, I meant *when*," she said. "What year?"

He studied her, his beer briefly forgotten. Her face was white and lined, her eyes dark, with deep shadows under them. She looked scared. "You really don't remember?"

Kaia shook her head, and pulled the covers close. "I'm cold," she said. "I was dreaming, and it was summer in the old land, and there were olive groves, and my sisters were there, and wine, and dust. And now I'm not sure . . . "

"2012," Bull said. "Christian calendar." His hand felt cold, and he remembered his beer. He popped the top; drained it in two swallows. Thin stuff, but it was hard to find the real thing anymore. Maybe he should figure out how to make his own. People did it. Couldn't be that hard.

Kaia wrapped the raggedy quilt tightly around herself. "Do you ever think about home?"

Bull belched, and crushed the beer can in his fist. "What's

home? I can't even remember how long we've been here anymore."

A breeze stirred the leafless pear tree outside the window. Both of them looked out into the night. Kaia coughed, a thin, ugly sound. From the corner of his eye, Bull saw her snake one arm out from under the covers and grab a tissue from the nightstand. She wiped her lips, and crumpled it quickly, but he didn't need to see. The smell was enough.

"Blood," he said, trying to keep his voice even. "How long?"

Kaia looked lost. "Forever, maybe? I don't remember. I've . . . lost things, Bull." Her fingers worked restlessly on the quilt, bunching it up, pinching the nap, rubbing it between her fingertips. "I need to go home. Soon."

Home. Bull tried to think about it, but nothing much came, except the nightmare of stone walls and carrion. How long had it been? Too long. Not long enough. Kaia, though . . . he sneaked another glance at her, cocooned and shivering in her quilt. Her eyes were closed, and her lips moved as though she was praying, but he couldn't make out the words. And shit, anyway, who would she pray to? Been nobody listening for longer than he could remember.

Maybe it was time to talk to someone else.

• • •

You had to know about the place to get in. Bull knew, all right. He'd just never wanted to get in before. The kind of people who hung out in Sanctuary—stupid name for a nightclub—weren't his crowd. All the black and the velvet, and they wanted you to think they were dangerous, but they acted like a bunch of fags instead.

• • •

The door was one of those heavy steel jobs you got in warehouses. There was a little camera over it, and if you looked real close, the word 'Sanctuary' was scratched into the rusted metal door, like how someone might do it with a pen-knife. The door opened if they wanted you. It stayed closed if they didn't.

Bull didn't have a real lot of time for that. He stood there, in the pool of ugly neon light, long enough for the camera to look him over, and maybe a minute or two more just to be polite. But they weren't buying, so he knocked. For real, with his balled-up fist, so as to leave a serious dent in the top half of the door.

That got some attention. Someone yanked the door open, and a guy in a long black coat stepped into the doorway. He pulled out a shotgun. Stupid. Bull took it away from him and snapped it across his knee, all the time with his eyes locked on the guy in the coat. "Lizzy," Bull growled. "I wanna talk to Lizzy."

Coat-guy, though, he wasn't done. "Beast-creature beware!" he cried, and a couple of really sharp-looking knives popped into his hands, like magic. "The Lady is not for you. Only death awaits!"

He was fast. The knives zipped back and forth like swallows, slicing Bull across the arms, cutting up his best leather jacket. Bull stepped into the place, ducking to get under the doorframe, and drove his fist into coat-guy's belly, all the way up to the wrist. "Just wanna talk," he said, patiently as he could, as coat-guy sank to his knees. "Lizzy knows me, okay?"

"Enough, Toro," came a voice like honey and silk and cats. "James will trouble you no further."

Bull glanced down, where the coat-guy was spewing up a bellyful of sour, red wine all over the nice parquet floor. "Don't think he could anyhow," he said. "Sorry, James."

He looked across to see Lizzy, and she was just the same as always. Long dark hair, red lips, pale skin, big eyes, big titties: that was Lizzy's package, and she knew how to use it. This time she wore red velvet, fitted real tight, and black suede boots. She licked her lips. Bull felt the blood pound in his cock, and he laughed. "Don't you start that," he said. "We'll be here all night."

"Not a social call, then?" She took Bull lightly by the arm, and led him past a mess of pale, hostile faces, to a curtained booth by the bar. He didn't miss the way she signalled with her hand, though, and he gave the other two guys in long black coats the same flat, ugly stare they tried to give him. He was better at it. They turned away even before Lizzy pulled the curtain across.

"Nuh," he said then, as they sat. "You're all kinds of trouble." He could say things like that to her. It was part of their history. "But there's less of us around all the time, eh? You heard about Angel, maybe?"

Her face didn't change, but he didn't expect that anyway. That's why he was sitting close, leaning across the table. Not staring at her titties there, but catching her scent, and it told him what he needed to know. He leaned back.

"I was sad to hear about Angel," she said. "You know that, Toro."

Bull watched her for a moment. "Yeah," he said finally. "I know. And it's just Bull, these days. Nothin' fancy." He ducked his head and grinned. "Sorry about your door, there. And that James guy."

"Not your fault. And I'm Lizaveta again," she said. "With the accent. They love it, you know?" She looked more carefully at his head. "The horns?"

"Filed back," he said, though he hadn't had to do it in an awful long time. "Saves trouble. But you've still got the teeth?"

"Assuredly," she said, and flashed him a mouthful of ivory razors. "They are expected of me."

He leaned back against the leather upholstery. Lizzy twitched the curtain, and right away, a skinny, pale girl dressed like one of them French maids showed up. "My friend will have a beer," Lizzy told her. "A heavy stout. Not Guinness. Something sweeter. Some . . . red wine, for me." The French maid did a little curtsey thing, and disappeared. Lizzy leaned back and smiled at Bull again. "So, what brings you here?"

"Kaia," he said. "She's sick. She needs to go home."

"Home," said Lizzy. Her eyes glittered. "Interesting."

"Greece, I think," said Bull. "She dreams about olive groves. Talks in her sleep."

Lizzy folded her hands. "So. My part?"

Bull hunched his shoulders. He hadn't thought too much about the next bit. "Well. You're doing okay. Got your own place. You got people. We don't—we don't got papers, nothin'. Back when we come here, they didn't ask much. We're sort of . . . outside the whole thing, you know? But now, you wanna travel anywhere, there's all sorts of stuff. And money, I guess, but we can get that."

The French maid came back with the drinks. The beer was good: thick, bittersweet, cool but not too cold. Bull put away the whole pint before he thought better of it, and eyed the empty glass sadly. Lizzy smiled, and did the hand-signal trick again. Maybe there would be another.

"I don't think going home will help her," said Lizzy. Her expression didn't change, but somehow her voice sounded sad. "Not everyone adapts, Bull. Look at Angel. Look at the Sphinx."

"Angel was weak," grumbled Bull. "Sphinx was just stupid."

"Michael was the strongest of us once," Lizzy said. "And at one time, even I feared the Sphinx. But they couldn't find new ways to be themselves, and so they died. If you want Kaia to live, you should look to the dragons."

"Dragons," Bull snorted. The French maid returned with a new pint, and he seized it, but made himself wait. "Ain't no dragons no more."

"Powerful creatures," said Lizzy. "Creatures who gather great treasure to themselves, rapaciously destroying entire nations. And the treasure itself takes on the poison of the dragon, so that those who see it are ensorcelled and enslaved, desperate to own it. They will kill even their loved ones to keep it. Are you certain there are no such creatures, Bull?"

An idea came, but it was funny. He laughed a little, blowing foam off his beer. "Sounds like a bunch of investment bankers," he said. "Pricks."

Lizzy's slow smile made his eyes widen.

"Bankers," he said. Could the old drakes really . . . ? "No."

"Why don't you go try to take their treasure? See what happens?" She sipped her drink. It wasn't wine. Bull could smell it. But he hadn't really expected her to drink wine. She almost never did.

"Dragons," he said, his head buzzing. "How'd that happen?"

"They stayed true to their nature," said Lizzy. "They found a niche. As have I."

"Me and Kaia," Bull said. "We're getting kinda squeezed out." Working as a stevedore, a bouncer, anything that took muscle and size. Except machines did most of it better, these days. And Kaia, in the gardens, always with the plants. Nobody much cared about that kind of thing anymore. "And the new ones. Like them as did for Angel. They don't show respect. Hockey masks and chainsaws; shit like that don't scare me none, but Kaia . . . I ain't always home. I can't, you know. Always look after her."

Lizzy looked at him with infinite sadness. "That is the way of it, Bull. The old move on, making room for the new. Unicorns die, and blind, albino sewer alligators are born. If you want to live, you find a way. There is nothing else."

Bull shook his head. "Kaia's right. We get her back to the old land, she'll be okay. It's different there."

"If you say so," said Lizzy. She paused, staring at him like she saw something interesting. "Maybe," she said. "Maybe. You desire my help? There is, perhaps, something you can do for me. Something—" She licked her lips, and her teeth showed, just for an instant. "Something in keeping with your nature."

Again, that rush of blood. He got dizzy for a moment. Felt like the horns were back on his head, heavy and hard and proud. He hadn't felt that way in a long time. He didn't like how it felt *good*. Putting his hands on the table, Bull stood up. "Yeah, no," he said, the words spilling in a rush. "Okay, this was maybe a mistake. But it's good you're still here, Lizzy. I gotta go. Kaia, she needs my help sometimes. I gotta get back."

She didn't move, except to nod her head a little. "All right, Bull," she said. "But if you change your mind . . . "

He was gone before she finished the sentence.

• • •

"What are you doing?" Kaia looked thin and tired. The quilt was always wrapped around her now. She never used to complain about the cold. Always said winter was part of life.

Bull pushed the untidy pile of papers away from him, across the littered table. His head felt real bad. Reading and writing. He still wasn't much good at it. But Kaia had showed him, an age or two ago, and she'd been right. It was important. So he learned, and he practised. "Stuff I'm tryin' ta figure out," he said. "Papers. So's we can travel. It's not how it used to be. Now they got people checking everything. Wouldn't be good, we got put in one of them places for illegals."

She pushed a chair round the table so she could sit near him. "In the old days, they would help us. For love of me, for fear of you."

"Old times, long gone," said Bull. "Hey, you hear about the dragons? Lizzy told me—" he broke off.

Kaia stared at him. "You went to the Lamia? You did this?"

Caught, Bull nodded.

"Oh, Bull." She slumped. "I'm so sorry. You're worried about me, aren't you?"

He nodded again, his throat too thick for speech, and she sneaked an arm out from under the quilt, sliding it all cool and smooth around him. She rubbed her face against the heavy mat of hair on his chest. "It's not so bad, Bull," she said. "I'll get better in the springtime. I always do, don't I?"

But springtime wasn't what it used to be, was it? Even the birds and the flowers got it wrong, coming and going too early, too late. The air smelled wrong. It always did, lately. "I'm gonna do it," he said, touching her hair, twining it through his fingers. Red streaks in the green, brown in the red. More this year than ever before, maybe. "I'm gonna take you back home. You can see spring there, and summer. And your sisters, yeah."

"My sisters," she murmured, her voice soft, like she was tired. "Don't go to the Lamia, Bull. She helps no-one. There is no giving in her anywhere, only taking. Not love. Just death."

"She knows people," Bull murmured, tilting his head to snuff the rich, leaf-mould scent of her hair. "She's got power. She could get us out."

"Not her," said Kaia, her voice softer still as she nuzzled into his chest. "Never her. There must be others. The great Roc, perhaps? If we ask, it will carry us. Surely."

"Thunderbird," responded Bull. "That's what they called the big ones over here. But they're gone. Long time gone."

She pulled back from him, and looked up. "Gone? The Roc? Did I not see his great shadow only last . . . only last . . . " she faltered, and a look of misery came upon her. "I've forgotten again, haven't I?"

Bull said nothing, but pulled her head back to his chest and held her there, trying to warm her with the fires of his body.

"Not the Lamia," she murmured. "There must be another."

He held her like that until she passed into sleep. Then he carried her back to the bed, and lay her down. She was light in his hands, and stiff, like dry branches. When he pulled the covers around her, he saw her other arm, the one she hadn't put around him. The one she'd kept hidden.

He stared at it. Went to touch it, the rough surface of her forearm, all brown and cracked and dry, like . . . like bark. Pulled his hand away again.

Then he brought the covers up under her chin, and tucked her in, very gently.

Sanctuary had a new door. It looked like the old one, rust and all, but it was thicker and heavier. There wasn't no dent in the top half, either. Bull thought about maybe changing that, but this time, the door opened for him.

• • •

The new man on the door had that smell. The one they all had, all the Strangers Bull had met in a long, long life. Like a whiff of ozone, and the smell of hot coals. Even Angel used to have it, under the frankincense. Bull looked at the man carefully. He was tall and thin, made out of angles and sharp points, and he wore a lot of black. "Ain't seen you before," said Bull. "You're new."

The red-eyed man doffed his crooked top hat, and offered Bull a bow that wasn't quite a joke. Good thing, too, or Lizzy'd lose her another doorman.

"You're not new," said the man, straightening. "I can feel that. Privileged to meet you, Old One."

"Bull," said Bull. All the titles and the polite stuff made him uneasy. Always had. "My name. You can use it."

"Jack," said the other, and almost, he smiled. But not quite. "The Baroness said you would return."

Bull craned his neck, and peered into the red-lit night-club. "She around? I gotta talk."

"My instructions are to convey you to her at once," said Jack. He did the hand-signal thing, and one of the black-coat boys popped up. "You have the door, William," said Jack. "Don't lose it, eh?" William didn't look like he thought that was funny, so Bull made a point of chuckling. That got him an actual smile out of Jack. It looked like someone had slashed his face with a razor, then filled the wound with teeth.

They went through a door at the back of the bar, into a big space like the inside of a warehouse. It was done up fancy, with lights and plants and carpets and furniture, big video-screens and the rest. There was some kind of party going on, with dancing. Bull smelled marijuana and opium among the sweat and the reek of booze. Lizzy was by herself in a big clawfoot tub in a tiled corner. Her hair was all piled up on her head, and her big titties floated on the milky water, red nipples peeking.

"Bull," she said, and pulled herself out of the tub. "You're just in time!" She didn't have no hair at her crotch, and he could see the fat, pale lips of her quim. It made him tense and uncomfortable.

"It's Kaia," he said. "She's worse. We gotta go. Real soon. I got some money. You can have it all. We need papers, tickets. You got people can get stuff like that."

She towelled herself down, titties wobbling, like she didn't know he was there. Then she shrugged into a little wisp of a black silk robe that barely covered her butt, and she smiled. "Quid pro quo, Bull," she said. "I like you. I will get the things you need, but in exchange, you will do for me a thing for which you are peculiarly suited."

He was ready for this. He'd thought about what to say. "I been with Kaia a long time. She makes things grow. She likes stuff that's alive. She don't hold with killing no-one. I made a promise to her, see? But . . . " Bull took a deep breath. "Like you say. It's my nature. I ain't no good at much else. So—I'll do it. This killing. But then I'm goin' with Kaia to the old land, and I ain't coming back, so you best make sure it's someone you want proper killed."

The look she got on her face, Bull thought he'd gone too far. But then it changed, and he saw she weren't angry or anything. For real, it looked like she was trying not to laugh. "Who spoke of killing, Bull?" she said. "You may yet have murder in you, but in these times, who doesn't? Killing is easy as—" She glanced around, pointed out a man dancing alone, under one of the flashing lights. "Easy as that," she said, and snapped her fingers.

Quick as a snake, that guy Jack crossed the floor through all them dancing, drugged-up people. He grabbed the one she pointed at, and in all of one move, just cut his throat. Slashed it right across with a big old razor, blood everywhere, and all the time him smiling that ugly smile, and Lizzy not even looking his way. Just keeping her eyes on Bull, and licking at her lips.

And nobody cared. Some of 'em looked over at the dying guy, and Jack there, but they looked away again. Right there in the middle of the dancing, that crazy Jack did a murder and nobody did nothing about it.

"That's right, Bull," said Lizzy. "Nobody cares about that sort of thing now. Have you seen their movies? Their television shows? Once upon a time, you were the beast in the labyrinth, the primeval rage kept secret inside every man. Now? The labyrinth is gone, and the beast is loose. Being a killer is nothing special. Everyone's a killer now."

THE BULL IN WINTER • DIRK FLINTHART

He didn't know what to say to that. He thought of Angel, cut up and nailed to the wall. He thought of Kaia, and then he found words. "Okay. Okay. But you still want something. From me. So what is it?"

Lizzy's eyes glittered in the shifting light, and she slid close to him. The little silk robe gaped, and she pressed her hand against his crotch, sliding it along the thickening length of his cock. "Bull," she said. "They're still afraid of *this*, you know," and she squeezed him, digging in with her nails.

Lamia. Queen of desire.

Bull groaned in real pain, and stepped back. He had to loosen up his clothes. He always wore cargo pants, with plenty of room, but when the rut came on him even they were no good. "Bitch," he cursed, fumbling with the band, breathing hard. He bent at the waist, hunching over as his cock stiffened, and throbbed, and rose. The constriction hurt. With a growl, he bunched his big hands in the tough cloth and ripped.

Long as a child's arm, thick as a fist, his cock sprang free. It quivered to his pulse, all purple and shiny, a single, clear drop hanging from the eye. A murmur went around the big room. People drew in breath, exclaimed like they never did when Jack killed the dancer. They saw his cock, and it shocked them like murder couldn't.

Lizzy laughed, a clear, tinkling note. "You see, Bull? It's your nature. Now, follow me." She turned and sashayed away, her smooth, white butt swinging from side to side. The woman-smell of her was hot in his nostrils, and he panted, his cock aching hard. She led him through a narrow, badly lit passage, out a door that led onto some kind of stage. The lights were bright in his eyes, and there were cameras, but he didn't care. All he could see was her titties, the pink slit of her quim peeking from under that robe.

He lunged at her, but she danced aside, laughing at his clumsy grab. "No, no," she said, and a spotlight came up, showing a girl chained to a big, heavy table. She was naked, splayed wide open. Bull stopped, confused. The heaviness in his cock mixed up with the pain in his head, and the woman-smell, and the stink of the crowd beyond the lights. He hunched his shoulders, and grabbed the base of his cock.

The audience *oohed*.

Bull couldn't see Lizzy no more, but the smell was still there, fizzing in his blood, making his breath hot in his throat. The girl on the table. She saw him. She looked at his cock, and her eyes got real big. She shook her head back and forth fast, so her curly red hair flew. She had gingery curls at her crotch, too. Bull took a step closer.

"That's right, Bull," said Lizzy, somewhere off in the dark. "She's there for you. All for you. A true virgin, like the old days. Take her, Toro, Taurus, Old Bull."

Bull tossed his head. He tried to think. What about Kaia? What would she say? He tried to remember her face, but the scent of Lizzy, the smell of the girl, the sharp tang of her fear, the delicious, pink folds glistening at her crotch—too much. He snorted, and stamped his foot.

"Take her," crooned Lizzy. "Let the Minotaur have his due!"

Bull threw back his head and *roared*.

• • •

When it was done, when Bull came back to himself, the girl was still there on the table. He couldn't see her proper, with the people crowded round. They were fighting to touch her between the legs. Some were scooping up the blood and jizz with their fingers, smearing it on each other, licking it off. A man even grabbed at Bull's cock, softer now but slick, hanging down his thigh. Bull backhanded him in the head, and he fell away, his eyebrow split and bloody.

Jack came up and took his arm, led him away from the madness into a quiet changing room. "That was well done, Old Bull," he said. "The Baroness is pleased. The footage is already going viral on the 'Net. You're a star. A *legend*."

Bull didn't want to think about that. He saw some pants on a peg. Big, khaki cargo pants. Numb in the head, he put them on, shoving his heavy cock down one leg, like always. The smell of sex clung to it, got on his hand, and he wiped it on a velvet curtain. "The girl," he said. "She okay?"

Jack giggled, high-pitched and crazy. "What do you think?" he said. "Don't worry. She got what she came for." He paused, and looked at Bull, his strange red eyes slitted. He pointed at Bull's head. "Would you like a hat, Old One?"

Bull stopped. He ran a hand over his head. His palm snagged twice, once on each side, above his ears and forward a little. Two hard, sharp projections. His horns, maybe an inch long each.

"Shit," said Bull. "Yeah. Gimme a hat. I gotta go." He frowned at Jack. "When do I get my papers?"

"Within the day, Minotaur."

It was Lizzy, come up from behind. He hadn't noticed her. She still wore the little bathrobe, but now Bull didn't much care. The emptiness and the ache that started in his balls filled up his whole body. He felt flat, bitter like coffee too long in the pot. "Send 'em to me," he said, turning away from her. Jack offered him a beat-up felt hat, shapeless from long use, and he clapped it onto his head, pulling it down hard so it covered the horns. He'd file them back again, later.

Lizzy slid in front of him, smiling. "You can return for the papers tonight, Minotaur," she said, leaning close. "There will be another virgin."

The smell of her, close in the little room, all musky and sweet . . . He got a half-flash, a fragment of a memory: the girl, screaming. The taste of her sweat, where he licked her face. The slickness of her, the tightness as he pounded into her . . .

Bull shuddered. "Not coming back," he said. "You send me the papers." He shouldered past Jack and Lizzy to a door with an 'Exit' sign over it. Looked back over his shoulder. "The Minotaur died a long time gone," he said. "My name is Bull."

• • •

The little house was empty when he got home. Like it had been when they found it, abandoned. Another mortgage swallowed up by the poison wyrms, the bankers. Nobody'd cared when they moved into it, him and Kaia.

• • •

He moved through the place in a daze, going from room to room, calling her name. Sniffing at the air. But there was just the fading green smell of her, no hint of ozone or fire.

Finally he thought to look in the wintry garden of the back yard. Twice he checked, the bitter wind freezing the tears onto his cheeks, but she wasn't there. Except now, there was an apple tree, old and twisted and leafless. He sat in the snow with his back to the gnarled trunk. Turned his head to rest his cheek against the rough bark.

Maybe it would blossom in the spring.

• • • • • • • • • • •

SATURDAY NIGHT AT THE MILK BAR

GARY KEMBLE

Vampires. The word hung on the screen, burning itself into my eyes. Around me the office carried on as usual: fingers stabbing at keyboards, stage-whispered phone conversations, the Chief of Staff cursing, and the babble of Sky News. It barely penetrated my bubble. I'd been drinking a lot. Too much? I don't know. How much is too much when you've just buried your family? They put Donna in the ground, and Meg's tiny coffin went down next to her. My olds wanted the funerals on different days. They wanted me to suit up two days running, just so "that bitch' wouldn't get the satisfaction. I said no. They turned up anyway. My step-brother spat on Donna's coffin.

I stared at the email, pointer hovering over delete. Vampires. Vampires in Brisbane. A secret club. A soundproof room in an industrial estate in the badlands out past Inala, where members gathered to feed. When you work in journalism, you hear rumours. Lots of them. Your inbox chokes on them. The TRUTH about THE REAL King of England. The SECRET CONSPIRATORS behind 9/11. Chemtrails, lizardmen. You learn to filter the crap. The crazies go first—anything with whole words in caps and multiple exclamation marks. The cadet can do it, and often does. The more mundane stuff is trickier. Councillors on the take. Police in cahoots with bikies. There's usually a nugget of truth in it. But like a prospector looking for gold, you have to ask yourself whether that nugget is worth the sweat involved in unearthing it. Usually, the answer is no.

This email should have gone straight in the Trash, but that day

I needed to believe that there were things more horrific than a woman drowning her baby and then dosing up on sleeping pills, climbing into the bath next to her, and slitting her wrists. I clicked reply. Later, staring down into that 44-gallon drum, I wished I'd clicked delete and got on with grieving like normal people do.

• • •

I stopped at the drive-thru on the way home, as summer storm clouds gathered in the west. The young guy working there knew me by name. It had only been a month.

—The usual?

—Yeah, plus a bottle of scotch. Something cheap.

He loaded the carton of VB and bottle of Vat 69 into my car and added it to my customer loyalty card.

I went home and drank. Drank as thunder crashed and wind tore at Donna's prayer flags on the front verandah. Drank as rain pelted down, saturating the boxes of baby toys by the front gate. By the second six-pack I was convinced the place was haunted. By the third, I could see their ghosts. Donna and Meg, playing peekaboo on the couch.

• • •

My phone bleated its chirpy harpy song. I swiped it away and fell out of bed, weeks of dirty laundry breaking my fall. I dropped back into my coma, oblivious to the funk of stale sweat, urine and cheap grog. An hour or so later my alarm went off. I stared at the time with bleary eyes, forced myself into the shower, tried to wash away the remnants of a blank, dreamless sleep that was somehow worse than nightmares.

It wasn't until I was at work, looking at the email, that I remembered the unanswered phone call. She'd sent me a link to a video on a peer-to-peer file-sharing network. I clicked the link, I rubbed my eyes. While I waited for it to download I went and got a coffee from a machine that had been at the Courier-Mail longer than I had.

I sat down, pulled out my phone, and saw the blinking message icon. I called MessageBank, sipped the coffee, grimaced, sipped again.

—Uh, hi. My name's Kay. I sent you the email. About, you know . . .

A woman. Maybe 40, maybe older. She had the rough-smooth

voice of someone on the game, but none of the confidence of someone who was good at it.

— . . . thanks for getting back to me. I want you to know this is real . . .

A noise in the background. Television. Some kids show. Multicoloured mutants. Something Donna put Meg down in front of when she was struggling to hold it together.

—I've sent you a link . . .

Something breaking. A glass on the floor.

— . . . I've gotta go. Watch the video. Don't tell anyone. They'll kill me if they know it was me.

I clicked play, dived for the volume control when the sound of panting blared from the speakers. Someone laughed, then realised whose computer it was coming from, and shut up. It's amazing what you can get away with when your wife and kid have just died. I plugged in my headphones, started the video again. There wasn't much video to be had, a pixellated blur of black on black. But what I'd first interpreted as moans of pleasure were moans of pain.

—Please, let me go.

She slurred her words, "please' was "pleash'. Drugs or grog. Maybe both. Men laughed. The camera shifted, tilted. A leg, trussed. Black and blue. A man in a suit stepped in front of her.

—Here, let me have a go.

He got down on his knees, his body obscuring the act. The woman moaned again, and this time, if not for the ropes and the state of her legs, it was almost the sound of pleasure. But it was wrong. The wrongness was baking off the screen. In the background, a baby cried; the sound so out of context I jerked, turning in my chair half-expecting to see Kyle's missus bringing their newborn in for a visit. But the view was the same as it always was. Chaz trying to sink wastepaper hoops from his desk. Morag at the front counter, feigning busyness.

The baby cried again. The hairs on the back of my neck stood up.

—Shut that fucker up.

More screams.

—I said, shut that little fucker up!

The video cut out.

• • •

On my second and last visit, the counsellor told me it wasn't my fault. I stared out the window of her high-rise office, watching light twinkling off the river, cars gliding across the Storey Bridge. I was bubbling with rage and confusion. Donna was sick, the counsellor said. Donna had depression, and it wasn't treated. I could almost deal with that. But Meg—what about Meg? My job was to protect her. Isn't that the whole fucking point? You protect your kid from the bad things, from the monsters, you teach them right from wrong, and one day you throw a fucking party and give them an oversized key. The counsellor said I shouldn't blame myself.

And I agreed with her. I lied, because I couldn't tell her the truth. I couldn't tell her about the daydream I used to have in the days after they died. The daydream was this: I arrived home from work. I walked down the hallway. The bathroom light was on and I could hear bathwater splish-splashing about. I slipped off my shoes so I could surprise them. I loved that look on Meg's face when I managed to sneak up on her. Initial fear replaced by a big grin. When I peered around the corner, Donna looked up at me. She'd been crying. I sighed, preparing myself for a night of telling her it was all going to be okay, we'd all get through it, things would look better in the morning. Then I saw Meg, lying at the bottom of the bathtub. And it was awful, it was horrifying, right? Even if you've never had kids, you can see that. But the worst thing? The worst thing was that I was already thinking about how we could cover it up, what we could say so that it would all be okay, the two of us would get through it, so that things would look better in the morning.

• • •

I entered the brothel clasping my notebook and pen like a shield. The door closed behind me with the noise of a sod of dirt slapping against a coffin lid. Cool air chilled my skin. After the humidity outside I felt feeling clammy and sick. I regretted the heart-starters I'd downed at the Aussie Nash on the way over. The overweight woman behind the counter raised a heavily pencilled eyebrow when I told her I was there to interview Kay.

—Kay will be right out when she's ready for her "interview', love.

She waved me over to a faux leather lounge suite, bathing in the light from a TV bolted to the wall. Daytime TV. Men dressed as babies. The day after I found Donna and Meg, Chaz turned up on my doorstep, notebook in one hand, voice recorder in the other, uncomfortable expression on his face.

—No hard feelings, Chaz, but fuck off.

I slammed the door. Didn't give him the opportunity to give me the spiel about how my story might help others. It never helped.

Kay stalked down the hallway on patent leather stilettos. Red, matching her stockings and teddy. Perfume that smelt expensive but probably wasn't. Lipstick smeared on, waxy and bloody. Eyes glinting out of deep, dark sockets.

She took me to her room. Heavy red curtains and a four-poster bed struggling to sustain the illusion of opulence over the reality of the stained carpet and threadbare sheets. Any fantasy scotched by the chair in the corner of the room, bathed in bright white light from a standard lamp. It was where they checked punters for disease. She sat on the bed, patted a spot beside her. I dropped down beside her. I could feel the heat radiating off her body.

—They meet once a month, to feed.

—I thought you said they were vampires, not werewolves.

She silenced me with a look.

—What do you mean, "feed'?

—I mean exactly that. Feed.

—Like, a fetishistic thing? The whole man-baby thing?

She shook her head, frustrated.

—The women are mothers. They have babies. You know?

She broke down, thrusting a hand against her mouth, heaved in a breath, trying to hold in the pain. It just made it worse. She keened, rocking backwards and forwards. I forgot about my notebook. I thought about the gruff voice on the video: Shut that little fucker up.

I put my arm around her, meaning to comfort her. But then my mouth was on hers, my hands running rough over satin and lace. I squeezed my eyes shut, tried to remember what it used to be like, with Donna. Before the depression got really bad. I tried to push Kay to the bed, but she twisted sideways and slid off the bed, shuffling between my legs. She undid my pants. I felt nauseous. Sweaty. High. With her mouth she brought me down.

• • •

My boss was a nervous man. He had a lot to worry about. Circulation figures. Advertising revenue. Defamation suits. He herded stationery around his desk like an Office Works jackaroo. To the left of the blotter, to the right of the blotter. They always ended up straight, edges lined up. Pens or pencils that were different lengths were relegated to the dead zone under his computer monitor, where online news mocked him from beneath the screensaver.

—You need to take some time off.

—I need to work.

—We tried that. It didn't work.

—I'm chasing something big.

—Oh yeah?

You could see the wheels turning. My welfare stacked up against circulation figures, circulation figures stacked against a potential lawsuit. Breach of duty of care. Or defamation if I screwed up and fingered the wrong person.

I laid it out for him in terms he could understand. Illegal immigrants. Locked up somewhere west of Brisbane. Playthings for anyone who had the money and could keep their mouths shut. He asked for the source, and I told him it was someone who'd seen it first-hand. I flashed back to that afternoon, brushing her sweaty hair off her face as she spat my come into her hand.

—Okay, he said. Keep me posted.

I was almost disappointed. I wanted an out. I wanted to chase the story on my terms, feel free to pull the pin when I felt like it. Now there was something riding on it.

• • •

I knew quite early on that Donna had depression. A couple of months after we started dating I went around to her place and she didn't want to see the movie we'd booked. She didn't want dinner. She wouldn't even look at me. So we lay on her bed, not talking, staring up at the white mozzie net.

I rolled onto my side and brushed her hair away from her forehead, fingertips sticking to her sweaty brow. It was an awkward gesture. She stared through me.

—I sometimes have bad thoughts.

—That's okay. We all do.

—I imagine that you're here, lying on the bed. It's hot. You're just wearing your boxers. I lay a cool washer over your face. Then I pick up the hammer and smash it into your face.

She said it monotone. No emotion. I hugged her because I couldn't bear to look at her. She didn't hug me back.

No-one else saw the depression. She hid it from them. She saved it for me. The counsellor said that's because she loved me, she could trust me. Yay for me. My gentle suggestions of "getting help' were brushed away. The more forceful suggestions met a brick wall. She always picked up. I thought maybe the trip to Greece would help. Maybe the wedding would help. Maybe the baby would help. But she needed a different kind of help. She needed drugs, she needed counselling. I ended up with both. She ended up dead.

• • •

Richo met me at Lutwyche Shopping Centre. Faded acrylic, filth-smeared windows, the wafting reek of a shitty nappy. Richo looked late 50s, head shaved to escape the comb-over. He had the stringy, tanned look of a concreter, and the tatts to match. Handshake an iron vice. Cheap deodorant masking sweat and tobacco.

I explained that I'd never done it before, but was keen. I told him I'd thought about it my whole life, since I was a kid. Lying was easy: I substituted my real obsession for a fake one. He saw the need in me; misinterpreted the source.

—Once you've had full cream, you won't go back, chief.

He slapped me on the shoulder. It was like a cosh.

We sat on a bench and worked out the details. I had to send money—not as much as I'd thought—to a Paypal account. I'd get an email from him telling me the date of the next "meeting'. Then a phone call, on the day, someone telling me the address. I guessed that someone was Richo, but he was coy when I asked.

—We work on a need-to-know basis, chief. There are people who, ah, don't understand.

He punctuated it with another jab to the ribs. A mother walked past. Baby strapped into a pouch. Another kid shuffling behind on a lead, snot streaming down his face. Richo raised his eyebrows, nudged me again. I wanted to vomit.

• • •

Another storm rolled in that night. I defied it, turning on the TV and the radio and every other device that could possibly be harmed by a lightning strike, plugging my laptop in, researching vampirism, heroin babies, and breastfeeding fetishes. I took notes, wrote a rough draft of everything that had happened. Lightning flashed, thunder boomed so loud that it reverberated through the VJ walls and the glass of whisky by my hand. I dared the storm to erase it all. And sip by sip, gulp by gulp, I tried to erase it from my own memory, but already it was indelibly marked.

An almighty crack tore through the air and the lights went out. The laptop's screen flickered, then came good. Cursor flicking off and on, off and on. I could see Donna and Meg watching me from the other side of the room, eyes glinting in the darkness.

—Leave me alone! Leave me the fuck alone! I tried. Okay? I tried!

They didn't respond. I sat there drinking, watching their eyes gleam, until I passed out.

• • •

I don't remember much of the following fortnight. When I was on the mend, trying to piece things together, I Googled myself. Apparently I wrote half a dozen stories during that time frame. Half a dozen that were published online. I don't remember writing them. I don't remember doing the interviews. All I remember of that time is my mate at the bottle shop, and his entreaties to use the back roads. I vaguely recall buying a ridiculously expensive bottle of Laphroaig 30. But maybe I dreamt it.

• • •

The call came on a Saturday night. I suspect it was Richo, talking through a dirty sock. He gave me an address for an industrial estate out past Inala. I tooled up the dusty freeway, past painted faces glaring from concrete sound barriers. Up an exit ramp. Through a wasteland of dry lawns glowing white in the moonlight. Peeling paint. Old cars. Rusty chain-link fences. Fading signage with typos. An abandoned service station, all smashed windows and tag-encrusted walls.

I followed the directions, streets turning in ever-more convoluted circlets, until finally I reached the end of the road—a row of low-set pre-fab workshops, backing onto a polluted creek. It looked like the sort of place where bad things happen at night. I climbed out of the car, grabbed my jacket from the back seat and slipped it over my sweaty shirt (the dress code was "smart casual'), grabbed my shoulder bag and switched on the recording devices. Red lights glowed, then faded, just as the guy from the surveillance firm told me they would. It wasn't strictly legal. It certainly wasn't ethical.

But if the story panned out, I didn't figure too many people would be taking me to court.

Richo greeted me at the heavy door, first through the peephole, then in person. He had a suit on, an ill-fitting, shiny grey sharkskin. He looked no less the concreter with it on. Sweat beaded on his forehead and upper lip. He grinned, eyes shifted to the bag.

—Some work stuff. I didn't want to leave it in the car.

I opened the bag. He told me that wasn't necessary, we were all friends, then poked around anyway.

There was a small ante-chamber. For a moment I worried he would ask me to leave the bag there, but he was already pushing through a heavy velveteen curtain.

—Welcome to the Milk Bar, he said, and ushered me through.

I walked into the room and turned, taking in the scene, letting the camera record it all. The half a dozen women were trussed in various positions, like living works of art. They were all colours, nationalities—I figured I wouldn't have the opportunity to quiz them on their creeds. They were united by their predicament and by their naked, filthy bodies, full breasts, sagging tummies, greasy hair, doped up expressions. Each had a sign over her head, printed in tacky fonts and laminated: Dragon Lady (heroin); Little Angel (PCP); The Real Thing (Cocaine); and so on. The ones on uppers were tied and gagged, eyes rolling like spooked horses. The ones on opiates were left to sprawl in armchairs and on cheap, chipboard beds. At the back of the room was another heavy curtain. The sign above the door made me shiver: The Nursery.

—They're all under a fortnight post-partum.

His tongue flicked at his lips.

None of the men took much notice of us. They were either guzzling milk out of the women or sprawled on lounge chairs or bean bags, looking doped out of their minds. I knew from my research that only about two per cent of the drug went through to the breast milk. And that dropped off rapidly the first two weeks after birth. They weren't high on drugs, the were high on filth, corruption, control.

There was no sex. Richo had told me that was the deal. Nothing sexual about it. But it was hard to imagine a bunch of randy, drugged up men and helpless naked women and there not be any fucking. But he was right. No sex. No sign of there having been any sex.

In hindsight, it's obvious I was having a mental breakdown. The breakdown had given me the story. There was no way I would have followed the initial lead, no way I could have duped Richo so convincingly, if I'd been totally sane. All I knew at the time was that I was having trouble keeping it together, and that if I lost it, losing the story would be the least of my worries. My lips trembled as I struggled to make Richo think I was cool with it all. I didn't want to look behind the final curtain. I knew I had to.

—I'm sorry. It's just . . . it's like a fantasy.

Richo nodded. He'd heard it all before.

—What's behind the curtain?

I started across the room, lips numb. I felt Richo's iron grip on my shoulder, managed to shrug out of it.

—Whoa, whoa, whoa big man. Let's have some fun out here first.

I walked faster, skirting a Melanesian woman bound to an old massage table. Richo didn't have time to stop me, not without creating a huge scene. And most of us—no matter how pure, no matter how evil—most of us hate making a scene. Sometimes— most of the time—I wish he had.

For a long time, I couldn't remember what happened after I pushed back the curtain. My next memory was of driving back to Brisbane along the Ipswich Motorway, mouth and nose burning with vomit, cheek throbbing, eye almost swollen shut. And blood. Blood everywhere.

Then the nightmares came. Babies, covered in blood. Asleep? A worn butcher's block, covered in bloodstained scalpels, syringes, carving knives. A rusty forty-four gallon drum. Donna, staring blank-eyed at the TV screen, blood pulsing out of her damaged nipple, while Meg screamed. A wet nurse cradling a baby to her breast with with one flabby, tattooed arm. Three fingers missing off her right hand. Donna, smashing a hammer down on Meg's body, over and over again. A balding man in a plastic raincoat, cradling a baby to his mouth with a wrinkled, liver spot-stained hand. I saw myself, peering into the drum and seeing Meg's blank eyes staring back at me.

—Shut that fucker up, shut that fucker up, shut that fucker up!

• • •

The police had lots of questions. Starting at the booze bus on the Ipswich Motorway (my blood alcohol reading), and ending in an interview room at Roma Street (the blood). There was lots of bad coffee. Questions. And panic. Because I really couldn't remember how I came to have blood on my shirt, or why my face was smashed up.

If it wasn't for my boss, and the illegal recording I'd made, I think I'd still be in custody. Lying on a bunk in a cell at the Brisbane Correctional Centre, wondering how I'd come to be drinking baby's blood, until I found the opportunity to hang myself with my towel. As it was, the police watched the video and my boss bailed me early next morning. He wanted to drop me home. He said I was in shock. I asked him to drop me at work; told him if he didn't, I'd just get a cab there anyway. So he drove me through the city as the sun crept over the horizon, muttering about health and safety over the easy listening bullshit on the radio. I wrote my story.

The men at the Milk Bar, all bar Richo, were caught and sent to jail. The guy out the back, drinking the baby's blood, was put into protective custody. Two months into his sentence he was found bludgeoned to death in his bunk. No-one shed a tear. The wet nurse—she was real, not some Lynchian hallucination—was found to be psychologically unstable, and as far as I know is still locked up at Wolston Park. And Richo, God bless him, Richo was dumped outside the emergency ward at the Royal Brisbane Hospital, dead before the doc even had time to diagnose the overdose.

And me? The story was nominated for an award, but didn't win. I stopped drinking. I got counselling. I don't believe in vampires anymore. Or ghosts. There's just illness, and violence, and evil. And some days—most days—that's enough.

•••••••••••

THE WITCH'S WARDROBE

EDDY BURGER

Our air is flesh
so warm and supple
flourish we beneath its weight

We merge our skins
our pores the sky
our bodies mated with the world

by Wredda Gruber, from the "Organic Preserve" suite

Our air is flesh. Little did the poet realise how close her metaphor was to the truth. So minuscule and pathetic do our greatest exploits now seem. For eons we had lived in ignorance. And in ignorance, we prospered. Life was comparatively blissful and good fortune smiled upon the privileged. Yet it was due to the fortunes of an ill-fated few that led me to the discovery of the horrible truth.

Over the years there had been mysterious disappearances. Some among us linked these disappearances with a place known as the 'Witch's Wardrobe'. It was little more than legend. Only a scarce few claimed to know its whereabouts, and little would they reveal for fear that it would only lead to more disappearances. It was reputed to be just a small place where there hung foul-smelling cloths. An insidious air was said to permeate the place. To even approach it beguiled the senses and filled one with dread.

After word spread of yet another disappearance, I resolved to make the journey to the Witch's Wardrobe. I was determined to finally put an end to the rumours and fallacies, and learn of its true nature. But great was its distance from my humble village, further than even I had ever travelled—I, the greatest explorer of our time. Heavy was the air and so shrouded the distance, it would be such an arduous task that many a man would grow weak from the mere thought of it.

I did find myself a guide, a doltish old fool whose company I would never have tolerated had he not been the only person I could find who admitted to knowing the Wardrobe's whereabouts. Yet even though he was to profit considerably from being in my employ, he attempted to dissuade me from the outset. "Dunnut go there, young master. You'll be swallowed up like the rest of 'em," he said.

"Spare me your old wives' tales!" I spat. "I intend to learn the truth!"

We headed out of the village, my guide bent double with provisions and I with my chest held high to receive the well-wishes of the throng that lined the streets. Yet so grave were their long faces. A superstitious old crone accosted me and shoved a trinket into my hand. "It will protect you from evil," she said.

"Begone!" I spat and shoved her aside. Yet I held onto her trinket. It was the paw of a black cat, secured to a chain. I hung it around my neck. Though I reviled such superstitious nonsense, I knew the journey would be perilous and I could nary afford to refuse aid regardless of what form it took. The trek alone was sure to be an absolute ball-buster, regardless of the dangers I might face along the way. And then there was the question of the disappearances. Perhaps a band of cut-throats resided in the vicinity of the wardrobe. Or perhaps a great deep pit lay hidden there, a remnant of some long forgotten civilisation, which continued to claim its victims. I would need to be on my guard, that was certain. Yet I had made many an epic journey, to lands populated by ferocious savages. Though perilous this expedition would be, I was certain I would endure.

• • •

After two days of hard toil, my guide thought it his place to warn me again. "Ya can't go lookin' in it without bein' swallowed up, young master."

"What a load of bullocks," I said.

He liked to call me 'young master'. Granted, I was young, scarcely in my fifties, yet my achievements had ranked me among the greatest of men. Apparently the old fool used to be employed as a servant. He had walked with a bent back even before I lade him with provisions, as if the weight of the air was too great for him. The air could be quite cumbersome at times, but it did shield one from the elements. With his head held in front of him like it was, at least he was less likely to stumble because he could see where he was headed before his feet got there.

"I seen it happen before," he persisted. "One day I showed it to a lass, and she walks in and neva came out. I waited for 'er for two hours. I couldn't bear ta wait no longer."

"What part of the Wardrobe did she actually walk into?"

"She went 'tween the sheets o' cloth, like it were a doorway."

"So why couldn't you wait longer?"

"There's somethin' strange 'bout the air in that place. It's as if it could've sucked me up wherever I was."

"But can you be sure he did not come out later? Two hours is but a short while."

"You'll know when ya see the place, young master. There just don't seem ta be no place she could've got to."

My guide's account of a fellow explorer's disappearance would have been unnerving to a lesser man than I. Yet I did feel the need to question him further. "Tell me then—What if I entered this Wardrobe and snagged my tunic on a branch and then lost my voice, or something of that nature—would you not come looking for me?"

"There ain't no branches 'round there. It's a funny part o' the world where we is headed, young master."

"But what if I trip and hit my head on a rock?"

"Maybe that's what happens when folks go in—they have some kind o' accident. That's all the more reason not ta go in. No-one who's gone in has eva come out. You'll neva get me goin' in there, no matter how much ya pays me."

"But that great explorer you abandoned might have been just inside the entrance with a broken leg or such. You might have spared him a terrible drawn out death if only you had poked your head in!"

"Who?"

"That person you had led, who you saw go in and never come out."

"But that weren't no *great explorer.*"

"Well he must be entitled to some recognition. He dared to enter where no man dares to tread."

"It weren't no *man.* She were a lass, like I says, and she was simply bein' curious. She was a *fool,* much like yerself."

"I take umbrage to that remark! Don't be such a smart arse. My point is that surely you could have done more. Were there any savages you could send in after her?"

"I wouldn't find no-one willin'. There was folks who lived not far from the Witch's Wardrobe who used ta think like you. They'd 'ave none o' this so-called *superstitious nunsense,* they said. They sent five folks in after someone once. None of 'em eva come back."

"But they must have been savages. Did they use ropes? You couldn't become lost if someone outside held a rope to which you were tied. Perhaps they had vines."

"Oh, they had strong and proper ropes, all right, tied to each part o' their bodies, with a dozen people outside holden onto 'em. But all them ropes jus' came undone."

"Poppycock! They *must* have been savages."

Of witches, wizards
and foul sprite,
though disbelieving,
do not take light
grave warnings of their spells and snares,
for such might clothe
real dangers there

by Addrwe Urbreg, from "Who the fool?"

Over the next few days journeying, I thought much about our curious destination, which was feared by so many. But the fact that so many individuals had apparently either entered or been up close to the Witch's Wardrobe did in no way diminish the greatness of my endeavour. Impregnable was the barrier of distance that divides the world's peoples. Great was the civilised world's thirst

THE WITCH'S WARDROBE • EDDY BURGER

for knowledge of that which has been hitherto unknown, and great was their respect for the explorer who risked his life to venture forth into the furthest flung reaches of our world. None had travelled as far as I, nor endured so great a peril.

"Young master," said my guide. "The last time I travelled from our village to the Witch's Wardrobe, I vowed neva to return. Let me implore you one last time to abandon this insanity!"

"Quiet, you blithering fool! No harm shall come to thee while you are with me—though I care for you not."

I could not tolerate weakness. I had seen too many men rendered impotent by fear. Perhaps that's why the Witch's Wardrobe stank so much—a few weak-kneed fools had lost their bladders at the sight of it. It was said that it stank like a beggar or old crone. Some fancied that it was inhabited by a witch or governed by a witch's spell, hence the name. But there was also a rumour that it smelt more like a man—a man's dirty laundry.

It irked me somewhat that my guide never mentioned witches or spells. I had half a mind to believe his stories. Though a fool he was, he seemed very smart.

Yet it was the *danger* that compelled me. I would not only visit the Witch's Wardrobe but I would enter it and come out again, myself thus immortalised, my deeds recorded among those of the greatest men in history. Nothing could be more perilous. And coupled with the epic task of just getting there in the first place, I was destined to fill several history books. It was over two dozen miles from my village to the Wardrobe, which was, of course, extremely arduous when one cannot see more than a few cubits in front. It was fortuitous that I had my guide to show me the way. He had a special tool for making a path through the air. It was like a giant tongue depressor—a paddle that he used for levering up the air as we went.

• • •

After several more days of incredible hardship, we eventually came into view of the Witch's Wardrobe. My guide had had to carry me for the last few hours, so arduous was the journey. Then he lay me down and crouched beside me, watching the Wardrobe intently. I could now see for myself the things my guide had described about the air being strange and how there was nowhere for people to disappear to. There were no trees or bushes in the vicinity, nor any grasses or rocks surrounding it, just a few of those small fancy fungi that are so common and are not large enough to conceal an elephant. The Witch's Wardrobe itself was no wider than a few cubits, made up of two large pieces of plain, overlapping cloth, light brown in colour. It did have a strong human smell about it. Yet its strangest characteristic was that it could only be viewed from one side. Once I was sufficiently revived, I walked around it with the depressor, but the air somehow obscured me from getting a complete view. It was as if the air was being drawn into it.

"I wouldn't go no closer, young master, if I was you."

"But you are not me, are you."

I hobbled around it a little longer just to spite him, yet I too found it disconcerting. I crouched down next to him. He still looked at the Wardrobe with the same concentrated expression.

"Are you watching for anything in particular?" I asked.

"Just keepin' me eyes on it. If it tries ta get either of us, hopefully I'll sees it comin'. Have ya been sufficiently discouraged, young master?"

"Not quite."

"I'll tell ya one thing I noticed. Those is diff'rent cloths than was 'ere last time."

"Are you sure?"

"They're a diff'rent colour. Last time they was bright red."

"Do you think it means anything?"

"Can't say. But don't ya be fooled by its appearance or stillness. It could've only just took someone, for all we knows."

"That is all the more reason for going in there and finding out what is really happening!"

"It won't do no good coz once ya go in you'll neva be tellin no-one 'bout it."

"I've faced worse adversaries than some smelly sheets! I have established trade routes through the most perilous and untamed environments! I have rid lands of many dangerous native species! Have no fear, I shall be returning from the witch's lair! I shall enter her womb for to erect my claim on her territory! She will shudder in the face of my potency! She will be rendered powerless and infertile! All knowledge shall be mine, and I shall give it to my people, my seed thus sewn, my name thus spread so all will praise my brave and noble deeds!"

My guide shook his head. He had done his best to dissuade me. I stood up and approached the sheets. The air certainly was strange, seeming to converge at a point above, where the two sheets parted. I prodded the sheets with the depressor then stood back. Nothing happened. Then I inserted the depressor between the sheets. Still nothing untoward befell me. I waved it around inside. If anything, I thought it would be filled with air, but I touched nothing. It was dark inside. And that was unaccountable considering that it seemed only one sided and occupied so small a space. I held the cloths apart and stood facing the darkness. I slowly inserted one of my arms. I inserted it in all the way up to my armpit. There was nothing but empty space. I crouched down and felt for a floor. It was covered with cloth but felt quite firm.

"You'd better stop there," said my guide. "That's just like what the last one did 'fore she dispeared. She looked in, put in 'er arm ta make sure it were all right to go in, then she went in and neva come out."

"Did she mention anything about a dark void?"

"I think I remember hearin' somethin like that."

"And the next thing she did was walk in and disappear?"

"Yep."

"Did she yell or voice her alarm in any manner?"

"I didn't hear nothin'."

"Has anyone ever yelled when they entered?"

"Not that I heard of."

There was nothing to suggest that the same misfortune would not befall myself. But how could I accept it? I was able bodied and strong willed. I was going to enter and nothing was going to bear me away.

I stood in front of the entrance and braced myself. Then I parted the cloths, put one foot inside and set it down. Nothing happened. I moved my head and torso inside, then I brought my other foot in. I was now wholly inside, standing right beside the entrance. Still nothing happened.

The great man stands erect
swelling with self-importance
but his hollow seeds will soon shrivel

and lay bare the true extent
of his flaccid legacy

by Drawde Regrub, from "The Flaccid Spectator"

I stepped forward and felt my surroundings. I was faced with masses of curly, tree-like growths. I climbed in among them and ultimately found that they sprouted from a great wall of air. But suddenly the cloth wall came thumping against me, squashing me against the air. Again and again it thumped and squashed. Then the whole place started heaving one way then the other and I was hurled around, buffeted between the tree-like growths, the air and the cloth. Then the thumping and squashing came on again. It all went on for an interminable time. I was getting seriously battered. But through all this calamity, which in itself created an uproarious noise unto my ears, I came to hear the occasional sounds of people talking, with voices that sounded vast and resonant. Finally the thumping and movement subsided.

"I've got crabs again, doctor," said a male voice. "A regular penile colony."

"So I suppose you're after more lotion," said a female voice.

Though I was surrounded by walls of air and cloth, I could hear their voices quite clearly. They sounded distant yet were of such volume, it was as if they came from some giant voice box.

"I'm still using the stuff you prescribed last time," said the male voice. "You gave me several repeat prescriptions."

"Oh yes. I remember now. So you still have crabs, even though you're using the lotion?"

"I get them only occasionally, and they've just come back now."

"This really is very odd. You might have contracted something else entirely. You'd better pull down your pants and let me have a look at you."

"Er . . . I'd rather not."

I could not believe my ears! Although it seemed the most absurd hypothesis one could possibly concoct, I came to the realisation that I was inside a giant man's underpants! I was the pubic infestation that he was complaining about!

I made my way upwards between flesh and fabric. Immediately the thumping and crushing started again, caused by scratching no doubt. I persisted, clinging onto the great thick hairs and using them like branches to climb my way up.

"Scratching will not reduce the symptoms, Mr Burger."

"But it gets so itchy!"

"Did this itchiness come on quickly or gradually?"

"Quickly. I wasn't feeling a thing till a few minutes ago, as I happened to walk past the clinic."

"Would you say that it feels like crabs?"

"I don't know. It doesn't actually sting like I'm being bitten down there, but I must have quite a rash, all the same."

"Well, you really should let me examine you."

"I'd still rather you didn't."

"There's no need to feel embarrassed, Mr Burger. Part of my job is to make sure that people's private parts are good and healthy."

Eventually I reached the waist, where the trouser belt pressed the material more firmly to the skin. Yet I was so tiny in proportion to this giant, I encountered only the occasional tight spot where I had to squeeze my way through. I soon exited the lower regions. Between two great curtains of cloth, his shirt front, I could see the uppermost rim of the trousers and the top edge of an enormous belt buckle.

"Would you rather see someone else?" asked the female voice.

"No."

"Are you embarrassed because I'm female?"

"No."

"Is it because of your religion?"

"No."

"Is it because of your moral convictions?"

"No."

I parted the shirt fabric, stepped out onto the rim and was faced with the greatest void I had ever seen. We were inside some kind of enormous structure, but through an opening I could see into the greater exterior world, and nowhere was the air composed of the soft fleshy substance or of anything else opaque and tangible.

"You needn't be embarrassed of any abnormalities, Mr Burger. You'd be surprised just how many people's private parts deviate from the *popular* model."

"Don't you remember what I told you the last time I came to see you?"

"Told me? Oh! Oh yes, I remember now. Correct me if I'm wrong, but I think you said that your penis is so big and cumbersome that you keep it in another world, though it is still attached to your body."

"It extends into another dimension."

"Really?"

"Yes. But I don't like talking about it. I once mentioned it to a couple of fellows, though I wish I hadn't. It happened one evening when I was in a pub, and I overheard one fellow say 'My dick's so big, I have to tuck it into my sock'. Then his mate said 'My dick's so big, it goes down one trouser leg and up again, then down and up the other leg, then up past my chest and around my neck a couple of times, and it finishes down in my jocks so I can still urinate in the usual way. Why else do you think I wear these high-neck sweaters all the time?' I must say, he did manage to conceal it well, though he must have had a very narrow neck. Anyway, then I said 'My dick's so big I have to keep it in another dimension'. But all they could do was laugh. It was very humiliating."

"I see."

"When I was a baby, I used to tuck it into my sock, but it soon became too big to fit anywhere."

"Anywhere but in this other dimension?"

"Yes. I have a portable portal in my underpants."

It was then that I finally realised the dreadful truth. Its implications were appalling. My whole world was filled with this man's penis! Our air really *was* flesh, as the poet had said. For as far back as I could remember, it had been a comfort to me, feeling its warmth and softness as it pressed down lightly upon me. But if any of us had known that our children were being raised in union with some giant man's genitalia, we would have died! It was abominable! No wonder no-one ever returned once they'd learned the truth. Who could ever face that penis again? Who could face that world again? All our achievements suddenly seemed so minuscule and trifling. So highly had we ranked the exploits of our world's great men! So highly had we ranked the epic journey's of our greatest explorers! Yet the furthest anyone had ever journeyed was no longer than the length of some guy's dick! And a flaccid one at that!

The doctor gave Mr Burger an injection in his arm.

"Just remain seated for a while, Mr Burger," she said. "Hopefully we will see some positive results soon."

"What kind of results?"

"I believe there might be a connection between your psychological condition and your erection problem."

"I've never been able to get an erection."

"And that is why you have this delusion about having a gigantic penis."

"What have you done to me?!"

Suddenly Mr Burger's penis began to grow. What had been soft now became harder and harder. He cried out in pain as it pushed with ever increasing pressure against the boundaries of my world. It pressed down upon the buildings and people till everything was totally flattened. Every person in my world was crushed to death.

•••••••••••

COMFORT GHOST

LEE BATTERSBY

Even on the hottest day, the grounds of the Arts Centre are bitterly cold. Emily doesn't care. She will never feel warm again. Even on the hottest day, she only has to think back to the hospital, to the shake of the nurse's head, the manufactured sympathy in the doctor's voice. All the warmth Emily had, she put into baby Susan's little body. It took forty weeks for her to die, pressed hard up against Emily's soul, deep inside her belly, and then: nothing. Emptiness. Cold, never ending. Emily spends her days hunched over, arms curled around her body, but nothing helps.

One thing. One thing helps.

The gate is open. The Centre is never closed, at least, not for Emily. She slips inside the compound, sealed off from the world by high limestone walls and a sudden drop in temperature. The change is a physical thing. She has watched people start as they enter, reach into bags to pull out jumpers, wrap shawls around themselves, rub at their arms. Even if the thick stone walls did not exist, Emily knows the reaction would be the same. The Arts Centre is a bubble of isolation and loss. It is why she comes. Only the building understands what she has endured. Nowhere in the city has experienced more loss. It has been an asylum, a homeless shelter, a military headquarters. Everything it has touched brought death. Even now, while one wing churns out books, and another houses exhibitions, a significant number of the buildings are dedicated to a museum: the dead and their achievements, pressed between glass like bacteria, entire lives reduced to the pause in a tour guide's speech. Emily's own life turned upon an instant, a glass slide of memory. If she could feel at home anywhere, it might be here.

Today is not hot. Winter keeps casual visitors away, and overnight rain has enclosed the centre of Fremantle in grey. It makes no difference to Emily. Weather, like so many things, is incidental. The lawns have kept the rain alive. Drops shine on the blades of grass. Emily stops inside the gate, and surveys the swathe of green. There is no sign to distinguish the spot she seeks. It will be a matter of time, and luck. Emily has all the time in the world. She picks a patch of lawn several feet up the slight incline, and steps towards it.

She is fortunate, today. She finds it on the third attempt. Some days, closing time thrusts her into the outside with nothing more than a wet skirt for her dedication. But not today. She has barely settled near a statue the size and shape of a melting child when the feeling engulfs her. Love. Comfort. Peace. Emily doesn't give it a name. She *can't* give it a shape. But it finds her, wraps her in invisible arms, brushes against her exposed skin. The air changes. She is no longer alone- an older, wiser presence protects her. A spirit of experience, attuned to her grief, drawn to her across the gulf of memory and death. Emily leans her head back against the rough mosaic statue, and lets tears join the droplets on the grass.

Emily cried for a single day after they told her about baby Susan. One day, and then whatever controlled her tears seized up, and no matter how painful the pressure behind her eyes, there was no release. No matter how sympathetic the sounds her family made, how angry and distant her husband became, the channels inside remained frozen. Eventually, only the ice remained: no family, no husband, no Emily. To become warm would mean facing all she had lost. Too easy to stay encased in ice. Until she found the Centre, and the grass, and the circle of warmth that could only be the ghost of someone who understood, who knew the same tearing loss.

"What do I do?" she whispers. "What do I do? What do I do?"

There is no answer. She doesn't expect one. It is enough to feel the love. It is enough to know that someone has been where she was, and left enough of themselves behind to give her warmth. Emily believes in ghosts. The whole world became ghosts once Susan died. She sits alone on the grass, and the pressure behind her eyes leaks through one drop at a time, until she can open them without seeing her baby's body, forever cold.

Someone is watching.

Ten metres away, in a wedge of shadow created by the corner of a covered walkway, an old woman stands, eyes fixed on Emily. Emily sits up straight, shivering as the ball of comfort slips away. She wraps her arms around her chest and watches the woman slink along the corridor, hunched over, gaze piercing her. There is something wrong with the old woman. Her grey hair is a mess, wild and unkempt. A deep stain lies across one side of her head, as if she has just finished rubbing it through the mud. She is barefoot and wears only a plain white shift that looks soiled and dirty. She clutches at her chest in a way that makes Emily notice her own posture and rearrange her arms. The old woman reaches the shadows at the far end of the walkway, fixes her with one final stare, and disappears.

Emily blinks in shock. In an instant she has found her feet and is running to the walkway. A door blocks the path of the old woman's journey. Emily grabs the handle, and twists. The door stays shut. She tries again, thumping against it with her shoulder. Again, the door resists. She is about to try a third time when someone behind her coughs politely.

"Can I help you?"

A blonde woman in a business suit stands a few steps away, her head cocked in enquiry. Emily steps away from the door.

"It's locked, I'm afraid," the newcomer says. "If you're after someone in particular . . . "

"There was a woman. An old woman." Emily touches the rough wood. The door is cold, painfully so. She sucks at her fingers. "She disappeared."

"You've seen her? The old mother?"

"What?"

The young woman takes Emily by the arm and steers her towards another door at the far end of the walkway. It is open, and Emily can see an office beyond, warm and inviting. "We call her that. Nobody knows her real name. She's supposed to have been here when this place was an asylum. Threw herself from the Investigator gallery window on the first floor when her baby was abducted. There's a display up there, actually. A whole series of photographs. This place is riddled with ghosts, you know. At least, that's what they say. Lots of people see things. Would you like to have a cup of coffee? We have a register, you can sign it if you like, write down what you saw. You should read it. The things people . . . "

"No. Thank you." Emily pulls her arm from the woman's grasp. "I . . . I have to go." She rushes away, pretending not to hear the other woman's chuckle. The streets outside are warm, but Emily doesn't feel it. She is freezing inside, and getting colder.

• • •

She stays away for a week. But she is cold, and the world is grey and empty, and soon enough she can't bear the lack of feeling any more. So there she stands, inside the gate, with no real memory of how she got there, trying to decide the best place to sit, while at the back of her mind the presence of the walkway sits immovable, constant.

In the end she chooses a spot about halfway along the gravel entry path, underneath a large gum tree, where she can keep the walkway in her peripheral vision. But there is no comfort there, and after half an hour she chooses again, and again, and when the loving ghost finally wraps its invisible arms around her she is tucked into a corner of the yard where the building's wing obscures all vision, and then she is too busy crying to take notice.

The following day she sits less than a foot from the walkway. Not even the appearance of the blonde secretary, coming out to ask after her welfare, stops the tears. And again the next day, and the next, and still the old woman refuses to materialise. Emily begins to arrive earlier each day, and leave later, until every visit is an obsession on two fronts, and even days spent wrapped in the arms of her ghost no longer satisfy her. Until one day, late in September, when she leans back against the mosaic-covered statue once more, and the old woman stares at her from the corner of the walkway.

This time, Emily makes no movement, simply watches as the stranger walks her circuit, eyes fixed upon Emily's tear-framed face, and disappears. When she is ready, she stands, and lays a hand upon the statue's head. It is warm, where the old woman's gaze has reste. Emily steps back, sees the child within the statue's shape. She nods, and understands. From now on, it will be easier.

• • •

December is hot, but it makes no difference to Emily. She stands on the road opposite the wide-flung gates of the Centre and watches several families make their way up the sloped road. It is bazaar day, an annual event. The Centre opens itself to craftspeople and textile makers; families come to buy pots and fabrics, to sit against statues and stare at glass-pressed photographs.

The lawns inside the centre are crowded. Families huddle together on blankets, rubbing uncovered arms in the cold air. Outside it is amongst the hottest days of the year, and all but Emily have dressed accordingly. She stops amongst the shoppers, surveying the grass. It no longer matters. She has all day, and only one spot is important. She spends half an hour in front of a stall selling baby clothes, gazing down at the jumpsuits and bibs.

"Are you going to buy something, or just stand there all day?"

Emily stares at the stallholder. A younger woman, all cornrows and piercings, frowning at her with hands bunched into fists on her hips. She moves away, lips frozen together, unable to reply.

A nearby stall sells handmade mirrors- shards of broken glass rearranged in patterns inside painted frames. Emily sees herself reflected in a thousand fragments- hair unbrushed and wild, with the first hints of grey beginning to encroach at the fringe; her face unadorned by make up; dressed in a simple white cotton dress. She turns away, crosses the lawn, sits with her back against the mosaic statue, digging the toes of her bare feet into the grass.

Some days. Since deciding on this singular resting place, some days the warmth visits. More often than not she goes home unreleased. But she has grown used to the days of numbness. It is only here that the woman appears, and she can see some sort of shared experience within another being's eyes. She rests her head against the statue, sets her gaze upon the walkway, and waits.

It takes three hours, but shortly after lunchtime, the warmth creeps across the grass and slides over Emily like a blanket. Invisible arms enfold her. The weight of a body presses into her back. Love washes over her like rising bathwater, thawing the frozen lump inside her body. She gasps, and slumps into herself. Tears begin. She reaches arms around her chest, and hugs the presence as best she can.

"Thank you," she whispers, oblivious to the stares of those

around her. She glances up, and in the darkness of the doorway, sees familiar eyes. Unhindered by surrounding bodies, the old woman begins her journey along the walkway. Emily matches her gaze. The old mother. Bereft of child, bereft of warmth. Emily feels a rush of sympathy, of understanding. To go through life, knowing only the cold substance of loss . . . she squeezes her eyes closed for a moment. To go through life, and then, after life, to continue to go through it. Such a weight to bear. Such a glacier to carry within you. The old woman is halfway along the walkway. Emily looks at her again, sees the frost inside the bent frame. She shudders, leans into the warmth wrapped around her. Some sliver of ice cracks within Emily's chest. She gasps, realising just how much she has salvaged, compared to the woman on the walkway.

"Wait," she says, and when the old woman does not acknowledge, she closes her eyes. The mantle of love grips her tightly. Emily bites her lip.

"Can you . . . " she begins, then tries again. "Can you go to her?" She unwraps her arms, reaches up to stroke at the empty air, indicates the lonely, shuffling figure. "Can you give her . . . this?"

There is no response, but like an abandoned blanket, the warmth around Emily begins to slide away, down the length of her body and into the grass. It brushes across her bare feet last, a final caress that leaves her shivering in the sudden cold. The old woman walks on, until she is almost across the corridor. Then she stiffens, and Emily fancies she can hear the merest whisper of a gasp. The old woman's eyes close. She leans into something invisible, wraps her arms around herself as if caressing the skin of an unexpected lover. Emily sees the way she balances herself against the weight of an unseen body, knows exactly how the curves and folds of that body fit. The old woman sketches something like a smile. When she opens her eyes again, Emily can see tears glistening along the creased skin of her cheeks. She takes another step, wrapped in intangible warmth, and disappears.

Emily sits alone, and stares at the barren space where the old woman has walked. The air that gusts along the walkway has changed—it has emptied, swept itself clean. The old woman is gone. Truly gone. Yet Emily can not move, can not take her eyes from the vacant air. All she has come here for, all she has hoped, all she has drawn comfort from—she is owed . . . something, please, let her have *something*.

Eventually, as the shadows lengthen and stallholders admit the end of the day and began to pack up, she sobs once, and bends over herself, hunching over the emptiness at her middle. She understands: there will be no reappearance, no thank you, no connection. The old woman has left, and taken with her the only kindness she has known. She will not share, not with Emily: warmth, understanding, experience. She will not share. Emily finds her feet, and pushes away from the statue. The air inside the Centre is frigid, and there is nobody left to wrap their arms around her, nobody to lean into and cry.

Behind Emily's eyes, ice begins to spread. She turns away from the unloving air and walks through the crowd, out of the Centre and into the cold world.

••••••••••

HUNGRY MAN

WILL ELLIOTT

When the redheaded woman with the baby carriage at last moved out of earshot, Phil said, "It's easy, just get it down the back of your pants. You saw me do it a hundred times, come on."

Lex looked nervously at the girl behind the newsagency counter and said, "She'll see me. We come here every other day and never *buy* anything."

"She doesn't care. For $12 an hour, think she cares if they're missing a couple magazines? C'mon go, she's not looking."

Phil made it look easy. In awe Lex had watched him walk out of shops with packets of corn chips stuffed in his shirt so he looked pregnant; watched him take show bags from stalls at the carnival, condoms from the chemist (they did nothing with them except leave them on the spouts of their school's drink fountains.) Phil stole cigarettes and sold them to the older kids who played coin-op games. He stole CDs, once a DVD set from JBHiFi. His prize catch: an ipod, one of those nice 32 gig ones with a digicam inside. Close call, the Target woman turned her back for just a moment after he'd got her to take it out of the case for a look at it, not even planning to steal it till she took her eyes off them. A security guard chased them out of there and they couldn't go back to Westfield Strathpine again any time in the next decade.

For his part Lex had stolen two packets of bubble gum. It had been from this very newsagency when the girl went out the back for a minute or two. "The register," Phil had urged. "Go! There's fifties in there."

Lex couldn't do it. People had been walking past the doorway, they'd have seen him. He took the gum instead. His hands shook for half an hour afterwards.

And right now the newsagency was busy. Old people buying lottery tickets. A creepy perverted dude by the porn mags who hadn't moved since they came in, probably had a big fat woody while he fumbled through the latest *Picture*. "Don't worry about that perv," Phil whispered. "That's the retard who walks up and down the road all night. If he sees you he won't even remember it five minutes from now."

"How do you know?"

"We threw rocks at him, me and Trent. He just looked at us, didn't even care. Next day we walked right past him, he didn't recognize us. So what are you worried about?"

I have a dad at home, Lex thought but didn't dare say. *Not like you. Your mother won't pull your pants right down right in front of everyone at any old excuse to do it and hit the crap out of your nude butt like it turns him on.*

Well no, Phil's dad wouldn't do that exactly. Phil's dad would visit once per week and his doped out mum would sit there in a valium cloud and list out stuff he'd done wrong during the week in a calm dreamy voice, while Phil's dad slowly undid his belt. *Alex I think you should go home now.* You'd hear it from three houses down: cries and pleads like Phil was being killed in there, whack, whack, whack. Every Tuesday. Visit Day.

Phil said, "Alex listen. You eat the stuff I steal, you keep half of it. You never take anything yourself. Bubble-gum? How badass. Come on. Go get us some titty mags and we're even."

Lex left Phil standing before the comics, sidled over to the magazine stand opposite the titty mags, looking nervously at the girl behind the counter, now selling smokes to some geezer who thought he was pretty funny. Lex snuck a glance at the glossy covers, where a woman who looked a little like his teacher posed on *Penthouse* with legs open, a white sheet draped between them; another on *Barely Legal* with pig-tails, in roller-skates with a lollypop in hand; another in this weird black leather outfit on *Babes & Bikes*. Suddenly he wanted each magazine very badly. He'd all but forgotten the pervy guy, who hadn't moved, still thumbing through the *Home Girls* section in *Picture*. The pervy guy was just a pillar of legs beside him, inhuman as concrete.

Lex grabbed a *Penthouse* and a *Playboy*. Down the back of his shorts they went, where they slipped and slid almost completely out till he tucked them in his underwear. Turning for the exit, not daring to look and see if anyone had witnessed, he walked head-first into the pervy guy's legs, his face striking the man's hip.

It was a long way to look up at the face staring down at him, half covered in black stubble. The man's wide mouth hung open, eyes just peering down with no way of telling if it was anger or anything else in them—all Lex saw was blankness. But he sensed something *else* there too, deeper within, a threat he didn't understand at all and one very different to the usual fear of getting into trouble with an adult.

"Hey Alex, let's go for a swim," Phil called innocently across at him from the newsagency counter. "Before it gets dark. Over at the nature strip. C'mon." Phil's voice seemed to break Lex out of a trance. He walked through the magazine rows, not daring to look sideways at the girl behind the counter, whose gaze he felt following him. The magazines down his pants were surely sticking out a mile.

At long last, blessedly, they were outside in the afternoon light. Cars whizzed by on Anzac Ave. Their bikes leant against the shop wall. "Don't pull em out yet you dink," Phil hissed as Lex adjusted the magazines' position. "Oh shit. Quick, get on your bike and go."

"What, why . . . ?"

The pervert guy, like a horror movie zombie, shuffled slowly out of the shop and headed their way. His mouth still hung open, his eyes dead as pebbles. "Catching flies, fuck head?" Phil said to him. "Shut your mouth, you look like a spastic." The man didn't say a word, just stared and shuffled closer. "I think he likes you Alex. Frigging weirdo."

They rode away, wheeling through traffic and many pissed off drivers, car horns blaring. Lex was so filled with sweet relief to be out of the newsagency he hardly noticed how close he came to getting run over.

• • •

Rumour had it that if you could get to the waterhole at night you'd sometimes see the bogan kids who got drunk in the Kallangur shop car parks doing it with their girlfriends, actually doing it right here in the long grass. They'd been out here one sleepover to test the theory, but had seen no such thing.

It had rained last night and now the quite frequent cars which swung down the nearby road's dip sloshed up water as they went. On the wide grassy platform a few meters above the water, Phil took out the Mars bar he'd slipped in his pocket right in front of the counter girl, while he'd joked with her about selling him the winning lotto ticket. He peeled back its wrapping which took much of the squished melted thing off with it, then stuffed the rest into his mouth. "Yeah I saw that retarded perv before," said Phil, examining the *Penthouse* centrefold. "Lives on Sheehan Street. Sometimes he just walks around at night, right down the middle of the road sometimes. Drivers have to go around him. Lives with these really old people, maybe his parents. Not right in the head. You can throw rocks at him or whatever and he just looks at you, doesn't even care. We did that once, me and that Nicholas kid, pelted him right in the face and he just *looked* at us."

"Maybe that's why he followed us out of the store. Because he remembered you."

"Doubt it. So are you going to jump in or not?"

Last time they'd come, Phil had ridden his bike off the ledge and into the water. It was now Lex's turn. From the seat of his black BMX the water was just a brown wedge visible over the sloping rise before the drop. Phil said, "You won't break your legs or anything. It's deep right down there."

"Not worried about my legs, I'm worried about the bike."

"It's *water* man jeez come on."

"I didn't get this bike for my birthday like you got yours. I delivered pamphlets on Saturdays in the heat and paid for it myself."

"Then you went and stole from the shops. What a good boy." Phil took the Playboy out of Lex's schoolbag. "If you don't jump I'm keeping this."

"Okay okay." Lex took off his shoes, put his glasses in their case, took a deep breath then pushed off, pumping hard on the pedals, the tyres bumping hard over the grassy ground. The water opened up into view three meters below, but it looked much higher than that . . . then he was airborne, letting go so the bike flung itself out ahead of him while he landed feet first in the water.

It was cold and not as deep as Phil had claimed, for his feet sank into the hideously soft mud at its bottom. He came up and used his first gasp of air to whoop in triumph. He swam forward to get the bike. "See that?" he laughed, spitting out a coppery mouthful.

"You didn't stay on your bike, doesn't count. Do it again."

"I'll do it again no problem, that was sweet!"

It was a slippery climb back up the rise. Nearing the top Lex heard other voices up on the grassy platform; someone laughing. "Oh shit," he heard Phil say. "Lex get up here okay? Hurry."

Still elated, Lex wheeled the bike around up the curving path, starting to feel a chill from the late afternoon air. There was at most an hour of daylight left.

When he got up there he saw why Phil had been worried. Craig Randall and Keith Hume, that was why. There was, Lex was quite aware, a chance for him to get back on the bike and ride it down the path and out of there. And he probably would have, if his schoolbag and shoes weren't up there with Phil, along with the precious magazines. Both these guys had been kicked out of school for beating people up. The last guy, Keith had rammed his head into a pole and put him in hospital and into neck brace. Keith's messy blonde hair hung down over his shoulders, muscled arms exposed in a singlet. His friend Craig was tall, fat, redheaded, with squinting eyes and skin entirely covered in freckles. They were both three years and many growth spurts older.

Craig casually took Lex's bike from him and sat on it in a way somehow devoid of aggression—just borrowing a seat. "Your friend's fucked," he said in his oddly high pitched voice. *Going to be a pretty good show, hey?* Craig smiled with no malice at all and produced a little bag of cask wine, which he put to his lips and sucked on. The wine's cheap stink filled the place.

Phil didn't move as Keith Hume stepped closer to him.

"Why do you have to hit him Keith?" Lex said. "We got no problem with you."

"Shut the fuck up Alex," Phil snapped at him.

Lex remembered what Phil had said about guys like this. They *would* beat you up now and then, face it. Just let them. Don't be a pussy about it and they'd mostly leave you alone from then on. "Get it over with," said Phil.

"What'd you say cunt?" Shove to the shoulder, fists up, here it came. Jab, jab, crack went knuckles on Phil's nose and cheek. They were fast economical punches. Long fast arms, punching machines made just for this. Phil's head rocked back. Lex almost felt it, almost saw the explosions of white stars. Craig chortled and slurped his wine. "Come on Keith that's enough hey," said Lex.

But it wasn't. Phil staggered and nearly fell but fought to keep on his feet. The "bully will respect you" theory, if you put up some kind of fight, but Lex knew it wouldn't work. "Stay down Phil for fuck's sake," he yelled, tears welling up in his eyes, a lump in his throat.

Craig got off the bike and with the same lack of malice gave it a shove toward the drop to the water. It rolled most of the way there balanced on its wheels as though with an invisible rider, then clattered on its side and slid over the edge.

Lex forgot about Phil and the *crack crack* of punches still rocking his friend's head back. There was just a long dark angry tunnel with Craig at the end of it. It was the casual way he'd done it, absolutely nothing personal in trashing his bike. All those mornings in the hot sun, barked at by dogs, once chased by one, riding up that hill on Gyp Court swooped by magpies, wasp nests in letter boxes, folding fucking Coles and Foodstore pamphlets together all Friday night till his fingers were dark with ink.

Lex's hand picked up the flat rectangular stone all by itself. He moved automatically as he drew it back and shoved it into that utterly hated squinting freckled face.

Craig grunted in surprise. That was the point Lex's memory erased what came next, which was of course his hand—so much smaller—being grabbed tight, the rock being taken out, and the favour returned with interest as Craig swung it down on his head. His body dropped in the long grass some way away from Phil's, and about ten seconds after.

• • •

When sight returned there were only the stars and clouds above, all of it spinning about slowly and lazily. A continent of thick grey cloud slowly swallowed the half-moon, dulling out its light. Crickets chirped. Pain throbbed down from the top of Lex's skull like Craig were right here thumping him with the rock every two seconds.

There was rustling nearby, the tickling touch of long grass, a faint lingering stink of cask wine. A gnawing, crunching sound. Like Phil's dog Jules, at work on a bone. Sucking, slurping. Crunching, gnawing.

He lifted his head—tried to, rather, but the spike of pain made him leave it resting where it was. Tenderly he touched his scalp, where there was a sticky tacky patch of blood. He moaned quietly. The background sounds—the eating sounds—ceased.

A listening, watchful silence ensued which instinct told him not to break. It went for a long time. There were footsteps padding through the long grass, going away from him, then toward him, then away. Slow, heavy steps.

Keith and Craig? he thought. *Both of them, still here?*

The footsteps stopped. The grass rustled. The eating sounds began again. There was a low murmur of someone's voice saying something mostly inarticulate, but amongst the babble he made out the words, "good, good."

Slowly Lex sat up, hardly disturbing the long thick blades of grass around him. A shape loomed ten or twelve meters away, set against the sky behind. A large man hunched forward on the shorter grass where Lex had ridden his bike over the drop. The large man had his back to Lex. The big hunched-over body was just a silhouette against the cloud. It moved in jerking, sawing motions.

A soft moan. Mournful, Lex thought, or maybe a note of pleasure. Though he knew he must stay quiet, he was too confused to be scared. He thought back to rumours about the bogan kids who came here with their girlfriends to screw. But that was no kid.

Up on his elbows Lex watched the man's strange movements, still not comprehending as the minutes passed. Not till he sat up, and the clouds shifted, the moon's light came out from hiding to reveal the large man crouched over Phil.

Phil was looking right at Lex, so it appeared, his eyes wide and unblinking and with a strange kind of grimacing smile, his lips peeled back from his slightly buck teeth. Lex gestured to him as if to say, *Are you okay? What's going on?*

Phil did not react at all. His head was in a strange position to the rest of him, a most unnatural angle. In fact as Lex's eyes adjusted he saw that it wasn't Phil at all but was actually some kind of doll, for the head had been pulled right off. He rubbed his eyes as if it might change things, but no, the head wasn't attached to the body at all.

A dark pool spread about the doll. Phil's chest and belly had been ripped open. The man by the corpse of his best friend was digging around in it, sawing off handfuls of flesh with a small knife and lifting them to his mouth. The sight did not quite register, did not make any kind of sense at all. Lex did not think he was really seeing it.

The man's head turned sideways and Lex could see the chewing motions of his jaw. Inarticulate sounds came from his chewing, gargling throat, interspersed with, "Good . . . good."

For Lex everything spun around again, very fast. His belly heaved; his head fell back down on the long grass, making it rustle.

The eating sounds stopped. The large man got to his feet. For a moment his heavy excited breathing was the only sound. Heavy footsteps padded, swish swish, through the grass. Lex felt and heard him coming, but didn't care or even particularly sense danger, only a sickening weirdness. He still didn't understand what he'd seen.

The man stood tall over him, stretching far above like a statue, legs that were concrete pillars. It was the man they'd seen in the newsagency ogling the magazines. For a long time, the longest minute in Lex's life, the man stared down at what the moonlight had revealed to him in the tall grass. His blood-smeared mouth hung open mutely, just as it had when he shambled out of the shop towards them.

A car swept past, swishing up puddles of water where the road dipped, its headlights sweeping the trees a stone's throw away, then it was gone.

The large man was trying, it seemed, to speak. Gibberish came out, a language of stuttering grunts, here and there peppered with words. Among the grunting noises Lex discerned only, "Where we come from . . . makes us hungry."

• • •

In long years later, on therapists' couches, in bed tearfully telling his wife about it for the first time after twenty-one years of marriage; after waking from every nightmare where he was again a kid lying in long grass next to the water . . .

All the while driving himself through business school, through board rooms, from success to success, ever higher and faster as though to get away from a shambling monster on the road behind him . . .

Through memories of the funeral, of police interviews, the witness stand with the monster blankly watching him answer questions in the trial, which eventually put the monster in a hospital, not in prison . . .

From trying to work out why, why *he* hadn't been taken as well, why *he'd* been spared after he passed out in the long grass, utterly at the monster's mercy, only to wake later and find what was left of his friend spread across the dewy ground . . .

Till he was an old man, rich and lonely, fading from life in his last days, bitterly wishing that, of all the memories his mind so eagerly shed, good and bad, why *those* memories above all others must remain till his very last day . . .

He would throughout all this seek some secret meaning in those words his ears had barely discerned amongst the grunts and stutters, which had burned those words—with whatever secret things they meant—in his mind, in his life, as a never fading scar.

• • • • • • • • • • •

THE COOK OF PEARL HOUSE, A MALAY SAILOR BY THE NAME OF MAURICE

R.J. ASTRUC

My name is Maurice Alaska
and by day I make crepes
consommé
bouillabaisse
soufflé
and sweet meringues
while Mishter Lusk looks for a leather apron
and the negro girls of Austin jump at shadows.

By night I fry a kidney (half)
in a cast iron skillet
and I eat it watching the white girls in Whitechapel
their fat gobble necks trembling
and the constables pecking at the dirt
for what scraps I leave
but I leave little.

They call me a ghost and I suppose I am
in the way that all sailors are ghosts
lost and wandering spirits
always moving on
to a new harbour.

They call me a doctor or butcher
but I say a cook knows best how to wield a knife
how to dice
and mince
the light meat and the dark.

In my kitchen I keep an axe
and the negro girls of Austin could tell you stories
about the way it shone when it came down
but that was long ago
and I have a new game to play
with the whore who robbed me of all I had
that whore and all the Whitechapel girls
oh Mishter Lusk you can have my knife
if only you wait a little longer
because it is not finished cutting yet

My name is Maurice Alaska
but I have many names

They said I ran away
but I moved on.

•••••••••••

THE LOQUACIOUS CADAVER

KYLA WARD

One night in the ghastly adolescence of the world, when men and women had learned enough to be sure they knew everything but were yet to take responsibility for themselves, the Beetle found a corpse in the desert. The desert had become the barren stretch between cities, scarred with steel rails and cracked concrete, and the Beetle had not encountered such a thing in many years.

"A corpse," she clicked, "Left for my tending. I will carry it away underground, so that it may transform and rise again."

"No," came a croaking and the Bird descended, flapping her black wings. "From high above I saw the human fall. I will bear it into the sky, so it may become a spirit."

"No," came a barking, and the Dog came running over the sand, "I tracked this human in dying, and now I shall take it to my master, who will judge its eternal fate."

The three ancient psychopomps sat and glared at each other, for as the desert had shrunk, opportunities to perform their sacred duties had become rare. But in the great cycles of existence, few problems are without precedent and such conflicts had been resolved before.

"At the very least," said the Beetle, "I will lay my eggs in its tongue."

"At the very least," said the Bird, "I will take its eyes."

"At the very least," said the Dog, "I will remove its hands and entrails."

At this, the corpse stirred and said, "Excuse me, but you will do no such thing. I'm waiting here for the police and would like to look my best when they arrive."

"Eek!" shrilled the Beetle, "Lie still! Lie still!"

"You must not move," scolded the Bird. "And corpses do not talk!"

"We talk," replied the corpse, "To coroners and detectives. I hope you appreciate the exception I'm making for you."

"Well, I don't see anyone else here," huffed the Dog, "Nor smell anything but you."

"They'll come: the story doesn't start until they come."

"What story?"

"The detective story: don't you watch television? Now get off me, you nasty vermin! Shoo!"

"We understand," said the Beetle patiently, "you're expecting the priests of your God to come. But it all comes down to one of three—"

"Not priests, police!"

"Well, what will these police do when they get here?" asked the Bird.

"Examine me to determine my identity and the cause of death. Then they'll put me in a van and take me away."

"Well, no wonder corpses are so hard to find! What happens to you then?"

"If I was murdered, then there's the hunt for the killer and the trial: it will be in the papers and everyone will talk about it. If it was an accident then not so much: still less if natural causes. But I get an obituary, that's the important thing."

"What happens then?"

"I'm taken to a room and burned."

"And?"

"And that's it," said the corpse.

"That's it?" The Dog frowned. "I don't understand."

"You become smoke," suggested the Bird. "You go up into the sky."

"You become ash," suggested the Beetle. "You go down into the earth."

"I become nothing and go nowhere: that's why the obituary is so important." The corpse settled back into its original position. "Now, if you'll kindly leave me be."

Faced with the corpse's instance, the psychopomps retreated.

"Load of tripe," grumbled the Dog, "I mean, we *know* that's not what happens!"

"Yes, but it seems they've forgotten," said the Bird.

"Forgotten very rigorously," said the Beetle, "We may have to give them a little prod. But first, we must wait."

So the three waited as the sun rose and brightened, then dimmed and sank, and the corpse reddened and swelled, then blackened and shrank and still no one came. At last, they approached the corpse again.

"Look," began the Beetle. "We don't mean to be insensitive, but you've been here a long while now."

"It will be harder for the detectives," the corpse slurred, "But that will only make the story more interesting."

"No one's coming," the Dog said bluntly, "No one comes here except people like you."

This struck the corpse sombrely. "I don't suppose one of you could take a message into the city?"

"I don't see why you're so set on becoming nothing," said the Bird.

"It's the only way I can remain what I was," said the corpse. "You really won't go and find them?"

"No," replied the three in unison.

"Then I will," said the corpse and sat bolt upright, causing the Dog and Bird to scatter and flinging the Beetle across the sand. All the parts that had once held together inside it jostled and jangled, but with a mighty effort of will, it contrived to stand.

Then across rails and over concrete, the corpse teetered and tottered but managed to keep moving towards the buildings that quickly rose around it. And all unnoticed, the Beetle rode on its shoulder, with the Dog trotting behind it and the Bird circling overhead. They accompanied the corpse down a long street where at first it drew only brief glances from such people as were too tired and poor to care. But as they continued, the glances grew longer and the people rich enough to scream and energetic enough to run, and finally the police arrived.

When the vans pulled up, the corpse waved and attempted to explain the situation, but they answered only with bullets. These failed to harm it, of course, but did nothing to improve its disposition. It took hold of a man by the shoulders and shook him, and a woman by the throat, but neither would listen and so it raged, overturning the vans and bending the guns into pretzels.

Eventually, the corpse decided it must seek for its obituary by itself and so it sought out the streets it had known in life. But no one there recognised it, even among those who were caught in corners and could not avoid looking in its face. So it attempted to visit a dentist and, after the dentist said she could not perform an x-ray because everything had come loose inside, to engage a private detective. But the private detective said he could not take its fingerprints because its fingers were already black, and besides, the corpse had lost its wallet. Everywhere it went, there was only screaming and running, and frantic excuses. At last, it saw a newspaper containing its picture, and thought that its search was over. But when it read the article, all it described was a walking corpse terrorising the city.

It sat down on the steps of the city hall. "It's too late!" it exclaimed. "I'm not what I was any more. I've changed so much that even the story is new!"

"Actually," said the Beetle, "I'm afraid it's very old."

"A corpse leaving the desert and rejoining the living world is rare," said the Bird, "But not new."

"You'll never be nothing now," said the Dog.

"So I might as well go with one of you," said the corpse. "Or all of you: I don't care."

"I'm afraid," said the Beetle, "that's no longer an option."

"What do you mean? You were fighting over me before!"

"But you not only started talking, you got up and walked," said the Bird. "That puts you beyond our reach."

"But you're right here beside me!"

"Here, the only thing we are is nasty vermin," said the Dog. "There really isn't anything we can do."

"But I only got up because of you!"

"I suppose that's true," said the Dog.

"Oh dear," said the Bird. "Silly us."

"But don't despair," said the Beetle. "Eventually people will get used to you. They'll grow curious and begin to follow."

"And they'll give me my obituary?" cried the corpse.

"Not yours, precisely," said the Beetle, "But I'm sure it will do."

So the corpse got up and continued walking, but slowly, avoiding the crowded places. Night came, and day came, and still it kept walking, looking for someone who would listen.

The psychopomps went their way, hungry but content. For they were ancient indeed, and had witnessed the founding of many religions. They knew that there is nothing like a walking, talking corpse to turn people's minds towards something rather than nothing and to go back into the desert, seeking wisdom.

•••••••••••

WHAT BOOKS SURVIVE

TANSY RAYNER ROBERTS

"Books are the carriers of civilization. Without books, history is silent, literature dumb, science crippled, thought and speculation at a standstill. They are engines of change, windows on the world, lighthouses erected in the sea of time."
Barbara W. Tuchman.

MY CHRONICLE DIARY HISTORICAL ACCOUNT OF WHAT HAPPENED AFTER THE INVADERS CAME, BY KATIE SCARLETT MARSDEN, AGE 16 ½
(and yes, that is a deliberate Adrian Mole reference, so there)

My brother Otis caught me, the first time I tried to sneak out through the barricade. I remember when he wasn't such a boy scout, but we're all different now.

"Don't be thick, tadpole," he said to me. I hated that nickname. It reminded me of the river we had lost; of the muddy, happy weekends before everything ended. "There's nothing out there any more."

"Nothing that you care about," I snapped, and went straight home so he would think he had won.

Everyone in town acted like the barricade was it; the thing that would save us from the invaders who had come crashing in from the skies. I guess it made them feel better. But how could the barricade be good when it cut us off from everyone and everything else?

Our family was lucky. At least our house was on the right side of the eight foot wall they built of broken things and piled earth and dead cars. We didn't even have to take in guests from the abandoned houses, because there were already five of us: Mum, me, Otis, his girlfriend Frances, and the baby.

Everyone's so busy being frightened, pretending that the barricade will fix everything, that no one ever talks about what was left behind. The stuff that's smaller than houses and roads and the river, anyway. The really important stuff.

They talk about how sensible it was to keep the town hall, so we have a central point for meetings, and we can use that for the school too, when there aren't town meetings (our town likes meetings, twice a week—as good as the barricade for making people feel safe).

No one talks about the fact that when we built the barricade, drawing the line along Wharton Street and Mansfield Avenue, we didn't just leave the school on the other side, and half the shops, and the river.

We left the library.

• • •

My house is full of books that don't work. That's the worst thing about the invasion. Well, okay. Not the worst thing. But it's not like people were shot out of the sky, bodies lying in the street or anything like that. The invaders don't care about us, as long as we stay behind our walls.

Meanwhile, nothing electronic functions. Computers, TV, phones. Our shelves are full of DVD cases full of shiny silver discs we can't watch. Everyone's acting like the world we knew is going to come back any minute.

What if it doesn't come back? We have a dozen actual paper books in our house, and I've read all of them. Most people have less. When they drew those big red lines in the map, they thought about space to hold school lessons once things are back to normal, but no one thought about what they were going to hold lessons with. Slate and chalk? What happens when all the ink runs out of the biros?

Anyway. That's not my problem. Not like I'm trying for a uni place now.

I just want to read the second half of *Wuthering Heights*.

• • •

There was a scream. Three weeks ago. Not a person screaming. It was like the sky filled with scream, from edge to edge. I was lying on my bed with some stupid soap blaring at me, and music drilling into half my brain through a single earbud, with my Kindle resting against my knees. One more book to go. I'd figured, reading all the Brontës, that was an easy project for my class reading assignment. There were only three of them, right?

Should have guessed from the smirk on Ms Hopkinson's face, what I was getting myself into. *The Tenant of Wildfell Hall* went okay, and then Jane-Eyre basically kicked my arse six ways from Sunday, and then it turned out that Charlotte (officially my LEAST favourite Brontë) had written tons of books. Screw that. One book per sister, I decided.

And I only had three days left, before the assignment was due.

But *Wuthering Heights* was brilliant. It was spooky and weird and kept changing voices. I hated everyone in it, and I wasn't sure what a moor actually was, but I couldn't stop reading.

Catherine died. Like, she actually died, and it was only halfway through the story. What the hell was that about? Was she going to come back as a zombie or something for the second act? I wouldn't put it past Em and her nasty sense of humour (me and Emily Brontë were on first name terms by now).

Then the sky screamed, and my TV flickered, and my iPod went silent. I saw something, on the screen of my Kindle, and then reflected in the TV screen too. A face. At least, I think it was a face. Whatever it was, it sure as hell was not human.

Wuthering Heights turned into a mess of pixels as the Kindle shut down, and then there was nothing there but one of those weird line drawings of dead authors. Only, it wasn't a dead author at all, was it? It was the same face that had stared out from the TV screen. The same face that stared out from every electronic screen, it turned out, when the sky screamed. Before the world stopped working.

• • •

The second time I sneaked through the barricade, Otis didn't stop me.

I felt like a criminal at first. I tried to walk really softly on the pavement, even though I was already wearing sneakers, and not exactly clomping around. I walked close to the side, near the fences of abandoned houses, so my shadow wouldn't give me away.

It was night, but there was a decent sized moon, enough for me to see the world. I was wearing dark jeans, the pair that already has a rip in them (and where am I going to get new ones?).

I used to walk this way every day. From home to school. It takes maybe seven minutes, unless I stop to chat or hover around the corner shop for too long.

There it was, the old corner shop. The windows were broken and the door half bashed in, from the embarrassing half-riot that had gone on during the building of the barricades, before everyone came over. The whole town went crazy for about ten minutes, then regretted it. I could see cans of food on the floor of the shop where they had been dropped in the panic. There was still a display of chocolate bars by the counter. They wouldn't be too gross, right? Not after only four weeks. But I couldn't bring myself to step inside.

It felt like they'd know. The invaders. Bad enough I was out on the wrong side of the barricade. They'd know as soon as I touched the chocolate. If I was going to get in trouble for stealing (rescuing!) something, it wasn't going to be junk food. It was going to be for a book.

My backpack hung loosely from my shoulders. I hadn't brought anything in it, not even water. I didn't want to waste an inch of space. My mouth was dry and yuck already, though, and I couldn't help thinking about the closed fridges in the shop, full of bottles of Coke. Sure, it would be room temperature, but it would still be Coke.

Later. Maybe. Books first.

• • •

The school looked undamaged at first. Empty, like on the first day of the holidays. But the thought of crossing that wide asphalt yard to get to it was too much. I already felt exposed, and there was moonlight sweeping across the black space. So I kept to the wall, following it around until I got to the front gate, with all the scrubby bushes and the gum trees. The windows were broken on this side, and the school looked a whole lot less okay.

Maybe this wasn't a good idea. Maybe there wasn't anything left worth saving inside.

But I had to try.

I scurried up the little path to the doors. They were locked, and barred. Of course they were. The adults might have been making some pretty dumb decisions lately, but they weren't completely stupid.

One of the windows had most of the glass missing, and I found a loose brick in the corner I could use to knock the rest of the pieces through, one by one. With every small crunch of glass, my stomach twisted hard, and I checked behind me a million and twelve times.

Finally, I clambered in over the window sill and landed on the glass-strewn lino.

Inside was safer. It had to be. The invaders didn't come within our walls. It was one of their rules, right? So I was okay. I was alone in my old school, only one staircase and a couple of corridors away from where I needed to go.

That was when I heard the music.

It was so quiet I wasn't sure at first, but as I got closer to the library . . . oh. It was coming from there.

The music didn't sound right. It was uneven and sort of scratchy, and one of those old fashioned tunes that they wouldn't even cover on *Glee*, something that lived in a black and white movie.

The music hit me full in the face as I opened the doors. It felt heavier than I was used to, from mp3s and e-videos. It vibrated through the carpet into my feet.

I want to be loved by you, just you and nobody else but you . . .

It was a record. I could see it now. An actual record playing on an actual record player. I'd seen them in the tip shop from time to time, but never actually seen one working. Even Nan has a CD player, and iTunes.

(I haven't heard from her since the invaders came. She lives in Newcastle, and it's just too far to hear from. I hope she's okay.)

The needle reached the end of the track and sort of jerked for a moment. Then a hand snaked out, and lifted it off the record.

I froze, but didn't yell or anything. I just backed up, towards the doors.

"You don't have to run anywhere," said a lazy male voice. "Safer in here."

"Oh, you think?" I said back, like I wasn't freaking out.

"Safest place in the world, libraries." There was a squeak as a chair spun around. I sidled around the desk, to get a look at him. Oh.

He was younger than I'd thought from his voice, but still older than me. Definitely out of high school. Not old enough to be a teacher. And I'd never seen him before, not ever. He wasn't one of us.

"What's your name?" he asked, leaning back in the chair, spinning it slowly around. He had a ponytail, and battered jeans. A jacket that had taken some damage, with charred marks around one sleeve. But maybe he just wore it to look cool, like he was all dangerous.

He didn't look cool, incidentally, scorched leather aside. He looked thirty or more years out of date.

"Ka—Amy," I said, too late realising that I didn't want to give him my name.

He raised his eyebrows, like I'd said something funny. "Nice to meet you, Kay-amy. Welcome to my castle."

"It's not yours," I said, angrier than I had expected to be, now I wasn't afraid of him. He looked like too much of a slacker to be dangerous.

"I bet you went to school here. Good girl, were you? Popped in to pick up your homework?"

"I came for a book," I said crossly.

He leaned forward, suddenly intent. "You came through the hole in the barricade on the far end of Mansfield, yeah? Walked down Susann Street to come in the front entrance of the school?"

That was creepy. Really creepy. "How did you know that?"

"Because," he said, shrugging back into his chair like my confirming his guess made me uninteresting all over again. "The other obvious way is around Mitchell Lane, and if you'd come that way, the Observers would have wiped you out."

What was a girl supposed to say to a line like that? "I don't believe you," I said, though I sort of did. I didn't want to think about it. How stupid was I? I'd heard the rumours, even without radio and TV. There was a reason all the adults were so hot on barricades, and a reason that the invaders hadn't just blown our new walls apart.

Observers, everyone called them. I wasn't even sure what they were—cameras, I guess, or mines, or something in between.

No one who ever saw one survived it.

The rule was, if we didn't move around, if we stayed inside the barricades, we stayed alive. I knew that. And I'd risked everything for a stupid book.

Well, not a stupid book. A really good book.

"Help yourself," he said, waving one hand. "Plenty of books here. Grab an e-reader while you're at it. Maybe you can trade it on the black market for some bubble gum."

"Funny," I said, glaring at him.

He put another record on, another stupid old song that I remembered from some Saturday afternoon old movie, and lost interest in me altogether.

I stomped off to the Classics section. What else was there to do?

My plan was to save the books. There were a good number of real books floating around of recent releases, if not in our town then in general, around the world. But classics . . . ever since they started loading hundreds of famous old books on to every e-reader they sold, I don't know anyone who bothered to buy the Brontës or Shakespeare in hard copy.

My mum used to have a whole lot of them, battered paperbacks and a few nice hardcovers. I hadn't read most of them, but I loved the bright covers all lined up unevenly on the shelves. My favourites were the Penguins, spine after spine in brilliant orange. So many books I was planning to read, when I got a chance.

One holiday, when I was staying at Nan's, Mum cleared off half her shelves, boxed up the books and took them off to the tip shop. "I've got them all on the Kindle," she said impatiently, when I yelled at her. "We needed the space."

I spent my whole allowance at the tip shop that week, buying back *The Three Musketeers* and *Playing Beatie Bow* and a whole row of Agatha Christies. She thought I was mad, but I liked looking at them, rearranging them on my shelves.

In the library, now, I stashed a handful of Jane Austens in my backpack. I wasn't a particular fan of Lizzy Bennet and that crowd, but they were my Mum's favourites, and she was going to need them.

I picked books out carefully. I wasn't sure if I was coming back here again, not after what the creep had said. Maybe he was lying and maybe he wasn't but . . .

Should I pick books because of posterity and shit like that, or should I just be selfish and save the ones I wanted to read? It wasn't like anyone else was coming to salvage anything from this library.

No one but me and him.

I stomped back to the main area of the library. He was still there, swinging his foot and listening to his stupid old record player. Where had he even got that from? He must have stolen it from the antique store or something. They wouldn't have one here in the school.

"How do you know about the Observers?" I snapped. "Or were you just trying to sound impressive?"

"Impressed you, did I?"

"Don't try so hard. No one's ever seen them. Not and survived."

"Maybe no one in your hick town. I know people. I hear things. I know what to look for."

I glared at him. "Fine. If you're so smart. Where's *Wuthering Heights*?"

He laughed at me. "Is that what you came all this way for? Emily Brontë? That's so earnest of you. If I was going to risk my life for an author, I'd stick to one who'd bothered to write more than one book."

"She died of consumption!" I yelled at him.

He shrugged and looked away. "Try to leave the Asterix comics when you make off with your backpack of contraband, yeah? I don't want to be left here completely without culture."

The school library had six copies of *Wuthering Heights*. I remember that. I remember looking at them on the shelf a month earlier and thinking it was kind of dumb, really, because there were so many e-readers and they all pretty much had it on there as a freebie. Why would they not be on the shelf now?

I didn't have time for this. I was going to get into so much trouble if I was caught. I whirled back and grabbed books quickly, filling my backpack. I grabbed history books, and poetry, and a bunch of Dorothy Sayers novels. I left some space at the top, just in case Emily Brontë turned up, and finally found what I wanted, several battered paperback copies of *Wuthering Heights*, hidden on the lower shelf of the Recent Returns (ha!) trolley. I picked the one in best shape and hugged it to my chest like it was a treasure map.

"I can tell you how it ends," said the creep as I walked past him, on my way out.

"Don't."

"If you really want to know . . . "

"I'm going to report you, when I get back."

"No, you're not," he said lightly.

"You could be a spy. I sneaked out, but that doesn't mean I'm not . . . "

"A patriot? A good girl? A law-abiding citizen?"

I stared at him for a moment. "Stupid. I'm not stupid."

"When you report me," he called after me as I left. "Call me Heathcliff. With two fs."

I gave him the middle finger, and went home. Slowly. By the safe route.

• • •

I hid the books under the bed for a month. I didn't realise it at first, but *Wuthering Heights* hadn't made it home with me. I searched my backpack three times, and asked if anyone had been in my room, but they all ignored me.

So much for my rescue mission. So much for Emily Brontë.

When they finally got around to setting up school lessons in the town hall, I volunteered to make a database of all the hard copy books owned by people in the town, as an independent project.

My teacher was delighted with the idea. We had three teachers. Which is odd, because the school had at least fifteen, and I'm pretty sure none of them died in the invasion. I would have heard. Maybe some of them didn't come inside the barricade. Maybe they were off somewhere selling black market copies of gothic novels for food and medicine.

Maybe they didn't want to be teachers any more. A lot of people refused to do their old jobs, now that the world was different, and our town was stuck behind a wall.

My brother Otis used to have an apprenticeship as a mechanic, but he stopped bothering when the invaders came. He didn't help Frances with the baby much either. He hung out with the other men who called themselves the town militia, and marched up and down the inside of the barricade, acting like tools.

He didn't care about books. Lots of people didn't care about books. They acted like I was crazy, most of them. My mum even got angry at me once, like collecting the books and keeping track of who owned what was somehow—admitting that the electricity was never coming back.

Then they moved the barricade.

I didn't realise at first, but Otis and Dad were gone for lunch, and I overheard them talking when they came back. "What do you mean, Martin Avenue is gone?"

"Town business," my dad muttered.

"That means it's everyone's business," I said sharply. "What happened?"

My dad shuffled off into the house, leaving Otis to tell me. "No one's heard from the Jacksons in three days. One of our patrols evacuated the rest of the families this morning. New barricade is more defensible."

I wanted to argue, to scream. Defensible against what? Either we're safe inside the barricade, or we're not.

"Are the Steeles okay?" I asked finally. "And the Hopkinsons?" I didn't want to think about the Jacksons, about what might have happened to them. Now they were on the other side of the barricade, so if they were okay, they wouldn't be for long.

"They had to leave a lot of their stuff behind, but they're alive. We're sorting out accommodation now."

Their stuff. I looked at him, stricken. "Their stuff? But 40% of the town's Mills and Boons were archived with Mrs Hopkinson. We're already running short!"

"Katie, when are you going to stop with all this book crap?" he roared at me. "We're trying to stay alive here. Survival doesn't have time to stop for a cup of tea and a nice bedtime story."

"Then what are we surviving FOR?" I retorted, and walked away from him.

• • •

So yeah, I went back. You saw that coming, right? Maybe I was crazy, maybe it was post-invasion syndrome or whatever they'd be calling it on TV if we still had working TVs.

But *Wuthering Heights* had vanished, and I knew there were more copies in that library. And. And the book supplies were getting smaller, and.

And.

And.

We weren't safe behind the barricade. We all knew that, now. I didn't know how to deal with that knowledge. I didn't even know how to deal with all the adults around me, pretending they weren't freaking out just as much as I was.

So after I sneaked through the barricade, on a night with barely a sliver of moon in the sky, I didn't go to the school by the same route I had used last time. I went the Mitchell Lane way.

People all said something different, about what observers looked like. They were CCTV cameras, they were spiky silver balls that hovered in the air, they were actual people, they were robots, they were . . .

I didn't see any of those things, that night. I walked slowly, keeping to the shadows, step after step, looking up at every window, the line of every roof.

Maybe he had just been screwing with me. That was a distinct possibility, right? It was the dickheadiest thing he could possibly have done, and I had no doubt he was capable of a lie like that, just to see what my reaction would be.

Then I saw it. A small, bright white smudge in the darkness. A pool of light that moved slowly across the road ahead of me, only there was nowhere for it to come from. It wasn't moonlight, or streetlight. It was something else.

It was growing. The whiteness spread like psychedelic milk spilled from a plastic bottle, out and out and out.

I turned and ran, and had no doubt that it was following me.

• • •

A few minutes later, I slammed the front door of the school behind me and leaned against it, gasping for breath. I had come here. Why had I come here?

Oh. Because an observer was following me, and I didn't want to lead it—them—it through the barricade. It made some sort of sense at the time, or maybe that was the adrenalin talking.

My chest hurt.

He was playing Elvis this time. Of course he was.

I knew these songs. I walked slowly, from the front door and up the stairs and along the corridors towards the library, and in that time I heard "Loving You", and "Got a Lot of Living To Do", and the stupid one about the teddy bear.

My dad used to sing that to my mum, when he thought we weren't listening. Which is weird, right? They're both far too young for Elvis. It was some kind of parent joke, that made them giggly and flirty in a way that made me and Otis want to stick our fingers in our ears and go, *Lalalalala*.

I couldn't remember the last time I saw my Mum smile.

Also, wasn't the front door of the school supposed to be locked? I didn't remember walking through it, but I must have done. I definitely didn't climb in through the window.

I stopped outside the library doors and thought about it.

The needle scratched its way along the record, and Lonesome Cowboy started up. It seemed appropriate enough music as I pushed open the doors and made my entrance.

• • •

He was sitting in the same place, with his feet up, as the last time I'd been here. Which was weeks ago. Also, there was no way I was going to call him Heathcliff. Even if he was as much of a douche as the original.

"Someone stole my *Wuthering Heights*," I said, though I didn't really think that was what had happened.

"Damn those post-apocalyptic book clubs," "Heathcliff' drawled without looking up. "Cut-throat to the last."

"I saw one of them," I blurted, and wondered why. I hadn't been planning to tell him. "An Observer."

He looked sharply at me, and then grinned. "Scary fuckers, yeah? Even though they don't look like anything at all."

"It might have followed me."

I expected him to be angry at my confession, but instead he laughed. "Yeah, no. Not in here. This is the one place that's completely safe from them."

That unsettled me. "You mean the one place outside the barricade," I corrected him.

He didn't flinch. "Do I?"

"You could come back to the town with me," I said, not sure why I was even offering this much. "They let in travellers, you know. At least, they did once." Hitch-hikers who had been stranded in the middle of the electro-magnetic pulse, and walked for weeks before they found us. They had been carrying two well-thumbed Harlequin romances, a ripped Archie comic, and a copy of Jack Kerouac's *On The Road* that didn't even have a crease in its spine.

His face closed over. "Didn't I make it clear? This is the only place that's safe. You're cute and all, with your mission to rescue the world's reading material, but I don't fancy the rest of your town moving in here with me."

I didn't know what to say to that, so I went back to the Recent Returns trolley, and fished out another copy of *Wuthering Heights*. If I was really superstitious, I'd sit here and read the whole thing, from beginning to end, just in case the next one I took got lost too.

There were three left. I took one, thought about it, then took the other two, then put one back. In case my backpack had some kind of *Wuthering Heights* eating vortex in it.

I didn't only pick fiction this time. I loaded up on some practical books about farming and making your own butter and shit like that. I thought about Frances, my brother's girlfriend, and how hard it was to get an appointment with the few health professionals left in our town, but sadly high school libraries aren't great on maternity and early childhood books. Not many picture books, either. When do babies start to read?

"We value your custom," drawled the creep as I walked past him.

My backpack felt lighter. Without a word, I sat down on the library floor and started unpacking it, book after book. The practical books had gone. So had *Wuthering Heights*. All I had left was the fiction, more Agatha Christies, a few familiar romances and the Sherlock Holmes novels I had added in at the last minute because if the baby didn't have picture books we were just going to have to start him on the classics early.

"What the hell?" I said, and then glared up at him. "Did you do this?"

He—whatever his name was—not Heathcliff, leaned over the desk. He looked kind of sad. "Nothing to do with me."

"I put the books in here."

"You can't take them with you."

"Why not?"

He sank back on to his chair, spinning it slowly around. "Figure it out, Kay-amy. What do they have in common, the books that you're allowed to take?"

I looked down at what looked like a pretty ordinary selection. Then it clicked. "I've read them before. All of these. I've read them before."

It felt like the library was pressing in on me, and the books were sucking all the air from the room. I was very small, in this giant space of bookshelves and Elvis music on a scratchy record player. "What did they do to the library, the invaders?" I asked, in a tiny voice.

"Absolutely nothing," he said. "I was asleep in the basement of the school, the night they came. My dad had kicked me out, and I was going to hitch across to the big city, but I didn't get further than two towns over. This was the easiest building to break into. So I was asleep when it hit, you know."

"The electro-magnetic pulse." The thing that stopped everything working, every electronic device, every television, every . . . every . . . every . . .

Something I was forgetting, on the tip of my tongue. Brain. Finger.

"It's funny," he said, in a tone that made it very clear that it wasn't, actually. "I figured it out later. The bit of basement I was dossing in was right here, beneath the library. It was like . . . the books protected me, when everyone else . . . "

"What happened to everyone else?" I whispered.

He looked so sad, so hollowed out, and I didn't even know what his name was. Maybe I should call him Heathcliff after all. It was the only name he'd ever given me.

"The wave—the pulse—whatever you want to call it. It killed them all. I walked out of the school into a ghost town. The buildings were dust, most of them. And the ones that weren't— some houses, a few shops. The antique shop, the newsagency. I figured it out, eventually. It was the buildings that had books in them. Real, paper books. All the rest of them were gone to dust. And all the people were dead. Dust and shadows."

"But that's not true," I argued. "Not this town. All the buildings are still standing. And everything behind the barricade is just fine."

"No," he said with a small smile. "It's really not, Kay-amy."

"Katie. My name is Katie."

"Huh," he said. "Did you know that's Scarlett O'Hara's real name, in *Gone with the Wind*? It's Katie Scarlett O'Hara."

"Yes," I said impatiently. "What's that got to do with anything?"

"Books are important."

"Not if we're all dead, they're not." I leaned in and tweaked his nose.

"Ow."

"See? I'm not dead. None of us are. You're just being stupid."

"I know what I saw," he said. "I saw a town full of people, gone to dust. And then—they all stood up again. They kept themselves busy, building a wall of air and imaginary things. I could walk right through them, and they never saw me. Whatever it is that pulse did to our electronics, it did something to people, too. We're not real any more. We're just memories that won't lie down."

I thought about Otis, and my Mum, and Frances and the baby. I didn't know what to think about them. All I knew was that they were going about their lives as they always had, only everything was smaller and fading and . . . maybe it was true.

"You were so worried about preserving the books, weren't you?" he said now. "But you didn't have to be. The invaders like books. Paper ones, especially. They have a reverence for them. They want to keep the books, store them and tend to them. It's human beings they don't plan on cataloguing."

His skin looked paler than before, almost a bright white. His skin shimmered like moonlight in the darkness. Like a spreading pool of milk.

"You're an Observer," I said, stepping backwards, tripping over my empty backpack and landing hard against the scattered pile of books I had already read.

He moved through the desk like he was a ghost, the milky whiteness of him parting and then reforming. "They made us," he said. "I don't think they meant to kill all the humans, with that first wave. But the bodies were so fragile. The thing that's left, the memory of humans, they're trying to figure out how to make a record of them, but they can only change a handful into something . . . permanent. They chose me because I was here. They thought I was a librarian, can you believe that? I promised them I would bring them someone who cared about the books, who could explain to them how they work. And here you are. You're the only one who came, while the rest of them were building that fucking wall. You're the only one who thought about the books."

I could hardly keep myself together. The tiny pieces of me were all clinging tightly, but I could burst apart at any moment.

"I won't get to read any new ones," I said.

"A small price to pay. You're the chosen one, Katie Scarlett. You're going to survive."

The fluorescent lights flicked off, and the only light in the room was the bright whiteness of him, and of me.

My arms looked like glowing moonlight, like milk, like crisp printing paper fresh from the packet.

I couldn't remember the baby's name. If I was real, if I was alive, I would remember his name, right? If all this was a lie, I should be able to remember something about my nephew. Something other than the yellow blanket they wrapped him in when he was born, and the book I bought him as a present, the touchy feely one made of plastic and crinkles and soft, soft felt.

His name was . . .

"Heathcliff," I said in a very small voice, knowing it wasn't the answer.

The Observer held a hand out to me. "We'll be the ones who save humanity. Who remember what being human was like. We'll make them remember, too. We'll save the books. There will be a record, at least, that we were here, that we had this history. They'll read about who we were. Once we teach them to read."

I stared up at him, and his outstretched, bone bright hand. I inhaled, and exhaled, though I no longer had any reason to do either of those things. The library breathed with me.

••••••••••

ORACLE'S TOWER

FAITH MUDGE

It stands at the heart of the forest, a grey tower pointing towards the skies, a stone finger raised in warning. The vines that once grew around its walls are withered and dead. The only life that clings to this place are the ravens which swoop and caw around the solitary window at the top of the tower, their mourning cries carrying on the sighing wind. This tower is my prison. The prison of the Oracle.

Listen. There is little time left to me. Listen to my story.

I was a wanderer, in my youth, and I wandered far, across every map I could find and off the edges into strange seas and stranger lands, where everything that I had believed was real became unreal. As I wandered, I learned things not told of in any book or scroll. I learned the tongues of bird and beast, the way to charm restless waters, how to shape the world around me to my will. I learned the dance of fire and the voice of the trees. My form shifted like clouds blown across the sky, melding, changing, reforming. I was powerful—so powerful!—but not as powerful as I wished myself to be.

So I travelled on, to places where the name of my native shore had never even been heard. In a land where the sun shone all day and night and the people spoke with their hands, I heard a tale that excited my curiosity. The story told of an orchard at the end of the world where the fruit the trees bore had magical powers. Whoever ate of the red tree would be granted beauty incomparable. Whoever ate of the blue tree would be granted vision unknowable. And whoever ate of the white tree would be granted power over all who saw and heard them. I desired those fruits more than anything I had known before, and I resolved to find them.

It took me years of searching and all the knowledge I had accumulated in my long travels, but find them I did. The three trees of legend grew in a place where one world met another, under the light of two suns and two moons, where the earth was split in two by a line of white fire. In that place, gazing through the crack between worlds, I looked into time itself. What marvels I saw! What wonders—what horrors. It was as if until that moment I had been blind and now I saw clearly. The future lay before me in all its terror and majesty, beyond my comprehension, beyond what I could even bear to witness. After my many years amassing knowledge, I saw how little I truly knew, and reeled from it, stunned, almost senseless.

My eyes, newly opened, fell on the trees themselves at this moment and I was filled with the deepest longing of my life. Theirs was a wonder to rival all others I had seen, a beauty that woke within me a desperate hunger the like of which cannot be described by any word in any tongue spoken upon the face of this world. But I was stronger now than my desires, and I took from those trees but one fruit each. Holding them safely in my arms, I left the orchard at the ends of the earth, determining that I would taste my bounty only when I set foot once more upon the soil of my birthland.

The voyage was long and hard. When at last I reached my native shores, I took the first of the fruits and cut them open, lifting the sweet dripping flesh to my lips to taste its juices. The scent alone was intoxicating. But before a single bite had touched my tongue, my sight cleared. I saw the future as surely as I saw the sky above me. Within these fruits lay power united, unlimited, unimaginable. To give in to that heady perfume, to taste those glistening juices, was to be corrupted. To use that power . . . the world would fall.

Appalled, I cast down the fruit I held, my hunger turning to revulsion. I buried the three fruits deep beneath the earth where they could not tempt the unwary, then lay down to sleep, believing that the danger I had brought with me was now negated. But it was not so. When I woke in the morning, my horrified eyes fell upon three shoots rising from the ground where I had buried the fruits. Power is not easily thwarted.

Fury possessed me. I tore up the shoots! I crushed them with my feet and with my knife slashed them into a thousand pieces. But the more I cut them down, the sooner they returned and the faster they grew. From shoots they became saplings, and from saplings, strong young trees. Despairing, I realised that my efforts to destroy them would come to nothing, so I built a high wall of stone around them and a cottage within those walls. There I stayed to guard the world from the horror I had unleashed.

Around my cottage I made a garden. In growing healing herbs I found renewed purpose, even contentment, in this life. I had spent so many years gathering knowledge like a miser hoarding gold; to share it was a new experience and to my surprise, a pleasurable one. A small hamlet existed close to the place I had made my home—in exchange for my plants and wisdom, they provided me with the goods I needed for living. But I never permitted anyone within my walls, and I never told a living soul of the fruits, for no one could be trusted; not even myself.

Just outside the hamlet, close to the forest, there lived a woodcutter and his wife. They were a handsome couple and arrogant in their youth, disdainfully patronising to the crotchety old woman they believed me to be. I knew that they longed for a baby and I offered my knowledge to the young wife, giving her herbs from my garden. In time she fell pregnant. I received no thanks from the delighted couple, who forgot my aid and advice the moment they discovered the happy news. I, likewise, forgot them. I should have known better.

One night I was woken by a sound from my garden. Taking my staff, I went to check my fruit trees, and discovered the woodcutter climbing down from their boughs, a filled basket in his arms. The trees bent and swayed to aid his progress; their treacherous wooden fingers had stretched to reach over the wall, beckoning, inviting the invader, whispering softly on a windless night.

My anger knew no bounds. The form I had worn for the years I had lived in this place fell from me and the woodcutter saw my true aspect. He fell to his knees.

"Have mercy upon me!" he begged. "My wife was passing your walls when the first fruit dropped at her feet. She could not resist it. The next day she came again, and the day after that, seeking more fruits—and they fell from the branches over the wall as if

— 443 —

in answer to her prayers. But now she longs for more, it is all she speaks of day and night, and I cannot deny her!"

I tore the basket from him and forced him to return with me to the cottage where he lived. His wife stood waiting for him by the window. With one glance I could see that the fruits had had no effect on her at all. I could not understand it. Then she appeared in the doorway, and I saw the truth of it. The power of the fruit had been concentrated entirely on the baby she carried within her.

I did what must be done. I was powerful—I could be terrifying. The woodcutter and his wife must have believed me a demon or djinn, some terrible being casting a curse upon them. My voice was dark and deep and dreadful as I told them I would spare their lives only if they paid for the fruit in full. They promised anything, anything at all. I told them I would take my prize in a se'nnight's time. Then I returned to my garden, to deal with the damage.

For all I knew of their danger, I realised the fruits had still enchanted me. True, the trees were powerful, but I had despaired of their destruction too easily. Now I bent my full powers to the task. A fire the like of which had never been seen before roared through my garden that night, hot enough to turn the stone walls to glass, razing every living thing within to ashes and burning those very ashes to dust. When the task was done I was wearied beyond belief, but the trees were gone. With what little strength I had remaining, I shifted my shape to that of a raven and perched on the roof of the woodcutter's house to rest and keep watch.

Seven days passed. On the seventh night the woman went into labour, and gave birth to a baby girl. The child came into the world not crying or screaming, but smiling, and she was as beautiful as the song of an angel. Her head was already covered in a soft golden down and her eyes were wide, wide blue. Her parents were smitten. And I, watching from the roof, glimpsed the future.

Swooping down, I took the form of an old woman once more and strode into the house. The mother shrank back from me, clutching her baby; the father moved to stand protective in front of them. They guessed at once what the price of the fruits would be, what I intended to claim. The woodcutter attempted to fight me—I threw him to the ground. The woman tried to run from me—I stilled her with a flick of my hand. Then I took the baby from her frozen arms. It looked up at me calmly and patiently, with a deep knowing that belonged to no true child, and I was filled with dread. There was no doubt in my mind. The baby must die.

Wings of feather and flesh unfurled from my back, breaking through the skin and flaring wide to meet wall and ceiling. I flew that night across the stars until I came to a lake, deep and still in the heart of an enormous forest, and over it I held the sleeping newborn child. But just as I loosened my grip, preparing to drop my bundle into the dark waters, its eyes opened and it began to wail, a high lost miserable wail.

Where is my mother, that sound seemed to cry. *Where is my warm bed and sweet milk? What is this dark, miserable place and who, who are you?*

The face that had been porcelain smooth was now screwed up and red with crying. The hair was tufty and sticky with sweat. Looking at the child I held, I saw only a small baby girl far from her home and parents, and I found that I could not harm her. Surely the effects of the fruit could not justify the slaughter of an innocent baby?

Instead, I sang to the bedrock of the lake and wrought from it a high, thin tower of stone. Into the tower I flew with the baby in my arms, and fashioned inside it a room where we could live. Then I changed her wrappings, fed her lakewater transformed into milk, and rocked her to sleep in my arms.

Perhaps, I thought, *this girl's future may be changed. With my wisdom and power, perhaps I can give her a different path.*

The tower had no doors or stairs and only a single window at the top. I summoned vines to grow over the stone walls, bearing grapes and pears and plums for us to eat, but I whispered thorns onto their smooth sides so they could not offer an escape when the child was old enough to think of it. And here, in utter isolation, I raised the baby I had stolen. I named her Rezuel.

She was beautiful. I must and will say it. She was lovelier than anything and anyone I had seen in all my long years of travelling. Her hair was a richer gold than the dying sun in all its glory, and softer than the finest silk. Her eyes could have been little circles cut from the sky, bluer than blue, and her voice . . . her voice brought every kind of bird from the forest to our window when she sang, to wonder at her.

From leaves and water I wrought garments for her; from stones, pretty jewellery; from twigs, a comb for her hair, and I loved to look at her. She, in her turn, was a delightful baby and a yet more delightful child. Whatever I asked of her, she hurried to comply. I was filled with hope. Each night as I combed out her long hair—already the length of her ankles and growing every day—I was sure that I had done right. No dark phantasmic visions could justify the taking of such a beautiful life.

Rezuel could not leave the tower. She often begged me to take her with me when I left, in winged form, through the window, but I always refused. My fears were quite different now to what they had been. The world could be in no danger from the little girl, but in her unthinking innocence she could be in terrible danger from the world. Savage beasts; poisonous plants; the deep lake that had already almost claimed her. In the tower she was safe.

One day, when she was nine years old, I had flown out to pick for her the wild berries she had asked for the previous night. It was midday when I returned. She was waiting for me at the window, her arms spread wide, as though to embrace me as I entered. But as I flew through into the room, my wings were caught and my body tangled inside the gleaming fibres of a golden net.

"Now you are the one who is caught," Rezuel cooed over my prone form, bending her lovely face close to the net. Its knots around me were nothing compared to the pain of my disillusioned heart as I saw my beautiful ward for what she was for the first time since I had brought her to the lake. The dark future I had seen at her birth was no phantasm; I had not changed her path.

I shifted my form to a beast with many spikes, cutting through the net of golden hair, then took my own shape and stood. Rezuel backed away from me, explanations tumbling from her lips—it had been a game, she promised me, and had I waited she would have set me free. How could she harm me, her dearest protector, who had loved and watched over her all these years? I longed to believe her sweet, innocent words, but the enchantment she had held over my senses all these years was broken. What she had intended to do with me, I was unsure—I could no longer tell what dwelt in her mind. Of course her first demand would have been for her freedom, but I knew there was no limitation on what else she might desire to have, or be, or do.

So I closed my ears to her weeping and flew from the tower to decide what had best be done.

She should have died on the night of her birth, had I not weakened at the last moment—but it was too late for such self-flagellation. Could I kill her now? I, who had been mother and father and sole friend to her from infancy? I knew I could not. A prisoner she must remain all her life, and I must be her guard. I summoned a flock of ravens to roost upon the tower so even when I was absent Rezuel would be watched. And I waited for the years to pass and set us both free with the gift of death. When the time came, my sorcery would die with me. The tower would crack and the lake would claim Rezuel as it should have done long ago.

Even knowing what she was, I could not stay away from her entirely, though I no longer dared to fly through the window for fear of another trap. Instead, I would sail a boat across the lake to the foot of the tower and call to her. If she wished to see me, she would wrap her hair around a hook by the window and release her long braid down the side of the tower. It was now long enough and thick enough for me to climb—a rope strong enough to support me, but which she could never use herself, for I had left no knife or scissors within the room for her to use against me. Her charms were danger enough. She would sit with me and talk, sometimes laughing and playful, other times solemn and sad, but always asking the same question.

Will you take me down? Will you let me come with you, and live with you, outside of this tower?

It cost me sorely to refuse her, but refuse her I did, and in climbing down again I would tell myself that this was the last time I would visit the tower, the last time I would be tempted by Rezuel's voice. But my resolve would not last. Her singing would carry across the lake and my heart, my stupid stubborn heart, would melt like ice beneath the sun.

For seven years, this pattern held, until the day I heard her screaming.

I was in the boat and across the lake before I knew what I was doing. Her long braid was waiting for me; I climbed it. As my fingers reached the sill, Rezuel's screams stopped, and I saw three things very clearly.

One, the body of one of my watch-ravens lying in the corner, its neck snapped.

Two, the braid that had been severed with the raven's sharp beak, tied to its hook.

The third—Rezuel standing at the window, her hair shorn roughly at the neck but still as lovely as ever, her smiling face tilted down to me and her hands reaching out towards my face.

They were full of thorns.

She put out my eyes. Blinded, I was helpless, and she dragged my aged, weakened body into the tower. Then she climbed down the braided rope dangling from the window, down to my boat, and once at the foot of the tower she set fire to the braid so that I could not follow her. By the time I hobbled to the window and called to my ravens, she was beyond their reach, and beyond mine.

I tried to fly, to follow her, but the forms I took were as old and decrepit and blind as my own true shape. In the years Rezuel had been growing tall and strong, I had faded to a shadow of my old power, never realising that it was happening—but she had. She was beautiful, and she was ingenious, and she was powerful.

And there was no one on this earth now who could stop her.

I stood at the window and through my ruined eyes saw the future once more. I saw Rezuel's lovely hair blowing in the wind and a horseman reining in wonder as he glimpsed her from afar. I saw her ride with him to the King's city and abandon him there with a shattered heart. I saw her ascend the steps of the palace and walk unhindered into the King's hall, enchanting his guards to powerlessness with a single smile from her flawless lips. The king would be instantly smitten, lost the moment he met her eyes. I saw him strangle his own wife on Rezuel's command—I saw the wedding held in his hall, the day Rezuel became his queen. The people of his kingdom would fall to their knees in worship of her beauty. They would vow to live for her, to die for her, to fight for her to the last man and the last breath . . .

And how those vows would be fulfilled.

Tears mingled with the blood streaming down my face, but there was no release from the visions of a future I had brought about by my own delusion. I saw Rezuel wage her war, reaching out her delicate hand to take whatever she so chose, no matter the cost. I saw whole armies fall to her while she stood apart, untouched by the blood spilled in her name. I saw her rule her world.

And I saw the arrow that could end it all. A single arrow, carved from the wood of three fruit trees at the end of the world, with the strength to fell power itself.

I saw it pierce her heart.

The hand that draws the bow is not my own; I must wait for the one who will hear me and learn the secret even Rezuel does not know, the secret of her death. It is a desperate chance, but I cling to it. I will die here, captive in the prison I made, alone in the heart of the forest, surrounded by my ravens. They alone have heard my final prophecy. They cry it to the keening wind—my warning, my story, the last words of the Oracle.

Listen. Listen to them.

There is hope.

••••••••••

NIGHTSIDE EYE

TERRY DOWLING

The fact that the guest lounge, ballroom, whatever it had originally been, was devoid of furniture only intensified the feeling of something waiting to happen.

Jared had read the latest tender updates for the old Hydro Majestic Hotel, knew that they all listed the Delfray Room as a minor function room.

"So that's it?" he said, indicating the mantel-piece above the handsome fireplace in the eastern wall.

"That's it," Susan answered, clearly intrigued, possibly even disconcerted at knowing someone who actually wore an eye-patch like the traditional black one over Jared's left eye. Jared was 36, lean enough, his features regular enough, to make him attractive to many women at first glance. The patch lent him an unexpectedly rakish air, friends and colleagues said. Susan Royce was in her late twenties, with ginger hair in a pixie crop, and was clearly taken with him—in spite of the patch, because of it, who could say? Now she led the way across the parquetry floor to the black iron fireplace, looking for a moment as if she were actually going to touch the unadorned marble ledge. "Put anything on it, it ends up on the floor."

Jared did reach out and touch the cold smooth marble. "But not immediately, I understand. It takes time."

"Not immediately, no." Susan seemed interested, well-intentioned. She was a different heritage representative to the one assigned to Martin Rathcar fifteen months before. Without

Rathcar's media brouhaha, the scale of that whole publicity circus to draw attention, she may have had only a token briefing on what this evening's proceedings were all about. "But an hour, two hours later. It always happens. Used to take days, weeks, months, but it's much more frequent now, a matter of hours, sometimes minutes. Even heavy weights end up being shifted. They say it's something electro-magnetic, a freak of nature."

"You've seen it?" Jared asked. Though he'd been hoping he'd get Cilla Paul, the same heritage rep Rathcar had dealt with, things seemed to be shaping up well regardless.

"Only on CCTV. I'm still pretty new."

The Delfray Room seemed larger from this angle than it actually was. Being painted a stylish off-white probably helped create that effect. At the far end, the western end near the double doors, four long sash windows were curtained with light brown drapes, gathered back with the same tasselled silken cords as on the other westward-facing windows in the hallways of the old Hydro Majestic. Like those hallway windows, these too looked out over the vastness of the Megalong Valley, gave the spectacular views that had made the place so famous in its hey-day. Now the Hydro was in its third year of being closed, officially awaiting restoration to all its former glory as a world-class spa resort if only the appropriate government, licensing and restoration bodies could agree. Having read the various tender documents, Jared knew how dauntingly expensive it was going to be. The old Victorian and Edwardian buildings made a gentle chevron along the ridge-line, set fifty metres in from the main highway that led across the Blue Mountains from Sydney out to Lithgow, Bathurst and beyond. It was the sort of white elephant that was so costly to maintain yet too dramatically part of the local landscape and local history to be ignored.

The late-autumn sun had already set beyond the last of the ranges. The famous view was gone from the long windows now, their old panes turned to so many mirror reflections by the light from the Deco wall sconces and the chandelier overhead. The black iron fireplace, clean but inevitably dusty, was the room's most distinctive feature, the mantel a modest afterthought by comparison, even more simple and functional than the CCTV footage had shown it to be.

"The previous owners must have become fed up with the whole thing," Jared said.

Susan nodded. "None of the various management groups ever said much about it but, you know, who wanted the publicity? It could happen at any time. It was always there. And, like I say, it's been getting more frequent."

"Hard to live with."

"They only used the Delfray Room as an overflow room for special occasions, last-minute wedding bookings, that sort of thing. They just made sure they put nothing on the mantel. Records show that the occurrences—you call them "events", don't you?—started soon after the hotel was first opened in 1891 as the Belgravia Hotel, though very infrequently then. When it became the Hydro, only a few people knew about them. Management had to consider their more refined and sensitive clientele, so hushed things up pretty quickly. There was originally a large mirror mounted over it, quite ornate, so no-one really questioned the lack of other adornment."

"Except the occasional guest who suddenly found his drink on the floor."

Susan laughed. "Exactly. The ultimate party trick. I imagine it's a bit like trying to sell or lease out a murder house. Something you just don't mention, just work around as best you can. Mr Ryan—Jared—if you'll excuse me asking. I understand that you're not blind in that eye. You're just masking it for what's being done tonight. Is what Cilla said true? This whole thing is about *seeing* what's doing it?"

"That's right."

"You don't mean it's someone? A person? A ghost?"

Jared shrugged. "We can't know. Martin Rathcar proceeded from the certainty that *something* was doing it—whether resident poltergeist or freak of nature. He found serious funding to develop a method for seeing anomalies like this a different way."

"But the patch. I understand that—"

"Dr Rathcar called it the Nightside Eye as a media drawcard in 2008, back when the funding proposals went in. Made it sound sexy, mysterious. He got the idea from one of those myth-buster programs on TV."

"Really. How so?"

"It seems veteran seamen aboard sailing ships in the 17th, 18th and 19th Centuries often wore a patch over one eye when they went below-deck. They swapped the patch from one eye to the other so they were nightsighted and could see immediately. It let them find things quickly, stopped them bumping their heads. Very practical."

Susan looked sceptical. "That really happened?"

"It's highly likely. Dr Rathcar expanded on the idea, kept one eye completely isolated from all the customary vision tasks for nine months, took injections of several quite powerful, very specific neurological regulators to intensify the "nightside" function in that particular optic nerve."

"Biased it?"

"Many claimed so, though the regulators weren't known to be hallucinogens. More like the drugs used in eye surgery, optical trauma events, sight retrieval situations. Increased receptivity and adaptivity. Intensification of the optic process."

"I remember now. Rathcar's the guy from Sydney University who wouldn't say what he saw. He took his own memories with another drug. I remember that interview on *60 Minutes*."

"That's the guy. Martin Rathcar."

"You're doing what he did?"

"As best I can." Jared touched the smooth marble ledge again. There were no frissons, no untoward sensations, nor had he expected any. He took his hand away. "When he injected the Trioparin, took his memories, he breached quite a few legal agreements. He ended up being locked out of his own facilities, forfeited his database and research material. But some preliminary theory was already published. There was even a popular article in *New Scientist* to generate interest. The rest of the procedure was relatively easy to duplicate. The main thing was getting access to the same location he used a year ago. You can see why I'm so grateful to you and your office."

Susan smiled. "Cilla briefed me as well as she could before she left for London. Her mum is unwell, all last minute. She said I just have to be here and watch. Make sure rules are followed."

"You're doing more than you realize. You and the security guards rostered on tonight become impartial observers as well."

"Hey, I like that. Independent witnesses!"

NIGHTSIDE EYE • TERRY DOWLING

"I'm glad you think so. I wonder if you'd be okay with us using your names in our observation log? It could really help."

"Sure. It's exciting. I'll ask Geoff and Amin later."

"My camera and sound people will be here soon, Sophie and Craig, my volunteer assistants and official witnesses. It's six o'clock now. Once we're set up, we'll begin at 7pm, the same time Dr Rathcar did fifteen months ago. We'll do the whole thing twice if we can, put several objects here on the mantel—a plastic bottle, a child's wooden block, a toy train—and simply record what happens. Second time through, if we *are* lucky tonight and the phenomenon occurs, the moment they're moved, disturbed in any way at all, I shift the patch from one eye to the other and see what I get. It shouldn't take long."

"You do that *once* it happens."

"As soon as it happens. As close to. The first time is a control to establish parameters: event frequency and duration, lighting levels, things like that. But the second time round I stand over here by the fireplace and shift the patch, just as Rathcar did."

"But the camcorders will only catch your reactions. Not *what* you see."

"Right. But whatever we get may match reactions in the CCTV footage from the Rathcar attempt. Rathcar's own footage hasn't been made available yet, but may be released once we do this. Rathcar called out a single word—"Kathy!"—his assistant's name. We don't know why now, and of course he can't tell us."

"Or won't."

"Or won't. But there may be some key detail or other that emerges. Later spectrographic analysis may show even more, who knows?"

"It's all very uncertain," Susan said, looking at him intently, or possibly at the eye-patch that was to play such a key role in what was about to happen.

"True. But it's all we can expect in a situation like this, and hopefully what we do tonight will actually duplicate Rathcar's results, whatever those ultimately were. All we know is that there was an event and that Dr Rathcar shifted his patch, reacted strongly to something, called out Kathy Nicholls' name, just her first name, then shifted the patch back. It's what he did afterwards that caused the fuss. Gave himself the injection."

"So you're doing this to help Dr Rathcar."

"In a sense. Not out of some noble motive or anything; I've never even met the man. But I have to allow that he saw *something*. A respected research scientist took his own memories of what seems to be the key moment in a serious experiment. Grandstanding aside, something probably significant happened to make him do that."

"The resident poltergeist," Susan said.

"I'll settle for that, whatever it is."

"You hope to see it?"

"That's the idea. Hopefully see something."

"So why do it at night? It happens in daylight too. Surely that'd be easier."

Jared had to smile. "Rathcar did it at night, so we do likewise. I think it was Channel 9's idea, having the night-shoot. Spookier. More dramatic."

"I can understand that. The smallest things are scarier at night."

"Exactly."

"But whatever you see may just be sensory overload. All those drugs you mentioned."

"I know. Large-scale perceptual trauma. But those optical regulators aren't known for that, have been deliberately tailored to avoid it in fact. Ah—here are my long-suffering volunteers!"

Sophie Mace and Craig Delmonte had appeared at the doorway to the Delfray Room, laden with camcorders, audio equipment and a portable lighting stand, assisted by Geoff and Amin, the security guards rostered on for the evening.

Jared and Susan walked back to the double doors, where Jared completed the introductions then helped the security men carry in chairs and a table so Craig and Sophie could set up their video monitors just inside the entrance. Susan left them to it, going outside to discuss the evening's schedule with the guards.

"Give us twenty minutes to get the settings," Craig said. "Won't take long."

"Listen, Craig—"

"Jared. Let's do this like we discussed. You're pumped, I can tell. It's only natural. Go for a walk and calm down! Sophie and I can handle this."

"Right."

They had talked about it, about remaining composed, focused, letting others help. This footage would be seen, closely scrutinised. Objectivity and detachment were everything.

Jared stepped out into the corridor, walked the short distance to the corner and turned left into the long axial hallway for the whole wing. It was dimly lit, and so quiet, stretching off into shadow at its farthest reaches. Jared started along it, moving soundlessly on the old carpet, with locked doors to his left and long darkened windows to the right. He knew that beyond the steady mirror reflections in those panes the land fell away over sheer crags, buttresses, blurrings of eucalypts, a great gulf of darkness, all invisible now. In daylight it was the sort of panoramic view that caught your breath, weakened you in the knees, made any attempts to capture it in photographs impossible. Photographs never caught the scale, the dimension, the vast uncaring emptiness.

Now that he was finally doing it, everything seemed intensely unreal, and he had to counter that feeling. He took several deep breaths, made himself consider where he was. The old spa complex was all around him, stretching away like a bleached wishbone here by the highway at Medlow Bath, an antique ivory clasp opened and laid out along the ridge, arms pushed back against the incredible drop. The phrase "abandoned in place' had never been more appropriate. This fabulous old hotel was meant to be restored, maintained, feted, if only as something as second-rate yet cherished as the Carrington Hotel in nearby Katoomba. But *used*, for heaven's sake. Though no-one was saying so officially, there was already the distinct feeling that it might all prove too hard, that these empty rooms, forgotten lounges, deserted balconies and silent staircases would stay like this indefinitely, the only thing moving in the halls by day the motes of dust glittering in the westering sunlight, by night the shadows made by the moon as it fell down the sky. Now and then security guards would come and go, trying the locks, checking the fire-doors, running the aircon in various rooms to counter mildew and mould, helping to replace the fire-extinguishers as they reached their use-by dates, escorting the planning people who seemed to come less and less frequently now.

Jared turned to face his own reflection in one of the long casements, stood distracted by the familiar shape with the eye-patch. For a moment it made him forget the great darkness beyond the glass, but then he forced himself to think of it, savour it: the fact that two things could be true at the same time, his image *and* the other. It calmed him, anchored him somehow.

When he finally did check his watch, he saw it was 6:51, time to get back. He re-traced his course, returned with the same silent tread to the Delfray Room, welcoming the soft murmur of voices as Sophie and Craig made final adjustments, calmly explaining what they were doing for Susan's benefit. The security guards were off making last-minute checks of the exits.

Everyone knew to leave Jared be now, and he distanced himself, found focus by reviewing how well it had gone so far. The Rathcar duplication was nearly complete: his taking the exact regulator doses across nine long months, the grooming of the monocular separation followed to the letter. The logistical requirements had been met too: securing the Hydro for the evening, keeping the costs well down. The guards were rostered on anyway. Only Susan had to be paid a fee for the two or three hours it should take, and she had turned out to be so interested that if he'd bothered to arrange to meet beforehand she might well have done it for free.

At 6:56, Jared called for Stand-by. Susan took out her mobile and contacted the security men. "Geoff, get Amin. We're about to start."

The guards appeared in the doorway moments later, took their places on the spare chairs, interested and attentive.

"All right," Jared said. "So everyone is clear on the sequencing, we roll cameras at 7:00 sharp, do the control run to make sure our visitor is with us. We set up our things on the mantel, let our guest have a free go at them. Once it happens, *if* it happens, we then take the thirty-eight minute break and do it all again, this time with me standing over by the mantel and swapping the patch as soon as I can after the event occurs."

"Is the thirty-eight minutes necessary?" Susan asked.

"Again, it's what Rathcar did. It wasn't planned. He just had more things to co-ordinate. But we're duplicating his sequencing as closely as possible."

"Understood."

"Okay, Sophie, Craig. It's 6:59. Begin recording. I'll go put the things on the mantel-piece."

Jared did so, once again crossing the empty dance-floor to the fireplace. First he stood the plastic bottle on its end, then set down the wooden block a short distance along from it, finally placed the red toy locomotive. Though tempted to stay by the mantel even for this first run, pulling his patch aside at the first sign of any disturbance, he made himself return to the monitors by the doors.

The vigil proper began at 7:02.

It was exciting at first, full of a new and understandable tension, an intensification of everything. The objects sat there—so ordinary, so comical in that ordinariness, both unreal yet super-real, but growing more and more unsettling, even disturbing somehow in their stillness.

As long minutes passed, the waiting soon became unbearable, of course. In most modern cultures, human senses were rarely accustomed to being strained this way. What once might have been essential for hunting and for vigilance in the face of danger and strife now brought only a worrying hypersensitivity. Jared watched the monitors, then the mantel across the room, monitors and mantel, glance up, glance down, the cycle repeating over and over. He found himself afraid to blink, straining to catch the slightest movement, the smallest disturbance, keenly aware of the gulf beyond the windows, of the chill autumn darkness all about them, thought of the empty rooms and hallways, the locked bars and dining rooms, the kitchens, closets, the empty pipes, the utterly still interiors of the Hotel outbuildings scattered along the ridge. He imagined movement a dozen, two dozen times, but there was nothing, certainly no confirmation from Craig and Sophie at their monitors, watching the test objects in both long-shot and close-up. Geoff and Amin sat quietly behind him, Susan to his right, close by the monitor screens, no doubt staring too.

Jared had not forbidden talking, but that's what had resulted. There was barely a sound.

Ten minutes became twenty, thirty, and the silence grew to be a layered thing. Sounds not noticed at first gained a striking new intensity: the hum of the recording equipment, the smallest cough, the rhythmic cycle of their breathing, the occasional tick of temperatures shifting, of masonry cooling, old pipes settling, whatever traces came in from the great emptiness beyond the windows.

It was so sudden when it happened—as alarming, dramatic and violent as everyone had said it would be. One moment the objects sat unmoving, exactly as placed. The next they were gone, clattering on the parquetry floor as if an unseen arm had swept them aside.

"First event, 7:46," Craig said for the audio log, then: "Stand by. Stand by. Counting to the thirty-eight minute repeat at 7:47—now!"

Everyone relaxed then, began talking all at once. It was happening. They were in the thirty-eight minute time-out.

To Jared's surprise, one of the security guards, Amin, was suddenly at his elbow, handing him a folded note. "When I started my rounds earlier, Jared, a guy parked out by the highway asked me to give you this the moment something happened."

"What's that?" Jared said, even as he took the note, opened and read it.

Mr Ryan

I am waiting in front of the Hotel in a white Camry. Please give me fifteen minutes of your time. It is very important that you do so.

Martin Rathcar.

Jared passed the note to Craig, said: "Keep to the count-down. I'll be back in time." Then he left the Delfray Room, hurried out to the front exit, out through the porte-cochère to where, sure enough, a solitary white Camry was parked by the highway. As Jared approached the vehicle, the passenger window lowered, revealed a man behind the wheel leaning over, smiling.

"Jared Ryan? I'm Martin Rathcar. Thanks for coming out. Please get in for a moment."

Jared climbed into the passenger seat and they shook hands. "Dr Rathcar, I have to say this is truly a surprise! Really quite marvellous! But why are you here?"

Martin Rathcar looked older than his fifty-two years. He sat with his hands on the steering wheel, his narrow face partly shadowed, partly lit by the highway lamps. His eyes glittered. "I know you don't have long. My one-time assistant, Kathy Nicholls, let me know that you'd duplicated the monocular separation and were doing this tonight."

"Using your Nightside Eye."

Rathcar gave a wry smile. "To call it that. I enjoyed the theatricality, I suppose."

"I've read all the interviews, all the *available* transcripts."

"That's all there are."

"I accept that. But I thought—since you asked to see me—that there was something you remembered and were prepared to share."

"Jared, I remember nothing of what I saw, just that it was enough to make me obliterate the memory of whatever it was. It's strange to find myself asking you to abandon the whole thing now when I have no memory of what it is I'm warning you away from. Feels a bit silly really, especially when it puts me in the position of wanting more than anything to know exactly what I *did* see. But I have to allow that there were vitally important reasons. Please reconsider going ahead with this."

The request surprised Jared. "What about your own reply to Sandra Cartwright on *60 Minutes* in July 2009? "This is science. Learning about the world.""

"I won't insult your intelligence by giving the line that was put to me in the same interview, that there are things we are simply not meant to know. I still hold with what I said. If we can know it, it's science and there to be known. It's only right that I should wonder now about what I saw that night that led me to take the final step. Theatricality is one thing, melodrama quite another, and I really do hate sounding this way after years of advocating rigorous investigation myself. But it had to have been important. I pretty well committed professional suicide with what I did."

"Surely not. It was always going to be a case of their having to take your word for whatever you saw. You just pissed off a lot of people. Deprived them of an answer to something they would have called inconclusive anyway."

"Which, nevertheless, many say was because I saw nothing. That this was my intention all along."

"Dr Rathcar—Martin—your reputation, your previous work in perception, suggests otherwise." Jared hesitated. "It really did take your memory of it?" He had never been truly convinced, he realized.

"That's the thing, isn't it? I should have insisted on a second subject doing it with me from the beginning, or at least waited until whatever I saw could be verified in a subsequent procedure. But Trioparin is effective only on recent memory. I was told it affected only an hour, ninety minutes tops. It's like a mind-shock that way, very different to Diprovan and other amnesiacs. Whatever I saw made me decide that I could *not* by any means wait for subsequent verification."

"It bothered you that much."

"I have to allow that it did. I desperately needed to forget. Anyway, the drug worked better than expected. My short-term memory of the twenty-six hours preceding the injection was lost. Twenty-six hours, can you believe it? Far longer than anyone expected. Part of me wants to know what it was I saw, now more than ever given your intentions tonight, I can't deny it. But I have to accept that I gave myself that injection knowing what it was I did."

"But to have arranged for that contingency in the first place, you must have seriously suspected—sensed—that something could go wrong. Trioparin is a last-resort trauma amnesiac. Prohibitively expensive."

Rathcar nodded. "At the time I simply allowed that there could be intense trans-perceptual trauma. It seemed entirely likely. You deprive one eye of its normal tasks for months on end, suppress at least three key neurotransmitters in doing so, then suddenly restore sight to that—let's use the pop term—Nightside Eye. Well, you know the outcome, though now I wish I'd never *mentioned* arranging such a precaution. The media seized on it, had a field day."

Though he hadn't automatically expected it, Jared found himself liking this man. "You didn't just accept that whatever you saw might be dismissed as hallucination, hyper-perception. It suggests you *believed* what you saw."

"It does, doesn't it? I'm glad you think so."

"You wanted it *all* gone regardless, though you knew in advance that it would be intolerable for you afterwards. The *not* knowing."

Rathcar gave a forbearing smile. "That's what made me drive up here tonight and ask to see you. Weird position to find myself in, like I say, but I have to allow that it really is as serious, as important, as my subsequent behaviour suggests. I was never much given to pranks or over-reaction, believe me."

"But what could it be? What must you have seen—even as an hallucination—that could possibly make you want to forget it forever?"

Rathcar sat with his hands on the wheel for a time, staring at nothing. Then, noticing Jared glance at his watch, he continued. "You understand my dilemma. I have to allow that it was either an hallucination for me, something purely subjective, or a reality for us all. They're the alternatives, the least I can claim. But, Jared, you stand to face the problem I faced: failing in your duty as a scientist. I clearly didn't want even the *possibility* of it being real in the objective sense. You see the extremes here, why I can't help but be fascinated with what you're about to do. I knew it might happen in time, but now, tonight, I keep reproaching myself for not seeking corroboration *before* taking my memories of what I saw."

Jared smiled grimly at the implications. "It really must have been something."

"Well, no matter. At least you're doing it at the same place I did. And I understand you've duplicated my procedures for fostering the Eye precisely."

"That was the whole point, duplicating what you did."

"Again, I'd be lying if I didn't say that I'm fascinated to know what will happen. Maybe I was wrong to do what I did. But that's the other reason I wanted to see you. Would you consider using a lethophoric like Trioparin to take your memories?"

"Frankly, Martin, I'm more the budget operation. You had institutional funding. I can't afford luxuries like that."

Rathcar smiled again. It was a good smile. They truly did like each other. He took one hand from the wheel, patted the pocket of his jacket. "I have some here in case. The last of my supply, pocketed that night, thank goodness. Everything else was confiscated. I'll wait out here in the car."

"Come inside."

"No, I must *not* be in there. You must appear unbiased. But just remember that it's here. I'm here."

"If I do come out to you, you won't ask what I've seen?"

"I'll want to more than anything in the world. But, no. I promise I won't. I must believe in myself to that extent. You say you're not doing this for me, and I believe you. In a sense, I'm not just doing this for you either. It's because I have to trust myself—trust that I acted for the right reasons. I do not need to know what you see. But if you come out and ask for the Trioparin, I will at least know that you've seen something as unbearable and that I was right in doing what I did that night. Right now that means everything."

• • •

Jared made it back to the Delfray Room with seven minutes to spare. Both Sophie and Craig wanted to ask about what had happened, but Jared raised a hand.

"He just wanted to wish me luck and try to talk me out of going through with it."

"Really?" Sophie said. "No insights?"

"Unfortunately not a thing," Jared told her. "But we can talk about this later. It's nearly time."

At 8:24, Jared crossed to the fireplace again, retrieved the bottle, the wooden block and the toy locomotive from the floor where they had fallen, and began setting them back on the mantel, making sure that the placing of the train coincided with Craig's 3-2-1 countdown to 8:25 exactly. Jared then moved to the right of the fireplace, watching the three objects, wondering how long it would be—*if* at all.

It was a different sort of vigil now, of course, marked by a wholly new kind of tension, such a definite—*pressure* was the only word. Jared's breathing was so loud in his ears. He could feel his heart thumping, his pulse racing, was aware again of the silence out in the room, of how far away the others were across the dull sheen of the parquetry. A quick glance showed Sophie and Craig at their monitors, faces ghost-lit just a touch, showed Susan looking up from the screens to him, the screens then him. Geoff and Amin sat behind them, darker shapes in the open doorway, eyes fixed and glinting.

The pressure became everything. It could happen at any moment, any instant. He felt he could almost guess when. It was like the waiting tension in a game of Snap or that kids' game where closed fists were placed knuckle to knuckle against one another, and the kid who was it got to hit the other's hand before it could be snatched away.

Jared's thoughts raced. What was it? *Who* was it? Was it really something as simple as electro-magnetic fluxes, atmospheric and geomorphic glitches, nothing supernatural at all? Or was there motivation behind it? Purpose? That was the real question here. What was out there drawing ever nearer, was even now preparing to sweep the objects aside, so dramatically, so brutally. Where did it come from? How far did it have to travel to do this simple mindless thing? Is that what the delay meant, or was this poltergeist always here, holding back out of a sense of mischief? But *why* did it have to be done—this furious sweeping aside? That remained the issue. The real priority wasn't just shifting the patch to see what there was *after* the event, but shifting it in time to catch who or what was doing it *just as it was about to happen*!

It would be departing from Rathcar's procedure, certainly, but this was about finding answers, seeing the process as process. *Complete* process, with more than just an ending, an outcome. With a beginning, a definite lead-up and possibly—could it be?— with intent.

The pressure *was* building, definitely growing stronger, Jared was sure of it. Something was about to happen, was beginning even now out there in the room, there to be seen if he dared risk it, dared throw it all away on a conviction, this *felt* certainty, totally unprovable.

Jared felt his hand clench, felt himself preparing to take that risk, commit that violation.

This was what it needed to be! Knowing what it was *before* it happened, *as* it happened, not afterwards. Seeing the cause, not the effect.

The pressure was too much.

His hand was at the patch, shifting it from one eye to the other, uncovering the different kind of seeing.

• • •

Jared reeled at what he saw, had to reach out and steady himself with one hand on the mantel edge.

There was no sign of Susan or the others, none of the equipment, not even the spotlight. The room was crowded, too crowded, with row upon row of dead-white forms, pallid near-human shapes pressing shoulder to shoulder with not a space between them, dozens, hundreds of sexless, minimalist things like mannequins, but with mouths hanging open and dull red eyes fixed mindlessly ahead, looking beyond him, fixed on nothing.

He was frantically registering the enormity of what he was seeing when there was a commotion in the throng, a sudden rippling forward as someone, something came pushing through, finally thrusting aside the figures in the foremost row to stand slavering, heaving. It was another of the pallid shapes, but this one had eyes that were wildly animated, blazing red, and a mouth stretched wide in a grotesque toothless grin.

No sooner was it there than it raised one long white arm and swept everything from the mantel. The familiar clatter echoed in the room, in no way muffled by the crowding forms.

Jared stared in utter dread. It wasn't just the dead-white face, the grinning, gaping mouth, the imbecilic, red-eyed glare. It was the idiot glee in those eyes, the look of absolute manic delight at having done this single, simple, stupid thing yet again. It was like a puppy waiting for the next throw of a ball, a witless automaton for whom only this had meaning.

And worse still was the sense that the rest of the crowding, slack-faced throng had their special things too, tasks waiting to be triggered and just as mindlessly resolved, whatever they were, however long they had to wait, however long it took.

"Susan!" he shouted, not to Sophie or Craig, but to the young woman who was nearest in his thoughts, had been the focus of so much recent attention.

And there she was, visible now, moving from the back of the shapes, moving forward *through* all the still figures, but not alone. One of the pallid, gaping forms moved with her, followed close behind, in attendance, her eager companion.

We all have them, Jared realized. Following, always following, always there, biding their time.

Are they what waits for us? All that is left of us? What simply wears us down, brings us to death, what?

There was no way of knowing. But *this* was what Rathcar had seen. What Martin Rathcar had understood.

Jared couldn't help himself. He reached up, snatched the patch back over the Nightside Eye so the room, the hotel, the world became normal again.

Seemed to.

"What was it?" Susan asked, still moving towards him across the empty, never-empty room. "What did you see?"

"Nothing," Jared managed, giving the beautiful lie. "There was nothing. It was too much of a shock. Just too much disorientation for the brain. It didn't work."

And he gazed out at the welcome emptiness, the normal world, knowing it could never be that again, knowing that Rathcar was right and realizing what had to be done.

If Rathcar had waited, kept his word, was still out by the highway.

Jared ran to the double doors, rushed out to the main entrance. Susan hurried behind. Sophie and Craig abandoned their monitors and ran after him. Geoff and Amin exchanged glances and followed.

Behind them the abandoned equipment hummed quietly. The things from the mantel lay scattered where they had fallen. The windows reflected only the empty room, showed not a trace of the darkness beyond the old, old panes.

• • • • • • • • • • •

ABOUT THE CONTRIBUTORS

JOANNE ANDERTON is speculative fiction writer living in Sydney. Her publications include the collection *The Bone Chime Song and Other Stories*, and the novels *Debris* and *Suited*. She had been shortlisted for multiple awards, and won the 2012 Ditmar for Best New Talent. Visit her at **joanneanderton.com**

R.J. ASTRUC's latest books are a young adult novel about censorship, *Banned Books*, and a collection of science fiction stories about international terrorists called *Signs over the Pacific*. You can find more of RJ's fiction here: **rachelastruc.com**.

LEE BATTERSBY is the author of the novels *The Corpse-Rat King* (Angry Robot, 2012) and *Marching Dead* (Angry Robot, 2013). He blogs at the Battersblog (**battersblog.blogspot.com**).

ALAN BAXTER is a Ditmar Award-nominated British-Australian author. He writes dark fantasy, sci-fi and horror, rides a motorcycle and loves his dog. He also teaches Kung Fu. He is the author of novels *RealmShift* and *MageSign*, and co-authored the short horror novel, *Dark Rite*, with David Wood. Read his work and more at his website **www.alanbaxteronline.com**.

JENNY BLACKFORD's short stories have appeared in places as diverse as *Westerly* and *Cosmos*. She grew up reading and rereading H.G. Wells, and is thrilled to have "A Moveable Feast" reprinted here from Amanda Pillar's lovely anthology *Bloodstones*, and a second Wells hommage, "New Miracle Celebrity Weight Loss Diet", in the June 2013 *Penumbra*.

EDDY BURGER is a Melbourne writer of funny and experimental fiction, poetry and plays. His work has appeared in local and overseas journals and anthologies including *Sleepers Almanac*, *Dark Edifice*, *Forever Shores*, *Going Down Swinging*, *Meanjin* and *Bewildering Stories*. Eddy is an anti realist, post modernist and champion of the imagination.

ISOBELLE CARMODY is one of Australia's most highly regarded and prominent authors of fantasy. A consummate and much-loved storyteller, Isobelle has written over thirty novels and many short stories. She has a host of award-winning novels to her credit. Isobelle divides her time between her home on the Great Ocean Road Australia and Prague in the Czech Republic.

JAY CASELBERG, an Australian author based in Europe, has appeared in multiple venues worldwide and in several languages. His next novel *Empties* "a novel of brutal psychological horror" is due out soon and there are a number of short stories forthcoming. More can be found at **jaycaselberg.com**

STEPHEN DEDMAN sold his first short story in 1977 and his first novel in 1995. That novel, *The Art of Arrow Cutting*, was shortlisted for a Bram Stoker Award. His short stories have won two Aurealis awards and a Ditmar, and been nominated for the British Science Fiction Association Award, the Sidewise Award, the Seiun Award and the Spectrum Award. **www.stephendedman.com.**

Melbourne based FELICITY DOWKER is a Ditmar and Chronos Award winner and an Aurealis and Australian Shadows Award finalist. Felicity is a founder and contributing editor at dark fiction news and reviews site Thirteen O'Clock (**thirteenoclock.com.au**). Felicity's debut collection is *Bread and Circuses* (Ticonderoga).

TERRY DOWLING has been called "Australia's finest writer of horror" by *Locus*, its "premier writer of dark fantasy" by *All Hallows* and its "most acclaimed writer of the dark fantastic" by *Cemetery Dance* magazine. His collection *Basic Black* won the International Horror Guild Award and is regarded as "one of the best recent collections of contemporary horror" by the American Library Association. **terrydowling.com**

TOM DULLEMOND stumbled out of university with a double degree in Medieval/Renaissance studies and Software Engineering. Tom was a co-editor of *The Complete Guide to Writing Fantasy* and has sold short fiction to a handful of anthologies, including *Danse Macabre: Close Encounters with the Reaper*. He writes a regular flash fiction column for *The Helix* science magazine.

THORAIYA DYER is a three-time Aurealis Award-winning, three-time Ditmar Award-winning Australian writer based in the Hunter Valley, NSW. Her short fiction has appeared in *Clarkesworld*, *Apex*, *Nature* and *Cosmos* and is forthcoming in *Analog*. A petite collection of four original stories, "Asymmetry," is available from Twelfth Planet Press. Find her online at Goodreads or **thoraiyadyer. com**.

WILL ELLIOTT won the ABC manuscript award with *The Pilo Family Circus*, which also won the 2006 Golden Aurealis Award, the Aurealis for Best Horror, the Ditmar, the Australian Shadows Award and in 2011 won the Spanish Nocte for Best International Book. The book was turned into a play by the Godlight Theatre Company in New York in 2012. He has written seven other books and is published in ten countries. He lives in Brisbane.

JASON FISCHER lives near Adelaide, South Australia. He has a passion for godawful puns, and is known to sing karaoke until the small hours. He is the author of over thirty published short stories and a novel, with a short story collection *Everything is a Graveyard* forthcoming from Ticonderoga Publications. Jason can be found online at **jasonfischer.com.au**

DIRK FLINTHART resides in Tasmania, where he admires echidnas and platypuses, battles wallabies and rabbits, and raises annoying children. He is currently undertaking an MA in creative stuff at Tas U, and is at work on two novels, a ridiculously epic poem, and a filmscript. Plus some stories. Also, he now owns a nice top hat.

LISA L. HANNETT hails from Ottawa, Canada but now lives in Adelaide, South Australia—city of churches, bizarre murders and pie floaters. She has won three Aurealis Awards, including Best Collection for her first book, *Bluegrass Symphony* (Ticonderoga). *Midnight and Moonshine*, co-authored with Angela Slatter, was published in 2012. Lisa has a PhD in medieval Icelandic literature, and is a graduate of Clarion South. You can find her online at **lisahannett.com**.

NARRELLE M. HARRIS writes crime, horror, fantasy, erotica and non-fiction. Her collection, *Showtime*, is in Twelfth Planet Press's 12 Planets series. Her Melbourne-based vampire books The *Opposite of Life* and *Walking Shadows*, have been praised for their fresh approach to the genre. Narrelle's current project is *Kitty and Cadaver*—an online novel told in weekly installments with music, art and craft components. Find out more at www.narrellemharris.com.

KATHLEEN JENNINGS is a writer and illustrator from Brisbane. She loves how pieces of stories and worlds, maps and fears, superstitions and technologies can be braided together into new tales. She is online at **tanaudel.wordpress.com.**

GARY KEMBLE is an award-winning speculative fiction writer. His stories have been published in magazines, anthologies and online. He lives in Brisbane with his wife, two kids, and a family of determined scrub turkeys. You can follow him on Twitter: @garykemble

MARGO LANAGAN's critically acclaimed North American debut, *Black Juice*, is a Michael L. Printz Honor Book and won two World Fantasy Awards. *Black Juice* also received the Victorian Premier's Literary Awards Prize for Young Adult Fiction, a Golden Aurealis Award for Best Young Adult Short Story, and a Bram Stoker Award nomination from the Horror Writers of America.

Perth-based writer MARTIN LIVINGS has had nearly eighty short stories published in a variety of magazines and anthologies. His first novel, *Carnies*, was published by Hachette Livre in 2006, and his first short story collection, *Living With the Dead*, was published in 2012 by Dark Prints Press. http://www.martinlivings.com

PENELOPE LOVE is an Australian writer whose work has recently appeared in *One Small Step, Damnation and Dames* and *Bloodstones*. She is currently working on the re-launch of 'Horror on the Orient Express', a classic *Call of Cthulhu* role-playing supplement she first helped create in 1991.

ANDREW J. MCKIERNAN is a writer and illustrator living and working on the Central Coast of NSW. First published in 2007, his stories have since been nominated for multiple Aurealis, Australian Shadows and Ditmar Awards. His illustrations have appeared in, and on the covers of, various books and magazines and he was Art Director of *Aurealis* Magazine for eight years.

KAREN MARIC's dark fiction has appeared in numerous magazines and anthologies in Australia and the US. She is currently working on a novel set in a time and place close to her heart, during the break-up of the former Yugoslavia. Visit **www.karenmaric.com** for more.

FAITH MUDGE is a Queensland writer with a passion for fantasy, folk tales and mythology from all over the world. Her stories feature in FableCroft's anthologies *To Spin a Darker Stair* and *One Small Step* and Ticonderoga's *Dreaming of Djinn*. More of her work can be found on her blog at **beyondthedreamline.wordpress.com**.

NICOLE MURPHY has been a primary school teacher, bookstore owner, journalist and checkout chick. She grew up reading Tolkien, Lewis and Le Guin and lives her love of SF and fantasy through the Conflux conventions. Her urban fantasy trilogy Dream of Asarlai is published in Australia/NZ by HarperVoyager. **nicolermurphy.com**.

Former Queenslander JASON NAHRUNG works as an editor and journalist to support his travel addiction. His most recent books are the Gothic tale *Salvage* (Twelfth Planet Press) and outback vampire thriller *Blood and Dust* (Xoum). He lives in Ballarat with his wife, the writer Kirstyn McDermott, and online at **jasonnahrung.com**.

TANSY RAYNER ROBERTS is the award-winning author of the Creature Court trilogy: *Power and Majesty*, *The Shattered City* and *Reign of Beasts*. Her short story collection *Love and Romanpunk* was published by Twelfth Planet Press in 2011. You can find her at her blog (**tansyrr.com**). Tansy lives in Tasmania, Australia with a Silent Producer and two superhero daughters.

ANGELA SLATTER writes dark fantasy and horror. She is the author of the Aurealis Award-winning *The Girl with No Hands and Other Tales*, the WFA-shortlisted *Sourdough and Other Stories*, and the collection/mosaic novel (with Lisa L Hannett), *Midnight and Moonshine*. She has a British Fantasy Award, a PhD in Creative Writing and blogs at**angelaslatter.com**. In 2013 she was awarded an inaugural Queensland Writers Fellowship.

ANNA TAMBOUR's latest novel is *Crandolin* (Chomu Press, 2012). For short stories to come in 2013 see a paean to parrots in *Postscripts #30/31 Memoryville Blues* (PS Publishing) and another to the beautiful and wild words of the Scots language in *Caledonian Dreamin'* (Eibonvale Press). **annatambour.net**

KYLA WARD is a Sydney-based creative who works in many modes. Her latest release is *The Land of Bad Dreams*, a collection of dark poetry. Her novel *Prismatic* (co-authored as Edwina Grey) won an Aurealis Award. Her short fiction has appeared on *Gothic.net* and in the *Macabre* and *New Hero* anthologies. To see some very strange things, try **www.tabula-rasa.info**.

Shirley Jackson Award winning author KAARON WARREN has three novels in print (the multi-award-winning *Slights*, *Walking the Tree* and *Mistification*) and four short story collections. *Through Splintered Walls* won a Canberra Critic's Circle Award for Fiction, two Ditmar Awards, two Australian Shadows Awards, an Aurealis Award and a Shirley Jackson Award. Her next book is the reprint e-book, *The Gate Theory*, from Cohesion Press.

RECOMMENDED READING LIST

Joanne Anderton, "High Density", *Andromeda Spaceways
Inflight Magazine #53*
———"The Bone Chime Song", *Light Touch Paper Stand Clear*
Daniel Baker, "At The Crossroads", *Aurealis #51*
Alan Baxter, "Cephalopoda Obsessia", *Bloodstones*
———"Crossroads and Carousels", *The Red Penny Papers*
———"Fear is the Sin", *From Stage Door Shadows*
———and Felicity Dowker, "Burning, Always Burning",
Damnation and Dames,
Eddy Burger, "Domestic Berserker", *Dark Edifice 3*
Jenny Blackford, "The Sacrifice", *Aurealis #47*
James Bradley, "Beauty's Sister", *Penguin*
Isobelle Carmody, "The Wolf Prince", *Metro Winds*
———"Metro Winds", *Metro Winds*
Jay Caselberg, "Blind Pig", *Damnation and Dames*
Steve Cameron, "If You Give This Girl a Ride", *Cover of
Darkness 11*
David Conyers and Brian M. Sammons, "The R'lyeh Singularity",
Cthulhu Unbound 3.
Terry Dowling , "Mariners' Round", *Postscripts 28/29: Exotic
Gothic 4*
———"The Way the Red Clown Hunts You", *Subterranean*, Winter
2012
Thoraiya Dyer, "The Second Card Of The Major Arcana", *Apex*
———"Faet's Fire", *Light Touch Paper, Stand Clear*
———"Surviving Film", *Bloodstones*
Jacob Edwards, "Salt & Pepper", *Polluto 9¾: Witchfinders Vs The
Evil Red*
Marina Finlayson, "The Family Business", *Andromeda Spaceways
Inflight Magazine #55*

Joanna Galbraith, "The Keeper's Heart", *The Coloured Lens* #3

Michelle Goldsmith, "The Hound of Henry Hortinger", *Pandemonium: Stories of the Smoke*

"The Skin of the World", Stephanie Gunn, *Bloodstones*

————"Ghosts", *Epilogue*

Lisa L. Hannett, Angela Slatter, "The Red Wedding", *Midnight and Moonshine*

————"Warp And Weft", *Midnight and Moonshine*

————"Prohibition Blues", *Damnation and Dames*

Richard Harland, "A Mother's Love", *Bloodstones*

Narrelle M. Harris, "Thrall", *Showtime*

Robert Hood, "Escena de un Asesinato", *Postscripts 28/29: Exotic Gothic 4*

————"Walking the Dead Beat", *Damnation and Dames*

"First They Came . . .", Deborah Kalin, *Andromeda Spaceways Inflight Magazine* #55

Pete Kempshall, "Dead Inside", *Bloodstones*

————"Sound and Fury", *Damnation and Dames*

Margo Lanagan, "Isles Of The Sun", *Cracklescape*

————"Titty Anne and the Very, Very Hairy Man", *Meanjin*, Volume 71, Number 4.

————"Significant Dust", *Cracklescape*

————"Bajazzle", *Cracklescape*

S. G. Larner, "Duck Creek Road", *Bloody Parchment: Hidden Things, Lost Things and other stories*

Martin Livings, "Birthday Suit", *Living with the Dead*

————"The Ar-Dub", *Living with the Dead*

Tracie McBride, "Drive, She Said", *Lovecraft eZine 14*

Andrew J. McKiernan, "They Don't Know That We Know What They Know", *Midnight Echo 8*

————"The Final Degustation of Doctor Ernest Blenheim", *Midnight Echo 7*

Kelly Matsuura, "Hours on the Voodoo Clock", *Free Flash Fiction*

Nicole Murphy, "Euryale", *Bloodstones*

Jason Nahrung, "The Mornington Ride", *Epilogue*

————"Breaking the Wire", *Aurealis* #47

Ian Nichols, "In the Dark", *Apex Magazine 37*

Shauna O'Meara, "Blood Lillies", *Midnight Echo 8*

Christopher Sequeria, "The Adventure of the Lost Specialist", *Sherlock Holmes: The Crossovers Casebook*

Helen Stubbs, "Sayuri's Revenge", *Tales From the Bell Club*

Anna Tambour, "King Wolf", *A Season in Carcosa*
Kaaron Warren, "The Pickwick Syndrome", *Stories Of The Smoke*
————"Sky", *Through Splintered Walls*
————"Creek", *Through Splintered Walls*
————"The Lighthouse Keepers' Club", *Postscripts 28/29: Exotic Gothic 4*

AUSTRALIAN & NEW ZEALAND FANTASY & HORROR AWARDS

THE AUSTRALIAN SF "DITMAR" AWARDS

BEST NOVEL

Sea Hearts, Margo Lanagan (Allen & Unwin)
NOMINEES
Bitter Greens, Kate Forsyth (Random House Australia)
Suited (The Veiled Worlds 2), Jo Anderton (Angry Robot)
Salvage, Jason Nahrung (Twelfth Planet Press)
Perfections, Kirstyn McDermott (Xoum)
The Corpse-Rat King, Lee Battersby (Angry Robot)

BEST NOVELLA OR NOVELETTE

"Sky", Kaaron Warren (*Through Splintered Walls*, Twelfth Planet)
NOMINEES
"Flight 404", Simon Petrie, *Flight 404/The Hunt for Red Leicester*
    (Peggy Bright)
"Significant Dust", Margo Lanagan, *Cracklescape* (Twelfth Planet)

BEST SHORT STORY

"The Wisdom of Ants", Thoraiya Dyer (*Clarkesworld 75*)
NOMINEES
"Sanaa's Army", Joanne Anderton, in *Bloodstones* (Ticonderoga)
"The Bone Chime Song", Joanne Anderton, in *Light Touch Paper Stand Clear* (Peggy Bright)
"Oracle's Tower", Faith Mudge, in *To Spin a Darker Stair* (FableCroft)

BEST COLLECTED WORK

Through Splintered Walls, Kaaron Warren (Twelfth Planet)

NOMINEES

Cracklescape, Margo Lanagan (Twelfth Planet)

Epilogue, Tehani Wessely, ed. (FableCroft)

Light Touch Paper Stand Clear, Edwina Harvey and Simon Petrie, eds. (Peggy Bright)

Midnight and Moonshine, Lisa L. Hannett and Angela Slatter (Ticonderoga)

The Year's Best Australian Fantasy and Horror 2011, Liz Grzyb & Talie Helene, eds. (Ticonderoga)

BEST ARTWORK

Cover art, Kathleen Jennings, *Midnight and Moonshine* (Ticonderoga)

NOMINEES

Cover art, Nick Stathopoulos, *Andromeda Spaceways Inflight Magazine 56* (ASIM)

Illustrations, Adam Browne, *Pyrotechnicon* (Coeur de Lion)

Cover art and illustrations, Kathleen Jennings, *To Spin a Darker Stair* (FableCroft)

Cover art, Les Petersen, *Light Touch Paper Stand Clear* (Peggy Bright)

BEST NEW TALENT

David McDonald

NOMINEES

Faith Mudge

Steve Cameron

Stacey Larner

AUREALIS AWARDS

FANTASY NOVEL

***Sea Hearts*, Margo Lanagan (Allen & Unwin)**

NOMINEES

Bitter Greens, Kate Forsyth (Random House Australia)

Stormdancer, Jay Kristoff (Tor UK)

Flame of Sevenwaters, Juliet Marillier (Pan Macmillan Australia)

Winter Be My Shield, Jo Spurrier (Harper Voyager)

FANTASY SHORT STORY

"Bajazzle", Margo Lanagan (*Cracklescape*, Twelfth Planet)

NOMINEES

"Sanaa's Army", Joanne Anderton (*Bloodstones*, Ticonderoga)

"The Stone Witch", Isobelle Carmody (*Under My Hat*, Random House)

"First They Came", Deborah Kalin (*Andromeda Spaceways Inflight Magazine 55*)

"The Isles of the Sun", Margo Lanagan (*Cracklescape*, Twelfth Planet)

BEST HORROR NOVEL

Perfections, **Kirstyn McDermott (Xoum)**
NOMINEES
Bloody Waters, Jason Franks (Possible Press)
Blood and Dust, Jason Nahrung (Xoum)
Salvage, Jason Nahrung (Twelfth Planet)

BEST HORROR SHORT STORY

"Sky", Kaaron Warren (*Through Splintered Walls*, Twelfth Planet)
NOMINEES
"Sanaa's Army", Joanne Anderton (*Bloodstones*, Ticonderoga)
"Elyora", Jodi Cleghorn (*Review of Australian Fiction*)
"To Wish Upon a Clockwork Heart", Felicity Dowker (*Bread and Circuses*, Ticonderoga)
"Escena de un Asesinato", Robert Hood (*Postscripts 28/29: Exotic Gothic 4*)

BEST COLLECTION

That Book Your Mad Ancestor Wrote, **K.J. Bishop (self-published)**
NOMINEES
Metro Winds, Isobelle Carmody (Allen & Unwin)
Midnight and Moonshine, Lisa L. Hanett & Angela Slatter (Ticonderoga)
Living With the Dead, Martin Livings (Dark Prints)
Through Splintered Walls, Kaaron Warren (Twelfth Planet)

BEST ANTHOLOGY

The Best Science Fiction and Fantasy of the Year: Volume 6, **Jonathan Strahan, ed. (Night Shade)**
NOMINEES
The Year's Best Australian Fantasy and Horror 2011, Liz Grzyb & Talie Helene, eds. (Ticonderoga)
Bloodstones, Amanda Pillar, ed. (Ticonderoga)
Under My Hat, Jonathan Strahan, ed. (Random House)
Edge of Infinity, Jonathan Strahan, ed. (Solaris)

BEST CHILDREN'S FICTION (TOLD PRIMARILY THROUGH WORDS)

Brotherband: The Hunters, **John Flanagan (Random House Australia)**
NOMINEES
Princess Betony and the Unicorn, Pamela Freeman (Walker)
The Silver Door, Emily Rodda (Scholastic)
Irina the Wolf Queen, Leah Swann (Xoum)

BEST CHILDREN'S FICTION (TOLD PRIMARILY THROUGH PICTURES)

Little Elephants, **Graeme Base (author and illustrator) (Viking Penguin)**
NOMINEES
The Boy Who Grew Into a Tree, Gary Crew (author) & Ross Watkins (illustrator) (Penguin Group Australia)

In the Beech Forest, Gary Crew (author) & Den Scheer (illustrator) (Ford Street)
Inside the World of Tom Roberts, Mark Wilson (author and illustrator) (Lothian Children's Books)

YOUNG ADULT SHORT STORY

"The Wisdom of the Ants", Thoraiya Dyer (*Clarkesworld* 12/12)
NOMINEES
"Stilled Lifes x 11", Justin D'Ath (*Trust Me Too*)
"Rats", Jack Heath (*Trust Me Too*)
"The Statues of Melbourne", Jack Nicholls (*Andromeda Spaceways Inflight Magazine 56*)
"The Worry Man", Adrienne Tam (self-published)

BEST YOUNG ADULT NOVEL

Dead, Actually, **Kaz Delaney (Allen & Unwin)**
Sea Hearts, **Margo Lanaga (Allen & Unwin)**
NOMINEES
And All The Stars, Andrea K. Host (self-published)
The Interrogation of Ashala Wolf, Amberlin Kwaymullina (Walker)
Into That Forest, Louis Nowra (Allen & Unwin)

BEST ILLUSTRATED BOOK/GRAPHIC NOVEL

Blue, **Pat Grant (author and illustrator) (Top Shelf Comix)**
NOMINEES
It Shines and Shakes and Laughs, Tim Molloy (author and illustrator) (Milk Shadow)
Changing Ways #2, Justin Randall (author and illustrator) (Gestalt)

BEST SCIENCE FICTION SHORT STORY

"Significant Dust", Margo Lanagan (*Cracklescape*)
NOMINEES
"Visitors", James Bradley (*Review of Australian Fiction*)
"Beyond Winter's Shadow", Greg Mellor (*Wild Chrome*)
"The Trouble with Memes", Greg Mellor (*Wild Chrome*)
"The Lighthouse Keepers' Club", Kaaron Warren (*Exotic Gothic 4*)

BEST SCIENCE FICTION NOVEL

The Rook, **Daniel O'Malley (Harper Collins)**
NOMINEES
Suited, Jo Anderton (Angry Robot)
The Last City, Nina D'Aleo (Momentum)
And All The Stars, Andrea K. Host (self-published)
The Interrogation of Ashala Wolf, Amberlin Kwaymullina (Walker)
A Confusion of Princes, Garth Nix (Allen & Unwin)

PETER MCNAMARA CONVENORS' AWARD

Kate Eltham

AUSTRALIAN SHADOWS AWARDS

NOVEL

Perfections, Kirstyn McDermott (Xoum)
NOMINEES
Blood and Dust, Jason Nahrung (Xoum)
The Corpse-Rat King, Lee Battersby (Angry Robot)

LONG FICTION

"Sky", Kaaron Warren (*Through Splintered Walls*, Twelfth Planet)
NOMINEES
"Critique", Daniel I. Russell (*Ishtar*, Gilgamesh)
"Escena de un Asesinato", Robert Hood (*Exotic Gothic 4*)

COLLECTION

Through Splintered Walls, Kaaron Warren (Twelfth Planet)
NOMINEES
Bread and Circuses, Felicity Dowker (Ticonderoga)
Living With the Dead, Martin Livings (Dark Prints)

EDITED PUBLICATION

Surviving The End, Craig Bezant, ed. (Dark Prints)
NOMINEES
The Year's Best Australian Fantasy & Horror 2011, Liz Grzyb and Talie
    Helene eds. (Ticonderoga)
Cthulhu Unbound 3, David Conyers, Brian M. Sammons, eds.
    (Permuted)

SHORT FICTION

"Birthday Suit", Martin Livings (*Living With The Dead*, Dark Prints)
NOMINEES
"To Wish Upon a Clockwork Heart", Felicity Dowker (*Bread and
    Circuses*, Ticonderoga)
"Pigroot Flat", Jason Fischer (*Midnight Echo 8*, AHWA)
"They Don't Know That We Know What They Know", Andrew J.
    McKiernan (*Midnight Echo 8*, AHWA)
"Creek", Kaaron Warren (*Through Splintered Walls*, Twelfth Planet)
"Mountain" (*Through Splintered Walls*, Twelfth Planet)
"Road" (*Through Splintered Walls*, Twelfth Planet)
"A Monstrous Touch", Marty Young (*Dangers Untold*, Alliteration
    Ink)

SIR JULIUS VOGEL AWARDS

BEST NOVEL

Queen of Iron Years, Lyn McConchie and Sharman Horwood (Kite Hil Publishing)
NOMINEES
Dead Radiance T.G. Ayer (Evolved)
Growing Disenchantments, K.D. Berry (Bluewood)
Empire State, Adam Christopher (Angry Robot)
Tropic of Skorpeo, Michael Morrissey (Steam Press)
Don't Be A Hero, Chris Strange (Cheeky Minion)

BEST YOUTH NOVEL

The Prince of Soul and the Lighthouse, Frederik Brounéus (Steam Press)
NOMINEES
Red Rocks, Rachael King (Random House NZ)
Guardians of the Shimmer: Dream Time, Garth Lawless (Ocean)
Shadowfell, Juliet Marillier (Pan Macmillan Australia)
The Enchanted Flute, James Norcliffe (Random House)
Wizard's Guide to Wellington, A.J. Ponder (Coombe House)

BEST NOVELLA / NOVELETTE

"Flight 404", Simon Petrie (*Flight 404/The Hunt for Red Leicester*, Peggy Bright)
NOMINEES
"Fire, Escape", M. Darusha Wehm (self published)
"The Hunt for Red Leicester", Simon Petrie (*Flight 404/The Hunt for Red Leicester*, Peggy Bright)

BEST SHORT STORY

"Hope is the thing with feathers", Lee Murray (*Royal Society of New Zealand*)
NOMINEES
"Dying for the Record", A.J. Ponder (*Arc/The Tomorrow Paper*)
"Paint By Numbers", Dan Rabarts (*Andromeda Spaceways Inflight Magazine 56*)
"Wearing the Star Cloak", Dan Rabarts (*Wilywriters*)
"Better Phones", Grant Stone (*Andromeda Spaceways Inflight Magazine 56*)

BEST COLLECTED WORK

Mansfield with Monsters, Matt and Debbie Cowens, eds. (Steam Press)
NOMINEES
I got his blood on me, Lawrence Patchett (VUP)

Avenir Eclectia, Grace Bridges (Splashdown)
Steam Pressed Shorts, Matt and Debbie Cowens (self published)

BEST PROFESSIONAL ARTWORK

Cover art, Les Petersen, *Light Touch Paper Stand Clear* (Peggy Bright)
NOMINEE
Cover art, Matt Cowens, *Steam Pressed Shorts* (self published)

BEST PROFESSIONAL PRODUCTION/PUBLICATION

The Hobbit: An Unexpected Journey: Chronicles—Art and Design,
Daniel Falconer (WetaNZ)
NOMINEE
Triumph: Unnecessarily Violent Tales of Science Adventure for the
Simple and Unfortunate, Greg Broadmore (WetaNZ)
The Comic Strip Companion: The Unofficial and Unauthorised Guide
to Doctor Who in Comics: 1964–1979 , Paul Scones (Telos)

BEST DRAMATIC PRESENTATION

***The Hobbit: An Unexpected Journey*, Peter Jackson, Philippa Boyens,**
Fran Walsh, Guillermo del Toro, screenplay (New Line, MGM,
Wingnut)
NOMINEES
The Almighty Johnsons Series 2, Simon Bennett, prod. James Griffin and
Rachel Lang, creators (South Pacific)

ACKNOWLEDGEMENTS

"Tied To The Waste" © Joanne Anderton 2012. First published in *Tales of the Talisman*, March 2012, edited by David Lee Summers.

"The Cook of Pearl House, A Malay Sailor by the Name of Maurice" © R.J. Astruc 2012. First published in *Dark Edifice 2*, edited by Dayle Robert Grixti.

"Comfort Ghost" © Lee Battersby 2012. First published in *Andromeda Spaceways Inflight Magazine 56*, ASIM Collective.

"Tiny Lives" © Alan Baxter 2012. First published in *Daily Science Fiction*, edited by Michele-Lee Barasso and Jonathan Laden.

"A Moveable Feast" © Jenny Blackford 2012. First published in *Bloodstones*, edited by Amanda Pillar, Ticonderoga.

"The Witch's Wardrobe" © Eddy Burger 2012. First published in *Dark Edifice 3*, edited by Dayle Robert Grixti.

"The Stone Witch" © Isobelle Carmody 2012. First published in *Under My Hat*, edited by Jonathan Strahan, Random House.

"Beautiful" © Jay Caselberg 2012. First published in *The Washington Pastime*, edited by Mark Vidafar.

"The Fall" © Stephen Dedman 2012. First published in *Postscripts 28/29: Exotic Gothic 4* , edited by Daniel Olson.

"To Wish On A Clockwork Heart" © Felicity Dowker 2012. First published in *Bread and Circuses*, Ticonderoga.

"Nightside Eye" © Terry Dowling 2012. First published in *Cemetery Dance 66*, edited by Richard Chizmar.

"Population Management" © Tom Dullemond 2012. First published in *Danse Macabre: Close Encounters With The Reaper*, edited by Nancy Kilpatrick.

"Sleeping Beauty" © Thoraiya Dyer 2012. First published in *Epilogue*, edited by Tehani Wessely, Fablecroft.

"Hungry Man" © Will Elliot 2012. First published in *The Apex Book of World SF*, edited by Lavie Tidhar, Apex; and *The One That Got Away*, edited by Craig Bezant, Dark Prints.

"Pigroot Flat" © Jason Fischer 2012. First published in *Midnight Echo 8*, edited by Amanda J Spedding, Mark Farrugia and Marty Young.

"The Bull In Winter" © Dirk Flinthart 2012. First published in *Bloodstones*, edited by Amanda Pillar, Ticonderoga.

"Sweet Subtleties" © Lisa L. Hannett 2012. First published in *Clarkesworld*, edited by Neil Clarke.

"Bella Beaufort Goes To War" © Lisa L. Hannett and Angela Slatter 2012. First published in *Midnight and Moonshine*, Ticonderoga.

"Stalemate" © Narrelle Harris 2012. First published in *Showtime*, Twelfth Planet.

"Kindling" © Kathleen Jennings 2012. First published in *Light Touch Paper Stand Clear*, edited by Simon Petrie and Edwina Harvey, Peggy Bright.

"Saturday Night at the Milkbar" © Gary Kemble 2012. First published in *Midnight Echo 7*, edited by Daniel I. Russell.

"Crow And Caper, Caper And Crow" © Margo Lanagan 2012. First published in *Under My Hat*, edited by Jonathan Strahan, Random House.

"You Ain't Heard Nothing Yet" © Martin Livings 2012. First published in *Living With The Dead*, Dark Prints.

"A Small Bad Thing" © Penelope Love 2012. First published in *Bloodstones*, edited by Amanda Pillar, Ticonderoga.

"Torch Song" © Andrew J. McKiernan 2012. First published in *From Stage Door Shadows*, edited by Jodi Cleghorn, eMergent.

"Anvil Of The Sun" © Karen Maric 2012. First published in *Aurealis 54*, edited by Michael Pryor.

"Oracle's Tower" © Faith Mudge 2012. First published in *To Spin A Darker Stair*, Fablecroft.

"The Black Star Killer" © Nicole Murphy 2012. First published in *Damnation and Dames*, edited by Liz Grzyb and Amanda Pillar, Ticonderoga.

"The Last Boat To Eden" © Jason Nahrung 2012. First published in *Surviving the End*, edited by Craig Bezant, Dark Prints.

"What Books Survive" © Tansy Rayner Roberts 2012. First published in *Epilogue*, edited by Tehani Wessely, Fablecroft.

"Jimmy Dean, Jimmy Dean" © Angela Slatter 2012. First published in *This is Horror*, edited by Michael Wilson.

"The Dog Who Wished He'd Never Heard Of Lovecraft" © Anna Tambour 2012. First published in *The Lovecraft eZine*, edited by Mike Davis.

"The Loquacious Cadaver" © Kyla Ward 2012. First published in *The Lion and the Aardvark: Aesop's Modern Fables*, edited by Robin D. Laws, Stoneskin.

"River Of Memory" © Kaaron Warren 2012. First published in *Zombies Vs Robots: Women on War!*, edited by Jeff Conner, IDW.

978-0-9586856-6-5	Troy by Simon Brown (tpb)
978-0-9586856-7-2	The Workers' Paradise eds Farr & Evans (tpb)
978-0-9586856-8-9	Fantastic Wonder Stories ed Russell B. Farr (tpb)
978-0-9803531-0-5	Love in Vain by Lewis Shiner (tpb)
978-0-9803531-2-9	Belong ed Russell B. Farr (tpb)
978-0-9803531-3-6	Ghost Seas by Steven Utley (hc)
978-0-9803531-4-3	Ghost Seas by Steven Utley (tpb)
978-0-9803531-6-7	Magic Dirt: the best of Sean Williams (tpb)
978-0-9803531-7-4	The Lady of Situations by Stephen Dedman (hc)
978-0-9803531-8-1	The Lady of Situations by Stephen Dedman (tpb)
978-0-9806288-2-1	Basic Black by Terry Dowling (tpb)
978-0-9806288-3-8	Make Believe by Terry Dowling (tpb)
978-0-9806288-4-5	Scary Kisses ed Liz Grzyb (tpb)
978-0-9806288-6-9	Dead Sea Fruit by Kaaron Warren (tpb)
978-0-9806288-8-3	The Girl With No Hands by Angela Slatter (tpb)
978-0-9807813-1-1	Dead Red Heart ed Russell B. Farr (tpb)
978-0-9807813-2-8	More Scary Kisses ed Liz Grzyb (tpb)
978-0-9807813-4-2	Heliotrope by Justina Robson (tpb)
978-0-9807813-7-3	Matilda Told Such Dreadful Lies by Lucy Sussex (tpb)
978-1-921857-01-0	Bluegrass Symphony by Lisa L. Hannett (tpb)
978-1-921857-05-8	The Hall of Lost Footsteps by Sara Douglass (hc)
978-1-921857-06-5	The Hall of Lost Footsteps by Sara Douglass (tpb)
978-1-921857-03-4	Damnation and Dames eds Liz Grzyb & Amanda Pillar (tpb)
978-1-921857-08-9	Bread and Circuses by Felicity Dowker (tpb)
978-1-921857-16-4	The 400-Million-Year Itch by Steven Utley (hc)
978-1-921857-17-1	The 400-Million-Year Itch by Steven Utley (tpb)
978-1-921857-24-9	Wild Chrome by Greg Mellor (tpb)
978-1-921857-27-0	Bloodstones ed Amanda Pillar (tpb)
978-1-921857-30-0	Midnight and Moonshine by Lisa L. Hannett & Angela Slatter (tpb)
978-1-921857-10-2	Mage Heart by Jane Routley (hc)
978-1-921857-65-2	Mage Heart by Jane Routley (tpb)
978-1-921857-11-9	Fire Angels by Jane Routley (hc)
978-1-921857-66-9	Fire Angels by Jane Routley (tpb)
978-1-921857-12-6	Aramaya by Jane Routley (hc)
978-1-921857-67-6	Aramaya by Jane Routley (tpb)
978-1-921857-86-7	Magic Dirt: the best of Sean Williams (hc)
978-1-921857-35-5	Dreaming of Djinn ed Liz Grzyb (tpb)
978-1-921857-38-6	Prickle Moon by Juliet Marillier (tpb)
978-1-921857-39-3	Prickle Moon by Juliet Marillier (hc)
978-1-921857-42-3	The Bride Price by Cat Sparks (hc)
978-1-921857-43-0	The Bride Price by Cat Sparks (tpb)
978-1-921857-46-1	The Year of Ancient Ghosts by Kim Wilkins (tpb)
978-1-921857-47-8	The Year of Ancient Ghosts by Kim Wilkins (hc)
978-1-921857-32-4	Invisible Kingdoms by Steven Utley (hc)
978-1-921857-33-1	Invisible Kingdoms by Steven Utley (tpb)
978-1-921857-69-0	Havenstar by Glenda Larke (hc)
978-1-921857-70-6	Havenstar by Glenda Larke (tpb)

TICONDEROGA PUBLICATIONS LIMITED HARDCOVER EDITIONS

978-0-9586856-9-6   Love in Vain BY Lewis Shiner
978-0-9803531-1-2   Belong ED Russell B. Farr
978-0-9803531-9-8   Basic Black BY Terry Dowling
978-0-9806288-0-7   Make Believe BY Terry Dowling
978-0-9806288-1-4   The Infernal BY Kim Wilkins
978-0-9806288-5-2   Dead Sea Fruit BY Kaaron Warren
978-0-9806288-7-6   The Girl With No Hands BY Angela Slatter
978-0-9807813-0-4   Dead Red Heart ED Russell B. Farr
978-0-9807813-3-5   Heliotrope BY Justina Robson
978-0-9807813-6-6   Matilda Told Such Dreadful Lies BY Lucy Sussex
978-1-921857-00-3   Bluegrass Symphony BY Lisa L. Hannett
978-1-921857-07-2   Bread and Circuses BY Felicity Dowker
978-1-921857-23-2   Wild Chrome BY Greg Mellor
978-1-921857-27-0   Midnight and Moonshine BY Lisa L. Hannett & Angela Slatter
978-1-921857-37-9   Prickle Moon BY Juliet Marillier
978-1-921857-41-6   The Bride Price BY Cat Sparks
978-1-921857-45-4   The Year of Ancient Ghosts BY Kim Wilkins
978-1-921857-68-3   Havenstar BY Glenda Larke

TICONDEROGA PUBLICATIONS EBOOKS

978-0-9803531-5-0   Ghost Seas BY Steven Utley
978-1-921857-93-5   The Girl With No Hands BY Angela Slatter
978-1-921857-99-7   Dead RED Heart ED Russell B. Farr
978-1-921857-94-2   More Scary Kisses ED Liz Grzyb
978-0-9807813-5-9   Heliotrope BY Justina Robson
978-1-921857-98-0   Year's Best Australian F&H EDS Grzyb & Helene
978-1-921857-36-2   Dreaming of Djinn ED Liz Grzyb
978-1-921857-40-9   Prickle Moon BY Juliet Marillier
978-1-921857-92-8   The Year of Ancient Ghosts BY Kim Wilkins
978-1-921857-28-7   Bloodstones ED Amanda Pillar (tpb)

THE YEAR'S BEST AUSTRALIAN FANTASY & HORROR SERIES
EDITED BY LIZ GRZYB & TALIE HELENE

978-0-9807813-8-0   Year's Best Australian Fantasy & Horror 2010 (hc)
978-0-9807813-9-7   Year's Best Australian Fantasy & Horror 2010 (tpb)
978-0-921057-13-3   Year's Best Australian Fantasy & Horror 2011 (hc)
978-0-921057-14-0   Year's Best Australian Fantasy & Horror 2011 (tpb)

WWW.TICONDEROGAPUBLICATIONS.COM

THANK YOU

The publisher would sincerely like to thank:

Elizabeth Grzyb, Talie Helene, Joanne Anderton, R.J. Astruc, Lee Battersby, Alan Baxter, Jenny Blackford, Eddy Burger, Isobelle Carmody, Jay Caselberg, Stephen Dedman, Felicity Dowker, Terry Dowling, Tom Dullemond, Thoraiya Dyer, Will Elliot, Jason Fischer, Dirk Flinthart, Lisa L. Hannett, Narrelle M. Harris, Kathleen Jennings, Gary Kemble, Margo Lanagan, Martin Livings, Penelope Love, Andrew J. McKiernan, Karen Maric, Faith Mudge, Nicole Murphy, Jason Nahrung, Tansy Rayner Roberts, Angela Slatter, Anna Tambour, Kyla Ward, Kaaron Warren, Cat Sparks, Donna Maree Hanson, Robert Hood, Pete Kempshall, Karen Brooks, Jeremy G. Byrne, Kim Wilkins, Marianne de Pierres, Jonathan Strahan, Peter McNamara, Ellen Datlow, Grant Stone, Sean Williams, Simon Brown, Garth Nix, David Cake, Simon Oxwell, Grant Watson, Sue Manning, Steven Utley, Lewis Shiner, Bill Congreve, Jack Dann, Janeen Webb, Lucy Sussex, the Mt Lawley Mafia, the Nedlands Yakuza, Shane Jiraiya Cummings, Angela Challis, Kate Williams, Andrew Williams, Kathryn Linge, Al Chan, Alisa and Tehani, Mel & Phil, Jennifer Sudbury, Paul Pryztula, Helen Grzyb, Hayley Lane, Georgina Walpole, Rushelle Lister, Nerida Fearnley, everyone we've missed . . .

. . . and you.

IN MEMORY OF
Eve Johnson (1945–2011)
Sara Douglass (1957–2011)
Steven Utley (1948–2013)

www.ingramcontent.com/pod-product-compliance
Lightning Source LLC
Chambersburg PA
CBHW020825030726
47496CB00001B/89